'I've started ma... need,' she said. '...ings like sarsaparilla and laudanum—and we might need a gun—'

'A gun? I don't want a gun.'

Lily looked at her soberly. 'We wouldn't have to shoot anyone,' she said, 'not unless they were actually trying to kill us. I think if we just waved the gun, they would know we weren't defenceless. I mean, we won't be all on our own out there. There will be Patrick and this Henry and the cousins—'

'*If* we catch up with them.'

'Oh. But we must,' said Lily, startled. 'We could never manage on our own. Oh Kate, I suppose this *is* all happening? We're not dreaming, are we?'

'We're *not* dreaming,' Kate assured her with a grin. 'At least, I hope not. We're all going to California to make our fortunes and no one is going to stop us!'

LILY GOLIGHTLY

Pamela Oldfield

ARROW BOOKS

Arrow Books Limited
62–65 Chandos Place, London WC2N 4NW

An imprint of Century Hutchinson Limited

London Melbourne Sydney Auckland
Johannesburg and agencies throughout
the world

First published in Great Britain by Century 1987
Arrow edition 1988

Printed and bound in Great Britain by
Anchor Brendon Limited, Tiptree, Essex

ISBN 0 09 953720 6

Chapter One

As Lily guided her pupil's small fingers, her attention was elsewhere.

'Thumb, first finger, second finger, swing your hand round like *this*, then thumb again, first again and second again . . .'

She was listening for the postman.

'Now watch me, dear. I'll do it once more. It's really quite easy.'

Lily watched her own slim fingers as they demonstrated the fingering for the key of C. A small neat hand with well-manicured fingers. A ringless right hand. Ah, but the *left* hand! A faint smile softened her expression as she glanced at the gold band on her left hand. 'I am a married woman,' she reminded herself. 'I am Mrs *Patrick* Golightly.' It still sounded unfamiliar; she still felt like Lily Freedman. Her lips curved into a wry smile as she took hold of the small podgy fingers of five-year-old Maurice's right hand and placed them carefully on the correct keys.

'Now,' she said to him, 'we'll try it again, shall we? Don't fret, I'll help you. So, it's thumb, first finger, second finger, swing it under – that's splendid . . .'

This was Maurice Dent's first lesson and with any luck it might also be his last, she thought. As soon as Patrick's letter came, she would be off to the United States of America. She had written to the parents of all her pupils explaining the situation and recommending Miss Perring as a worthy

1

replacement. Miss Perring was nearly sixty and her fingers were stiff with rheumatism, but she had taught hundreds of children to play the piano, including Lily herself. Doubtless she would go on teaching until she died.

Lily watched the small fingers as they stumbled over the notes and glanced sideways at Maurice's fair head and the expression on his face. 'I will never *make* my son learn to play the piano,' she vowed, then amended it hastily to 'our child'. If they ever had a son he would almost certainly have dark hair like hers and Patrick's for, as Mrs Harrington frequently remarked, except for the fact that Patrick's eyes were brown they could have been brother and sister. Her own hair was a glossy black, her blue eyes were large and her nose and mouth were small and finely shaped. Her skin was clear, unblemished and so pale that her father often described her as 'a delicate Dresden shepherdess', but her looks belied her. Despite her father's belief to the contrary, Lily was surprisingly robust. She wore her hair parted in the centre and drawn back into two plaits which she then wound over her head and looked every inch a parson's daughter, demure and sensitive. She had led a very sheltered life and any other qualities she possessed had never been put to the test.

She sighed. When, *when* would Patrick's letter come? She had been waiting for it for nearly two months, her hopes high each morning and dashed again by mid-afternoon.

'Well done, Maurice,' she said. 'Now I would like you to do that once more and then we will try it with the other hand. Are you ready? Now then, thumb, first finger, second finger . . . Oh, Maurice! What's the matter, dear?'

The boy turned brimming blue eyes towards her. 'I want Mama,' he whispered. The rosebud mouth trembled and two large tears ran down his plump cheeks.

Lily resisted the urge to put her arm round him and instead smiled reassuringly.

'Only a few more minutes,' she told him briskly. 'Your Mama isn't far away. She's in there' – she pointed towards the front parlour – 'waiting while you have your lesson. You do *want* to learn to play the piano, don't you?'

2

After a moment's hesitation, he shook his head.

'Of course you do,' said Lily. 'Your Mama told me so herself. Have you got a handkerchief, dear? Oh well, I'll find mine and we'll wipe away those tears. There we are. That's better, isn't it? You're a big boy now, Maurice. Five, isn't it? Nearly six. So we'll try the scale with your left hand and then it will be time to go back to your mother. See the clock on the mantelpiece? Just five more minutes.'

Maurice gave a long shuddering sigh and turned his attention to the white keys in front of him.

'Thumb, first finger . . .' Lily began again. 'Don't hurry it.'

She did not feel at all like a married woman because after a honeymoon lasting only seven days, Patrick had left for the United States of America where he would join his uncle's firm in New York as a very junior accountant. Uncle Albert, who was childless, had promised that if Patrick showed the proper aptitude, the firm would eventually pass into his hands. It was this glittering prospect which had persuaded Patrick to leave England and all that was safe and familiar and put his trust in a new country. Patrick had called it 'the New World' and he had spoken with such enthusiasm that Lily, hopelessly in love with him, had been unable to disappoint him by saying she did not relish the idea. So she had reluctantly agreed to leave her father and make a new life with her husband thousands of miles from England.

All the time she was with Patrick the prospect had seemed reasonable, but his departure had left her a prey to all manner of doubts and fears and at times Lily felt her courage slipping away. As soon as the letter arrived she would, she felt sure, experience a renewal of enthusiasm for the project but as weeks became months she began to nurse a secret hope that something had happened to bring about a change of plan. Perhaps Patrick and his uncle did not get along as well as they had expected. Perhaps Patrick did not like the United States. More likely still, he might have taken a dislike to the Americans themselves for, if she believed all she had read on the subject, they were a somewhat uncouth people, notoriously outspoken and quick to take offence.

In preparation for her emigration, Lily had studied

3

accounts of life in America – one by Mrs Trollope and another by Captain Basil Hull – and she fancied the people might not be at all to her husband's liking. As more time passed and still no letter arrived, she allowed herself to speculate on the possibility that Patrick's enthusiasm had waned and that when he did write it would be to tell her that he was coming home to England.

However, Lily did not share this secret hope with anyone else, but gave the impression of a cheerful young wife, eager to join her husband and share his new life in 'foreign parts'.

The last faltering piano note died and Lily smiled at her small pupil.

'Splendid!' she told him. 'That wasn't really so bad, was it? You have made a very good start, Maurice. Let's go and tell your Mama, shall we?'

As she closed the lid of the piano the boy slid thankfully to the floor, dislodging the red velvet cushion as he did so. He picked it up fearfully and Lily's heart ached for him. So young and vulnerable, she thought, and so afraid of the unfamiliar. A first piano lesson with a strange woman in a strange house must have appeared as daunting to young Maurice as her own projected trip to America.

She held out her hand and Maurice took it and allowed himself to be led into the next room where he hurled himself towards his mother who hugged him protectively.

'Was he all right?' she asked anxiously. 'He didn't cry, did he?'

'Of course not,' said Lily loyally. 'He made a very promising start. Very promising.'

'Did he really?' She looked relieved. 'There, Morry, what did I tell you, eh? I said you would like it.' She turned to Lily. 'It's his grandmother on my husband's side,' she confided. 'She's paying for the lessons, otherwise I would have waited until he was a little older, but she was so determined and my husband gives in to her.'

Maurice was rapidly recovering his composure and as he now stared round curiously at the large high-ceilinged room, Lily tried to see it through his eyes. It was on the east side of the parsonage, overshadowed by tall trees which kept out

4

the sun and made it gloomy even on the brightest day. To Maurice it was the room where he was reunited with his mother, but to Lily it was the Sunday School room, the Bible Reading room, the Knitting Circle room and the room where the confirmation classes were held.

'I have explained to him about practising daily,' said Lily, 'but he tells me you have no piano?'

'He will practise at his grandmother's house,' the young mother assured her. 'They live just round the corner, so it won't be difficult. And we shall be getting a piano of our own as soon as we can afford one. Well, I'm glad you think he has made a good start. It's fortunate for us that you're still here. When you said you were going to Australia, I said to my husband –'

'America,' Lily corrected her. 'I'm going to New York to join my husband. I expect to receive news any day now, which is why I explained to you that I may not be able to continue Maurice's lessons.'

Maurice's mother looked at her with awe.

'America!' she said. 'My word! You *are* brave. Wild horses wouldn't drag me over there. And all those weeks at sea!'

'Not so very many,' Lily told her. 'The Black Ball packets are very fast and they run twice a month.'

'But aren't you nervous?' Mrs Dent persisted. 'Can you swim?'

Lily laughed. 'No, I can't, but I'm hoping that won't be necessary. I don't think we shall sink. Patrick – that's my husband – says the ships are as safe as houses.'

Mrs Dent appeared unconvinced by Lily's assurances. 'But all that way alone?'

Lily shook her head. 'I won't be alone,' she said. 'I shall be travelling with an acquaintance. My husband's aunt by marriage has a sister who is going over to visit and we shall travel together for moral support. She will be taking her maid with her; I'm sure it will be a wonderful experience.'

Mrs Dent shook her head. 'Well, I wish you luck, that's all I can say. Still,' she brightened visibly, 'you will be joining your husband and that's the main thing. I don't know where I'd be without my Alfred.'

Maurice took his mother's hand and began to tug her in the direction of the door and Mrs Dent pressed a sixpence into Lily's hand.

Lily hesitated. 'By the way,' she said reluctantly, 'my father asked me to mention the Sunday School. I don't know if perhaps Maurice . . . ?'

Mrs Dent looked embarrassed and lowered her voice. 'We're chapel,' she said, almost apologetically. 'His grandmother takes him to chapel twice every Sunday. I really don't think – '

'Oh no, no,' Lily said hastily. 'I quite understand, and of course it doesn't matter. My father always likes me to ask, that's all.'

Reaching up, she tugged the bell-rope and Mrs Spencer, the housekeeper, appeared.

'Mrs Dent is leaving,' Lily told her with a farewell smile for her little pupil. 'I'll see you at the same time next Friday, Maurice. And remember to practise. Thumb, first finger, second finger, then swing your hand and start again. You'll soon get used to it.'

Mrs Dent edged out of the door, pushing Maurice before her. As the housekeeper reached for the door handle, there were footsteps on the path outside and Lily's heart gave the familiar jump.

The postman handed several letters to the housekeeper, but she did not glance at them until the Dents had departed and she could close the door.

'Is there one for me?' cried Lily. 'Oh, give them to me, Mrs Spencer. You know you can't read without your specs. Oh!' She clapped a hand to her mouth. 'There *is*! It's from Patrick. And so is this. Two letters! And one for Papa.'

'Oh, Miss Lily!' cried the housekeeper (Mrs Spencer could never remember that she was now a married woman), but Lily had decided to open the letters in the privacy of her bedroom and now ran upstairs, her face flushed, her eyes bright with excitement. Once in her room, she closed the door and leaned back against it.

'Oh, my dearest Patrick!' she whispered, kissing the envelopes. 'You've written at last.' She checked the postmarks and then hastily tore open the earlier letter. This was the moment she had dreaded, when she must leave her home and her father. But she would be with Patrick again, she reminded herself, and she must not be so faint-hearted. With trembling fingers she opened the letter and sitting on the edge of the bed, began to read.

12 December 1848

My own dear wife,

Forgive me for the delay, but the time has passed so quickly and my days have been so full – but oh, how I have missed you, my dear sweet Lily! But soon we will be together again *in our own little home!* Yes, I have found a furnished flat (they call it an apartment) for us to rent, with a tiny garden. It is on the north side of the town and not at all bad and you will make it homely. Aunt Mabel says it needs a woman's touch. You will like her, I'm sure, when you get used to her . . .

Lily frowned, reading between the lines. What was wrong with Aunt Mabel, she wondered uneasily as she read on.

Uncle Albert is rather gruff at the office, but he has a kind heart and they are both longing to meet you. I am finding the work interesting, but my position as nephew to the 'boss' is not easy for the other clerks to appreciate, so I come in for some ragging, but they dare not say much . . .

'Oh dear!' whispered Lily, wondering exactly how much he was telling her. Was it just 'ragging', or were the clerks making his life a misery? Would he ever admit that the whole venture was a mistake? No, she rebuked herself, she was being foolish. Her imagination was getting the better of her. Of course they would tease him a little; they would most likely tease *any* new clerk.

To answer your last letter, dearest, yes, they *do* spit over here – that is, a lot of them do – but no one takes

7

it at all amiss and yes, I suppose they are loud of mouth and somewhat vulgar, but that is their way and they mean no offence to anyone by it. Some women do smoke but others, more enlightened, frown upon them for it. Please don't worry, Lily, and on no account let anyone poison your mind against this wonderful country. What it lacks in one respect it compensates for in another and *we will be together*, so the rest of the world can go hang! My sweet, gentle Lily, do come quickly. Believe me, we can make a grand life here if we make up our minds to like it. I know our honeymoon was disappointing, but I do believe circumstances were against us and when we are truly alone in our own home everything will be as it should be. Trust me, Lily. You will never regret the day you said you would be my wife.

Later we will find a house of our own, for Uncle Albert has hinted that my income will keep pace with our family! I am longing to show you off to the men at the office. Ned, my immediate superior, is married to a very homely girl and she is with child. Henry Simms is a year older than me, but still single and recovering from a recent heartache. More of that story when we meet; he is such a romantic. You will like him. He assures me that from what I tell of you he is half in love with you already!

So, my darling, buy your ticket and pack your trunk. Take plenty of food for the trip (they serve very little) and if the sea is rough, grin and bear it for my sake and tell yourself that it will be all worth while when you set foot in the United States. As to your final question, I have not seen any woman to equal you, so have no fear on that score. For me, you are the only woman in the whole world and I promise everything will come right between us. A few more weeks, Mrs Golightly, and we will be in each other's arms. Your ever loving husband,

Patrick Golightly.

Lily took a deep breath. So it was all going to happen at last; she really was going to America! Now she must follow the instructions Patrick had left her and notify Alice

Harrington so that they could finalize their travel arrangements. Alice Harrington was Mabel Golightly's widowed sister and she was going to America to stay with the Golightlys for an extended holiday. She would take her maid, Kate, with her and Lily would join them at Liverpool. Fifteen days at sea – or twenty if the winds were against them – and she would be with her husband. Then the rest of the world could indeed 'go hang' as Patrick put it. As to their honeymoon, she gave it no thought; of course everything would be different next time.

Jumping to her feet, Lily prepared to run downstairs to the study to share the news with her father; but then she remembered the second letter. It was slimmer than the first and she opened it curiously, wondering what had prompted him to write again so quickly. Opening the single sheet she read the hastily scrawled words; then with a whispered 'Dear God!' she sat down again, her face drained of all its colour, her heart hammering uncomfortably.

Lily,
    They really *have* found gold in the north-west. It is there for the taking and Henry and I mean to take some! We shall go first to Buffalo, where Henry has two cousins who we hope will join us in the venture. Four people can work a claim more profitably than two. Most likely we shall stay with them for a few days. From Buffalo we shall go via the lakes to Chicago and down river from there to St Louis and Independence. This really is the most splendid opportunity and will change our whole lives. *Do not tell your father*, but come to New York as planned. The rent of the apartment is paid for six months and you will bring some money with you. We have applied by post to join a company called the Brown Bears and will find them when we reach Independence. I believe you might also reach me by letter at Fort Kearny or Fort Laramie. I will be away for perhaps a year, but will write when I get to Independence. Forgive me, dearest, and trust me. I know this will be a shock to you, but do try to understand that I must go. I will come home *a rich man*, Lily!

9

In great haste to be among the 'early birds'!

                              Your affec. husband, Patrick G.

As a postscript he had added the cousin's address in Buffalo, with a request that she write to him there.

Gold in the north-west? She had heard the rumours, but knew almost nothing about the far side of the great American continent.

'No,' she whispered, 'this isn't happening. I don't believe it.' Had her husband *really* abandoned his wonderful prospects with his uncle's accountancy firm on the east side of America in order to go in search of gold on the opposite side?

'You're mad, Patrick,' she told him. 'You must be mad to believe in gold for the taking. And who on earth is Henry?' With an effort, she pulled herself together and re-read the first letter. Ah, yes. Henry, a year older than Patrick, unattached and somewhat of a romantic. Her lips tightened. So presumably it was Henry's idea to throw security out of the window and rush off on this wild-goose chase.

'If ever I set eyes on you, Mr Simms,' she said grimly, 'I'll strangle you with my bare hands.' It was true that Patrick was very trusting and easily led, she reflected, but this whole gold idea was quite preposterous. She tried to imagine small, dapper Patrick with a pick and shovel, hacking at a rock face in the bowels of the earth, but somehow the picture was a hazy one.

'Dear God!' she said, 'what have I done to deserve this?'

She sat frowning and at once other more sinister considerations crowded in. Was this Patrick's way out? Was he afraid to face her? She re-read the note. He was going to be away for a whole year! What sort of marriage was this turning out to be? 'Oh Patrick, you coward!' she thought miserably.

For a long time she sat on the bed with a letter in each hand, staring into space and trying to come to terms with this traumatic turn of events. She had never told her father a lie and her whole being shrank from the prospect, but if she showed him Patrick's second letter, he would most certainly forbid her to go to America. Then she would have to stay

10

on at the parsonage until Patrick came home – if he ever did. She covered her face with her hands and prayed for guidance.

After a while she slowly straightened her back and began to refold the letters with trembling fingers.

'Somehow I must pretend that everything is all right,' she told herself. 'I won't panic and I won't confide in anyone. I must go to America, I must find Patrick and I must persuade him to give up this mad idea.'

The more Lily considered the invidious position in which Patrick had placed her, the more angry she became. How dare he treat her so casually, deciding to throw up a secure means of financial support without so much as a word to his wife. It was irresponsible, to say the least. It really was unpardonable. He was expecting her to sit alone in her apartment for a whole year (possibly more!) twiddling her thumbs and waiting patiently for his return. Lily imagined him telling Henry Simms the neat plan he had made to keep her quiet while he went off on his harebrained adventure. Well, she was *not* a piece of inanimate property to be lightly abandoned, nor was she a meek obedient wife.

*

After much soul-searching Lily showed her father Patrick's first letter and went ahead with her plans to go to New York. She decided to find out exactly what Patrick had undertaken. Secretly, she made a few discreet inquiries and with the help of an atlas and a talkative American at the Black Ball shipping line, she learned a little more about California and the madness which had gripped so many men, her husband included.

'North-west' meant California, which until recently had been part of Mexico. A two-year war had just ended and, on its conclusion, California had been handed over to the United States. It was by all accounts a primitive area, undeveloped apart from a few settlements along the Pacific coast, but at the end of January a man called James Marshall had found gold in a stream on land belonging to someone called Sutter. Newspapers then took up the story and a steady

11

trickle of hopeful Americans set off to find out for themselves if the rumours were true. In December 1848 the President of the United States announced to a startled world that gold *had* been found in California – along the American, the Feather and the Yuba rivers – and more significantly, that it had been found in large quantities. The President's endorsement of the claim had made the affair respectable and many more men had promptly sold all their worldly goods to finance the trip west. Apparently Patrick and Henry were only two of many thousands infected with what was now being called 'gold fever'.

Intrigued in spite of herself, Lily purchased and read a report written by John Charles Frémont, who described his explorations in the west before the discovery of gold. As she read this, she became fired with a certain cautious enthusiasm. Perhaps she ought not to dissuade Patrick from his planned trip. Perhaps she should give it her blessing. When she had finished the account, she read it again, and long before she reached the final pages she had come to a momentous decision. She would not wait at home for Patrick's triumphant return; instead she would go with him. She would catch up with him and travel with him to California! Patrick Golightly would discover that he could not so easily cast her aside, she told herself grimly. She had married for better or for worse and if there were dangers ahead on the road to California, they would face them together. If the worst happened, she would rather die with Patrick than be left a grieving widow.

'If you are going west, Patrick, then so am I!' she declared and her small chin jutted defiantly.

Lily was used to getting her own way. Her mother had died giving birth to her and her maiden aunt, Florence Freedman, had moved in to keep house for them. 'Aunt Florrie' had doted on her and her father had also spoiled her. Later, after her aunt's death, Mary Spencer had been employed as housekeeper and although she was much less forbearing, Lily's character was already formed.

Now Lily had made up her mind and, once the decision was made, she felt as though a great weight had been lifted from her shoulders. Her earlier doubts gave way to a cautious but rapidly growing optimism.

*

6 February 1849

Kate Lester groaned and rolled over. Her stomach heaved and she began to count to a hundred in an attempt to distract her thoughts from the threatening nausea. Some mornings this worked, but at other times it failed. Her body was uneasy and lethargic but her mind was horribly active, her imagination working overtime as she tried to grapple with her problem. Outside, the nearby church clock struck five.

'Damn and blast!' she muttered and pulled herself up into a sitting position from which she could see out of the grimy attic window and across the endless expanse of sooty London roof-tops.

Kate was the fourth daughter of a family of nine girls, only six of whom survived their first year of infancy. There would almost certainly have been more daughters if her bricklayer father had not been killed in a drunken brawl just before the birth of the last child, a still-born boy. The destitute widow and four of the children had moved into the workhouse and it was from there that Kate had graduated, like her sisters before her, into domestic service.

Kate, at seventeen, was of a wayward disposition and before coming to work for Mrs Harrington had lost three similar positions through 'cheek', but bitter experience had curbed her tongue somewhat and a sneaking respect for her present employer had made her try a little harder to moderate her behaviour. She groaned again and thought of the young policeman whose child she was carrying. Of course he had taken fright when she broke the news of her 'trouble' – Kate had not expected anything else. It was her own stupid fault for allowing herself to be 'sweet-talked', but she had an eye for the men and had enjoyed many secret assignations. Now she must live with the consequences. She wasn't the first servant to fall from grace and wouldn't be the last. The trouble was that she hated children and babies in particular;

13

she was definitely not the motherly kind, but what to do about it? That was the question which filled her waking hours. She had tried all the usual remedies without success and the pregnancy persisted.

Rubbing her eyes wearily, she pushed down the bedclothes. She was a tall girl with an angular body and broad hips. Her reddish-gold hair, fine and inclined to be frizzy, was tied in bunches on either side of her face and framed a high broad forehead. Her mouth was thin and her green eyes were set wide apart. Not the face to launch a thousand ships, but fair enough to interest the young constable – not to mention several others before him. Kate's offer to marry him and make a home for him and the child had been turned down on the grounds that he was too young and marriage would spoil his chances of promotion. She had not been too upset by his rejection, for she had seen what marriage did to a woman and was not particularly keen to follow in her mother's footsteps.

Now with a resigned shrug of her shoulders, Kate slid out of bed and made use of the chamber-pot. She then poured cold water into the chipped china bowl that stood on the washstand and gave her hands and face a perfunctory wash before emptying the water, along with the contents of the chamber-pot, into the slop-pail. She dressed hastily, wriggling into a coarse blue dress. From five until six in the morning her appearance went unnoticed, for no one else would be up and about. Later she would comb her hair and change into her second-best dress, adding white cuffs and a white apron and covering her head with a square of lace in anticipation of the cook's inspection.

As she went downstairs with the slops, her nausea became unbearable and she hurried outside into the back garden where, bending low beside a stunted rhododendron, she put a finger down her throat and brought up a small amount of green bile. At once she felt much better and emptied the slop-pail over the grass, rinsed it under the pump and made her way back inside the house. She stole a slice of bread and ate it dry and was immediately restored to a positively hopeful frame of mind. Food had that effect on her, she had discovered.

'Something will turn up,' she told herself as she set about her early-morning chores. She lit the fire and filled the kettles and because it was Monday, she also filled and lit the copper. She whitened the front steps, set the breakfast trays and laid the dining table. When the kettles boiled she made a pot of tea and carried it up to the cook on a breakfast tray containing bread, butter and marmalade. It was five-past six and the day had only just begun.

*

Alice Harrington toyed with her poached egg, eating it in small quantities and washing her teeth round with frequent mouthfuls of very sweet tea.

'Don't fidget, Kate,' she told the maid. 'I don't know what's the matter with you these days. Stand up straight, girl! Why do you think the Lord gave you a spine? And take that expression off your face.'

'What expression, ma'am?' Kate protested.

'You look impatient and sullen and I don't know what else. You'll have to change your ways, my girl, or I shall change my mind about taking you with me.'

Kate looked at her blankly. 'Taking me?' she echoed.

'Yes, taking you.'

'Taking me where, ma'am?'

Mrs Harrington snorted with irritation. 'Why, to the United States, of course. The United States of America. That is *where*, as you put it. And don't look so surprised. I told you months ago that I was thinking of taking you with me.'

Kate was staring at her employer with her mouth open. 'America, ma'am? But I never give it another thought. The United States of America. Ooh, ma'am!'

Mrs Harrington's expression was disapproving.

' "Ooh, ma'am"?' she echoed sarcastically. 'Really, Kate. What a way to talk! I told you I would be visiting my sister in New York, and you will be coming with me. I've been waiting to hear about a companion for the journey and I heard yesterday. My sister thought it would be pleasant for

15

us to travel out together. The girl – Lilian – is joining her husband who now works for my brother-in-law. I thought – '

She broke off in surprise, for Kate's manner had undergone a transformation. 'The United States of America, ma'am!' she cried. 'Crikey! Me going to America – I can't hardly believe it.'

Mrs Harrington's face relaxed into a thin smile. 'That's cheered you up, has it? Thank goodness for that, then, but don't get too excited just yet, Kate. From all accounts the United States are not at all what we're used to. Here in Kent we are accustomed to a certain way of life, a certain standard of living. England is *civilized*, Kate. America is not. America is a young nation . . . but you wouldn't understand.' She shrugged. 'My sister assures me that I shall have all the comforts to which I am accustomed, but I have my doubts. She is very keen for me to go and no doubt has glossed over some of the country's failings. However . . .' she sighed, 'I have said I will go and I shall keep my word, but if I don't like it there I shall not stay – I shall come straight back to England, sister or no sister.'

But Kate clasped her hands rapturously, refusing to be brought down to earth by this threat. 'Will we go on a boat, ma'am? A ship, I mean?'

'Well, we certainly won't swim across the Atlantic,' Mrs Harrington assured her tartly, 'and we have no wings, so we certainly can't fly there. Of course we'll go on a boat, you silly girl – a steam packet, to be exact. I shall go to London tomorrow and purchase two tickets.' She surveyed her grinning maid sternly. 'It's *not* going to be fun, Kate,' she told her with a shake of her head. 'The packet will no doubt be crowded and full of fumes from the engine and if the weather's rough, we shall have all the miseries of sea-sickness to contend with.'

Kate, familiar with the miseries of morning sickness, was not deterred by her employer's warning.

'But I've never been on a ship, ma'am,' she cried, her eyes gleaming. 'Have you?'

'I've been over to Boulogne in France on two occasions,'

Mrs Harrington admitted, 'but I suspect that hardly prepares one for the rigours of an Atlantic crossing. What I have heard from my poor sister does not encourage me to look forward to the journey, but it can't last for ever.' She wagged an admonitory finger. 'But you, Kate, will have to be on your very *best* behaviour every minute of the time. None of your foolish sulks, Kate, and no lapses into bad language. And take your bible with you; we shall make time to read from it at least once a day.'

'I'll do that, ma'am,' cried Kate, 'and I won't sulk. Oh, ma'am, the United States of America! It sounds too good to be true.'

Mrs Harrington drank the last mouthful of tea and pushed aside the remains of her poached egg. 'I see there is no honey on the table,' she said. 'Have we no honey?'

'No, ma'am, I don't think so. Should I ask Cook?'

Mrs Harrington put a hand to her head. 'I slept badly,' she said. 'I feel quite exhausted this morning. Yes, ask Cook for some honey; it always gives me renewed energy. And a fresh pot of tea, Kate please, and some toast.'

As the maid departed in a whirl of excitement, Mrs Harrington sighed. It would have been so much more enjoyable if her husband had been spared to share it with her. Now it all seemed such a chore – so many friends and tradesmen to be notified, new clothes to be purchased and arrangements made for the journey itself. The trouble with journeying to America, she reflected, was the awful prospect of the same wearisome journey back. She did so hope she had been wise to accept her sister's invitation. She did so hope that America was not going to be a mistake.

*

11 February 1849

Edmund Freedman looked up from his painting, screwing up his eyes in a vain attempt to see more clearly in the fast-failing light. The oil painting on his easel showed the view from the window, a view he had painted three times before. Once in the spring of 1844 when a rough wind had stripped

17

the brown leaves from the chestnut tree; again at the end of the previous June when the rhododendrons were at their best; and now in the cold winter light, when the clouds loomed overhead, slate-grey and threatening rain.

Painting in oils was the only luxury he allowed himself and the time he could devote to it was precious little. He was a dedicated parson who loved his flock and he worked a long day, from seven each morning until eight or nine each evening. When he did sit down to paint, he did so for a variety of reasons, the least of these being to gratify his own creative desires. Sometimes it was to calm himself after an upsetting visit to a bereaved family and sometimes to gather strength for a forthcoming battle with authority on behalf of one of the weaker members of his congregation. Occasionally he took up his brush to think about his wife, long dead, and recall the short time they had spent together before her death. He had married Emma late in life, when all his friends had marked him down as a bachelor.

Today he was painting to occupy his mind so that he need not think about his only child, Lily, who was completing her packing; the daughter he might never see again in this life. He stared at the far hedge and added a touch of grey to the painting, then regarded the result critically. At that moment Lily entered the room and he glanced up with feigned cheerfulness.

'Oh, it's you, my dear,' he said. 'Have you finished your last-minute packing?'

'Yes, Papa.' She thought, with a pang, how frail he looked. His seventy-five years sat heavily upon his thin, angular frame and his hair and beard were white. Years of study in his youth had ruined his eyesight and his spectacles perched insecurely on his nose. Her throat tightened as she wondered yet again whether she should leave him, but there was Patrick and her first duty surely was to her husband. She had come very close to telling her father the truth, but now she was afraid of the result of such honesty. When she was safely on the boat, and no one could stop her from going to America, she intended to write to him and confess everything. He was

18

a God-fearing man and hopefully he would forgive her the deception.

She crossed the room to stand beside him and looked at the half-finished picture, comparing the view from the window with his interpretation of it. He waited anxiously for her comments.

'I'm trying to get that hint of blue shadow in front of the far hedge,' he told her. 'I'm not happy with it, I'm afraid; I think I've made it too heavy. It's really more of a haze than a shadow. A *hint* of blue is all I wanted, but I'm not capturing it at all. My mind's wandering.'

A sudden deep sigh shook his frame and at once Lily put an arm round his shoulders.

'Why not leave it for today?' she suggested. 'We could wrap up well and take a stroll in the garden. It's cold but there's no wind. Do you feel like some fresh air, Papa?'

'A walk in the garden! What a capital idea,' he said, abandoning his brush and rising to his feet. 'I shall miss our little strolls in the garden. Oh, my dear . . .' His voice faltered and Lily knew how hard the separation would be for him. They had been constant companions for so many years with rarely a cross word. It would be hard for her also, but she had a new life to look forward to while her father had only his parish and she feared he would fill the gap in his life by work and more work. She had tried in vain to persuade him to let a younger man take over, but now she was glad in one way that he would have something to occupy his time.

As they walked arm-in-arm in the garden, Lily talked as cheerfully as she could about the days ahead and sometimes spoke wistfully of the past. She had been born in the rambling parsonage and had never known any other home.

Her father stopped suddenly and shook his head in mock despair.

'Who will play croquet with me now?' he asked, surveying the iron hoops that dotted the lawn.

'Why, Mr Downey of course,' said Lily. 'You know he will always be glad to give you a game.'

Mr Downey, an elderly solicitor, was Edmund's closest friend.

'But Mr Downey doesn't let me win!' he protested.

They both laughed as they walked on down the brick-paved path and through the small rose garden which later would be a source of great pride when the summer blooms scented the air.

'I wonder what your mother would say,' her father said, 'if she knew I was letting you go gallivanting off to the other side of the world!'

Lily smiled. 'I'm hardly gallivanting!' she told him. 'I'm sailing to join my husband. I'm a respectable married lady now, Papa. As soon as we can afford it, we will come home and visit you – or else you could visit us. Oh, I know your views about foreign parts, Papa, but we shall be there to take care of you. If Mrs Harrington can go to America to visit her sister, surely you can come and visit us? We would send you the fare and then you could paint the view from *our* window in New York. Think of that! The church would survive your absence, Papa. Just for a bit.'

'The church might,' he agreed, 'but what about my parishioners? My poor little flock? How could I leave them? No one else understands them as I do. No one else would care. I could not abandon them to a stranger, not even for a short time. Poor old Ellen, with her hare-lip – no one else can understand a word she says! – and the Beakes with that dreadful son of theirs. So difficult, poor lad. And what about my nature study lessons at the school? I know you mean well, Lily, but it just wouldn't do, my dear. Besides, I'd be a poor sailor – I feel it in my bones!'

Lily squeezed his arm and forbore to argue the point with him. 'Then we shall come back to England to see you,' she promised. 'I shall start saving up my pennies – or cents! – as soon as I get out there. Oh, Papa, I do love you, you know. You do forgive me for leaving England, don't you? I need to be reassured that you don't resent my going.'

'Resent your going? Certainly not!' he cried. 'If all I have heard is true, then it's a land of opportunity and if Patrick thinks it best for you to go, then I must trust his judgement. I know I was reluctant to let you marry and I still think it was a *little* hasty, but there – I want your happiness above everything. Patrick is young, but he will learn wisdom under his uncle's firm guidance, I am certain of that. Patrick will take good care of you, I'm sure. If I thought otherwise, I would never have let you marry him.'

He turned to look at her suddenly. 'But I would like to see my grandchildren before I die. That would give me great pleasure.'

He looked at her keenly and Lily found herself blushing. She knew that during the week she and Patrick had spent together before he sailed she could not possibly have conceived, but her father could not know that and he had dropped several subtle hints. However, she was not with child and now she knew it would be a long time before a child became even a remote possibility, because first she must find Patrick. However, she did not want to disillusion her father so she said, 'As soon as a grandchild is on the way, I will write and tell you. That will be an excitement, Papa. And if it's a boy, we will call him Patrick *Edmund* Golightly.'

His face lit up with pleasure. 'Ah! That *would* be something to tell Mr Downey. Patrick Edmund! It has a nice steady sound, I think. And the first girl?'

'Why, Emma, of course, after Mama.'

He nodded and Lily knew that they had unwittingly stumbled on the one subject that would ease the parting for him.

'Just imagine,' she went on, 'in a few years – not too far distant if Patrick prospers – you will be waiting at the parsonage gate to greet not just me and Patrick, but a whole brood of grandchildren!'

'I shall live for that moment,' he assured her.

They reached the old wooden summer-house and paused before turning back towards the house.

'Do you remember your seventh birthday?' he asked. 'It was so cold but you were determined to have the party tea in the summer-house and your poor Aunt Florrie and I were so worried. January in the summer-house! Do you recall that, Lily?'

Lily nodded. 'I do indeed. Mr Downey's niece came and we were both wrapped in shawls and wore mittens to keep

21

our fingers warm.' She laughed at the memory. 'Poor Papa! Was I a great trial to you?'

'A trial? Never!' he said. 'A little wayward at times, maybe, but I daresay we were not strict enough. Mr Downey assured me so on many occasions, I recall. Spare the rod and spoil the child!' He laughed. 'Poor Florrie, it wasn't easy for her at first. She had been a spinster for such a long time.'

'She was wonderful,' said Lily. 'She loved us both so much. I've been very lucky.'

She stood back to stare up at the summer-house roof. The wooden shingles were rotting and several had been blown off in the recent high winds.

Her father, following the direction of her gaze, said, 'Dear me, I must see to that roof. I say that every time I see it and then it slips my mind again until the next time I notice it! I really must have it mended before it gets any worse.'

'Oh yes, you must, Papa,' said Lily. 'Where will young Emma Golightly have her tea-party if the summer-house roof has fallen in?'

'Emma Golightly?' he repeated blankly.

She saw her father's expression change as the name registered and he smiled broadly. 'Ah! Little Emma. Where indeed?' he said. 'I shall set about seeing to its repair next week without fail.'

Chapter Two

On the thirteenth of February the clipper *Western Queen* slipped her moorings and edged slowly out of the dock into the Mersey and down towards the open sea. Already Mrs Harrington had retired to her cabin to lie down, her stomach unsettled by the swaying of the ship even when at anchor. Kate and Lily stood at the rails, clutching their hats which were threatened by the rough wind gusting in off the Irish Sea. With the rest of the passengers they watched Liverpool receding into the pall of smoke that somehow still hung over the town. A growing expanse of water separated the ship from the stone wall which divided docks and city, while above the walls the grim warehouses huddled together, dark and forbidding.

'Good riddance!' muttered Kate. 'Honestly, ma'am, I think Liverpool's a *horrible* place. I thought London was bad enough, but Liverpool!' She raised her voice a little. 'Thank goodness we were in a decent hotel. I shall remember the Adelphi. At least it was clean and the food was good.'

Kate had never before stayed overnight in an hotel and she wanted the rest of the passengers to understand that she was the sort of person who did so.

Lily nodded. 'And all those beggars in the town. I couldn't bear it,' she said. 'I had no idea there was still such poverty. It's truly terrible.'

Kate decided to change the subject.

'Well, we're leaving all that, ma'am,' she said. 'We've got a fine ship to take us to the United States.' She glanced up-

23

wards, shielding her eyes from the brightness. 'Just look at all those masts and things. When the sails are hoisted – or whatever they do to them – the *Western Queen* is going to look a real picture. I wonder how long she is?' she added loudly for the benefit of a passing seaman who was eyeing her boldly.

'One hundred and ninety feet, ma'am,' he told her. 'She's one of our biggest. And that mast there,' he pointed upwards, '*with* the main top mast, is a hundred and twenty feet high. When we get her in full sail, she'll fly like a bird.'

He moved on to answer a question from another passenger and Kate grinned at Lily.

'Nice fellow,' she said. 'I think he fancied me, ma'am. Not that I'd marry a sailor. Not never! They're never there, are they? They get shore leave, put you in the family way and then 'op it back to sea again!'

As Lily only nodded, Kate gave her a sideways glance. 'Feeling homesick?' she asked kindly. 'Missing your Pa, are you?'

'I'm worrying about him,' Lily confessed. 'He looked so old and frail when I left him. I wonder whether my departure will be too much for him to bear. Oh dear, I must go to be with my husband, but I am so afraid I shall never see my father again.'

Kate was not impressed. 'Think yourself lucky, ma'am, that you've got someone who's going to miss you,' she said, 'and a husband waiting for you in New York. Nobody cares a fig about me. I could drop dead one day and no one would hardly notice! But it's no good moping or feeling sorry for meself, is it?'

Lily said, 'Mrs Harrington seems quite fond of you, Kate. You have a good employer and that's something to be thankful for.'

'Oh, I *am* thankful,' said Kate. 'I could be worse off; a lot worse. So could you.' She lowered her voice. 'We *could* be travelling steerage,' she said, 'then we'd be worse off. At least we've got a *bit* of privacy, even if the partitions don't go all the way up.' She giggled. 'Mrs Harrington's making me sleep in the top bunk in case the folks next door peep over. Not that I'll get much sleep. Crikey! She does snore! Still, I'm not complaining . . . hullo! Something's happening!'

Above them nimble-footed sailors began to ascend the rigging and with the sound of snapping canvas, the sails suddenly billowed one after the other – like a spray of white flowers bursting into bloom, thought Lily. The passengers felt the motion of the boat change and quicken as the wind took possession of the ship and, steadily and relentlessly, the shoreline began to fade into the distance as the *Western Queen* cut a path through the cold grey sea which now surrounded them on all sides, whipped into angry white crests by the wind. Too late Lily put up a restraining hand as her hair was blown free of its hairpins. Kate's red hair was safe inside a bonnet and she laughed at Lily's predicament.

'You'd best make yourself a bonnet, ma'am,' she remarked. 'I think there will be plenty of windy days on this trip. Crikey, it'll be a miracle if no one gets blown into the sea!'

She looked round her. One by one the passengers were relinquishing the last view of Liverpool and making their way below decks.

'I'd best go down and see if Mrs Harrington needs me,' said Kate reluctantly, and she too went below.

Lily, with a few other passengers, remained at the rail while the crew scurried to and fro like ants, intent on their various tasks, and the officers strode the heaving decks to ensure that no one slackened.

Later on, at the Captain's insistence, the ship would be sailed at speeds which tested her to the utmost limits and Lily, with the rest of the passengers, would find the crossing uncomfortable in the extreme. The trip from England to America would prove an experience best forgotten but now Lily, blissfully unaware of this fact, finally followed the example of her fellow passengers and went below.

*

New York
7 March 1849

My dearest and most beloved Papa,

I write to say that with God's help we have arrived in New York. I am thankful the crossing is over. The cabin was very cramped but I should not complain for many passengers had a worse time of it, sharing the gloom below decks with a variety of hens, pigs and sheep which are kept to provide a little fresh foodstuffs for passengers like us who enjoy the comparative luxury of individual cabins. The weather was rough most of the time and poor Mrs Harrington was indisposed for the entire journey. I was seasick for nearly a week, but then my body adjusted to the constant rolling and I was more comfortable. Mrs Harrington's maid, Kate, got a piece of soot in her eye from the funnel but fortunately the ship's surgeon removed it for her. We have talked at some length. She seems a pleasant girl and very cheerful company.

When it was possible I went up on deck for some air but I did not venture far and held on tightly to the rail. With the wind filling the sails and the birds wheeling overhead against the sky, it would have made a fine subject for one of your paintings. Unfortunately the wind was so strong it would have blown you and your brushes into the sea! At the very least you and your canvas would have been drenched with the spray which soon drove me below deck again to the stale air and the groans of the less fortunate passengers. It seemed on occasions that our captain was a lunatic, or else determined to drown us all, for he would – even in the most huge seas – urge the men to crowd on more sail until even the crew muttered that we would end up at the bottom of the sea.

Mostly the passengers played cards or gambled and others drank spirits (which is against the ship's rules but is still indulged in) so there was some unruly behaviour.

But enough of all that Papa. We arrived safely and I am settled in the apartment.

Now Papa, I come to the hardest part of my letter. I swear it is as hard for me to write as it will be for you to read. The truth is that for the first time in my life I have deceived you and that knowledge is a heavy burden for me to bear. When the letter arrived from Patrick, a second letter came with it which I kept from you. In it he told me he was going to California, to the newly discovered

26

gold fields we have heard about. He instructed me to wait in New York for his return and he left me amply provided for, but I cannot do as he suggested, Papa. I am determined to accompany him in this venture. A few women *are* going West and many immigrants have already travelled most of the route on their way to Oregon. There will be no danger. You must understand that it is not such a risk as might be imagined from reading the newspapers. I shall break the news of my intentions to the Golightlys when I call on them again, tho' I am certain that it will not be well received by them. No doubt they are already distressed by Patrick's departure and that of his colleague, Henry Simms, who goes with him. I hope most sincerely that we do find gold, because he has almost certainly forfeited his uncle's goodwill and I doubt if there will be a place for him with the firm when he returns from California.

He and his companion, Henry Simms, have gone ahead to Buffalo to join up with cousins of Mr Simms and I hope to catch up with them there, so do not be anxious on that score.

I will write whenever I can to inform you of my whereabouts and I beg you not to fret on my account, for I shall look on it as a grand adventure. If we find gold, we will be able to visit you that much sooner.

I love you dearly and the thought that you might be anxious on my account is all that troubles me. Pray for me and we will be reunited again before too long.

If you write to the Golightlys' address, which I gave you before I left, they will no doubt forward it to me somehow.

Please give my kindest regards to all my friends. God bless you and be with you always, Papa. You will always be in my thoughts.

Your most loving daughter
Lilian.

As Lily made her way towards the Golightlys' house she did not relish the thought of what lay ahead. They had been so kind to her on her arrival and at great pains to help her feel at home, but behind the smiles she had sensed the deep hurt which Patrick's extraordinary behaviour had caused them. Yet they had not reproached her, although Lily could appreciate how great a temptation it must have been to unbraid *her* for her husband's betrayal. Betrayal, thought Lily, was not too strong a word. They had offered a nephew the prospect of advancement that normally would have gone to a son and Patrick had dismissed their generosity as though it was of no consequence. Lily had apologized profusely on his behalf, but she knew that nothing she could do or say would heal the wound. Now she was about to add insult to injury.

When she reached their neat clapboard house and knocked, the door was opened by Kate.

'Hullo, Kate,' said Lily in some surprise.

'Come in, ma'am,' said Kate with a noticeable lack of enthusiasm.

It was strange to be mistress and maid once more after the earlier and more equal companionship of fellow passengers on a difficult and tedious sea journey.

Lily stepped inside the Golightlys' house, which was furnished in quiet good taste, and found herself wondering if she and Patrick would ever own such a charming home. If they found gold they would!

'I'll tell them you're here, ma'am,' said Kate.

Looking at her closely, Lily saw that her eyes were red and her manner rather subdued.

'Is anything wrong?' she whispered.

Kate shrugged. 'You might say so,' she said. 'There's been a bit of a barney, that's all.'

'You do look rather . . . pale.'

'And no wonder,' was the uncompromising reply. 'I'm in a bit of bother — but still, worse things happen at sea, I suppose.'

Lily nodded. She was strongly tempted to go away again without seeing the Golightlys. If there had been some kind of domestic upheaval, it was hardly a good time to tell them of her own change of plans.

She had not been idle during the two days she had been in New York, but had read all the newspapers she could find

28

which contained articles on the gold fields. From her reading, it seemed to her that only fur trappers *chose* to live among the inhospitable plains and mountains, for the first settlers of 1841 had hurried through it on their way to Oregon, experiencing all manner of hardships along the way. Did Patrick really have any idea of the difficulties of such a trip? She doubted it. He was young, impetuous and easily persuaded and Lily became more convinced than ever that the terrible Henry Simms must have talked him into the venture. She suspected that neither of them fully understood the hazards that awaited them and her heart quailed at the thought that she, too, would share the dangers ahead. Common sense urged her to stay in New York as instructed, but an innate stubbornness drove her on. She resented being told to stay at home like a good wife while Patrick risked his life, and she did not want to fritter away months of her life waiting for the occasional letter from a husband who had taken this momentous decision without first consulting her.

However, as she hesitated on the doorstep of the Golightlys' house, she believed she could face all manner of hardships on the trail more easily than she could face the Golightlys!

'Perhaps I should come back tomorrow – ' she began, but at that moment Mabel Golightly came to the door of the dining room.

'Oh, it's you,' she said distractedly. She turned and called 'It's Patrick's wife come to see us.'

Lily heard a whispered exchange and then Uncle Albert appeared, hands outstretched in greeting.

'Lily,' he said. 'Come right in. We were just finishing lunch. Will you have some coffee?'

'No, thank you.' Lily was aware that Kate still hovered nearby. 'I would like to talk to you if I may, when you have all finished your coffee. I'm quite happy to wait out here.'

To her surprise Mrs Golightly said, 'Nonsense, child! I'll come into the parlour with you. I've finished my coffee.'

And she hurried Lily into the elegant parlour and closed the door behind them with elaborate care.

'My dear!' she began at once without even asking Lily to sit down. 'You've called at a most awkward time. You won't believe what's happened! I was *so* shocked and my poor sister is simply furious. It's Kate, her maid. She's in a *certain condition*. Can you imagine? And the girl not even married. Fancy the nerve of it, coming all this way without a word!'

'Poor Kate!' exclaimed Lily.

'*Poor* Kate?' Mrs Golightly drew herself up, stiff with disapproval. 'Isn't it poor Alice? She's brought the girl all this way and now she'll have to get rid of her. Really, it is quite unpardonable. A young policeman! A "bobby", as she calls him. Would you believe it?'

'The father, do you mean?'

'What else? Alice is quite beside herself and I must say I sympathize. At home the girl could be bundled off back to her parents, but out here . . .'

'She has no father,' said Lily, 'She told me so. And her mother's in the Union – that is, the workhouse.'

'I do know what a Union is,' said Mrs Golightly coldly, beginning to suspect that Lily's sympathies were not all with the unfortunate Mrs Harrington. 'I can tell you that if she had been one of my servants, I would have boxed her ears on the spot. The nerve of the girl!'

'But how did you find out?' Lily asked.

Mrs Golightly rolled expressive eyes. 'Why, she was giving my girl Annie a hand at table when she fainted clean away. Dropped one of my best tureens and went down like a log. We quite thought she was dead. As soon as she came round, she burst into tears.'

'Oh dear,' said Lily. 'How terribly sad!'

'That's hardly the word for it,' said Mrs Golightly severely. 'I cannot imagine what is to be done with her. My husband was just suggesting that she be sent back to England – it would be worth the fare just to get rid of her. And the wretch is so forward – not a word of regret except to say that she hates babies! Hates them! Can you imagine? My husband soon put a stop to that. He can be very forbidding and a few well-chosen words soon put her in her place. A girl like that must be made to see the error of her ways before she can even start to repent of her folly.'

Lily was frantically wondering how to avoid making her own confession. It certainly did seem that her visit was most untimely. On the other hand, she was longing to be done with deceit and it occurred to her that her news might distract some unwelcome attention from the unfortunate Kate.

She suddenly decided to brazen it out and took a deep breath. 'Perhaps my news will cheer you all up,' she said brightly. 'I've come to tell you that I'm not going to stay in the apartment. I'm following Patrick. I've decided I don't want to be left behind, so I shall go with my husband to California, I shall join him at Buffalo.'

It took a few seconds for her words to register, but then a glazed look came into Mrs Golightly's eyes and she groped for a chair and sat down heavily. Lily plunged on.

'I've thought it all out very carefully,' she said. 'Patrick is no good at cooking and will never wash his clothes or take care of his health. He's going to *need* me and he can't have gone far. I'm only a few weeks behind him and I can soon catch him up, then when we reach the gold fields, he and Henry can concentrate on the digging while I keep house for them – '

Mrs Golightly found her voice at last. 'Are you out of your mind?' she demanded. 'Go to California? Are you mad? Your husband would never agree and my husband will absolutely *forbid* it! Go to the gold fields? Why, you know nothing about it. *Nothing*. Maybe a few women *are* making the trek, but they're American born and bred and they belong to the land. You disappoint me, Lily. We did think Patrick had made a sensible marriage, if nothing else. A parson's daughter is too good for him! That's what my husband said; those were his very words.'

Lily bridled at this slur on her husband. 'Patrick is as good a man as you could find anywhere,' she protested. 'He has been talked into this trip by this wretched man Henry Simms, who – '

But Mrs Golightly was shaking her head emphatically. 'Oh no, Lily. That's not how it was. It was Patrick who came to us first, telling us he was off on this wild-goose chase. It was Patrick's idea.'

Lily gazed at her in disbelief.

'Oh, yes,' Mrs Golightly continued, enjoying Lily's discomfiture. 'It was your husband's idea. Henry only came to us three days later. Mind you, they are two of a pair. Dreamers, the pair of them. Mr Simms always was a little wild, but Albert thought he would settle down. Then Patrick had to turn his head. Oh yes, you have my word on it, Lily, your husband is to blame if anything happens – '

'He must have wanted to go,' cried Lily. 'Mr Simms, I mean. Patrick could not force him to go.'

Mrs Golightly sniffed disparagingly. 'How long have you known your husband, Lily?'

'Four months.' Lily spoke defiantly, guessing what was to come.

'And you have been married only a few weeks.' Mrs Golightly shook her head. 'Too short a time to get to know him, Lily. I was betrothed to Albert for five years! Young people today are so hasty. I'm surprised at your father allowing you to marry without a proper betrothal.'

Lily now flew to her father's defence. 'Papa *did* think the betrothal much too short,' she said. 'He wanted us to wait, but you had offered Patrick the position in the firm and that meant we either had to marry or be separated, possibly for years. I begged Papa to let us marry. He was very reluctant.'

'Then he should have said "No",' Mrs Golightly insisted. 'Why, you hardly know each other.'

'Of course we do!' cried Lily, stifling her doubts.

Mrs Golightly pounced. 'Do you? Do you really? Then how is it you were so surprised when you learned that Patrick was rushing off on a fool's errand?'

Lily was silent.

'And how come,' Mrs Golightly went on, 'Patrick saw you as a dutiful wife who would obey his instructions to stay in New York and await his return? You were surprised by his behaviour and he will be just as surprised by yours. You don't know him, Lily, you don't know each other at all.'

Lily could not argue with the logic of her reasoning. 'But

we do love each other,' she said lamely. 'That's more important, isn't it?'

'Do you think so?' Mrs Golightly shook her head at this further proof of Lily's foolishness. 'I'm sure you are making a mistake, Lily, and I think you should stay on in the apartment – at least he has made good provision for you, I'll grant him that much.'

'I can't,' said Lily, with a stubborn shake of her head. 'I won't be left behind, I'm going with him!'

'And if you *don't* catch up with him?'

'I will. I know the way he's going.'

'You're out of your mind!'

Lily shook her head, but made no comment. She was horribly afraid that Mrs Golightly's advice was sound and that she should take it. Her confidence was shaken, but she felt determined to prove Mrs Golightly wrong.

'I've been cosseted all my life,' she said suddenly.

'Well, I should hope so,' said Mrs Golightly. 'A well-bred young lady *should* be cosseted.'

'I don't know what goes on out there – in the rest of the world. Maybe that's how Patrick is thinking! That's what *he* wants to know.'

Mrs Golightly put a despairing hand to her forehead. 'Lily, this is all so foolish.'

'But perhaps this is what made him decide to go. Maybe it's not just the gold,' cried Lily. 'Maybe I don't know Patrick yet – you are right there – but I'm learning quickly. Maybe what he wants is to know another way of life. A new experience, good or bad.' She stood up abruptly. 'I must go with him, Mrs Golightly – don't you see? He'll be a different person when he comes back. If he's going to change, then I must change with him.'

Mrs Golightly stood up with a look of resigned defeat.

'I don't know why I waste my time with you,' she said wearily. 'You are every bit as bad as your husband. I shall write to your poor father and tell him exactly how I feel about this whole affair. I'm really disappointed in you, Lily.'

Lily smiled faintly. 'I'm sorry,' she said. 'You have actually done me a great favour, if only you knew it. I think I was determined to go from the moment I read Patrick's letter, but I was going for the wrong reasons. You've helped me tremendously.'

Impulsively, she leaned forward and kissed the older woman lightly on the side of her face.

'Try not to think too badly of us,' she said and hurrying out of the house, made her way back to the apartment with feet as light as her heart.

*

The next two days passed for Lily in a whirl of activity. She had not yet unpacked, so she did not do so. She attended one of the many lectures being given on the subject of the gold area and she re-read Frémont's book and began to read *What I Saw in California* by Edwin Bryant, who had been there in 1846. She had also ordered a copy of Ware's *Emigrants' Guide* which the bookseller assured her was 'the most valuable source book for gold seekers travelling over-land' and included such useful information as how to cross rivers and assay gold!

Lily was nothing if not thorough and she was beginning to enjoy herself. She visited the offices of the *Intelligencer*, where she spent a whole morning reading through back copies of the newspaper. From these she learned that the gold strikes were both real and sometimes astonishing. Someone had found a lump of gold weighing seven pounds! Someone else had acquired twelve thousand dollars' worth of gold in six days! Barques, schooners, steamers and brigantines were apparently sailing from all the major ports in America bound for California and mining companies were being formed as fast as the articles of constitution could be laid down.

It appeared that the jumping-off points for the overland trek were either Independence or St Joseph. Beyond these two points the land was unsettled and only two isolated government posts existed along the long westward trail – Fort Kearny and Fort Laramie.

From the map it seemed that she must go by train to Buffalo on Lake Erie. There she hoped to find Patrick and

34

his companions, but if she missed them she would travel on by steamer through Lake Huron and down through Lake Michigan to Chicago; and from there down the Illinois River to the Missouri and thence to Independence. Lily anticipated that Patrick would be delayed there for some time. Companies were being formed, but they would all have to wait until the spring grass appeared on the prairie which would provide vital feed for the cattle and horses. Lily was sure that if she missed Patrick at Buffalo she could reach Independence before he moved out, but she thought it prudent to make plans in case she missed him again. In that case she, too, would have to buy into one of the companies. Beyond that she could only guess at the possibilities; she would put her faith in God and take one step at a time. But she would certainly need all the money she could raise and to this purpose she found a jeweller and sold the only items of any value she owned. There was a gold locket which had belonged to her grandmother and a ring which had been in the possession of her father's family for several generations. Her father had given her a silver-backed hair brush and Aunt Florrie had left her a pearl brooch. Lily let them all go – not without a twinge of regret – but the money raised was nearly seven hundred dollars which, with the money she had brought with her from England, gave her a more comfortable total of nine hundred and forty dollars.

She then broke the news to her landlord that she would not after all be keeping the apartment for six months and asked for a refund of Patrick's money. At first he was unwilling, but Lily finally persuaded him by agreeing to pay a month's rent after she moved out. That way he did not stand to lose any money and in fact would most probably make a profit, since accommodation was hard to find in New York and he would relet the apartment without difficulty.

Lily knew she was not properly dressed for life on the trail, but decided she would purchase new and more suitable clothing when she reached Independence. There, apparently, she could buy anything she needed.

On her fourth evening in New York, she was once more

35

bent over the map when there was a knock at the door. Kate Lester stood outside, clutching a faded carpet-bag.

'Kate!' said Lily, startled.

Kate's expression was grim.

'I heard what you told Mrs Golightly,' she said breathlessly, 'and I'm coming with you to California, so you can say "No", ma'am, till the cows come home, but I shall come anyway. I shall just follow you wherever you go. I have a little money and I can pay my way. You can't stop me.'

Lily was speechless as they stared at each other in the long silence that followed Kate's speech.

'I'm coming, I tell you,' she repeated desperately. 'If you can go, ma'am, then so can I. They want to send me back to England, but I won't go back to the workhouse. I'm telling you straight. I'm coming with you.' She stopped and glared defiantly at Lily.

'You'd better come in,' said Lily.

Kate walked past, her head high, but Lily had seen the anguish in her eyes. So Mrs Harrington had decided to send her back to the workhouse. Not a very pleasant prospect. 'In her place, thought Lily, 'I'd do exactly the same.'

'Look, Kate . . .' she began. 'Oh, do put down that bag!'

'I got the fare to England,' said Kate, still clutching the bag. 'I made them give it me instead of the sailing ticket, so I can pay my way to California. I'll find enough gold for me and the baby. I can work as hard as anyone – harder than most.'

Gently Lily took the bag from her and nodded towards a chair. Kate sat down abruptly.

'I won't go back to England,' she repeated. 'I'd rather die, and that's the truth. I won't be any trouble to you, if that's what you're thinking, and when you find your man I'll keep meself to meself. The money's not a lot, but I can be your maid: cook and wash the clothes for you and your husband – and I won't want no wages, just my food.'

Lily looked at her helplessly. 'Kate, no one travels to California with a *maid*,' she said. 'It's just not like that.'

'Well, I'll be your companion then. A lady like yourself – a parson's daughter – should have a companion.'

Lily shook her head. 'No maid, no companion,' she stated.

Kate swallowed. 'I tell you, I'm coming to California,' she repeated, her voice rising.

'Kate, please listen to me,' said Lily. 'I understand how you feel, but it's out of the question. You must see that. I don't know what I'm letting myself in for – not really. How can I allow you to come with me in your condition? It would be madness.'

'I could be your housekeeper,' said Kate. 'I could do your washing and cook your meals. Your sort *has* to have servants, you always do.'

'Not this time,' said Lily. 'We shall all have to fend for ourselves. It will be a hard life.'

'That's nothing new to me,' Kate insisted. 'I'm *used* to a hard life.'

She looked so pathetic, clutching her few possessions, that Lily was touched. She was also tempted to say 'Yes' because it would be rather pleasant to have a travelling companion. She hesitated. 'Look *if* you did come with me it would be as a friend,' she said. 'An equal. Do you understand? I'd be in no position to take responsibility for you or anyone else. It will be hard enough looking after myself. I expect to be reunited with my husband before the going gets too difficult, but there's no guarantee that that will happen. If for any reason it does not – if he's too far ahead – we would be on our own. That would be bad enough, but you're expecting a child, Kate. When is it due?'

'September maybe, or October. I'm not sure. It doesn't make no difference.'

'But it does,' Lily insisted. 'How would you look after a baby on the trail? It might die, Kate. You would be better off in England.'

'But I'll never be rich in England,' said Kate. 'The gold will make all the difference.'

'*If* we find any gold.'

Kate looked at her with desperation in her eyes.

'It *must* be there, ma'am,' she said. 'Your husband thinks it's there or he wouldn't be going. I want a chance the same as you and you can't stop me.'

Lily sat down and faced her across the table.

'Look, please don't keep calling me "ma'am",' she said. 'And try to understand. I *want* you to come with me, I really do, but I have to point out the disadvantages. If I encourage you and then the baby dies or something else dreadful happens . . .'

Kate grinned suddenly. 'Like I'm scalped by an Indian?'

Lily shuddered. 'Don't even *talk* about it,' she said. 'I just wanted to be sure you understand – then you can't say I didn't warn you.'

Kate considered Lily's words carefully and then said slowly, 'Are you saying I can come?'

Lily nodded. 'I suppose I am saying you can come and welcome, but only as an equal. We'll just be two women going to California together, helping each other and trying not to make too many mistakes. I don't know anything about babies – '

Kate laughed. 'And you don't want to, neither, ma'am. Turn your hair grey, they do. There was always a baby in our house – horrible screaming brats.' Kate looked round the room as though seeing it for the first time and then back at Lily. 'You mean it – I really can come?'

'Yes.'

'Crikey!' breathed Kate. 'That's a weight off my mind.' She hesitated. 'The only thing is, can I stay here until we go? I've nowhere else.'

'Of course you can.'

Lily knew she was being hasty and over-optimistic, but the prospect of a companion was irresistible. She knew very little about Kate, but had found her amusing company on the ship coming over. Somehow they would muddle along together – at least, she hoped they would. It was a chance they must take. On balance she was glad she had said 'Yes', but only time would tell whether or not she had made the right decision. Suddenly, her whole life seemed so unpredictable that one more gamble was neither here nor there! She had said Kate could come and she would hope for the best.

She smiled at Kate. 'We'll have a cup of tea, then we'll look at the map and I can show you where we're going.'

38

'I'll make the tea, ma'am,' said Kate, jumping to her feet.

Lily raised her eyebrows at the forbidden word and they both began to laugh.

'Equals,' said Lily, holding out her hand.

Kate shook it solemnly, although her eyes were smiling. 'Equals,' she agreed.

*

Later that evening they pored over the map and Lily explained the plan to a wondering Kate.

'We take the train as far as Buffalo,' she explained, 'and I'm fairly hopeful we can catch the men before they leave. In case we don't, I've worked out the rest of the route to Independence. We're sure to catch up with them there because the wagon trains will be waiting for the spring grass before they set out.'

Kate nodded. 'So if we have to find our own way to Independence?'

'We go by paddle steamer through the lakes here – first, Erie, then Huron and down through Michigan – '

'All that way by water!'

Lily shrugged. 'I'm just following Patrick and Henry,' she said. 'I'm sure they know best. After all, Henry Simms is American born so he should know. Then from Chicago we go by canal until it joins the Illinois River, then it's another river boat down the Illinois, along the Missouri to Independence.'

Kate looked at her dubiously. 'Lily, suppose we don't find them? Just *suppose*. What do we do then?'

'We go on until we do,' Lily told her. 'If the worst comes to the worst, we can join a company there and they'll provide a wagon and mules – '

'Mules!' cried Kate. 'You won't get me anywhere near one of them. They'll kick the daylights out of you as soon as look at you!'

'Something has to pull the wagons,' Lily reminded her.

'What's wrong with horses?'

'They're not very suitable for the long distance, apparently,' said Lily, delighted to air her newly acquired knowledge. 'Don't ask me why because I forget. Mules or oxen are best. Oxen are cheaper, but mules are stronger though harder to control. Mules have to have reins and be driven from the wagon seat. Oxen don't have bridles; they're yoked to the wagon tongue and you have to walk beside them, urging them on and cracking a whip. Take your pick!'

'The oxen get my vote,' said Kate after a moment's reflection. 'I rather fancy cracking a whip.'

'Oxen it is, then.'

'Just like that?'

Lily shrugged. 'Why not?' she laughed. 'In Independence we can buy all the things we need to take with us to California.'

'You do know an awful lot,' said Kate, impressed.

'I've learnt it all in the past weeks,' Lily told her. 'I badgered people to tell me anything and everything. I read back copies of the newspapers and they're full of letters from people who went last year. There really is gold, Kate, and I'm beginning to believe we just might find some of it. I'm getting an attack of gold fever!'

'We could pray for it,' said Kate. 'Mrs Harrington says that if you pray, your prayers get answered.'

Lily smiled. 'I don't think gold is a thing you should ask for, Kate. I mean, it would be greedy to pray for gold. I just want to get over there in one piece. After that, it's up to Patrick. He can find all the gold he likes!'

For a moment they were both lost in delightful daydreams, but then Lily remembered the business in hand.

'I've started making a list of things we shall need,' she said. 'Things like sarsaparilla and laudanum – and we might need a gun – '

'A gun? I don't want a gun.'

Lily shrugged. 'We might need them. It says there may be Indians. The Pawnees are supposed to be friendly, and so are the Shoshoni, but in some areas they might not be so friendly.'

'I'll have a gun!' said Kate. 'I've changed my mind.'

Lily looked at her soberly. 'We wouldn't have to shoot anyone,' she said, 'not unless they were actually trying to kill us. I think if we just waved the gun, they would know we weren't defenceless. I mean, we won't be all on our own out there. There will be Patrick and this Henry and the cousins – '

'*If* we catch up with them.'

'Oh. but we must,' said Lily, startled. 'We could never manage on our own. Oh Kate, I suppose this *is* all happening? We're not dreaming, are we?'

'We're *not* dreaming,' Kate assured her with a grin. 'At least, I hope not. We're all going to California to make our fortunes and no one is going to stop us!'

Chapter Three

On reaching Buffalo, Henry and Patrick were intensely disappointed to discover that the two cousins were not prepared to accompany them to California. The elder had just become betrothed and his wife-to-be was adamant that he remain at home. The younger cousin had enlisted in the cavalry only weeks earlier. Henry's letter warning the family of their imminent arrival and plans had somehow gone astray and their welcome was not as cordial as it might have been. They stayed for only a few hours, their enthusiasm only slightly dashed by their reception. They regretted the time they had wasted, but were otherwise undeterred. 'All the more gold for us!' Patrick asserted defiantly, and they made their way to the shipping office and set off towards Chicago.

They reached Independence on April the twenty-third and went at once to see Captain Douglas P. Becher. Becher was the leader of the Brown Bear Mining Company, a large man with a fierce hooked nose and dark eyes which stared out from beneath bushy eyebrows. He had been in the army and later a lawyer and he came straight to the point.

'Golightly and Simms?'

'Yes, sir.'

Becher extended a huge hand to each in turn and then motioned to them to sit down on an adjacent log. His 'office' was the small, well-trodden area of grass alongside his wagon and he was sitting on an upturned crate.

'So you want to join us,' he began. 'Well, you've made a wise choice although I say so myself. I don't believe in false modesty, so I can tell you I aim to make this the most efficient company en route for the gold fields. We're well organized, well financed and we know what we're doing. You two don't look like miners, but then neither does half the company and it's not looks that count. By the time we reach California, you'll be as tough as you need to be. Which one of you is Simms?'

'I am, sir.'

'Hmm.'

Henry Simms smiled easily. He was nearly six feet tall with a narrow frame; his freckled face was plain but good-natured, and from the lines round his eyes he obviously smiled a lot. Pale lashes fringed blue eyes and his thick blond hair, which curled untidily, was parted on one side and reached just below his ears. He sported a moustache. His look said, 'I'm prepared to be friends,' and even in such unusual circumstances his attitude was at once relaxed and unafraid. His grey jacket was collared in black velvet and he wore a thin black tie knotted over a clean white shirt. He looked exactly what he was – a city boy.

'Any family, Mr Simms? Wife? Children?'

'No, sir.'

'Dependent relatives back home?'

'My parents are alive and well and run a grocery store in New York.'

'And you have your parents' approval?'

'Most certainly *not*, sir, but hell!' Henry laughed. 'I'm going anyway.'

Becher laughed with him and then turned his attention to Patrick.

'And you, Mr Golightly?'

Patrick faced him eagerly and the contrast between the two young men could hardly have been more striking. Three inches shorter than Henry, Patrick was as dark as Henry was fair. His fine dark hair was brushed smooth from a centre parting and he wore it short. His dark eyes were fixed anxiously on Becher's face as he leaned forward to answer his question, hesitating fractionally as he searched his mind for phrases which would impress. He held his hat in his lap and his fingers toyed with the brim.

'A wife, sir, but no children.'

Becher, recognizing the accent, raised his eyebrows. 'And you are an Englishman, Mr Golightly?'

'That's right, sir. I came to America to take up a job with my uncle, but then decided to try my luck in California. I talked Mr Simms into joining me and here we are.'

'And your wife?'

'She's still in England, sir,' said Patrick. 'At least she was, but by now she'll be on her way across on the Black Ball packet. She's going to live in New York until I get back.'

'And she's willing to wait for you? Have you left her well provided for?'

Patrick, agitated by the line of questioning, was seized by a sudden panic. This man was going to accept Henry but turn *him* down! Had he given up his opportunity with Golightly and Brown, quarrelled with his uncle and rushed to Independence, only to be rejected?

'*Very* well provided for,' he lied vigorously. 'The rent is paid for a year in advance and she will be living near to an aunt and uncle of mine who are very fond of her. She's one hundred per cent behind me in this venture, sir.' He hoped he didn't look as guilty as he felt and dared not meet Henry's eyes. 'She knows what a wonderful chance it is for us to amass some real capital.'

Becher said. 'And you said no children?'

'No children, sir.' This must surely be a point in his favour, thought Patrick. 'We've only been married for a few months . . .'

'And you're leaving her alone for a long and indefinite period?'

'She is keen for me to go, sir,' Patrick insisted. 'I can assure you, Lily is a very sensible girl.'

Becher made no answer but pursed his lips thoughtfully. Patrick's palms were sweating and his heart almost stopped beating. Becher *was* going to reject him. Anger snapped within him – the man had no right to blight his chances of a fortune. He opened his mouth to say so, but fortunately at that moment Becher shrugged and smiled.

'Well, gentlemen, it looks as though we might be in business,' he said and the two younger men exchanged triumphant looks. 'The stake money is two hundred and fifty dollars a head and that gives you a share in the equipment and provisions. By equipment, I include purchase of wagons, horses or oxen, tools and medical supplies. Food will be basic supplies that can travel two thousand miles without rotting – that is, beans, flour, bacon, dried fruit and so on. We'll aim to supplement the rations with fresh game. Do either of you shoot?'

'No, sir,' said Patrick.

'Can't wait to learn,' grinned Henry. 'Are we expecting trouble with Indians?'

'Hopefully not,' said Becher. 'There's been very little trouble so far. They like to trade, of course, but last year some of them died of white man's diseases. They are very vulnerable to smallpox and cholera, so they're understandably wary of us.' He consulted the paper on his desk. 'Now let me see. The company so far is forty-two, now risen to forty-four. That's six messes – '

'Messes?'

'Groups. A group of men mess together and cook for themselves – it's a damned sight easier than trying to cook for forty-two or each man cooking for himself, but everyone takes a share of the general duties such as lookout, supervision of animals etc. The Brown Bears is my company and what I say goes. My second in command is Mr Pritty – Rodman Pritty, known as Rod. Any questions so far?'

Patrick said eagerly. 'The route, sir?'

'The route, yes.' Becher closed his eyes and recited. 'We follow the Oregon trail for much of the way – Platte River, Fort Kearny, Ash Hollow, Fort Laramie, as far as South Pass, then skirting Great Salt Lake we pick up the Humboldt River and then probably Lassen's Cut-Off. It will take four or five months.' Seeing their blank looks, Becher said sharply, 'Get yourself a map, for Christ's sake! No one's going to spoon-feed you on this trip!'

'We will, sir,' said Patrick hastily. 'Er, does that mean . . . I mean are we definitely coming? Are we *with* your company?'

Becher laughed. 'When I see the colour of your money,' he said. 'Yes, I see no reason why not. If you're both fit and willing and can put up your stake, I guess we can add your names to the roll.'

He pushed back his chair and stood up. 'Call in tomorrow at the Blue Goose saloon – down the street to the right as you go out of here – and ask for Rod Pritty. And don't let the name fool you. Pritty has spent five years in the area, trading with the Indians, and he knows it well. He's got all the experience; I'm the brains, you might say. My legal background's essential in a venture like this. Large funds are involved and have to be properly managed. If people invest their life's sayings, they won't want to see it go down the drain before we're half-way across. I've drawn up legal contracts and you can both sign one tomorrow. It lays down your rights as well as your obligations. Anyway, just ask for Rod Pritty, give him your stake money and a few details – home address, next of kin and so on. We have to be prepared for all emergencies on this venture, I can promise you that.' He glanced at Henry. 'You're not saying much, Mr Simms,' he remarked.

'I think a lot,' Henry smiled, rising to his feet. 'I guess you've covered most things.' He held out his hand. 'And thank you, sir. Glad to be a member of your team.'

As they shook hands, Patrick rose also. 'Honoured to be a member of the Brown Bear Company, Mr Becher,' he said and his own neat hand was crushed briefly in Becher's firm handshake.

As they moved towards the door, Becher said, 'There has to be discipline or we shall never make it. You will not like it, but it's vital.'

Patrick nodded. 'I appreciate that,' he said. 'Are you an Army man, sir?'

Becher smiled grimly. 'I was,' he replied, 'and you'll be glad of it!'

Henry nodded. 'How soon do we start? We have to get ourselves kitted out.'

'You've got until the twenty-eighth, but Rod Pritty will help you. Now, if you'll excuse me, gentlemen?'

A moment or two later, Patrick and Henry exchanged delighted grins, momentarily silenced by their good fortune. It had all happened so quickly. They had arrived in Independence as green as grass, but within three hours had found the company willing to enrol them and almost ready to move out! Henry let out a war-whoop and clapped Patrick on the shoulder.

'We're going to California,' he cried. 'We're going to be rich!'

Patrick's eyes glowed. 'Gold!' he exclaimed. 'We're going to find gold!' Then his expression changed suddenly. 'About Lily,' he said. 'I *had* to say all that; I had to pretend she was keen.'

Henry shrugged. 'So who's to know?'

'*I* know.'

Henry laughed. 'You worry too much,' he told him. 'Come on, I'll buy you a drink. To celebrate. Members of the Brown Bear Company! How does that sound to you? Isn't it terrific?'

'Wonderful!' Patrick agreed. 'Well then, just one drink to celebrate and then I must write to poor Lily. I hope to God she'll forgive me for all this.'

Henry looked at his friend and his eyes were shrewd. 'And if you thought she wouldn't?' he asked. 'If you thought she wouldn't forgive you – what then, Patrick? Would you want to back out?'

Patrick wrestled with his finer feelings. 'To tell you the truth, Henry,' he said, 'I don't think I could give up now. Not if she begged me on bended knees. Oh God, Henry – if anything was to stop me now, I think I'd die of disappointment. I've *got* to go. I might get lost in the desert or scalped by Indians but as God is my witness, I've got to go through with it.'

Five minutes later they were leaning on the bar of the Blue Goose saloon, glasses raised.

'To us two brown bears!' toasted Henry, with an exultant grin.

'I'll drink to that,' said Patrick.

*

Lily and Kate reached Buffalo on April the sixteenth and immediately went to the address Patrick had given Lily. They approached the large house with some trepidation, and Lily's fingers were firmly crossed behind her back as she pulled on the door-bell.

'They *must* be still here,' she whispered.

Kate grinned. 'I'm looking forward to meeting your Patrick,' she said. 'If he's as handsome as you say he is, I'll be quite bowled over!'

A plump maid opened the door and Lily explained who they were. They were shown into a spacious parlour where they exchanged anxious looks.

'It's very quiet,' said Lily. 'No sound of excited voices or packing or anything. I have a nasty feeling we're too late.'

Kate was determined to look on the bright side, however. 'Maybe they're all out in the back garden,' she suggested.

Lily sat down on the well-stuffed sofa, but Kate darted curiously around the room exclaiming over the various objects on display.

'Look at this! Dead butterflies pinned on to a velvet cushion in a glass case. Poor little things! And this – it must be the biggest vase in the whole world! Ooh! Look here, Lily! All bits of stone and stuff – one of them looks like gold. Do come and see – we ought to know what gold actually looks like.'

Together they stood in front of the glass-fronted cabinet and admired the selection of rock specimens – the yellow-green serpentine, glossy black obsidian, milky-white opal and bright blue-green chrysocolla.

'That one looks like gold,' said Kate, pointing excitedly, 'but its name begins with "p" so it can't be.'

A voice behind them made them both jump. 'It's pyrites and we call it fool's gold.'

Lily and Kate turned to see a very tall, very elderly man regarding them with a strange expression. There was no hint of welcome as he stood fingering his long white beard. Lily began to explain who they were and their circumstances, but he interrupted her with a dismissive wave of his hand.

'You have missed them by the best part of a week,' he

told her. 'In and out of here like scalded cats, they were. Wouldn't listen to reason, so we had to let them go, but I wasn't letting my grandsons join them. Fool's gold is about the right name for it, in my opinion, and I smelled death as soon as they walked in. Give it up while you've still time, I told them. I've lived a lot longer than you or them and I know. A fool's errand, that's what it is. There's nothing comes free in this world that's worth a fig. You want something, you work for it and that's how it should be. Wealth never comes easy. Only greedy men believe it does.'

He glared at Lily who, dismayed by this tirade, felt bound to say something in their defence.

'But the President himself confirmed that –' she stammered.

'The President?' The old man drew his eyebrows together in a scowl and his faded blue eyes were dark with disapproval. 'What does the President know about gold? Has he been there? Has he panned for it himself? What does he know of heartache and disappointment?' He shook his head. 'But *I* know and I'll tell you for nothing. There's more folk going to lose money in California than make it and there's plenty will lose everything – health as well as wealth. California is a fool's paradise, a mecca for greedy men, and I don't thank anyone who comes here trying to turn my grandsons' heads with fancy notions of treasure trove.' He nodded towards the collection of rocks. 'They're the only treasures I want to see and I've collected them myself.' His voice softened a little as he approached the cabinet. 'That was my hobby when I was a youngster. Beautiful, aren't they? Look at that azurite – did you ever see such a blue? And the jasper – so warm and red. And the jade here – not much colour to that until it's cut and polished.'

For a moment he was absorbed in his collection and the girls were able to exchange rueful looks behind his back, but then he straightened up suddenly and said, 'Everyone's out visiting but me. Will you stay for a cup of tea and a slice of cake?'

'No, thank you,' said Lily. 'We shall have to hurry if we are to catch up with my husband.'

49

The strange expression returned to his face. 'You find him and you talk him out of it – that's the best thing you can do for him! Talk some sense into the pair of them before it's too late. Gold fever! I never thought I'd live to see such a thing. The world's gone mad and that's about the truth of it.' He pointed a bony finger in Lily's direction. 'If you know what's good for you, you'll take that husband of yours back where he belongs before it's too late. I smelt death the minute they walked in.'

There was a shocked silence.

'Death?' echoed Lily. 'What do you mean?'

'Exactly what I said,' the old man insisted. 'I can smell it. Always could, even as a boy. I remember when my father died I knew the moment he came down that morning, hale and hearty and in the prime of life. Forty-one years old and never had a day's sickness. But I smelled it as he passed me by and ruffled my hair with his hand. He was dead by the evening, sure enough, and everyone surprised but me.'

'But how did it happen?' echoed Lily, her throat suddenly dry.

'Thrown off his horse.' He shook his head. 'Killed outright in the prime of life. Broke my mother's heart. Same thing when my older sister died. Doctor said it was nothing to fret about – a bit of a cough, he called it – but I smelled death on her and she was gone before the month was out.'

Lily's eyes were fixed on his face, wide and frightened. 'And which of the two men was it? I mean – the smell of death. Which of the . . .'

Her voice trailed off as he lifted his bony shoulders in a shrug.

'Couldn't make out which one it was,' he admitted, 'but it was there right enough. Sweet and yet heavy. Hangs in the air like –'

'Oh, please stop!' cried Lily. 'I don't want to hear any more.'

She threw Kate an anguished glance and said hurriedly, 'Perhaps we should be going.'

The old man rang for the maid without another word and made no further comment as they were ushered out. As they went down the front steps and along the drive, they saw that he was watching them from the window. Neither spoke until they were outside the gates, then Kate snorted.

'What a terrible old man!' she said. 'He gave me the shivers.'

Lily nodded, reluctant to admit how much the old man's words had frightened her. She stood in the road, her hands clasped nervously, her expression troubled. Seeing her distress, Kate gave her arm a reassuring squeeze.

'Take no notice of him, Lily,' she said. 'He was a bit . . . you know . . .' She put a forefinger to her forehead and squinted horribly, so that Lily had to laugh in spite of her misgivings.

'Stop it, Kate!' she begged. 'You look terrible!'

'Well, he was,' said Kate, relaxing. 'I could see it in his eyes. A bit fey, my ma used to call it. How could he know anything?'

'I don't know,' said Lily, 'but I couldn't bear to stay there another minute. Suddenly I just wanted to get away from him.'

'A cup of tea would have gone down a treat, though,' said Kate wistfully, 'not to mention a piece of cake. I'm starving!'

'I am, too,' said Lily with an effort. 'We'll book ourselves a passage on the next steamer going to Detroit and then we'll see about something to eat.'

She spoke briskly enough, but the old man's words lingered uneasily in her mind and returned from time to time to trouble her.

*

The trip to Detroit in the *London* was uneventful and was followed by a further trip on the *Michigan* which took them to Chicago.

A hundred miles of canal linked Chicago with the township of Peru, so Lily and Kate once more transferred themselves and their baggage, from the *Michigan* to a canal boat fifty feet long, nine feet wide and barely seven feet high. They watched with the rest of the passengers as a team of mules was hitched up to the narrow canal boat and as they began

51

to move slowly along the towpath Kate groaned in pretended despair. 'Just look at 'em!' she demanded. 'How will we ever get to California at this rate? I could walk it faster.'

Their fellow passengers laughingly agreed. 'There'll be no gold left by the time we get out there,' said one of them.

Lily and Kate, two of the few women on the boat, were pleasantly surprised by the unfailing courtesy shown them by their fellow passengers. One young man, Amos Carp by name, was particularly attentive and seemed to take a special interest in Kate, much to her secret delight. Like ninety-nine per cent of the passengers, Amos Carp was also on his way to look for gold and had thrown up a promising teaching career to do so. Lily and Kate had noticed him when they were on board the *Michigan*, where he and two friends had spent most of their time playing monte. Amos lost most of his money at one stage, but won it all back again plus a little more.

Lily was a little sceptical of his story and could not imagine him as a teacher, but when she said as much Kate would not hear a word against him.

'He's as straight as a die,' she insisted. 'He's just trying his wings – first time away from home and no one to tell him when to blow his nose.'

'He seems to like you,' said Lily.

Kate grinned ruefully. 'He does,' she said, 'but then he doesn't know the half of it.'

Lily lowered her voice. 'The baby, you mean?'

'The same. I don't think I'll tell him.'

'No one would ever guess.'

Kate laughed. 'It's the binder,' she confided. 'Yards of it! I'm wrapped up like an Egyptian mummy.'

'Doesn't it hurt the child?' asked Lily, intrigued.

''Course not! My ma bound herself with all hers. Don't you know anything about babies?'

'I'm afraid not. I'm an only child.'

'You're lucky, then!'

'It can be lonely, being the only one,' Lily told her.

'I bet you were spoiled half to death!'

'I was,' Lily confessed with a laugh.

52

At that moment Amos joined them on deck with a cheerful smile. 'Good morning! How did you two ladies sleep?' he asked.

Although his frock-coat was crumpled his dark hair was well slicked down and his wide-brimmed hat was set at a jaunty angle.

Lily grimaced. 'Not well at all,' she confessed. 'I've never been so cramped in my life. It was like sleeping on a wooden shelf!'

'I had to make do on the floor,' he told them, 'with about twenty others. It was pretty rough.' He looked out of the window at the toiling mules and shook his head in wonder. 'All these weeks and we haven't reached the Missouri frontier,' he said. 'It's going to take for ever to get there.'

'To Independence, you mean?'

'I mean just that,' Amos agreed. 'After that, it's Indian territory!' He grinned. 'You sure you two ladies want to come along?'

'We're sure,' said Kate firmly.

'Can you shoot?' he asked. 'I could teach you.'

Kate and Lily exchanged doubtful looks. 'We have no guns yet,' said Lily. 'I think maybe later we shall have to learn.'

'Just say the word,' he said. 'There'll be plenty of time once we're under way.'

Giving Lily a sly look, Kate said pointedly, 'Lily's *husband* will be teaching her to shoot, but I'll be glad of some help, Mr Carp.'

'Her husband? Oh, yes, I forgot. But last night I was talking to a gunsmith, name of Parks, and I know a bit about guns. I could put you right on what's best for you ladies to buy.'

Kate fixed him with an admiring look. 'Could you, Mr Carp? We'd be ever so grateful.'

Delighted by her reply, Amos frowned, considering the matter.

'Well, don't let anyone talk you into a Hawken rifle,' he advised. 'See, they're pretty old now, twenty-five years or more, and they're weighty. You'd never handle one. You'd be better off with a light squirrel rifle, maybe, or even a double-barrelled shotgun.'

'A shotgun!' Kate rolled her eyes in pretended alarm. 'Ooh, I don't think so, Mr Carp. I don't like the sound of that. Isn't there anything smaller?'

'Like a revolver, you mean?' Amos nodded. 'There are a few on the market if you can get hold of one. The Colt.38 might do for you. It's Navy issue, but well-balanced. It has six chambers, you see. You measure the powder into each chamber, seat the ball on it, cover it with lard, and prime it with – '

'Cover it with *lard?*' Kate queried. 'Whatever for?'

He smiled at her ignorance. 'Seals it off. Otherwise when one chamber is fired they would all go. A sort of chain reaction. Don't worry, it's not as complicated as it sounds. You'll get the hang of it. A gun can be a good friend.'

They relapsed into a thoughtful silence, watching the landscape unfold in the early morning haze – a wide plain grazed by cattle who straggled across the gently rolling acres of broad soft grassland. Behind them in the crowded cabin other passengers were rousing up for the new day, stretching stiff limbs and rubbing their eyes. Some still snored, others coughed and grunted into wakefulness.

'It would be good if you ladies were in the same company as us,' Amos said at last. 'We've already joined one,' he went on. 'The Western Hope Mining Company. They advertised in our local paper in Iowa and I wrote away at once. They aim to leave Independence round about May the eighteenth. It's a proper joint-stock company, run by a man named Wallis – Captain Matt Wallis – and it's to be well-run on military lines. We all have a list of regulations and they like us to dress alike with long boots, blue pants and red shirt and a neckerchief. I'll buy mine in Independence.'

Kate said eagerly. 'We'd look nice in blue and red, wouldn't we, Lily, if they let us join?'

'We'll be joining Patrick's group,' Lily reminded her.

'If we catch them up. If we don't, we could join up with Amos's company.' Kate looked hopeful.

'I suppose we could,' agreed Lily.

Amos was obviously pleased by this possibility and gave Kate a warm smile. 'The three of us could mess together,' he said without much hope.

'No!' said Lily firmly. 'Kate and I would have our own wagon if there were no other women to share with.'

'But the wagons sleep four,' he protested. 'It says so in the regulations.'

'I'm sure it says four *men* to a wagon,' said Lily. 'No mention of men and women.'

He grinned broadly. 'It was worth a try,' he said.

Kate nudged Lily and smiled at Amos. 'Tell us about the Western Hope Mining Company,' she suggested.

Amos was only too eager to do so. 'It's very well run,' he assured them earnestly. 'And the folks in it are specially chosen – blacksmiths to help maintain the wagons, three or four doctors in case of sickness, carpenters and wheelwrights to repair the wagons. There's even a gunsmith!'

'And a teacher!' said Lily. 'You.'

'And maybe two English ladies will join us,' Amos said and looked at them inquiringly.

Kate said, 'I was in service and Lily's a parson's daughter.'

'I married an accountant's clerk,' laughed Lily, 'but apparently I'm now married to a gold prospector.'

As she began to explain, several staccato shots rang out and they turned, startled, to see a flurry of birds rise from the river bank in alarm. It appeared that some of the passengers were getting in a little shooting practice and had climbed up on top of the cabin roof. Perched on top of the luggage, they were taking 'pot-shots' at the wild life. There was no shortage of targets from small birds to wild geese and muskrats.

Relieved that it was nothing to worry about, Lily, Kate and Amos watched for a moment and then made their way to the small rear deck and watched for a while as the sun broke through the mist.

Kate asked casually, 'Are you married, Mr Carp?'

'No, ma'am,' he said emphatically. 'No such luck! But when I've made my pile, I shall be looking out for a wife.'

'There's no one waiting at home, then?'

'No one at all – except my ma and pa.'

Kate tossed her head. 'We're in the same boat then, Mr Carp,' she said. 'I'm fancy-free too.'

Lily, recognizing the way the conversation was going, tore her gaze away from the toiling mules on the towpath ahead of them and winked at Kate. 'Well, I've a letter half-written to my father,' she said. 'So, if you will excuse me, I'll go inside and finish it.' She smiled at Amos. 'I leave Kate in your hands,' she told him and earned from Kate a look of deep gratitude. When she had gone, Kate took a long breath and continued the little speech she had prepared for such a moment.

'I like America,' she told Amos. 'I shall never go back to England. My pa's dead and my ma won't live much longer.' She had decided not to mention the fact that her mother was in the workhouse, so that he need not know of her humble origins. 'It's her lungs. Same with my grandma and her ma before that – be the same with me, most likely.'

'Don't talk on death,' Amos warned. 'It's unlucky.'

'Is it? Well, I won't then.' She looked at him curiously. 'Those two men you were with – are they teachers too?'

'Gabby and Bart? No. They're two brothers – sons of one of our neighbours. Kept talking about going to California, but didn't do anything until I said I was off and then they wanted to tag along.'

'Is either of them married or promised?'

Amos hesitated, afraid that if he confessed to the contrary Kate might transfer her attention to one of them. '*Kind* of promised,' he told her cautiously. 'Leastways, Gabby's been walking out for nearly a year and she said she'll wait for him, but he's not so sure she will. Women are funny like that. Bart's aiming to get away from his girl – says he's had enough of petticoats for the time being. You wouldn't get anywhere with Bart.'

'Me? With Bart? Now what gives you the idea that I'm looking for a husband?' She looked at him with convincing indignation.

'I never said you were,' he said hastily. 'Nothing wrong in it, though. I might be looking for a wife.'

Kate held her breath. 'And are you?'

'Maybe.'

'Well then, maybe I'm looking for a husband – but it's only maybe.'

Studiously, they each stared towards the river bank, afraid to give too much away.

'So you don't reckon much on England?' asked Amos at last.

Kate shrugged. 'I'd stay in America if I met the right man,' she stated.

Amos said, 'I'd be looking for a girl with a trim waist . . .'

Silently Kate cursed her yards of binding. Once she had had a trim waist, she reflected wistfully, but men had been her undoing.

'And sweet-talking,' he went on. 'I can't bear a nagging woman – and she'd have to be faithful and hard-working and careful with the housekeeping and tidy about her person and not too much book-learning and a light hand with bread – '

'Crikey! You don't want much!' cried Kate, dismayed by this catalogue.

'And green eyes,' Amos added hastily, 'and gingery hair tied in bunches . . .'

Kate struggled to hide her elation. 'Well, I hope you find someone to suit you,' she said lightly, then turning to survey the confusion in the cabin behind them she played her trump card. 'But with all these men going to California and so few women, I should think you might find it hard to get any wife at all!'

The inference – not lost on him – was that *she*, among so many men, would be in the enviable position of turning down offers all day long. Before he could think out his next move, however, they were joined by another man. He was short, with small blue eyes, ruddy cheeks and the beginnings of a dark beard; his dark hair curled close to his head. Reluctantly, Amos introduced him as Bart Smith. Kate smiled at him boldly and to her delight he took off his hat with a flourish, bent his head and kissed her hand.

'Pleased to meet you, Mr Smith,' said Kate demurely.

She was beginning to enjoy herself. If *only* she had not encouraged Ernest Bailey, she thought ruefully, the trip to California would be full of such excitements. But then if she had not been pregnant, she would never have been threatened with disgrace and would still be in New York ministering to Mrs Harrington. Fate was very awkward, she thought with a sigh. The real problem was that in another month or two her pregnancy would become obvious to everyone and then her chances of finding a husband would be drastically reduced. Her only hope, she thought, was for someone to fall hopelessly in love with her *soon*. Then she could risk a confession about the child and it might be accepted but until then she would have to keep silent on the subject. It was all very difficult, but her life so far had been full of difficulties and she had never expected it to be otherwise.

'My pleasure, ma'am,' said Bart and turned to Amos. 'So this is what's keeping you away from the cards. You sly dog! Not that I blame you. If I had such a charming companion, I'd keep her to myself.'

He looked at Kate with unfeigned admiration and she felt the familiar tingle inside her. 'This is how it felt when I first met Ernest,' she thought and eyed Bart speculatively.

'So you've had enough of women, Mr Smith,' she said with a provocative tilt of her head. 'Amos has just been telling me.'

Amos burst out laughing to hide his confusion and Bart grinned.

'The hell he has!' he exclaimed. 'I'll deal with him later. What's he been saying?'

'That you already have a lady friend, but you're not very keen.'

'She's a nice enough girl,' Bart said, 'but stodgy, like her mother. I don't think we were suited. I like a girl with a mind of her own – an *adventurous* girl. Are you adventurous, Miss Lester?'

'I'm off to California, aren't I?' she demanded. 'You can't get more adventurous than that! A gipsy told my fortune once – said I had a lucky face. Stick by me, Mr Smith, if you want to strike gold. I've got the face for it, see!'

'And your friend?' he asked. 'Is she going to dig for gold, too?'

'We're both joining up with her husband,' Kate told him. Then to change the subject, she said, 'Amos was just telling me about his ideal wife. A list of virtues as long as your arm! What's your ideal woman like, Mr Smith?'

Bart looked at her carefully, a frown on his face, his thumbs hooked casually into the waistband of his trousers. He gave Kate a long simmering look and said, 'I reckon she looks a lot like you, ma'am.'

Kate, smiling radiantly, thought she had never been happier.

1 May 1849

Hester Cooper shook the pan and the pancake freed itself from the base and was flipped over with a quick jerk of her capable wrists. She was a thin, stringy woman with a hard mouth and grey hair pulled back into an uncompromising bun.

'How hungry are you?' Hester asked her husband.

There was no answer and she repeated the question.

'Hungry enough,' said Charlie, his eyes on the newspaper spread out in front of him. He was short and wiry, with greasy brown hair and pale brown eyes. His face wore a permanent frown and was already deeply lined.

'Why d'you always ask that, Ma?' asked Ella petulantly.

Their daughter, who took after her father, was just eighteen and pregnant with her second child. The first, a boy of three and a half, sat on her lap with his thumb in his mouth, his eyes rolling vacantly. 'You ask Pa, "How hungry?" ' she went on, 'and he says "Hungry enough!" You know he's going to say it, so why ask him? It gets to me, you know that? It just *gets* to me.'

'You shut your trap,' said Charlie. 'Your ma has a right to say what she likes in her own kitchen.'

Hester gave him a sharp look but said nothing. Her own kitchen was no different from any other to be found on a small and unrewarding Missouri homestead. The floor was of rough-hewn but well-trodden timber, the walls were the same. Furniture was scanty. There was an iron cooking range surrounded by a selection of pans and kettles and a large scrubbed table with four stools set round it – the latter made by Charlie himself many years earlier. A single rocking-chair offered a promise of comfort, its back and seat upholstered in hide. The only rug was also hand-made by Hester's industrious fingers during the first year of her marriage and was of circular design, woven from strips of calico cut from outgrown clothing. It had seen many years of service and was badly frayed and likely to trip anyone who stepped across it without due caution. Several flat-irons stood beside the range. A spinning wheel stood in a corner of the room with a mass of wool in a box beside it, waiting to be used, and above it on the wall an embroidered cloth pocket bulged with scissors, a pair of slippers and various odds and ends which had found no other home. There was a wooden butter-maker behind the door and a set of shallow shelves had been fixed to the wall; each of these had been lined with news-paper cut to a decorative pattern of points which hung down an inch or so and gave the shelves an almost frivolous look strangely at odds with the spartan appearance of the rest of the room. A kerosene lamp, hung from a hook in the ceiling, was their only source of light.

Ella pulled a sour face. 'That same old question gets to me,' she insisted. She looked at the boy in her lap and sighed uneasily. 'All this kid does is loll about. I wish he'd crawl or talk or do *something!* May Patten's Stevie is like greased lightning compared to this one.' She shook him half-heartedly. 'Come on, Will! Wake your ideas up, why don't you?'

'Leave him be.' said Hester. 'The doc said he was a bit slow.'

'He may be slow but he don't even *try*.' Ella frowned and sighed again. Then she looked up at her mother. 'He's *odd*,' she said flatly. 'I *know* he is. Never mind what the doc said. He's odd and he's never going to . . .' She swallowed and her eyes on Hester's were full of misery. 'He's always going to be odd. Different. He's never going to do *anything*. Just like now. I *know* it, Ma, I just know it!'

Hester refused to meet her gaze. 'He's kind of slow,' she conceded warily, 'but lots of kids are slow.'

'Not like this!' cried Ella. 'Not even talking or walking. Not even *trying* to. If he's not lazy then he's . . . odd.' She dropped her eyes to the child on her lap. 'I know it, Ma, so you might as well stop pretending.'

Hester turned to her at last, one hand on her hip. 'You shouldn't talk like that about your own son,' she said sharply. 'You don't *know* for sure; he could pick up some.'

They both regarded Will hopefully, but he continued to loll back against his mother while a thin trickle of saliva descended his chin. Ella wiped it away impatiently.

'If only he'd *try*,' she repeated. 'Jess says I do too much for him but I have to, don't I. If I don't feed him, who will? He can't feed himself. Does he want the poor kid to starve to death? If I don't dress him . . .' She stopped.

Charlie looked up suddenly and said, 'Least said, soonest mended.'

She looked at him in surprise. 'What?' she asked.

'You heard.' He returned to his newspaper.

'Thanks a lot,' said Ella bitterly. 'That's a real help. I'm worrying myself sick and all you can say is – '

Here she caught a warning look from Hester and subsided into a resentful silence. For a while no one spoke, then Charlie looked up.

'What I mean is,' he said, 'that this ain't the time for airing your views about the kid. We got more important things to think about. He may be kind of slow, but there's plenty time for him to spark up. There ain't plenty time for us to decide whether we're going or not.'

The two women groaned with exasperation.

'Here we go again,' muttered Ella, her attention momentarily diverted from her son.

'Well, hell, we got to make a decision,' insisted Charlie.

Hester slid the pancake on to a tin plate and pushed it into the oven with the others to keep warm. Adding a knob of lard to the pan, she began to crack eggs into it.

'Let's decide right now then,' said Hester. 'I say we go!'

'How can we?' snapped her husband. 'How can we go without Ella and Jess? They say they won't go but if we stay here, I reckon we'll go under in less than a year.'

'We won't go under,' said Ella. 'Jess says we'll get by.'

Jess was Ella's husband. He had gone into Independence to the market to buy a milk cow, with strict instructions from his father-in-law as to the kind of animal to look for and woe betide him if he came back with one that did not meet with Charlie's full approval. 'A large udder,' he had said, 'high-legged at the back and short in front and none of your fancy colours, either. Pale colours is best – go for something mousey. Always *do* get more milk from a pale cow. Don't ask me why, but you do.'

Jess had listened with that sullen look on his face, no doubt believing that he knew as much as the older man but afraid to say so. It didn't take much to start an argument between the two men and Jess was eager to be off away from the restrictions of the homestead and among the livelier company he would find in the town.

Charlie snorted. 'So Jess says we'll get by and he knows better'n I do, does he?'

'He's entitled to his own opinion,' said Ella.

'So's your pa,' put in Hester.

'And my opinion,' said Charlie, 'is that we give up this whole darned – '

'But Jess says – '

'To hell with Jess!' her father told her angrily. 'Maybe we'll just up and go without you and Jess. If he doesn't have the guts, he can stay behind and you with him, and you can stay poor for the rest of your lives. Me, I'd rather have a tough time of it for a year and then sit back and enjoy my gold. Hard work never killed anyone and there's gold out there for them as wants it.'

Ella leaned forward and wagged a furious finger at her father. 'We're not afraid of hard work, Pa, you know that, but we've got Will to think of and another on the way. We've got responsibilities. You two only got yourselves to think about, so don't go bawling me out about hard work and suchlike. Jess can match you any day of the week.'

'He works, but he's got no guts,' Charlie insisted.

'He has, too!' screamed Ella and then she burst into tears. Lowering Will roughly to the floor, she jumped up and ran outside, slamming the door behind her. The boy sat where his mother had left him, whimpering uneasily.

Hester looked at him and said in a low voice, 'There *is* summat wrong with that kid, Charlie.'

Her husband wasn't listening. 'I got a pain in my gut,' he said. 'I had it since last evening.'

'How bad?'

'Real bad.'

Hester was still looking at her grandson. 'There's peppermint and laudanum in the cupboard,' she said. 'Take some, Charlie.'

An uneasy silence followed this remark. A 'pain in the gut' could be nothing or it could be something. There was cholera in Independence and the Cooper spread was only six miles from the town. The local people blamed the gold seekers who had descended on the town in vast numbers, living in insanitary overcrowded conditions while they waited for the spring grass to appear on the plain and signal their departure. So far only a handful of strangers had succumbed to the dread disease, but how long would it be before the contagion spread to the town's residents? Some people would be very glad to see the back of the visitors, but others argued that the strangers had money and the town was glad enough to relieve them of some of it. Before the gold rush to California it had been the emigrants headed for Oregon. Independence would never again be the sleepy town the old folks remembered. Exploration westward had changed all that for ever.

Hester served up pancake and eggs and placed it before her husband, then sat beside him with her own smaller helping. They ate in silence for a few minutes and then Charlie spoke. 'She'll want some breakfast. She's like a scalded cat lately.'

'Ella's jumpy,' said Hester. 'We all are. I wish to God we

could get things settled one way or the other. Anything in the paper today?'

'Usual stuff. Prices of everything going up. Shortage of mules and oxen. Number of deaths. A shooting in St Joseph.' He glanced towards the door as they heard the rattle of an approaching wagon which heralded the return of their son-in-law from the town.

Hester's expression hardened as she heard Ella talking to Jess, her voice high and plaintive. 'I'm so sick of all this arguing,' she told Charlie. 'For my part, we can get up and go.'

After a moment the door swung open and the young couple came in without any greeting from Jess, who was slight with small dark eyes, mid-brown hair and a weak mouth. Hester and Charlie gave him a nod and continued to eat. Ella, red-eyed and grim-faced, sat young Will on a chair and dished up three helpings of food. They all ate in silence until it was broken at last by Charlie.

'You get the cow?'

'I got her,' said Jess. 'Course I got her.'

'And?'

'I got like you said. Mousey, big udders. She's in the barn.'

'She's a real pretty cow,' said Ella.

'She'd better be,' rejoined Charlie sourly.

Jess said, 'Go see for yourself,' and Hester looked at him suspiciously, puzzled by his mild reply. She would have expected a boastful account of the deal Jess had struck with the cow's previous owner.

'I will,' said Charlie. 'Soon as I've finished my food.'

He, too, looked at his son-in-law with narrowed eyes, aware of something different in his manner. He drank his coffee noisily, belched loudly and patted his stomach. Slowly he stood up and then, catching Hester's eye, sat down again, his expression wary.

'So what's new, Jess?' Hester asked. 'In the town, I mean . . .'

'Town's getting worse,' Jess told them through a mouthful of pancake. 'Folks everywhere. Tents and wagons all along the river bank as far as you can see. Smells terrible, too.

Shops crowded out, mules and wagons everywhere you look.'
He cut himself a hunk of bread and dipped it into his egg-
yolk. 'Half of 'em have never driven before, nor sat a horse,
neither. Talk about greenhorns! I've never seen anything like
it. They say one fellow there, learning to shoot, shot his own
partner in the leg!'

A smile fluttered briefly across Ella's face as she spooned
egg into her son's unwilling mouth. 'Shot his own partner?'
she said. 'I don't believe it.'

'It's gospel!' cried Jess. 'And some young fellow's tried to
hang himself in his hotel room, but they cut him down in
time. Been gambling; lost all the money he'd brought with
him, so now he can't go to California.'

Ella shook her head and said, 'Poor fool! Any more sickness?' She could not bring herself to say 'cholera'.

'Plenty,' he told her. 'And still coming in on the river
boats. It was so bad on one boat the passengers abandoned
it — just went ashore and wouldn't go back! Laudanum,
camphor and ammonia's clean sold out. No more until the
next boat puts in. I met Doc Pearson. Worked off his feet,
but says he'll be a rich man before this gold rush ends. He
says he don't *need* to go to California to get rich!'

There was another long silence during which Hester
poured more coffee. Jess cleaned his plate and wiped it clean
with another hunk of bread.

'Could have sold my horse easy,' he told them casually.
'Going broke, some of 'em, just fitting out for the journey.
You can patch up any old wagon and get a fair price for it.'
He shook his head. 'Wish I had a dollar for the number of
times I've been asked to sell my horse.' He paused and looked
around at the three faces turned towards him. 'Oh, and I
called in at the Pattens' place.'

'And?' Ella prompted.

'They've headed out.'

They all stared at him open-mouthed.

'Headed out?' echoed Charlie.

'The Pattens?' cried Ella in disbelief. 'Gone to California,
d'you mean?'

Jess nodded. 'Upped and gone. Joined up with the Brown Bear Company or some such name.'

His words created exactly the sensation he had intended and he grinned as Hester and Charlie exchanged startled looks. Ella found her voice first.

'But they *swore* they never would!' she cried. 'How could they go like that, and without a word to anyone? Downright sly, that is. Not telling us, and how long we known them?' She shook her head, utterly bewildered. 'Headed out and never a word. Just like that!'

'But all their stock?' exclaimed Hester. 'The farm?'

'Sold out to his brother-in-law,' stated Jess, 'for six hundred dollars.'

'Jesus!' said Charlie. 'Sold out the farm? Now I've heard everything!'

'But the old grandfather?' cried Hester. 'He'll never make it, not at his age. He's over eighty! It'll kill him!'

Jess wiped his hand across his mouth to remove some surplus egg-yolk. 'He's gone to his sister in St Joseph's,' he told her.

'Jesus!' said Charlie. 'That beats everything.'

Jess looked sideways at Ella. 'So maybe we *should* go,' he said slowly. 'What do you say, Ella? Shall we go to California?'

Her mouth fell open. 'Jess Cash! Are you serious? After all you said?'

He shrugged defensively. 'I can change my mind, can't I?' he said. 'Hell! I just don't want to be mouldering here if the Pattens come back from California with a sack full of gold.'

Charlie and Hester were astonished by this about-face on the part of their son-in-law.

'There's gold,' said Charlie quickly, 'and there's enough for all, but the longer we take to make up our minds, the less there'll be when we get there.' He looked round at his family. Hester, raw-boned and tough as any man; pretty Ella, spoilt but good-hearted – she'd work if she had to; Jess, a weedy specimen but willing enough, and he could shoot better than some men twice his age.

'We could take the new cow and some chickens in a coop,' Jess went on. 'We got horses and stuff to trade.'

Hester said breathlessly, 'It's the first of May today. If we're going, let's look smart about it.'

There was a shocked silence as the enormity of her words sank in.

'Do we go, then?' asked Charlie and they all looked at Jess.

'Why not?' said Jess with a sheepish grin. 'We could all get rich.'

The decision was made at last.

'We're going to get us some gold!' cried Charlie and he began to laugh.

Soon they were all laughing hysterically, and hugging each other. Only Will seemed unimpressed. To everyone's amazement, he puckered up his face and began to cry.

Chapter Four

A few days after the Coopers had decided to go west, Lily and Kate reached Peru where they exchanged the cramped quarters of the canal boat for a larger but equally crowded river steamer which took them along the Illinois River to St Louis. There, after an uncomfortable night's sleep in a dubious lodging-house, they prepared to change vessels for the last time and board the *River Queen*, the paddle steamer which would take them along the Missouri to Independence. They waited on the levée feeling tired and depressed. The novelty of the adventure had worn off a little and the gold still seemed a long way away. With growing irritation they waited, faces turned towards the bend in the river round which the boat would eventually appear. It was already a quarter of an hour late and they were not the only people fidgeting with impatience, anticipating its arrival. The river bank was crowded with people, and baggage of every description fought for space amongst wagons and animals, all jumbled together in the chaos to which they were all becoming accustomed if not reconciled. Singing, shouting and swearing, the men jostled and pushed each other while those of a more placid disposition sat playing cards or smoking, or queued with varying degrees of impatience to take a look through a telescope mounted on an iron stand which offered them a view of the opposite bank and the chance to study the river traffic in greater detail. Dogs barked and children wailed and Lily felt that she was rapidly losing her love of humanity. In the last few weeks she had almost forgotten the meaning of the word 'privacy' and could only recall the tranquillity of the parsonage with the utmost difficulty.

The weather, fortunately, was mild — rain would have proved the final straw. Lily watched the broad slow river as it flowed between low banks bordered by willow and cottonwood trees. Amos and his friends were nowhere to be seen and this fact added to Kate's discontent, for she had grown used to their company and worried in case their absence reflected a diminishing interest in her. She hid her feelings, however, by pretending indifference, even relief, at their defection, confiding to Lily that it was nice to be rid of their stupid chatter.

Lily nodded absentmindedly without comment, her thoughts elsewhere, and Kate's gloom deepened at what she believed to be a further proof of her own unworthiness.

'Where on earth is it, then?' Kate demanded after a further ten minutes had passed. 'Sunk, most likely. That would be just our blooming luck!'

Lily said, 'It won't be much longer,' but she did not sound very convincing.

'How d'you know it won't?' Kate pulled her shawl tighter around her shoulders and glared in the direction of the missing paddle steamer. 'Might have run aground,' she suggested. 'Or maybe the engine's broken down.'

Lily managed a smile. 'Or the crew's mutinied,' she said, 'or they've been boarded by pirates!'

Kate chose not to be amused. 'It's all right for you,' she grumbled, 'but my back aches, standing around here like a blooming lemon.'

'No one asked you to stand,' said Lily with a rare lack of sympathy. 'You can sit on the baggage.'

With a loud sigh Kate had just taken this advice when a noise made her jump to her feet again. It was the unmistakable sound of a calliope. To Lily's trained ears the music was wheezy and discordant, but the well-loved strains of 'Camp Town Races' set everyone singing, stamping or snapping their fingers. The quality of the sound was distinctive, unlike anything Lily had ever heard. Some of the steam from the ship's engine was passed to the calliope – an ingenious arrangement of valves and whistles of varying sizes so that each note was accompanied by a puff of steam. It was raucous and shrill, but it had a certain magic and once heard was never forgotten.

'It's coming!' shouted Kate and the cry was immediately taken up by hundreds of other eager voices as all heads turned to watch the glorious and long-awaited sight. The wheezy, jaunty strains of 'Milenburg Joys' next echoed across the water, filling the air with its jangling harmonies, and a great cheer went up from the crowd as the majestic stern-wheeler finally rounded the bend. She was an undeniably beautiful sight, one that lifted the hearts of all who saw her, for here was the next move in their grand design; this was their transportation to Independence!

The *River Queen* was broad-bottomed, nearly three hundred feet long and fifty feet wide. She sat well down and rode the muddy water like a swan. Her white paintwork gleamed, outlined here and there in red, and a series of bright flags fluttered in a row from her roof. Two tall but narrow pipe-stacks rose into the air, emitting twin trails of dark smoke, and her name was blazoned in large red and gold letters along the side. At the stern her giant red paddlewheel churned the brown water into a mass of flittering white froth, with a rhythmic beat that grew steadily louder as the vessel slowed down and prepared to draw alongside.

'Make it slow amidships!'

'Coming ahead slow, sir.'

'All stop . . . Back it in slow!'

Her three-tiered decks were lined with waving passengers, but the people on the shore had no time for them. Their interest in the ship's beauty waned suddenly and there was a concerted rush to seize baggage and round up straying animals, children and friends.

To Kate's relief Amos, Gabby and Bart materialized beside them and suddenly life seemed not only bearable again but positively enjoyable.

Lily alone stood unmoving, watching the *River Queen* as she came to a halt and the crew leaped ashore to make her fast. Her errant husband had stood here, she thought, or somewhere nearby. He too had watched a similar boat and she wondered if his heart had been touched, as hers was, not by the ship alone but by a combination of ship, water and sky – by the sheer immensity of it all. Still the ragged music played on, assailing her senses, but now it was 'Skip to My Lou' which was played at the same fierce speed as though the musician could not wait to be done with it.

'Lily! Stop gawking!' cried Kate, giving her a nudge and with a start Lily reluctantly relinquished the magic and returned to the mundane problem of her luggage.

As Lily struggled after Kate the music stopped abruptly as the player, at a shout from the captain, returned to his other less colourful duties. But in years to come, inexplicably the scene would return to Lily – bright, clean and unforgettable – and the haunting sound of the calliope would drift in and out of her dreams.

*

They were still three days from Independence when the rumour began that two cases of cholera had been identified on board the boat. Alarmed, Kate and Lily went in search of Amos.

'True enough,' he told them. 'It's a young man from New Jersey – travelling with his uncle, who is also unwell.'

'And is a doctor attending them?' asked Lily.

'He was there when I came by,' said Bart. 'They were rubbing him down with hot drops and brandy and tincture of lobelia. They say he was raving like a lunatic last evening. Nothing else to do now but hope.'

'And his uncle, too?' asked Kate soberly. Her earlier euphoria had vanished with the news of the dread disease.

'Well, he's shivering pretty bad and has pains in his gut,' said Bart. 'They're in the same company as us. Let's hope it doesn't spread.'

'Let's hope they don't die,' said Lily. 'I wonder if there's anything I could do to help. I've done a bit of nursing in the village at home and I could – '

Kate clutched her arm. 'Lily Golightly, don't you dare!'

71

she cried. 'You could catch it yourself! Leave it to the doctors. Tell her, Mr Carp.'

'She's right,' said Amos. 'They're probably going to die anyway, so why risk your life? Leave it to the doctors – no point in you dying as well as them.'

'They might not die.'

'Everyone expects them to,' said Amos. 'Maybe the doctor too.'

'But that's terrible,' protested Lily.

'Which company was the doctor with?' asked Kate.

'Don't keep talking about them as though they're all already dead!' cried Lily. 'Can't we look on the bright side?'

Amos shrugged. 'We'd only be fooling ourselves if we pretended they were going to survive,' he said. 'The only way to survive cholera is not to catch it! That's what they say.'

They were all silent, staring out across the water, uncomfortably aware that the spectre of death now stalked the boat and that any one of them might be its next victim.

They didn't refer to it again, but less than an hour later the boat suddenly changed course and instead of steaming parallel to the river bank, it swung into mid-stream and headed for a small, uninhabited island. A few inquiries elicited the dreadful news that the young cholera victim had died and was to be buried there. The shocked passengers watched in horror as the body, hastily wrapped in a blanket, was lowered over the rail to two of the boat's crew, who laid it aside and began to dig a shallow grave. Their movements were hurried and uncaring and Lily felt her throat tighten. A hopeful young man, another Amos or Bart, had been reduced in a few short hours to a shapeless, nameless bundle wrapped in a blanket. A mother and father had lost their son, who only weeks earlier had left home in high spirits and with hopes of a fortune. When they learned of his death, their world would be shattered and his loss would haunt them for the rest of their lives. Had the young man set out west with his parents' approval or with their reproaches? She hoped the parting had been amiable, for if not a deep remorse would doubtless be added to the burden of their grief.

Soil flew from the two spades and Lily longed to turn away, but the dreary sight hypnotized her and she was still looking on when the two men picked up the limp bundle and lowered it unceremoniously into his grave. She could not find it in her heart to blame the two sailors for their haste, for merely by handling the dead man they were taking a serious risk and could hardly be blamed for wanting to be through with their unenviable task as quickly as possible. Another aspect, however, did trouble her and she turned to a nearby member of the ship's crew.

'Isn't he going to have a proper burial service?' she asked.

'No, ma'am,' he told her. 'Time's short and we've work to do. Never heard of a schedule?' He eyed her truculently. 'You English?'

She nodded.

'Well, keep your nose out of what don't concern you, then. This is the United States and over here we do things *our* way.'

'But not to have so much as a prayer . . .' she persisted. 'That's terrible.'

The man grabbed her arm and pointed along the deck. 'That man over there, with the ginger beard – he's the captain. You got a complaint, ma'am, you take it up with him – and the best of luck! You'll need it.'

Angrily Lily pulled her arm free from his grasp, feeling her face burn with embarrassment and anger.

Kate whispered, 'He's right, Lily. It's not our business. Leave it be.'

'It might be Amos or Bart,' Lily replied angrily. 'Or you, Kate, or me. Would you like to go to your maker without even a prayer?'

'You're just as dead,' Kate insisted, 'whether you had a prayer said over you or not.'

But Lily took no notice. She pushed a way through the crowd until she reached the captain.

'That young man,' she began, 'the one your men are burying – isn't anyone going to say a prayer over him?'

'No, ma'am, I guess not.' He did not take his eyes from the scene below him.

'Isn't there a parson on board?'

'No ma'am, there ain't.' He was a burly man with an ugly pock-marked face and hard blue eyes. 'You offering, are you?' he asked sarcastically.

Lily hesitated. 'I'm a parson's daughter,' she told him, straightening up. 'If no one else will, then I suppose I could do it.'

'You ain't getting off this boat,' he told her firmly.

Lily's jaw tightened. 'You can't really stop me,' she told him.

At last he turned to look at her, his head on one side. 'Nope,' he said slowly, 'but I *can* stop you getting back on board again.'

Lily could see by the cold look in his eyes that he meant exactly what he said. If she climbed down to the graveside, he would leave her there. Desperately, she tried to imagine what her father would do if he were in her place. He would *not* lose his temper, she thought, and with an effort she managed a faint shrug.

'You're the captain,' she said, 'but it just seems sad that a young man should go to his grave without a few Christian words spoken over him. Even the Lord's Prayer would be better than nothing.'

He waved a hand airily. 'You want to say it, go ahead,' he said, 'but you'll have to say it from this here rail.'

Lily was beginning to regret her impetuosity. She did not want to be the centre of attention, but she had raised the issue and now she would have to see it through.

'Thank you,' she said and pushed her way back through the crowd of spectators until she reached the rail. She looked down at the scene below where the men were shovelling earth over the body.

'Friend of yours, ma'am?' asked a man beside her.

'No,' said Lily, 'but I thought perhaps . . .' Her voice faltered, but then she steeled herself and turned to those nearest her. 'Don't you think we could say a prayer for him?' she asked. 'It's such a sad way to go.'

There were a few nods and here and there a murmur of agreement so she turned back to the scene below. Already the body in its makeshift grave had vanished beneath the soil. Lily closed her eyes and put her hands together.

'Our Father,' she began softly, then cleared her throat and began again as firmly as she could. 'Our Father, which art in Heaven, hallowed be Thy name . . .'

The man who had asked if the victim was a friend of hers suddenly joined in, his head bowed, his voice loud and clear booming out with her own.

'Thy Kingdom come, Thy will be done . . .'

Gradually more voices joined them and by the time the prayer was concluded, it sounded to Lily as though most of the passengers had shared in the small tribute. She felt a hand on her shoulder and opened her eyes. A man she did not recognize said, 'Well done, ma'am!' and several others echoed his sentiments.

The two crew members were then hauled back on board, the boat moved out again into mid-stream and the first casualty of the Western Hope Miners was left behind.

By the time they reached Independence, the young man's uncle had also succumbed to the disease, but his death went unnoticed as the eager passengers waited for the gang-plank to be lowered. Once it was in place, the captain's plea for an orderly disembarkation was ignored and a cheerful pandemonium reigned. Passengers laden with bundles and boxes elbowed their way towards the landing place, their voices shrill, their hopes high, for now they were in Independence and the great adventure was about to begin. Animals and livestock were unloaded with squeals and squawks and an assortment of wagons was rolled down the ramps to be claimed by their distracted owners. Stores and baggage were carried ashore by sweating stevedores. In the rush Lily and Kate were separated from their new-found friends but, discovering that the town itself was four miles away, set off at once to walk there.

Lily kept her eyes open for a glimpse of her husband, although it seemed unlikely that she would find him here. It was much more probable, they were told, that they would find him encamped on the far side of the town.

The four miles seemed interminable and Lily realized very quickly that the shoes she was wearing were unsuited to walking any distance. First priority would be the purchase of some more serviceable footwear. Flimsy buttoned boots would never carry her two thousand miles to California!

Independence itself was crowded with people and the noise was incredible as the hundreds of new arrivals joined those already in the town. Kate kept her eyes open for a glimpse of Bart, Gabby or Amos while Lily asked repeatedly for news of Patrick Golightly and Henry Simms. When Kate complained of a painful cramp in her side, Lily left her sitting on the wooden sidewalk while she pursued her investigations. At last, from one of the town's many blacksmiths, she heard the news she had dreaded – Patrick and the Brown Bears had already left Independence.

'I know because I shod the last of their oxen ten minutes before they moved out,' he told Lily, bellowing above the noise of his own hammer blows which rained ceaselessly down upon what looked like half a horseshoe. 'They jumped the gun a bit, know what I mean?'

Lily shook her head. Beside the blacksmith a young blond man waited with an ox, a dark brown beast with short curling horns, impassive brown eyes and ears that twitched nervously.

'Itchy feet,' the young man told her. 'As soon as the grass is showing, they want to be first to go. They all want to be first away. Human nature, that is.'

The blacksmith paused in his hammering to wipe the sweat from his forehead with the back of a brawny right arm. 'Me, I'm getting rich right here!' he told them. 'Never shod so many beasts in my whole darned life, and it's never going to stop! From dawn till dark they just keep coming. If it's not mules, it's horses, and if it's not horses, it's oxen! Let 'em all come, I love it. They're making me a rich man and I don't have to do no searching for gold!' He grinned cheerfully at Lily and drowned her answer in a renewed flurry of blows. Suddenly the blacksmith straightened up, gave a nod to the owner of the ox and moved to join him beside it. With a concerted movement they took hold of the startled animal and deftly threw it to the ground, where it lowed plaintively but made no effort to get up. Lily, who had opened her mouth to protest, now closed it hastily, assuming correctly that the men knew what they were doing. Catching her eye, the young man grinned.

'This is how we shoe oxen,' he told her. 'They don't stand like horses. It don't hurt them none.'

The blacksmith asked, 'D'you want to watch?' but Lily, remembering the urgency of her mission, shook her head reluctantly, and left them to their work.

For a while she wandered aimlessly, reconsidering their position, oblivious to the milling crowds which jostled about her. Patrick and Henry had gone ahead; they had missed them by several weeks so they must join them later. It was too late to turn back. She and Kate must go on, and probably they would be wise to stay with the friends they had made on the boat. The Western Hope Mining Company – that was the 'outfit' they had joined. She squared her shoulders determinedly and set off once more. She must find Captain Wallis and ask him for permission to travel with his company.

Lily found him at last in a makeshift tent. He was stockily built, with a red-gold beard which made it hard to guess his age, but Lily thought he must be in his early thirties. His hair was slightly darker than his beard and curled down the back of his neck; his weather-beaten face was set in firm lines. There was a small slanting scar across the right side of his jaw and the hand that held the pen was muscular and covered with the same red-gold hair as his beard. He made no effort to disguise his reluctance when Lily put her proposition to him. She recognized the look in his cold grey eyes and did not miss the sudden tightening of his mouth.

'It would only be until we catch up with the Brown Bear Company,' she said. 'We're both sensible people and we wouldn't be troubling you for too long.'

She laid a faint emphasis on the word 'troubling' and he did not miss it.

'And if we don't catch up with them?' he asked, eyeing her intently.

'Then you might have to put up with us for the whole journey,' Lily answered as calmly as she could.

'That's what I'm afraid of,' he told her. 'This is no joy-ride, Mrs Golightly; it is not suitable for women travelling alone. If women travel with their husbands, that makes them their husband's responsibility. If they are killed by Indians or bitten by snakes, I shall be sorry, but I shall know that if their husbands allowed them to make such a hazardous trip, they must take the consequences. You and your companion do *not* have husbands and I should therefore feel a certain amount of responsibility for you. I shall have my hands full as it is, without playing nursemaid to two women – and English women at that!'

Infuriated, Lily bit back an angry retort with difficulty, knowing that if she antagonized him he would almost certainly say 'No' and they would have to try again with another company.

She spoke as steadily as she could. 'I don't quite see that being English has anything to do with it. Our money is as good as anyone else's. We can pay our way for the time we are with you.'

'Do you ride?' he asked. 'Are you used to dealing with mules or oxen?'

'No, but – '

'Are you used to roughing it? There'll be no feather beds, no fancy food. Can you cook over an open fire? Can you skin a rabbit? Ever had to cope with a broken wagon wheel? Even seen an Indian?'

Although she knew he was goading her deliberately, she was unable to hold back and her anger flared suddenly.

'No, no and no!' she cried. 'Maybe we are from *civilized* homes, but that doesn't mean we can't *learn*. There has to be a first time for everything. We're not dull or stupid, Mr Wallis – '

'*Captain* Wallis,' he corrected her coolly. 'No, you don't look dull or stupid, but everyone has to pull their weight and I don't reckon you'll be able to do that.'

'We'll have to prove you wrong, then,' snapped Lily. He was making her feel a complete fool.

'Do you shoot?' he asked.

'No, but –'

'Ever seen cholera?'

'No, but I have done a little nursing.'

'A *little nursing!*' he mocked. 'Mrs Golightly, it's going to be *tough*. You have no idea how tough. I'm telling you for your own good. I don't think you are cut out for what lies ahead.'

'I don't care what lies ahead,' said Lily. 'I want to join my husband in his company. As soon as we can, we shall leave you and you'll be rid of us. Surely just a week or two . . .'

He leaned forward and put his elbows on the table, then said more gently. 'You look very frail, if you'll pardon my saying so.'

Lily felt a flutter of hope. 'My looks belie me,' she said firmly. 'I'm perfectly fit. And strong,' she added.

He raised his eyebrows, apparently amused by this last suggestion, and she felt her cheeks burn. An insolent, ignorant pig, she decided angrily. He continued to look at her thoughtfully, then leaned back in his chair.

'Do you think you'll be safe among so many men?' he asked.

Lily counted to ten. 'I am perfectly able to look after myself, Mr – *Captain* Wallis. I shall not hold you responsible for my honour, if that's what you mean.'

To her annoynace he laughed aloud and then picked up the pen. 'Jesus!' he remarked. 'A parson's daughter and a lady's maid. I must be mad.' He began to write in the book which lay open on the table before him.

Lily's hopes soared. 'Are you saying you'll take us?' she asked.

'I guess so,' he agreed, throwing down the pen. 'We'll discuss the money side of it when I have more time. Just keep out of trouble if you can.'

Incensed by this patronizing remark, Lily fought back a strong desire to lean over and slap his face. Instead, she stood up and smoothed her dress.

'I can assure you, Captain, we will be no trouble at all. The sooner we can leave your company the better I shall like it.'

He eyed her levelly. 'For a moment I thought you were going to thank me for taking you on,' he remarked.

Lily swallowed hard. 'I'm sorry,' she said. 'You are right. I should have thanked you and I *do*. It's just that I object to your – '

But he stood up suddenly, gave her a dismissive nod and turned away.

Lily gazed at his broad back with mounting fury. Why was this man so determined to humiliate her?

He turned back to face her. 'Is there something else?' he asked.

Lily glared at him, then shook her head. 'No, nothing else,' she said and stepped outside the tent, where she added uncharacteristically 'Just go to hell, Captain Wallis!'

*

Independence, on the Missouri River
12 May 1849

Dearest Papa,

This may be the last letter you receive from me for some time, but I beg you not to be concerned. The reason is that once out of Independence and on the trail there are no postal collections until we reach the military outpost of Fort Kearny, but I will send you a letter from there.

You will be pleased to hear that I am not travelling alone, as Kate Lester (Mrs Harrington's maid) decided to come with me and Mrs Harrington made no objections. She is a sensible girl and pleasant company.

Yesterday we each bought a stake in the Western Hope Miners (a very well-run company of prospectors) and we now own a light wagon (painted yellow) and a team of four oxen – Durham steers – they are the very best. You can imagine, Papa, how earnestly Kate and I concern ourselves with the animals' welfare and training, for they are not used to drawing a wagon (being reared locally for the plough), but we persevere. We could have chosen mules, but they cost three times as much as the oxen and are frisky and of uncertain temper. We did not care for the sound of them.

The wagon is about ten feet long and has a cover tied over curved hickory bows and at each end a drawstring pulls it close to keep out the weather. The cover is made of osnaburg and we have made it waterproof by applying a mixture of linseed oil and beeswax. It was messy work, but well worth the effort. Kate painted our number on the cover and I greased the wheels with tallow.

Kettles and buckets hang outside the wagon and inside we have such necessities as coffee grinder, skillet, coffee and tea-pots, a stout knife, tin plates and mugs, tallow for our candles, scissors, needle and thread, liniments and bandage and much more, so you see we are well prepared for any emergency.

I learned that Patrick's company left Independence on the 28th April, so I only just missed him. Our own company leader understands that I am expecting to join my husband and has agreed to refund a fair part of our money when finally we make the move. I thought we would have moved out before this, but there are so many delays. I try not to be impatient but you know the way I am, Papa!

We are also learning to shoot, but I pray God we will never need to use the rifles except perhaps for game to supplement our rations. Of this last the company has plenty in bulk – salt pork, rice, dried beef, flour and meal, dried apples and baking soda, molasses, vinegar, hard tack (whatever that might be) and dried beans. You see we will not go hungry!

Independence is so crowded with tents, wagons and animals everywhere, and it will be a relief to everyone when we can set out on our journey. There must be hundreds or even thousands of gold seekers in and around the town. It is an awesome sight. When the scouts report that the grass is high enough, we will be on our way. It is such a long journey that all the companies must leave by the end of May or they will not reach California before

81

the autumn sets in, when snow will make the mountains impassable.

We have met some pleasant people, in particular three young men who seem to look upon themselves as our protectors – their names are Amos Carp and Bart and Gabby Smith. They are kind and respectful, so have no fears on that score. Amos helped us when we first yoked the oxen and Gabby gives us shooting lessons. There is one man in our company who does not have enough money for a wagon, so has all his belongings on a pack-mule and will *walk* all the way. His name is Adam Best and I cannot but admire such determination. Other men will ride horses and lead pack-mules. It all seems a very far cry from home and at times when I look around me, I can hardly believe it is real. I confess to a growing excitement and do not for one moment regret my decision to follow Patrick. The general enthusiasm is infectious and I firmly believe that when we reach California we will find gold.

Enough now about me, Papa. How are you keeping? I expect by now the painting is finished. Are you pleased with it? Have you seen Miss Perring? I dreamed of young Maurice last night and woke wondering about him.

Please remember me to all my friends and say that I am in good health and spirits. Oh yes, we have several doctors with the company in case of sickness.

I have made inquiries about the dispatch of letters and if you write to me, address your letter to Fort Kearny (which rhymes with blarney!) and later Fort Laramie. Later still, a letter addressed to Sutter's Fort, California might find me.

Now, Papa, I must end my letter as it is getting too dark to write, and I do not want to light a candle as Kate is already asleep and I might wake her. Try to imagine me as I write, perched on the driving seat of the wagon with our oxen tethered nearby. Other wagons and teams are on all sides and many people cooking a late supper over their fires.

I pray God will take care of you. Don't be anxious on

my behalf, for I shall soon be with Patrick and then, come what may, I shall be content.

> Your most affectionate daughter,
> Lily.

Lily re-read the letter with a prickle of conscience, for she had not told her father of Kate's pregnancy nor had she referred to the two deaths from cholera, but she told herself these were sins of omission and hopefully pardonable. There was no point in worrying him any more than was necessary.

Kate murmured in her sleep and Lily glanced at her with some amusement as she sprawled untidily in her makeshift bed, arms thrown out, the blankets twisted tightly round her. They had given up their hotel room like many others, partly to save money but also to acclimatize themselves to the rigours of life on the trail. The company, like so many others, was camped alongside the river just outside the town and most of the members now slept in tents or in their newly purchased wagons.

Lily shook her head, still bemused by the situation in which she found herself. Then she slipped down into her own bed – a straw-filled mattress covered with blankets – and gave herself up to the luxury of thoughts of home. She needed to remember who and what she was, for here in Independence she was just one more gold seeker and a name on the company list – a statistic. Deliberately, she closed her eyes and remembered herself walking in the parsonage garden with her father; taking calves's-foot jelly to a sick child in the village; reading the lesson at church; comforting a bereaved widow. Her life in Kent had been a series of small events – a patchwork. Contained and predictable, it had been a sheltered existence. There had been nothing in her life so far to prepare her for the coming months ahead. Hands clasped, she closed her eyes in prayer. She would put herself in God's hands.

Kate cried out suddenly in her sleep – an unintelligible jumble of words – then relapsed again into silence and Lily found herself wondering afresh about her. What had Captain Wallis said? A parson's daughter and a lady's maid. They knew so little about each other. How would they stand up to trail life, she wondered? Would it bring out the best or the worst in each of them? At least a servant was more prepared for hardships than a parson's daughter. Lily sighed. She would do her best not to give Captain Wallis cause to regret his decision. Now that she understood more about trail life, she had begun to appreciate his reluctance to take them along. Two unaccompanied women with no experience *were* a responsibility and she was grateful that he had accepted them. Her early antagonism had faded a little as the days passed and she saw the calm but firm way in which he dealt with the numerous problems which already beset the wagon train. She saw, too, that the men respected him. He might be brusque and intractable and rather unapproachable, but already Lily had complete faith in him. She hoped the Brown Bears leader would be equally suited to his responsibilities.

*

On the evening of May the twentieth, the entire company of the Western Hope Miners – or Western Hopers, as they now called themselves – was gathered together for the last briefing. The long-awaited departure was set for the following morning. Matt Wallis, perched on the driving seat of his wagon, surveyed his ill-assorted company and waited for the murmurings and whispers to die away. He wore the rig that he advocated for the rest of the Western Hopers: serviceable blue trousers, red woollen shirt and a dark knee-length coat. A red scarf was knotted round his neck and his trousers were tucked into high boots.

Matt Wallis had given himself the title of Captain not from vanity, but from an awareness of the need for strong leadership. He had made the trip to Oregon the previous year with a group of settlers and had learned from that experience.

Now he stared down at all the upturned faces and wondered how many would fall by the wayside before they reached their destination. Now they looked to him with trust and the very best intentions, but later he knew it would be a different story. Deprivation, exhaustion, danger and difficulties would all take their toll and many of those people would crack under the strain. He recognized some of them – the farmers, three generations of them who had only just joined in time; the three young men from Iowa who had been among the first to sign on – 'eager beavers', he called them, but they would knuckle down and were young and healthy. Then there were the two English women, who, thank God, were only temporary members. He'd been hard on Mrs Golightly and was unsure why. She was doing her best to prove herself capable and he had several times resisted the urge to offer his assistance. Almost certainly she would refuse it, he thought wryly. They had said very little to each other since their first encounter and he sensed that the rift still existed between them. Now he caught her eye momentarily as she sat with the rest of the company and she met his gaze coolly. Already she had changed – her newly purchased clothes were of more durable quality and plainly cut, and the fresh air and sunshine had put some warm colour into her skin. Beside her Kate Lester chatted with Amos Carp, her face animated, her frizzy hair free of its ribbons. He frowned uneasily. A single woman among so many men! It was a recipe for disaster.

His gaze moved on. Adam Best, the solitary walker – he was not a full member, but wanted to start off with them. Almost certainly he would fall behind and ally himself with other wagon trains as they overtook him. To his right there was an elderly man, an ex-tin miner whose health was already giving concern, but his previous experience would no doubt serve him well if he did reach the gold fields. Then there was Daniel Miller – he would keep a watchful eye on him! And so many more.

'I wanted to get you all together,' he began, 'before we start out so that we all know where we stand. The conditions could be better – we're having even more rain than is normal for May, so the trail's muddy and will be slow going, but the scouts tell me the grass is well up so we'll do fine for feed for the animals. We shall leave tomorrow as soon as it's daylight and head out to the south-west along the Santa

Fé trail. Later we turn off from that trail, cross the Kansas River and head for Fort Kearny. Any questions so far?'

Amos Carp raised his hand. 'How long do you reckon that will take?' he asked.

Wallis shrugged. 'Three weeks barring accidents.' He waited, but there were no more questions. 'You can send letters from Fort Kearny. The mail goes out twice a month from there for the military. We'll be in Indian territory and maybe see a few Indians, but they are not hostile so don't provoke any kind of trouble. They're Shawnee and Potawatomis. Later on when we reach Pawnee country, things may look a little different, but then again they may not. They might be too busy fighting the Sioux to bother with us.'

Someone cried, 'Let's hope so!' but others protested that they were eager to get in some rifle practice.

Charlie Cooper raised a hand. 'What sort of country can we expect?'

'Prairie at first,' Wallis told him. 'Later when we leave Fort Kearny it'll be valley all along the Platte River, then a drop at Ash Hollow into plains.'

'And then?'

He smiled. 'That's enough for now.' Leaning forward, he rested huge hands on his knees. 'Now, for Christ's sake try to get along with each other,' he warned. 'I'm here to get us safely to the gold fields and not to solve tin-pot arguments. We're members of the same company and the idea is that we *help* each other. You're all in small groups but if you don't like your messmates, don't tell me. I'm not a wet-nurse and you're all big enough to solve your own problems. I don't want to know; just sort it out amicably between yourselves. The food will be given out weekly to each mess and you can arrange between yourselves who cooks it. You use whatever fuel is available, but for much of the time it will be dried buffalo dung – known as chips. Don't turn up your noses – it burns without odour and gives a good heat. We start at daybreak each day, stop at noon for an hour or so to rest the animals, and knock off while there's still enough daylight to set up camp for the night. Some among you will be glad to know there won't be too much water for washing when we aren't passing near to the rivers or crossing over them. I know,' he said, anticipating protest 'that wherever possible the trail follows the river, but that doesn't mean we're right alongside it. We might be a mile away, we might be two miles.' He shrugged. 'Water is *precious*. It's *vital* and we don't waste it on washing.' He paused, but no hands went up so he continued. 'If anyone is taken sick, I want to know about it. I won't beat about the bush; cholera is always a possibility and we know it can be a killer. Don't wait until it's too late. We've got medical supplies and we have doctors with us. Can they stand up and introduce themselves?'

Four men stood up, announced themselves as Bonner, Scarfe, Perry and Fisher, and sat down again.

Wallis thanked them and went on. 'It will take a few days or maybe weeks for us to shake down together, so don't let's be too impatient. Oh, and before anyone asks me, it's not our policy to travel on the Sabbath, but we will if we lose a lot of travelling time in any one week. We can't afford to fall back, because those ahead of us will eat the grass, use the wood and shoot the game. There won't be too much left for the stragglers.'

He paused for breath, but there were no queries so he went on. 'By now I think you're all familiar with the way we shall organize the train. We're sixteen wagons and they are all numbered. Mine is number one and it always goes in front, followed by the rest of the supplies in an unnumbered wagon. On the first day, I'm followed by the number two wagon and so on. Next day number two goes to the back and three is behind me. That's because there will be plenty of dust on the trail and the further back you are in the train, the worse it will be. This way everyone gets a chance to be at the head of the train in the clearer air. If it rains, it'll lay the dust but we'll have mud instead.' There were a few good-natured groans and he smiled briefly. 'We have elected a committee of six men, as you know. At the end of the first month you can change any member of it by a democratic vote. After that you're stuck with them.' He took another deep breath and continued. 'Now, I'm going to get you to California, make no mistake about it, but once we get there you're on your own. We'll have a grand share-out of whatever money is left and then the company will be dissolved. Right? Any more questions? No?'

Someone called out, 'Then here's to the Western Hopers and may God speed us all to California!'

There was a ragged cheer and a few whistles and the meeting broke up in cheerful disorder. Lily, Kate and the three young men walked back to their wagons which were parked next to each other. Amos had an arm round Kate's shoulders; Gabby and Bart walked on either side of Lily. Already Kate and Lily were aware of the extreme shortage of women and that for a man even to be in a woman's company gave him a slight edge over his fellows who must make do with male companions.

'So we're off at last,' said Gabby. 'Hard to believe, isn't it?'

'It's a terribly early start,' said Lily. 'Half-past four!'

'That's not early,' said Kate. 'Not if you've been in service! I've been up at five for years. Don't worry. You'll get used to it.'

Amos suggested, 'I'll give you two ladies a call, if you like. It's no trouble.'

Kate giggled. 'What, wake us with a kiss like Prince Charming! Ooh, that'd be a bit of all right, wouldn't it, Lily?'

'I think we'll be awake,' said Lily cautiously.

Kate groaned. 'You've no soul, Lily Golightly,' she complained. 'None at all.'

Bart said. 'Amos offering to wake *you*? That's a joke! We have a job to prise his eyelids open.' He winked at Lily. 'Don't worry,' he told her. 'There'll be no Prince Charming, I'll bet my bottom dollar on it.'

Amos protested, but after a few further moments of conversation, Lily said she was going to bed and Gabby and Bart also took themselves off, which left Kate and Amos together.

As soon as they were alone, he turned to her and she was surprised by the serious expression on his face.

'Kate,' he said, 'if a man named Daniel Miller talks to

you, give him his marching orders. If ever there was a rotten apple, it's him.'

Kate was immediately intrigued. 'Which one's Miller?' she asked curiously. 'Do I know him?'

'He knows you.' Amos looked uncomfortable and would not meet her eyes. 'He's short and dark and kind of rough. Squashy nose.'

Kate still looked puzzled.

'He's got a whippet and he wears buckskin pants which he got from a trade with a tame Indian back in Independence.'

Amos was secretly envious of the buckskin trousers and had made up his mind to try and acquire a similar pair for himself.

'Oh, *him!*' said Kate. 'Is his name Daniel Miller? I've seen the dog but I've never spoken to the man. How is he a rotten apple?'

Amos stared at the ground and shuffled his feet. 'I can't say, not to a respectable girl like yourself, but just be on your guard, Kate. Don't get yourself alone with him. He talks . . .' He shrugged. 'You won't like what he says, Kate. Take my word on it. Just don't listen to him.'

Kate was becoming more and not less interested in Mr Miller.

'Has he taken a fancy to me, Amos?' she asked. 'Is that what you're on about?'

Amos shook his head. 'No, he hasn't. Leastways, not in the way you mean.'

Eyes narrowed, Kate stared at him, bristling. 'What's he said about me?' she demanded. 'What does he know? How can he say anything about me? He doesn't even know me. Amos, what has he said to you? I've got a right to know.'

He was looking very ill-at-ease and said irritably, 'Look, just forget it, will you? Talk to him if you must.'

'Amos!' Kate's tone was reproachful as she put a hand on his arm. 'Don't take on. I'm just curious. You obviously know something you won't tell me so it stands to reason I'll be curious.'

'I don't want to offend you,' he said.

'I won't be offended, I promise you.'

'You *will*.'

'Amos!' she shouted. 'Tell me what he said or I'll go right out and find him and ask him myself.'

Amos swore under his breath and took a few steps away from her. Then he swung round and came back to her, his face grim.

'Miller wants to make a bit of money and he sees his chance in you. He wants to *sell* you, got it?'

'Sell me?' She stared at him, uncomprehending. 'Does someone want to buy me?'

'Sell you to the men. There are dozens of men here and no unmarried ladies. You're the exception.'

Still her expression was blank and he took a deep breath.

'Look, ma'am, he wants to offer a woman for so much an hour. You'd split the money two ways. Don't you see?'

Kate gasped with shock.

'Split the money,' she repeated. 'You mean, I let them — and he takes half! Blooming cheek!' Suddenly she began to laugh. 'He's got a nerve, I must say. Daniel Miller! So that's his game, is it?'

Amos stared at her in relief. 'I thought you'd be upset,' he said. 'I didn't want to tell you. I just wanted to warn you in case he came direct to you. I know you'd never agree to such a thing. When he asked me if I thought you'd be willing, I knocked him down.'

Kate stopped laughing. 'You what? You *hit* him, on my account? Oh, Amos!' She threw her arms round his neck and kissed him then drew back, her eyes shining. 'You really *hit* him for *me*?'

'Certainly I did,' he told her. 'I told him you were a respectable girl and he was to stay right away from you. He took it badly — said he'd every right to speak to you if he wanted to. I'm afraid he might, so I wanted you to be ready for him.' He took her hand and looked at her earnestly. 'If he comes near you, Kate, you tell me and I'll give him a hiding he won't forget. I'm real sorry it's been such a shock for you, a respectable girl like you . . .'

Her animation had faded. 'Oh, Amos!' she said, her tone

anguished. 'I suppose I'll have to tell you. I'm not as . . .' she stopped, unable to go on.

'Not what?'

'Nothing.' She sighed deeply.

'Not as what?' he insisted, puzzled by her changed manner.

She searched quickly for a way out. 'Not as *shocked*,' she invented. 'I mean, I've been brought up rough, not like Lily. Nothing shocks me, that's what I meant.'

'Oh.' He looked relieved. 'Then you aren't offended with me for telling you.'

'Course I'm not, silly. Not a bit of it. How could I be offended when you knocked him down! I think that was wonderful of you, Amos, really I do.'

He grinned. 'It was nothing, ma'am. I'd do it again for you.'

'You would? Oh, Amos, I don't know what to say.'

His grin broadened. 'There's no need to say anything, but you can kiss me again if you've a mind to.'

Slowly she moved forward and raised her face to him. He put his arms round her waist as hers went round his neck. The kiss was long and satisfying and left them both breathless.

'I must go,' Kate told him reluctantly. 'Lily will be wondering.'

'She's not your mother.'

'No, but she's been very good to me.'

He nodded. 'I'll see you in the morning then. Kate, I – '

Quickly she put a finger to her lips. 'Don't say anything!' she said, keeping her tone light.

'But – '

'No, Amos!'

Before he could insist, she blew him a kiss. 'See you in the morning!' she said and climbed hastily into the wagon.

Kate lay sleepless for a long time, considering her relationship with Amos Carp. He was obviously very fond of her and he might even want to *marry* her! She could not let matters go any further without telling him about the baby and Constable Bailey. But how, she wondered desperately, could she shatter his illusions about her? He had called her 'a respectable girl' and had actually defended her honour, but Daniel Miller's opinion of her was nearer to the truth. She had given herself to several men, but for love and not money. Would that make any difference to Amos when she told him? She rehearsed several speeches, but they all lacked conviction and finally she gave up in despair. It was no good. Amos Carp was a respectable young man – a teacher, no less! He was not going to marry a pregnant runaway servant. Still, there were other pebbles on the beach and Daniel Miller was right about one thing. She *was* the only single girl in the company and there *were* a lot of single men. One of them might be willing to consider her even with a child. 'If I can't find a husband between here and California, I never will!' she told herself firmly. 'If Amos doesn't want me, he can go hang!'

But her heart was heavy as she settled herself for sleep. Amos Carp had knocked down a man in her defence. Amos was the man for her.

Chapter Five

The next day was to appear, in retrospect, the longest day in Lily's life. She was awakened by a fist drumming on the outside of the wagon.

'Rouse up! Look lively!'

She recognized Matt Wallis's voice and opened her eyes to hear Kate, already dressed, shouting a cheerful 'Thank you!' in return. Outside it was still dark, for dawn was yet some way off. Lily groaned and sat up, then felt a rush of excitement strongly laced with fear. But no doubt Patrick had experienced the same intoxicating mix of emotions, she reminded herself. They would have such fun comparing notes when they were together again.

Kate turned to grin at her, eyes large in the half-light.

'Come on!' she urged. 'We've got to yoke up the oxen and I'll never lift that blooming yoke on my own. It weighs a ton.'

'But what about breakfast?' Lily began.

'There's no time to eat,' said Kate. 'Oh, do come on, Lily. We're number five, remember? We daren't keep the rest of them waiting.'

As Kate scrambled out into the darkness Lily threw back the blankets and rolled them up into an unwieldy bundle which she stuffed into a corner. Should she eat something, she wondered, as she pulled on her clothes with trembling fingers that seemed suddenly unused to the most familiar task. Buttons would not button and laces refused to be tied as Lily tried to hurry. Outside the camp was coming alive with urgent sounds as the other members of the Western Hopers abandoned their beds and prepared to make the first day's journey towards their long-awaited goal.

'The very first day,' Lily muttered as she rubbed her face with a damp flannel. There would be countless other days, but none like this one. She pulled a comb through her hair, but the hairpins would not obey her fumbling fingers so she tossed them aside and tied her hair back in one bunch with a ribbon hastily pulled from the left cuff of her blouse. The thought of doing such a thing would never have occurred to her in England but this was America, she reminded herself, and today they were leaving civilization behind them. One ribbon more or less would count for little in the new scheme of things!

All around her she could hear eager voices as oxen and mules were coaxed and bullied into position before the wagons. Dogs barked excitedly, men shouted, there was the muffled sound of innumerable hooves and the occasional rattle of pans. Somewhere a child began to cry and Lily was thankful that she had only herself to look after.

She climbed down into a fine, misty rain and went forward to help Kate who was struggling with the first pair of oxen.

'Stupid things,' Kate grumbled as she whacked the rump of one of them. 'Get over, will you! Get over!' She heaved and jostled the reluctant animal and with Lily's help, laid the heavy wooden yoke over the first ox and placed the U-shaped stay under the animal's neck, locking it through the two slots in the yoke. Lily held the yoke steady while Kate tugged the second ox into position. When they were ready, the two girls repeated the operation with the second pair of oxen and finally all four were yoked and ready. They grinned at each other, secretly proud of their achievement, for they had agreed earlier that wherever possible they would manage without enlisting aid from the men, no matter how willingly such help might be offered.

'We did it!' whispered Kate and gave each animal a kindly pat. 'They do try,' she assured Lily. 'I'm sure they do. I thought we could give them names. These two could be Big and Bonny – Bonny has the crooked horn – and the others could be Dan and Duffy. What do you think?'

Lily laughed. 'How do we tell Dan and Duffy apart?'

'Dan is slightly smaller and has longer eyelashes – ' She broke off as Amos appeared beside them, carrying a lantern.

'Do you ladies need any help?' he asked hopefully.

They assured him proudly that they did not.

'Are you all ready?' Lily asked him.

'We are,' he assured her, 'though I have to admit my breakfast is lying like lead in my belly. Bacon, beans and coffee,' he said. 'We've been up since just after three. There's some coffee left if you fancy some!'

On being told that they most certainly *did*, he went away and came back with two tin mugs full of steaming coffee.

'You're an angel,' said Kate as the two girls sipped gratefully.

'Seriously,' he said, 'you ought to rouse up in time for breakfast. I was talking to a man called Charlie Cooper and he swears by a decent meal to start the day. He says you never know what's coming that might delay the noon-time break and it's real bad to travel on an empty stomach.'

As he was speaking, Matt Willis rode up. 'Any problems?' he asked. 'All hitched?'

'Yes,' they chorused.

'We'll take it reasonably slow today,' he said, steadying his horse which rolled its eyes nervously in the gloom. 'Give the teams a chance to settle down – give us all time to find our feet. We'll aim for ten to twelve miles, but it's chilly going and there's more rain heading this way. Could be a slow haul today, but we'll make better time as we go on.'

He smiled suddenly, his teeth white in the lantern light. 'We'll get there,' he said, his eyes on Lily.

Lily smiled back. 'Don't worry about us,' she told him. 'We're fine, aren't we, Kate?'

Kate nodded.

Amos asked, 'Any rivers to cross today?'

'We might make the Blue,' Wallis answered, 'if we get that far. It's a poor sort of bridge as I remember it, but it'll hold up. Later on there'll be no bridges, so make the most of this one!'

'No bridges?' Kate was astonished. 'But how – '

'Rafts,' he told her briefly. 'Or we'll drive across if it's shallow enough. And we swim the animals, of course.'

He raised his hand and spurred on his horse and they heard him greet the people in the next wagon.

'Rafts?' Kate repeated dubiously. She looked at Lily, who shrugged.

'Don't ask me,' she laughed. 'We'll have to wait and see.'

Amos said, 'He knows what he's about. I'd trust that man with my life.'

Just then there was a shout from Gabby Smith.

'I must go,' said Amos and was off with a hasty, 'Good luck!'

*

The wagon train moved off in an orderly fashion an hour later than planned, just as the dawn was breaking. Kate and Lily walked one each side of Big and Bonny, saying little but filled with an almost unbearable excitement. The general mood was one of exhilaration that at last, after weeks of endless preparation and last-minute delays, they were actually on their way.

Lily strode along, watching the preceding wagon as it swayed and creaked over the muddy trail. The first few miles of the journey led southward and so the rising sun appeared on her left, lightening the sombre sky with a warm coral flush, picking out the fine trailing clouds and gilding them with colour.

She glanced back at the town of Independence and saw the rest of the company stretched out, wagon after wagon, on the trail behind her. To her right the land was dark and empty and from time to time the last cries arose from nocturnal creatures, but these would finally be silenced by the coming of daylight.

Lily drew a deep breath and exhaled slowly in an attempt to calm her fluttering nerves. For one frightening moment her resolve almost deserted her. She wondered, terrified, what she was doing there and saw herself as she was – a small and insignificant speck moving across the vast untamed continent of America.

'Oh God, please help me. Stay with me!' she prayed frantically and just as suddenly as the fear had flared, it subsided. She squared her shoulders and spoke sternly to herself.

'You wanted to come on this hare-brained trek, Lily Golightly, and as usual you've got your own way. Whatever happens, you have only yourself to blame, so pull yourself together and don't you *dare* complain. Don't you *dare* whine. Don't ever say you're cold or tired or afraid. You *chose* to come and you can jolly well put up with it – whatever it is! You are going to find Patrick and then you are going to put your marriage to rights. With God's help – '

Unfortunately, at that moment His attention proved to be elsewhere and Lily stepped into a deep and unexpected puddle. Losing her balance, she fell full-length in the mud where she lay for a few seconds, but no one had seen her tumble and so nobody came to help her. While she lay there, shaken and breathless, the second pair of oxen passed her and she had to roll quickly sideways to avoid being run over by the wheels of their wagon. As the yellow spokes whirled past she scrambled to her feet and surveyed her muddied clothes. Seizing her skirt, she wiped splashes of mud from her face.

'So be it!' she thought furiously. 'If that's the way it's going to be, I can take it as well as the next man!' And, ignoring the impulse to clean herself up, she set her face determinedly, ran back to her place beside Bonny and plodded grimly on. For Lily, one of the worst aspects of the journey would be the lack of privacy, but she hoped she would grow accustomed to the communal life and her education in this area had already begun. The sight of a man's back, legs apart, no longer embarrassed her and the stream of urine had ceased to shock. She still dreaded the moment when it would be her turn to answer the call of nature, but Kate had laughed at her squeamishness. 'We'll just scurry off into the bushes,' she had told Lily. Lily had suggested that there might be a distinct shortage of bushes out on the prairie. 'So I'll hold out my skirts to hide you and you do the same for me. You worry too much,' said Kate. 'I reckon that'll be the least of our worries.'

And Lily was forced to agree that Kate was probably right.

*

At midday they 'nooned', making an hour-long halt to rest the teams. Lily unhitched the four oxen and tethered them in the grass alongside the trail. While she did this, Kate lit a fire with dry sticks and grass brought along for the purpose. The Smiths and Amos had invited them to share their fire, but Lily had insisted that for the first few days at least they must manage alone. Aware that Matt Wallis had not been enthusiastic about allowing them to join, they were determined to tackle every task, only asking for help where brute strength was required. On those occasions pride would be a foolish luxury.

The rain had stopped and a watery sun shone down as they sat round the small blaze sipping gratefully at hot sweet coffee and eating bacon and yesterday's bread rolls. Kate looked up at Lily and said triumphantly, 'Well, we've put some of the journey behind us. How far d'you think we've walked?'

'It feels like a hundred miles,' said Lily with a laugh. 'But maybe four. I don't think I've ever walked so far in my life – or if I have, then not in such uncomfortable circumstances.'

'If folks back home could see you now!' Kate giggled. 'You do look a sight. What happened? Did you fall over?'

Lily noddded. 'Flat on my face,' she said with a smile.

'You look horrible,' Kate assured her. 'Almost as bad as I feel. I suppose the dust will wash off.' She frowned. 'How *do* we do the washing out here?'

Lily shrugged. 'Wash in the river, I suppose,' she said.

'But if we're not near a river?' Kate insisted.

'As Captain Wallis said, then we won't wash.'

'Crikey! We shall stink!'

Lily laughed. 'Everyone else will be in the same boat,' she reminded Kate, 'so we won't feel too dreadful.'

'And the men won't be able to shave.'

'They're all growing beards – haven't you noticed? Some have started already.'

Kate said wistfully, 'Amos will look nice with a beard.'

'Yes, I think he will.'

Kate, guessing intuitively that Lily was about to comment on Amos's obvious affection for her, quickly changed the subject.

'That little boy in wagon seven,' she said, 'he's so big, but he's still like a baby – can't feed himself, can't talk, can't walk.' She sighed. 'He's just a poor little lump of nothing.' She swallowed. 'I'd hate to have a child like that!'

'There's no reason why you should,' said Lily. 'It's pretty rare, I should think.'

'But that poor girl, his mother I mean. She lugs him round on her hip and he must weigh a ton! And he just stares as though he doesn't know what's going on.'

Lily drained her mug and refilled it. She bit hungrily into a second roll and wrinkled her nose. 'They're a bit stale,' she said, 'but no doubt we shall eat a lot worse. We'll have to learn how to make bread. Oh dear, my legs are beginning to ache and there's still all the afternoon to get through.'

'It's my back that aches,' Kate confided. 'I shall be glad when it's bedtime.'

Lily tried to think of something encouraging. 'We have to remember it's only our first day,' she said. 'We'll get used to walking and we'll get tougher and healthier. All this fresh air!'

She waved a hand and they both paused to look around them. The land rose and fell, green and beautiful, and there was a freshness in the air. Lily sighed deeply with a sudden feeling of contentment. This was America and she, Lily Golightly, was part of the big migration west.

Fleetingly, she turned back the clock and imagined herself seated at the piano beside young Maurice Dent and heard herself murmur, 'Thumb, first finger, second finger . . .' She smiled at the thought.

Kate opened her mouth to say, 'A penny for them' but was interrupted by a clatter of hooves and they looked up to see Matt Wallis beside them. The sun behind him made a halo of his hair and Lily was reluctantly impressed by the directness of his gaze. Even to her inexperienced eyes he sat a horse well and looking up at him she was suddenly reassured. This was a man to be trusted.

'You ladies still making out?' he asked.

Kate and Lily answered together. 'Yes, thank you.'

'No problems?' he insisted, as though surprised – or disappointed.

'None so far,' said Lily. She stood up. 'Actually, there is one thing I've been meaning to ask and that's about milk. Would it be acceptable for us to buy milk from anyone who would sell it?'

Kate scrambled furiously to her feet. 'Lily, I've *told* you!' she cried. 'I don't *want* milk. I don't want to be fussed over. I'm fine.'

Matt Wallis looked at her in surprise and Lily gave her a meaningful look and said quickly, 'It's for *both* of us, Kate, although you're the one with the funny digestion.'

Kate collected her wits and said, 'Oh yes, I am. Real funny it is at times, but I don't like to fuss about it,' and she sat down again, her face flushed.

'You can inquire around,' he told them. 'The family in wagon fourteen have a couple of goats – also the Harpers, but they've got boys. The folks in fourteen might be glad of a bit of extra cash. The Coopers have a cow, too, but they also have a child. Ask them, anyway. They might sell you some; then again, they might not!'

He touched the brim of his hat and rode off.

'He's a handsome devil,' said Kate, watching him go, 'but sort of scary. D'you know what I mean?'

'No,' said Lily, 'but I'll take your word for it.'

'I'm sorry,' said Kate, 'shouting off like that about the milk. It was stupid of me, but I thought you were going to tell him about the baby.'

'I wouldn't do that,' Lily assured her.

'Do you think he's guessed about me?'

'I don't think so. Can men tell about these things?'

'I suppose the milk *is* for me.'

100

'Of course it is. Someone has to look after you and *you* don't seem inclined to bother.'

At this small rebuke, Kate's face assumed a slightly sullen look which Lily had learned to ignore. She stood up and stretched her arms above her head and then bent to rub her aching leg muscles.

'I shall be glad when the first week's over,' she remarked. 'By then I think my body will be used to the new way of life.'

'I'll be glad when *today's* over!' said Kate, also getting to her feet. 'I feel as though I've got a blister coming.'

'Wear thicker stockings,' Lily suggested, but it seemed Kate was wearing the thickest ones she had and was determined to grumble.

'My nose is full of dust and so are my ears!' she went on. 'It's even gone down inside my bodice, I can feel it all gritty and horrible.' She shook herself, the way a dog does, and said, 'Oh, for a nice hip-bath full of hot soapy water. That's what Mrs Harrington used to have. Once a week, regular as clock-work, with a lovely fire roaring up the chimney. Coo, did I hate bath nights! Weighed a ton, that bath did, and I had to lug it upstairs from the kitchen. Then it was up and down the stairs with jugs of hot and cold water. What a palaver!' She sighed at the memory. 'But it used to look so good, when she was actually in it. Course, I wasn't allowed to look until she was under the water, if you know what I mean, but then I had to wash her back and rub on all the potions and stuff she used on her skin. She should have been the most beautiful woman in the whole blooming world. Madame Vestris's complexion paste – that was one of them – a special wash to remove her freckles ... oh, and pearl water, that was another favourite. I used to make them all up for her. Quite fun, that was. Pearl water was Castile soap, water, alcohol and oil of rosemary. And something else – '

Lily laughed as she scattered the embers and trod out what remained of the fire.

'Sounds as though you could set up in business when you get to California,' she suggested. 'You could make and sell potions.'

'And oil of lavender,' said Kate triumphantly. 'Mix well, bottle and apply night and morning. Yes, that was pearl water, but there were plenty more. That was her favourite, though. Lordy, but I'd like a guinea for the number of times I've made pearl water!'

Lily was glad to see that Kate had resumed her former good humour. Together the two girls coaxed the oxen back into position on either side of the long wooden 'tongue' to which they were yoked.

'I wonder how the oxen will like California,' Lily mused, regarding them with growing affection.

'Probably won't notice the difference,' said Kate. 'Grass is grass, isn't it, and that's all they care about.'

Around them the midday halt was coming to an end. Fires were extinguished, utensils stowed away, animals reharnessed and last-minute adjustments made to the rigs. At last a cry rang out from the head of the train and it was passed back to the rear.

'We're moving out!'

A variety of voices carried the message from wagon to wagon, dogs barked and children whooped excitedly.

Kate, hearing them, grinned ruefully. 'Just think,' she said, 'my little lad is missing all the fun. He'll have gone right across America with the Western Hopers and he won't remember a thing.'

'Never mind,' comforted Lily. 'You'll be able to tell him all about it. Oh, it looks as though we're off!'

'I wish it was Christmas,' mused Kate. 'Then we'd *be* there!'

Lily laughed as she cracked her whip and urged the oxen foward.

'Christmas is a long way off,' she said.

'A hundred blisters away!' declared Kate. 'That's how I shall measure the journey!'

They fell silent as they walked on and above them a buzzard wheeled sluggishly in the still air. Lily tried to imagine a bird's-eye view of the Western Hopers – a straggling line of flimsy carts hauled by plodding beasts, driven by hopeful people who in turn were driven by the desire for the bright new future gold could bring. A narrow ribbon of hopeful humanity under a wavering pall of dust. Maybe not wildly impressive, she thought humbly, but she was suddenly grateful to be part of it.

*

While Lily was experiencing her first day out of Independence, Patrick was already half-way to Fort Kearny with the Brown Bears.

He stumbled on wearily beside the leading pair of oxen, whip in hand, head bent, finding it more of an effort than usual to drag his feet forward. His bowels rumbled uneasily and his breakfast of soda bread, bacon and coffee lay heavy in his stomach. Henry Simms watched him anxiously from the other side of the team.

'You don't look too good again,' he said. 'Still having problems?'

Patrick nodded, avoiding the effort of speech. Behind them a rear wheel encountered a deep rut making the wagon roll ominously and Henry cursed under his breath. It righted itself, however, and they plodded on.

'Did you take more physic?' Henry asked.

When Patrick made no answer, Henry repeated the question sharply and Patrick nodded again.

'Patrick! Speak, for Christ's sake!' snapped Henry. 'Don't just nod. What did you take? Is it doing you any good? Shouldn't you see the doc?'

Patrick turned dull eyes towards him. 'I'll be fine. I took laudanum with pepper – that'll cure it.'

'You look terrible,' cried Henry. 'You're really sick, you know that? I'm going to fetch Doc Baines.'

'No, Henry! Don't fuss. It's not cholera, I tell you; it's just a touch of dysentery.'

'How the hell do you know?' Henry demanded. 'You shouldn't take any chances – for your wife's sake, if not for your own. You look as though you can hardly walk.'

Patrick shook his head, afraid to admit even to himself the possibility of cholera. Three members of their company had died of the disease in the past five days and were buried in lonely graves alongside the trail. Out of four who had contracted it, only one had survived.

'Maybe I'll take some rhubarb at noon,' said Patrick. 'I think I'm on the mend.'

However, as though to disprove this assertion, his bowels contracted painfully and he was forced to abandon his place beside the oxen and run for the comparative privacy of the long grass. When he again caught up with the wagon, his face was pale and beads of sweat stood out on his skin.

'Why don't you rest up for a while?' Henry suggested. 'I'll manage.'

'I tell you I'm fine,' muttered Patrick stubbornly. 'Leave me alone, for God's sake, Henry! Talk about fuss! You're like an old woman.'

'Go to hell, then!' cried Henry. Offended, he stared straight ahead, ignoring Patrick's unsteady progress.

After a few hundred yards Patrick called, 'Henry!'

'What is it?' He turned to his friend with a show of reluctance.

'I've written a letter to Lily.'

'So?'

'If anything happens to me . . .'

Henry's patience was exhausted. 'If anything happens to you, you'll have no one to blame but your goddamn self!' he cried. 'Don't expect me to run round after you. There's a collection of mail goes from Fort Kearny. Hand you letter in when you get there – *if* you get there.'

At that moment a cry went up from one of the wagons ahead of them and word was passed back.

'Backtracker!'

Anyone who gave up along the way and turned back east was welcomed by those still heading west for a variety of reasons. He would carry messages from one company to another and was a useful source of information. A backtracker knew some of the hazards ahead – the quality of the grazing, for instance, the presence and mood of any Indians, the prevalence of cholera – and would even tell of a shortage of firewood.

People turned back for many reasons. Sometimes it was

ill-health which drove them to do so, sometimes a profound disillusionment or simply ill-luck. A few young men lost all their money and equipment gambling. No one asked why they turned back – there but for the grace of God . . .

The man reached Henry and, turning to walk beside him, said mechanically. 'Name's Jed. Got a bite to eat?'

A pathetically few belongings were strapped to his back – a couple of blankets, a water-bottle and what looked like a spare pair of boots. Patrick, seeing him, rallied enough to say, 'Take a letter back for me, will you? Post it at Independence? It's to my wife in New York.'

Jed dodged in front of the oxen and walked alongside Patrick, his hand held out.

'It'll cost you,' he said. He was walking west now, to keep up with the wagon which could not stop to accommodate a conversation, however brief. Patting his bulging pocket, he went on, 'I've got a whole heap of letters at a dollar a time.'

Henry knew how weak Patrick was. 'I'll get the money,' he offered and climbed back into the wagon.

Jed looked at Patrick suspiciously. 'You sick?' he asked.

'A touch of dysentery,' said Patrick. 'I'll be fine.'

Jed snorted derisively. 'That's what they all say,' he said. 'Next minute they're dead. I've seen it all – reckon you could say I've seen the elephant.'

Patrick looked puzzled. 'The elephant?' he repeated.

Jed looked at him in surprise. 'You ain't heard of the elephant? You some kind of a foreigner? You talk funny.'

'English,' said Henry.

'English, eh? I might've guessed as much. Well now, it's kind of a hard thing to explain, but if you set off to California, full of hope and then you get scalped by an Indian or bit by a rattlesnake, then you seen the elephant! See, there was this old farmer taking his stuff to market and he heard there was a circus in town with an elephant in it and he ain't never seen a elephant, so he drove on down to the circus and there's the elephant – so big it scared the farmer's horse and tipped up his cart and smashed all his eggs. "I don't give a damn!" says the farmer! "I seed the elephant." You get to see something, but it costs you. Or you get scared witless, and all for something that's not what you expected. Disappointing. See? You've seen the elephant. Oh, plenty of folks see it, you got my word on that. Once you've seen the elephant nothing looks quite the same. Me, I seen it. Got sick and got better, then got to playing poker with a couple of fellows. Cleaned me right out. Oh yes, I've seen it and you will too; you all will. Me, I've seen the error of it all.' He tapped his forehead. 'I come to my senses at last and I'm going home.'

He was obviously determined to make it appear that returning to Independence was the only sensible thing to do.

'What's it like up ahead?' Patrick asked him.

The young man shrugged. 'Tough,' he said unhelpfully. 'And that there gold – it'll be gone long before you get there. I'm not so dumb. I can see the writing on the wall. There's plenty of others that see it, too, but haven't got the guts to turn back.'

Henry climbed down with the money and Patrick took out the letter and gave it to Jed, who stuffed it into his top pocket without giving it a second glance.

'Here,' said Henry. He held out a handful of dried apples and a hunk of yesterday's bread. 'It's not much, but you're welcome.'

Jed's eyes gleamed. 'Thanks,' he said, stuffing the food into his pockets. 'I'll save it until later.'

Henry echoed Patrick's question. 'What's it like up ahead?'

'Getting tougher,' Jed said with relish.

'We've not sighted Indians so far,' said Henry. 'Any trouble spots?'

'Not what you'd call trouble. They're supposed to be signing some treaty or other, the Pawnees and Sioux. Kind of a breathing space. Leastways, they've stopped killing each other for the time being.'

'They're not attacking the wagon trains, then?'

'They rustle the stock when they can, but that's about it. You'll need a good guard on your beasts at night – I've just been telling your captain.'

'He's a good man,' said Henry.

Jed laughed shortly. 'They're all good men till something

goes wrong, then it's heave-ho. Oh yes, I passed a company back there that's all shot to hell; changed leaders twice and still squabbling. Everyone thinks he knows better'n the next man!' He spat derisively. 'I've had enough, I can tell you. You want California, you got it! You can have my share of the gold.'

Patrick raised a haggard face. 'Just post the letter to my wife,' he gasped, then doubled up in agony and made another rush into the long grass.

Jed's eyes narrowed. 'You want to watch him,' he said. 'I've seen 'em drop like flies. Cholera's a mean death. You can linger, but if you're lucky you go like that!' He snapped his fingers. 'Well, I'll be getting along.'

'Post his letter,' said Henry.

'I'll post it,' Jed promised.

With a brief wave, he turned again towards the east and a moment later Henry saw him talking to the Patten family whose wagon was a few hundred yards to the rear.

When at last Patrick came back, he could hardly stagger along and Henry's irritation gave way to fear. He *was* ill. Brushing aside Patrick's protests, he hauled him into the wagon and covered him with a couple of blankets. He then shouted ahead to the next wagon to pass on the message that wagon number eight had need of a doctor. It was passed on until Doc Baines rode up less than five minutes later and dismounted with a cheerful comment about the weather. He was a tubby good-humoured man not given to panic and he believed strongly in the recuperative powers of mind over matter.

'A bit of gut trouble?' he asked cheerfully as he surrendered the reins of his piebald pony into Henry's keeping. 'I'll take a look.'

Henry walked on as the wagon shuddered and shook with every irregularity of the track which had earlier been churned up and had now hardened into a tangle of ridges baked by the sun. One of the occupants of wagon nine, seeing the doctor, called to ask anxiously about the state of Patrick's health. Almost immediately, the man from wagon seven –

Abe Hanniker from Wisconsin – came up with a similar inquiry.

'A touch of dysentery,' Henry told him with as much conviction as he could muster.

'There's a lot of it about,' remarked Abe, not entirely convinced.

'The doc's a good man,' said Henry. 'He'll soon get him right.'

'Let's know how he gets on.'

'I will,' Henry promised.

He liked Abe and had learned that in most eventualities he could rely on his help. When one of the rear wheel-rims had worked loose, Abe lent a hand. When one of Abe's oxen had run away in the night, Henry and Patrick had helped him to find it. They were good neighbours united by a common goal but Henry suspected that if Patrick had cholera, it would be a different story and understandably so. Abe was travelling with his father, two brothers and a son of sixteen. Cholera was a killer and no man would willingly put his family at risk. No doubt the gap between the wagons would lengthen and contact between them would be reduced to a minimum.

'Please God, don't let it all end here,' Henry prayed silently as he trudged on beside the oxen. If Patrick had cholera, it would almost certainly attack him also for he and Patrick had been eating and sleeping together for the past weeks. There was a strong bond between them and if Patrick had cholera, Henry would nurse him despite the tremendous risk, but he knew he would almost certainly catch the disease himself.

Another horseman approached and Henry saw that it was Becher, a look of concern on his face.

'I hear you've got sickness here,' he said, reining in his horse sharply. He did not dismount, Henry noticed.

'Yes, sir,' said Henry. 'It's Patrick Golightly. Doc Baines is with him.'

'Does it look like cholera?'

'Dysentery, I think. I *hope*.'

'It's rife up ahead,' commented Becher. 'I think the bloody

backtrackers carry it. Generally speaking, it doesn't help to have too much to-ing and fro-ing. Tell the doctor to keep me informed. The sick man, Golightly, English, isn't he? They don't have the stamina.'

Henry bridled. 'He's as tough as I am,' he said. 'This whole trip was his idea.'

'Let's hope he doesn't leave you to it!'

'Oh God! I hope not.'

Becher, seeing the horror on Henry's face, softened a little. 'Forget it, I spoke out of turn,' he apologized, 'but that's the way it goes. We'll be crossing the river again in a few days if we keep up this progress. You won't manage it without your partner, but if he's still sick I'll send someone to give you a hand.'

'I'm much obliged.'

Becher raised his hand in salute, spurred his horse and rode away. A few moments later the doctor climbed down, his face grim.

'Cholera,' he said simply. 'I'll do all I can but if you're a praying man, you'd best start now.'

Patrick's condition deteriorated rapidly during the evening in spite of the doctor's application of a mustard plaster to his stomach and abdomen. By nightfall he began to vomit, retching with such violence that on one occasion he struck his head against the wooden side of the wagon and cut his forehead. Henry nursed him as well as he could, coaxing warm water between his lips, while his own stomach heaved at the stench. The accompanying fever gave way to intermittent chills and from time to time Patrick's lips moved soundlessly. Henry was not a religious man and he could not recall the words of any formal prayers, but he appealed directly to God with a simple fervour.

'Look down and be merciful,' he whispered. 'Patrick's a good man who has done no wrong. Give him strength to come through his ordeal. He has a wife and if You let him die he will be sadly missed.'

The terrible night hours passed and Patrick's temperature began to rise until his skin burned and his lips dried and split. His body was racked by violent spasms, his mind wandered and he talked urgently in a breathless manner. Most of it was incomprehensible to Henry, but shortly before midnight he became suddenly and astonishingly lucid. He opened his eyes and stared into Henry's face. His dark hair, wet with sweat, clung to his face and his shaking hands reached out to grasp Henry's. His voice was low but clear, and there was a sudden calmness about him that frightened Henry more than all his earlier ravings.

'Henry! My dearest friend. Forgive me,' he said.

Henry patted his hands. 'There's nothing to forgive,' he answered as steadily as he could. 'You're sick, but we'll pull you through.'

'I brought you into all this and now I'm going to desert you.'

'No! Don't talk like that,' Henry protested. 'We'll both reach California, you'll see.' He leaned over his friend and tried to smile. 'You don't think I'd let you die, do you? We're in this together, Patrick Golightly, and you're going to the gold fields with me. Like it or not. You hear me?'

Patrick's lips twitched in the ghost of a smile. 'I can't make it, Henry. I'm sorry.'

'You'll make it.'

'Write to Lily. She may not get my letter. Tell her. Say that I loved her. Say I died peacefully. I don't want her to know – '

He broke off suddenly and doubled up, clutching his stomach. A deep groan of pain was wrenched from his unwilling lips while Henry watched helplessly.

He reached for the water-bottle, waited until the spasm was over and then held it to Patrick's lips.

'Just a mouthful,' he urged. 'You must drink.'

Feebly Patrick moved his head, trying to avoid it. 'No use . . .' he said. 'You must tell Lily "Goodbye" for me . . .'

'Take a mouthful, *please*, Patrick,' cried Henry. 'The doctor said you were to take liquids. Sit up a bit. Let me help you.'

He slid an arm round Patrick's shoulders and tugged him into a semi-sitting position. 'Now just for me, Patrick, a mouthful of water? The doctor will be by later and he'll want to know that you've taken plenty of liquid.'

Patrick allowed the water to trickle into his mouth, but the acid vomit had seared his throat and he gasped painfully as the water went down. He waved a hand feebly to indicate the foul blankets. 'All this,' he whispered. 'It's so horrible. I'm so sorry, Henry. I couldn't . . .'

He sank back exhausted and Henry wiped his mouth gently.

'It doesn't matter,' he told him. 'You'd do it for me, Patrick, if I was ill. That's what friends are for. I'll give you a clean blanket as soon as the other one dries. I gave it a bit of a wash. Is that mustard plaster easing things at all?'

Patrick made no answer except to sigh deeply.

'Patrick?'

Patrick turned glittering eyes upon his friend and the cracked lips parted in a twisted smile; then his eyes closed wearily and his head fell to one side to rest heavily on Henry's shoulder.

'Patrick!' cried Henry. 'Jesus, Patrick, don't die!'

He took hold of Patrick's wrist and was surprised to find a pulse. Should he go in search of the doctor or stay with his friend? If he was dying, he shouldn't be alone, but perhaps the doctor could save him. As he agonized over the decision, it was answered for him. Footsteps sounded outside the wagon and Henry glimpsed the faint glow of a lantern. Seconds later the doctor was pulling himself aboard.

'I think he's dying,' blurted Henry. 'Please *do* something. You must save him. There must be something else you can do.'

The doctor's expression was not inspiring. 'Hold this,' he said tersely, handing Henry the lantern while he examined the patient.

'Hmn,' he said, his tone non-committal. 'I've brought this laudanum and camphor – a strong dose. It's kill or cure, I'm afraid. I suppose one day we shall understand this wretched disease, but at the moment it's anybody's guess.'

He opened his bag which contained the usual medicaments – spirits of camphor, tincture of capsicum, Dower's powders,

Wright's pills, calomel and essence of peppermint and a large bottle which he now withdrew. He poured some of the liquid into a spoon and managed to coax most of it into Patrick's mouth. 'It's simply swings and roundabouts,' he went on as he filled the spoon for the second time. 'What cures one patient fails with another. All you can do is try them all. If this keeps him alive until morning, I'll remove the plaster and try a friction rub, but at present I think he's took weak to stand it.'

He gave Patrick the second dose and then sat back. 'Is he still vomiting?'

'Yes, though he doesn't bring much up and the diarrhoea persists.'

The doctor rubbed his eyes tiredly and for a moment he too seemed to sway.

'Are you all right?' cried Henry, alarmed.

The doctor shook his head. 'I'm as right as I'll ever be,' he said. 'If I ever get to California it'll be a bloody miracle and I'll be too worn out to dig for gold.'

He put the cork back in the bottle and returned it to his pocket together with the spoon.

They both looked at Patrick, who gave a great shudder and then seemed to relax. Some of the tension faded from his face.

'It'll maybe give him a few hours' relief,' said the doctor.

Henry followed him out of the wagon and into the welcome fresh air. 'How is it that doctors don't catch the disease?' he asked.

'Oh, they do,' was the answer. 'I heard this morning that one of the doctors with the Wisconsin Rangers died two days ago.'

They both breathed deeply, filling their lungs with the cool night air.

Henry said, 'I can't even keep him *clean*. I feel so helpless. I've washed the other blanket, but it's still damp.'

'You're a good friend,' the doctor told him. 'You'd be surprised how quickly cholera can ruin a lifelong friendship. I heard last week from one of the backtrackers that up ahead, the other side of Fort Kearny, a young man was left to die by the roadside. Turned out of his wagon by his uncle without so much as a blanket. No food and no water. Terrible what fear can do.'

Henry shook his head and the doctor sighed. 'Well, I'll get back while there's still time to snatch a few hours' sleep,' he said. 'I'll be along again first thing in the morning.'

'Thanks,' said Henry, 'for all your help.'

'Wish I could do more.'

When he had gone, Henry stood in the darkness listening. The familiar sounds of the night camp came clearly to his ears – the creak of a wagon as the occupant turned in his makeshift bed; the rustle of the animals, the growl of a dog; the dying crackle of a late fire; a sudden burst of coughing. Beyond it all there was the heavy breath of a mounting wind and the ripple and gurgle of the water in the nearby river. Suddenly over it all he heard the old man's voice in far-off Buffalo. 'There's the smell of death on you. One or t'other. I smell it clearly. Go back to New York while there's still time.' Henry sighed. Maybe it was already too late.

He woke in the early hours of the morning and for a moment lay with his eyes closed, listening to the sound of rain on the canvas cover of the wagon as the dread memories flooded back into his mind. Patrick, his only real friend, was ill, maybe dying. He opened his eyes without turning his head to the far end of the wagon. He listened – and his heart skipped a beat as he realized that the heavy stertorous breathing was no longer audible. Hope fought with fear. Was Patrick now breathing naturally or had he stopped breathing?

'Jesus!' he whispered, not even daring to pray. Still he did not look at his friend, but the silence was ominous. As long as he didn't *see* Patrick was dead, there was still hope. Once he saw . . .

'Jesus!' he repeated helplessly. With a heavy heart he pulled himself up into a sitting position and slowly turned his head. All he saw was Patrick's shape huddled beneath the blanket.

Scrambling across the intervening space Henry knelt beside him, eyeing the blankets warily. They did not rise and fall. Tears filled his eyes.

'Please, no!' he begged.

Gently turning back the blanket, he stared into the face of his dead friend, his own rigid with shock. He had never encountered death before. Patrick's mouth was open and his eyes were screwed up. He looked as though he had died screaming, but Henry knew that was not possible; the sound would have woken him.

'Patrick! Oh, Jesus!'

Words failed him as he tried unsuccessfully to close his friend's gaping mouth and straighten the anguished contours of his face.

He wanted to tell him how sorry he was; how lonely he would be without him; how much he *loved* him. Anything. But no words came. The body was cold and stiff and Henry did not need the doctor to tell him that Patrick's life was at an end. He wanted to make a gesture of farewell, but nothing seemed appropriate. Blindly, he put out a shaking hand and ruffled Patrick's hair.

'I guess it's over, Patrick,' he said dazedly and raised a clenched fist heavenward in a mute gesture of rage and defeat. Then without a word, he took up a shovel and stumbled out of the wagon. Before anyone else was stirring, he had dug Patrick's grave. He wrapped him in the clean but still damp blanket and with shaking fingers, tied it up to form a secure shroud. The doctor arrived in time to help him lift the body into its final resting place. Henry had dug it deep and neither man spoke until the job was finished.

'I'm sorry,' said the doctor. 'I'll let Becher know.'

'You did your best,' said Henry. 'Thanks.'

When he was alone again he trod the grave, compacting the earth, then covered it with as many small rocks as he could find before searching for a small boulder to use as a marker for the grave. On it he scratched the following inscription:

Patrick Golightly. Aged 25.
From England. Beloved friend. Died May 21 1849.

Chapter Six

On the last day of May a weak sun shone down on Wallis's company as they took their midday meal – a few sitting inside their wagons, more squatting in groups alongside the stationary vehicles, enjoying the chance to exchange news and views with other members of the company. They had already endured eleven miles of heat, flies and dust and they faced the joyless prospect of another eight or nine miles before dusk. They had long since ceased to admire the views of rolling prairie and were aware only of the relentless discomforts of life on the trail. Ahead of them the line of earlier wagon trains stretched interminably, with the broad Kansas river to the north and boundless grassland to the south. Dust rose from the trail both ahead and behind the Western Hopers, dust stirred up by rolling wheels, plodding hooves and weary boots; brown dust that was part soil, part dung; pungent dust which clung to their skin, hair and clothes and filtered into their lungs. Ella Cash, troubled with a persistent cough, habitually wore a handkerchief tied over her mouth and nose, but now she had taken it off to eat. She dipped her bread into a cup of coffee. Her face was set in a disgruntled scowl as she leaned back against the wheel of the wagon, her legs spread out indecorously, her skirts pulled up to reveal puffy ankles.

'Look at them,' she grumbled. 'I should be riding *in* the wagon.'

Hester said, 'Do you good to walk a bit. Your limbs'll stiffen up, else.'

Ella tossed her head. 'I'd rather have stiff limbs than swollen feet.'

'It's not your feet, it's your ankles,' stated Jess.

'Same difference.'

'It's not!' said Jess.

Ella sucked noisily at the sodden bread and added, 'I wish I was back home, you know that.'

'So you keep saying.' Her father sat beside her on an upturned crate, both hands round his tin mug. 'You've done nothing but bellyache ever since we left Independence. I'm getting mighty sick of it.'

Jess now felt obliged to defend his wife against her father. 'Leave her be,' he said. 'She's bound to feel humpty the way she is.' He leaned across and patted her arm awkwardly. 'You take it easy for a while.'

'Take it easy?' cried Ella. 'What about poor Will? He's got no one to play with.' No one pointed out that Will was not capable of playing with anyone and Ella went on, 'I thought we might have caught up with the Pattens by now. Him and Stevie would be company for each other.'

'Catch up with the Pattens?' exclaimed Hester. 'You're hopeful, aren't you? They'll be miles ahead. Catch up with the Pattens!'

Jess gave his mother-in-law a withering look.

'Oh, that's terrific,' he said, his voice heavy with sarcasm. 'That's really terrific! Make her more miserable than she is already.' He rolled his eyes.

'I'm only putting her straight,' cried Hester. 'What's the point of hoping? We don't stand a chance in hell of catching up with the Pattens. They moved out on the twenty-eighth of April and we didn't move until the twenty-first of May. We'd have to run all the way to catch them up. You'd have to be really stupid to –' She broke off suddenly, seeing the tell-tale quiver of her daughter's lips. 'Oh, for Christ's sake, Ella, don't start bawling again. It gets to me, that does.'

Ella forced out a couple of tears, sniffed loudly and looked appealingly at her husband, but for once he pretended not to notice.

Charlie sighed heavily. 'Let's look on the bright side,' he

said. 'We're ten days out from Independence and, touch wood, no one's gone down with cholera. That's more than can be said for most of the companies, so let's be thankful for small mercies.'

'Your pa's right,' said Hester, already regretting her harsh words. She looked at her daughter thoughtfully. 'That English girl, a few wagons ahead of us — I reckon she's in the family way. She's got that look about her.'

'Which one?' asked Ella.

'The ginger one, not the married one.'

'She smiled at me yesterday,' said Ella. 'They're friendly with the folks in number twelve.'

'She can still be friendly with you, can't she? We shall need all the friends we can get before this journey's over.'

'But she's got no husband,' said Jess. 'The Smith brothers were saying — used to be a lady's maid, but she ran away.'

'Go on!' said Ella, intrigued.

Hester shrugged. 'Well, husband or no husband, I'll wager she's the same way as our Ella.' She smiled at her daughter. 'Walk along and say how-do. Get to know someone your own age — get out and mix instead of moping about in the wagon feeling sorry for yourself. They seem nice enough.'

'The dark one's a parson's daughter,' Charlie volunteered. 'Her husband's with the same company as the Pattens — she'll never catch him up.'

Surprised, Hester turned to him. 'How come you know so much, Charlie?'

'Keep my ears open, that's how,' he said airily. 'I may not say much, but I don't miss much either.'

'Funny,' said Ella. 'Her with one company and her husband with another.' She brightened up a little. 'Maybe I will walk along and have a word,' she decided, her fingers automatically tidying stray wisps of hair. She rubbed her eyes and sniffed again. 'I'll take Will,' she said. 'It'll make a change for him.'

Having made up her mind, she was suddenly eager to go and she drank the last of her coffee and climbed back into the wagon to rub a damp cloth around her face and put on a clean lace collar.

117

Jess, Sarah and Charlie watched her as she set off along the line of wagons with young Will (also tidied) settled as always on her left hip.

'She'll make out,' said Charlie.

'Let's hope so,' said Hester.

*

Kate was returning from answering the call of nature when she saw a woman with a child go up to Lily. She hastened her steps and the two women turned towards her.

'Kate, this is Ella Cash,' said Lily. 'Her family are a few wagons back.'

'Number seven,' said Ella.

Kate smiled and shook hands self-consciously. 'I've noticed you from time to time,' she told Ella, 'and kept meaning to say "hullo". I'm Kate Lester.' She smiled at the boy on Ella's hip and made clucking noises of encouragement, but the boy stared at her blankly.

'His name's William,' said Ella, 'but of course we call him Will. He's a funny kid, a bit . . . shy. Doesn't say much,' she said carefully. 'Best to take no notice of him really. There's another on the way, September time; I'm not real sure. I hope it's a girl.'

She waited for Kate to confide that she, too, was pregnant but an awkward silence followed her remarks.

'How old is Will?' Lily asked quickly, for something to say.

'Two and a bit,' Ella lied. 'He's a lazy lump, but Ma says he'll move when he's good and ready.'

She saw that the English woman regarded the boy doubtfully, but at that moment the cry of 'Backtracker!' came from further along the train.

'Not another one!' said Kate. 'That's the third this week. How can they do it when there's all that gold at the end of the trail? Wild horses wouldn't drag me back, not in a million years!' She turned to Lily. 'But he might take a letter home to your pa.'

'I gave it to the fellow who passed yesterday,' said Lily,

118

'but I'll have a word with him anyway. He might have news of Patrick.'

When she had gone, Kate and Ella looked at each other curiously.

'Your friend's married, then?' asked Ella.

Kate nodded. 'Yes. She was on her way out here to join her husband when he takes off for California! Sends her a letter to wait for him in New York, but she's not having it, so she says she'll follow him. She's got spirit, has Lily. She may look meek and mild but when she's made up her mind, nothing will shift her.'

'You're not sisters, then?' said Ella. 'I thought maybe . . .'

'Oh no, we're not related. Friends, that's all. I wanted to look for gold and she wanted to look for her husband, so we teamed up. That's all.'

Ella asked casually. 'So you're not married, then?'

'No such luck. Wish I was.'

Ella avoided her eye and said, 'My ma thought maybe you were.'

'Oh?' Kate gave her a sharp look. 'Why did she think that?'

The directness of the question confused Ella. 'She thought you . . . that is, she wondered . . .'

Kate's mouth tightened as Ella floundered on. 'She thought what?'

'Nothing,' Ella shrugged.

'She thought I ought to be married, is that it?'

'No. At least . . .'

Kate swallowed hard and fought down a longing to confide in her new acquaintance. Ella was also expecting a child and had given birth to another. She might be a useful ally. Lily was good-hearted and she had spirit, but what did she know about babies?

The awkward silence lengthened and finally Ella said, 'I'm sorry.'

Kate stared at her boots and took a deep breath. 'Well, your ma's right,' she said suddenly. 'I've a baby coming, but no husband.' She looked up. 'But if you tell a *soul*, I'll – ' Her anger evaporated and she sighed again. 'Well, I don't

119

want anyone to know just yet. I don't want everyone to talk about me the way people do.'

'I won't tell,' Ella assured her eagerly. 'I *swear* I won't.' She held up her right hand as though taking an oath.

'Not even your ma?'

'She knows already. She knew by looking at your face – she's funny like that – but the men wouldn't know.'

A shout from further along the trail warned them that the noontide break was over and the wagon train was preparing to move on. Lily hurried back to take her place on the right side of the leading oxen and Ella and Kate waited together on the left side. As soon as the wagon in front of them rolled forward, Lily cracked the whip and the animals leaned into their yokes, dug in their hooves and took up the strain once more.

Creaking in protest, the wheels turned and the wagon lurched forward. With another whip-crack, the wagon behind them also began to move.

Kate called across to Lily. 'Any news from the backtracker about Patrick?'

'I'm afraid not,' said Lily. 'He was a nice lad, name of Jed. He's collecting letters to post at Independence – he couldn't recall anyone by the name of Golightly, but he sees so many faces. Still, he *does* remember passing the Brown Bear Mining Company. He says they're about ten days ahead of us.'

'We've gained on them, then.'

'Yes. They had a couple of wagons break down and had to stop over while they were repaired. Had a lot of sickness, too.'

Ella said kindly. 'Soon be with your husband again, then.'

'I hope so,' answered Lily.

She walked with one hand resting lightly on the ox's broad warm back, enjoying the contact with the sturdy animal. She had lost her initial nervousness and was growing quite fond of them. It had become apparent, soon after leaving Independence, that they had made the right choice. Mules were bigger, but they were much less tractable and tended to shy at every passing bird; they also lashed out with their hind legs at the slightest provocation and had been known to bite people! The oxen, on the other hand, were always willing, almost trusting. Lily felt that they wanted to do their job well and would lumber willingly on until they dropped exhausted in their tracks. She took great pleasure in their performance and saw to their well-being; she talked to them and made encouraging noises and never used the whip except as a sign to start them off again after a stopover.

Ella watched Lily for a few moments, then said quietly to Kate, 'Guess she misses her husband. I'm lucky.'

'You are,' said Kate. 'Look, can I carry Will for a while? D'you think he'd come to me?'

'He might.' She hoisted Will up and said, 'Want to go to the nice lady, Will?'

He stared at Kate, his large blue eyes blank.

'He's a bit heavy,' warned Ella as Kate settled him on her hip.

They walked on in a companionable silence for a while until Ella began to cough.

'Dratted dust!' she exclaimed. 'I have to wear a scarf over my face. My lungs are real touchy.'

'Wear it, then,' said Kate. 'I don't mind.'

But Ella wanted to talk. 'D'you want to tell me?' she asked hopefully. 'About the baby's father?'

'No' was on the tip of Kate's tongue, but she surprised herself by saying 'Yes' instead and then it was too late. She launched into her story, modifying as she went along where necessary.

'See, I was a lady's maid in this big house,' she began. 'The Harringtons – that was their name. Ernest was the bobby on the beat. He took over from Constable Reed when he was promoted to Sergeant. Ernest is the baby's father: Police Constable Bailey, to be exact.' She tossed her head. 'He appeared one day at the top of the area steps just as I was going out to water the pansies in the window-box outside the kitchen – if you could call it a kitchen! It was more like a blooming dungeon, horribly dark and smelling of damp even in summer with the sun shining and all the windows wide open. And even in winter with a fire going and all the windows shut!'

'What are area steps?' asked Ella.

Kate paused. 'Well, they're steps going down to the basement. And the basement,' she went on, seeing Ella's bewilderment 'is part of the house that's below ground level. See, in London there's so many houses and not much room, so they build downwards and upwards. Anyway, there was Ernest.' She sighed at the memory. 'I just gaped. He was so handsome, but one of the smallest bobbies I'd ever seen. Just scraped in, he had, because he had an uncle at Scotland Yard who pulled strings. They have to be tall. He was always hungry, Ernest was, and I used to steal biscuits for him – almond crisps were his favourite, and almond cake, anything with almonds. I took a shine to him, I really did. One day I pretended I'd heard a prowler round the house at night and he promised to come back after he came off duty to investigate.' Ella nodded and Kate giggled. 'He was meant to investigate the prowler, but he ended up "investigating" me!'

Ella laughed.

'I crept downstairs after everyone had gone to bed and met him at the bottom of the area steps. He kissed me and . . . you know!'

Ella nodded. She did.

'After that, he came to the house quite often in the day and often late at night too. Then he started to get a bit too passionate and wouldn't take "no" for an answer. He was strong for his size and I couldn't stop him. One day Cook nearly caught us. Later, when it was all too late, I wished she had – but she didn't, and then it was too late. I was sure he'd do the decent thing by me, but he turned nasty. He even made out that the baby's father might be someone else – the butcher's boy or the postman – but I knew better.'

'A London *bobby*,' sighed Ella. 'How romantic!'

'Romantic, my foot!' rejoined Kate. 'I wish it had been the postman; *he* might have married me!'

'Do you hate him?' asked Ella. 'For what he did?'

'Not exactly.' She shrugged. 'I'd have liked to be married to a policeman, but it wasn't to be. Just my bad luck.'

'I've seen you with Mr Carp,' said Ella, giving Kate a sly look. 'He's a fine-looking man. He's handsome.'

'Oh, he is, isn't he?' Kate responded eagerly. 'He's as keen as mustard . . . but he doesn't know about the baby.'

'Will you tell him?'

''Course I will,' said Kate, 'I just keep putting it off. What's it like being married? I asked Lily, but she was only wed for a week and then her Patrick was off to America. Seemed like she didn't want to talk about it.'

Will began to whimper suddenly and Ella took him back.

'It's no great shakes being wed,' she said, 'but at least your ma and pa can't bawl you out so much – it's not as though you're still a kid. And Jess . . .' She hesitated, trying to find a suitable word to express her disillusionment. 'He doesn't bother me too much. He used to be fun but now he's not, though he likes kids.'

'Just as well,' laughed Kate.

Ella grinned and looked almost pretty. 'It was a shotgun wedding,' she confessed, 'but don't let on to anyone that I told you. Pa nearly went mad, but I didn't care. My friend, Mary Patten – we went to school together – she was married and having a baby and I wanted one. She's going to California with her folks with the Brown Bear Mining Company. If Jess hadn't been so against it at first, we could have gone with them and we'd be that much nearer the gold, but he was set against it and said *we* weren't going. Mind you, the Pattens said *they* weren't going and then one day they did.'

Kate winked at Will, but received no response. 'D'you think there's really gold?' she asked. 'Sounds too good to be true, but Amos swears to it. He reckons you can scrape great lumps of gold off the rocks with a knife. Sounds a bit unlikely to me, but that's what he says.'

Ella shrugged. 'Pa says you have a sort of pan and you put the gravel in it with some water and swirl it round. All the gravel and mud floats away and all the bits of gold get left in the pan.'

'Well, Gabby Smith – he's one of the two brothers with curly hair – '

'I've seen him around,' Ella put in.

'*He* says it's all lying in the bottom of the river, so you stand in the water with special boots on and scoop it up and you can tell it's gold by biting it and it's sort of soft – and if you hit it with a hammer, it doesn't break but goes flat. If it does break, it's just pyrites and that's no good – it looks like gold, but it isn't.'

'Jess says that some folk pick whole *lumps* of it out of the river or ravines. Real big lumps called nuggets. Captain Hollis was telling someone and Jess just *happened* to overhear!' Ella grinned. 'He was eavesdropping; Jess's good at that. He'd go into the saloon in Independence and *just happen* to hear all sorts of things.' She shook her head. 'Independence,' she mused. 'It seems so far away.' Petulantly, she scuffed up the dry earth and then stepped through the dust she had raised. 'So far away,' she repeated. 'We'll most likely never go back.'

'Who cares?' said Kate. 'The world's a big place.'

*

The wagons of the Brown Bear Mining Company reached Fort Kearny on the second of June with shouts and whistles of delight from its members. They now knew exactly where they were; they could point to a precise spot on the map; they could prove progress. The company had put an incredible three hundred miles or more between themselves and the frontier town of Independence. Of course, they could also calculate how many miles they still had to travel, but no one was in the mood to worry about that.

It was very obvious that other companies had passed through the fort before them, for a large area of the surrounding land was littered with their debris – not only their daily rubbish, but the numerous objects they had been forced to jettison in preparation for the next stage of the journey. The astonished Brown Bears saw abandoned furniture of all kinds; tools both large and small; bedding of every description; clothing in a variety of shapes and sizes, but mostly women's; rotting food; books, toys and ornaments!

The small fort had become a stopover for the companies while they took stock briefly and reassessed their priorities. By the time they reached the fort, the emigrants had learned that unnecessary weight made the wagons less manoeuvrable and thus slowed them down. Ahead of them beyond the plains lay mountains and desert. Nothing that was not vital should be carried further.

The inhabitants of Fort Kearny were still marvelling at the thousands of people who had already passed through, their faces set towards the gold fields, their hopes high, their courage and energy for the most part unabated. They had reached their first major landmark and if anything, their joint resolve was strengthened.

Alone of all the Brown Bears, Henry Simms debated whether or not to give up. He had said nothing to anyone else about his indecision, but the tragedy of Patrick's death had depressed his enthusiasm for the enterprise. Without Patrick the excitement of the venture had evaporated and he no longer cared about possible riches. He was shocked and lonely and he blamed himself for Patrick's death, convinced that he could and should have done more to save him. The doctor, the one person who could have reassured him, was now dead, also struck down by cholera, and Henry had helped to bury him too. The two deaths weighed heavily on his spirits and he could not shake off his melancholy. To Henry, Fort Kearny seemed as good a place as any to turn back. Once back in New York, he believed he might somehow free himself of the terrible memories. He had slept badly since Patrick's death and the vision of his friend's humble grave haunted him.

Fort Kearny had been established as a military outpost less than a year earlier, and the haste with which it was being erected was reflected in its untidy appearance. Several of the buildings were constructed with sods of turf and roofed with turf and brushwood; there was a scattering of makeshift wooden sheds and rows of tents which accommodated the lower ranks of the military. The government hoped that a military settlement in the area would help discourage the local Indians from harassing the emigrants who passed through the area, whether headed for Oregon or California. As yet, though, they had only a few cannon and little else in the way of fortifications. The rush westward in totally unprecedented numbers found the inhabitants of the newly established fort still reeling from the impact. Their resources were severely overtaxed by the never-ending line of wagon trains, but they continued to offer what help they could in the way of provisions, medical assistance and the use of their smithy.

As well as the daily disruption the emigrants caused to military routine, their passage through the fort created another problem for the fort's officers, for the young soldiers became excited by so much talk of gold and began to compare their own prospects with those of the gold seekers. There had been a number of desertions, but although some had been caught and brought back to camp a few had successfully 'lost' themselves and were now presumed to be on their way west.

On the evening of their arrival at Fort Kearny, Captain Becher and some of his committee dined with the camp's commander while the rest of the Brown Bears relaxed around their camp-fires or sought information from the soldiers about the various other companies which had preceded them through the fort. The one fear uppermost in everyone's mind was that the Californian gold would be gone before they arrived to claim their share of it.

Henry sat alone in his wagon nursing an aching head and trying for the third time to write to Lily. The first anguished letter, written on the day of Patrick's death, had later been rejected as too harrowing and torn up. The second, attempted a few days later and written in a more formal style, had seemed stilted and uncaring and had been thrown into the fire. Now two weeks had passed since Patrick had died and the initial horror had been dulled by time to an ache of self-reproach. But none of that, Henry told himself, must show in his letter. Patrick's wife would be stricken by the news of her husband's death and the wording of the letter must in no way add to her grief. After long deliberation, he began a third attempt:

Dear Mrs Golightly,
It is with a heavy heart that I take up my pen. I have to break to you the news of your husband's illness and death. Believe me when I tell you that I share your grief and would give my right arm if I could write otherwise, but hiding the truth from you will not be a kindness. I will come to the point to spare you the dread anticipation you must feel. Patrick was taken by cholera after a brief illness, but I want to reassure you that he was attended by a first-class physician who saw to it that he suffered very little pain . . .

As he wrote those last words, the picture of Patrick's agony rose up to reproach him for the lie, but he ignored it, determined to spare Lily's feelings as much as he could.

. . . He was rational up to the last and spoke of you constantly, asking me to tell you that he loved you. At the end he fell into a deep sleep and did not wake again.

He sighed and continued:

Patrick's grave, you will want to know, was deep and proper. I dug it myself as the last duty I could do for a good and well-loved friend. It is marked by a boulder and a suitable inscription.

When Patrick first mooted the idea of going west, I tried to dissuade him. Perhaps if I had not agreed to accompany him – but then he would have travelled alone, for he was determined to go, and no one would have been with him at the close of his life, so perhaps it was for the best that I agreed.
If it is any comfort to you, I will tell you that Patrick enjoyed the venture with all his heart and was happy in

127

spite of the hardships. Only when he was dying did he regret coming — and then only for your sake . . .

I am writing this from Fort Kearny, where the company is resting for forty-eight hours, but I will now turn back. In case anything happens to me, I will entrust this letter to the military express at the fort and I understand it should reach you in a matter of weeks. If I do return to New York I will call on you and answer any of your questions to the best of my ability.

My deepest regrets and sincere condolences to you. With Patrick's death you have lost a loving husband, I a good and loyal friend. We are both the losers.

Your obedient servant,
Henry Simms

Later when Henry entered the tent that served the company's leader as an office, he found not Becher but Rodman Pritty sitting on an upturned crate. He was a short, lean man with a swarthy face and small dark eyes; his dark hair hung to his shoulders and his worn buckskin jacket had fringed sleeves. He indicated a rickety stool and Henry sat down.

'Henry Simms, sir,' Henry introduced himself.

'Bad business about your friend,' said Pritty. 'It's not a good way to die.' He spoke in a flat monotone, his face expressionless. Henry thought he looked half-Indian.

'I'm sorry about Doc Baines,' said Henry.

'We've still got two doctors,' replied Pritty. 'If we lose them, we *will* be up the creek. Still, that's my worry, not yours. Becher tells me you're turning back. Sure that's what you want?'

'Yes, sir.'

'You don't sound too certain.'

Henry shrugged. 'It all seems a bit pointless now. It was all Patrick's idea and I just got carried away. Without him it's . . .'

He shrugged again and Pritty turned to a ledger and riffled through it. He read a few lines and said, 'He left a wife, I see. Have you written to her or should I?'

'I've written to her, sir, today, and handed it in at the fort. They said it should get to New York in about three weeks.'

'Have you met her?'

'No, sir. I said I'd call in on my return, just to talk to her about him.'

Pritty referred to the ledger again. 'He was English.'

'Yes. The wife, too.'

'Half the bloody world's heading for California!' Pritty exclaimed irritably. 'I've been talking to the fort commander.' He shook his head. 'Never been anything like it before. It's history whichever way you look at it. You sure you want out? There's gold there, you know. I reckon there's more gold than anyone knows.'

'I believe you,' said Henry. 'I just don't care any more.'

Pritty shrugged. 'I can't stop you from turning back, but I think you'll regret it. Still, why should I try to stop you? The more people who turn back, the more gold for those who make it!' He looked at Henry, his face impassive. 'You're definitely going back?'

'Yes, sir.'

Without another word, Pritty reached for a notebook and pen and assumed a more businesslike manner.

'How do you want to travel?' he asked. 'Pack or wagon?'

Henry looked at him blankly. 'I don't quite – '

'You taking your wagon and team, or d'you want to trade it for a horse and pack-mule? One or the other – you can't walk all the way.'

'Oh, I see. I hadn't thought. I suppose a horse and mule.'

'It's more manageable, but you'll have to sleep rough unless you can get hold of a tent. And don't hang about at the fort for too long after we're gone. The military only tolerate us, we're not exactly a bonus.'

'I'll make a start as soon as I'm organized.'

Pritty said, 'The Pattens in number four have got a spare horse and the fort might sell you a mule. When you've got what you need, we'll give you provisions and then settle the accounting. You'll have maybe a hundred dollars or so owing to you.'

Henry nodded wearily. His head throbbed and his throat

129

was sore. Pritty was making him feel very feeble, but he felt too ill to summon up any real resentment. He was going to cut loose from the adventure; that was what he wanted. He would put the whole crazy business behind him and return to reality.

He stood up. 'Thanks for your help, sir.'

'You're welcome, Mr Simms.' He frowned as he regarded Henry. 'You feeling all right?'

'A bit rough,' Henry admitted.

'You take care of yourself.' He began to write in the ledger.

'Writing me off,' thought Henry as he left the tent. 'Henry Simms – backtracker.'

His depression deepened, but he tightened his mouth grimly. He was returning to sanity; he had had enough of this nightmare journey. With a heartfelt sigh, he straightened his back. The Pattens were in wagon number four, so he would go at once before he changed his mind. Once the trade was made, it would be settled and he would feel better.

The Pattens were seated round their fire drinking coffee. A young woman held a sleeping child in her arms. Nearby another child, a tow-haired girl of about four years, was romping with a brown dog of indeterminate breed. A middle-aged woman threw a few more sticks on to the fire while her husband leaned back against an ancient leather trunk, both hands clasped round his steaming mug.

The older woman looked up and smiled. 'Cup of coffee, mister? Sit yourself.'

'Thank you.'

Henry was vaguely aware of a slight constraint, but he sat down and accepted a cup of lukewarm black coffee.

'My name's Simms,' he began. 'I'm wondering . . .'

The woman said, 'Thought as much. Lost your partner. That was tough!'

'Yes.'

'Cholera, was it?'

'Yes, it was.'

The young woman spoke sharply; 'My husband's got a touch of dysentery; he hasn't got cholera.'

130

The old man leaned forward. 'We don't know for sure unless the doctor tells us,' he pointed out.

'I tell you it's dysentery!' Her tone was bordering on the hysterical.

Henry looked inquiringly at the older woman.

'It's my son,' she said. 'May's husband. He's got the skitters and she won't have the doc look him over.'

'She' glared at her mother-in-law. 'I've got a name, you know,' she said. Turning to Henry, she held out a hand in a slightly dramatic gesture. 'I'm May Patten. Pleased to meet you, Mr Simms.'

Henry forced a smile, although the dread word 'cholera' had sent shivers down his spine and with difficulty he resisted the urge to jump up from the group and run.

'Poor Doc Baines,' said Henry. 'He did what he could for Patrick and then he went down with it himself.'

'They know the risks,' said the man, 'and they travel free in exchange for their services. Spare your sympathies. I'm Al Patten and this here's my wife Nellie. My son fell sick this morning. Most likely nothing, but you can't help wondering. Always expect the worst, that's my motto, then you don't get disappointed.'

'You should let the doc have a look at him just in case,' Henry suggested. 'They do save a few.'

'I tell you it's *dysentery!*' cried May. 'You'll wish the other on him, you will.'

Nellie's face stiffened. 'He's my son,' she said. 'I'll have the doc in if I want.'

'He's my husband,' said May, 'and I say it's nothing to . . .' Her voice faltered. 'It *can't* be that.' She looked at Henry through the first tears. 'I've got these two kids,' she said, 'and another one the way. Oh, Jesus!'

Her mother-in-law moved closer and put an arm round her and May began to cry in earnest.

'Fetch the doc,' mouthed the older woman to her husband and he jumped up with a guilty look at his sobbing daughter-in-law and hurried away.

Henry swallowed the last of the coffee, put down the mug and stood up.

131

'I'll come by later,' he began.

'Now's as good as any time,' she said. 'Turning back?'

Henry was startled. 'Yes, I am,' he replied. 'How did you know?'

'It's natural. Folks get low after a bereavement. What can we do for you?'

The dog squealed suddenly and she shouted to the little girl, 'Stop pulling that dog's tail! I won't tell you again.'

Henry explained that he wanted to trade his wagon for a horse.

'Reckon we could do with a new wagon,' said Nellie. 'The old one's already had a new tongue and a new rear-axle. Stands to reason, the wood's old and dry and this trail gives 'em such a pounding. You can't patch them up for ever. I'll send my husband round later on to have a look at it. The horses are over there. He might part with the sorrel.'

Henry left thankfully, for his encounter with the joyless Pattens had strengthened his resolve to go back to New York.

Later that evening he bought a mule from the fort and Al Patten agreed to take the wagon in exchange for the horse. It was an unequal trade in their favour, but Henry felt too ill to haggle and he went to bed with a sense of impending disaster. All he wanted was to get away before it was too late.

Chapter Seven

Nine days later – further back along the trail – the Western Hopers had reached the Big Blue River and found it misnamed, since it was only twenty yards wide. An enterprising group of men from an earlier wagon train had constructed a rough raft on which to ferry the wagons of anyone caring to part with two dollars, and everyone decided to avail themselves of the offer. Eventually it was the turn of Kate and Lily and with Amos and Gabby's help they pushed their wagon on to the raft and climbed aboard themselves. The oxen were tied to the raft by long ropes and would swim across. With much shouting and swearing two of the ferrymen leaned on their long poles while their colleagues on either bank of the river steadied the raft by means of further ropes.

'It's a far cry from a gondola,' Lily joked, but they regarded her blankly and she muttered, 'Never mind' and wished she had kept silent.

It was a haphazard method at best. The rafts were at the mercy of the currents, but the ferrymen were already quite skilful for they had ferried thirty-four wagons across the river in the past two days with only one serious mishap in which a frightened mule had capsized them. However, only the wagon had been lost and no one had drowned; the gold seekers had already learned to count their blessings.

Fortunately, the team of Durhams behaved themselves remarkably well and the raft reached the west bank without incident. Kate and Lily breathed a sigh of relief as the ferrymen helped them to rehitch the oxen and then they waited for the rest of the wagons to make the crossing. When the company was once more complete they moved on, keeping close to the river bank until they found a site for their overnight camp.

The camp was usually arranged with the wagons serving as the perimeter of a circle. Mules, horses and oxen could then later be brought in from grazing and enclosed for the night within the circle, safe from marauders whether human or animal. Today the animals of other wagon trains had eaten most of the grass which grew within easy reach of the water's edge, so Lily had to drive the animals for nearly a mile until she reached ungrazed prairie. There she settled down on a tree-stump to watch them. She was within calling distance of other people watching over their teams, but in spite of the beauty of the surrounding landscape, the scene held no great fascination for her – it had become part of the daily routine.

Instead she thought hungrily of the meal which Kate was preparing. Kate was becoming a very proficient cook and had begged a surprising number of recipes from various members of the company – both male and female. As Lily had no desire to sit hunched over a hot fire, she was only too pleased to take responsibility for the welfare of the animals and was, in her turn, becoming a very able 'herdswoman'.

Today they would eat frijoles – a simple but tasty meal of pinto beans cooked with cubed salt pork. They would follow it with stewed wild gooseberries which they had picked along the way. The inevitable coffee would wash it all down and bring the feast to an end. Compared with the food Lily was used to in England, the fare was plain, but she came to each meal with a ravenous appetite sharpened by life on the prairie.

Lily pulled a long grass and began to chew the end of it, allowing her body and mind to unwind after the rigours of the day. As usual, she thought about Patrick and wondered how long it would be before they were reunited.

Since making friends with Ella, Kate had hinted on more

than one occasion that she might prefer to stay with the Western Hopers instead of transferring to Patrick's company, and had suggested that maybe Patrick and Henry would like to join them.

'As long as we're together,' Lily now told her absent husband, 'I don't mind where we are.'

Kate spent a lot of her time with Ella's family and Lily did not regret this at all. She appreciated the opportunity to be alone. Kate was a cheerful girl, she performed her share of the chores without complaint and Lily admired her tremendously, but when Lily was in an introspective mood she found Kate's chatter irritating. If Kate wanted to spend time with Ella's family, it suited Lily very well.

She had often tried to imagine how she and Patrick would make love in the wagon and viewed the prospect with some misgiving. Their love-making had been unsuccessful in the feather bed at the parsonage, but Lily blamed their failure on the circumstances. Because Patrick was going to New York they had been short of both time and money, and had decided not to go away for their honeymoon but to stay in the parsonage. Her father had given up his double bed to the newlyweds and had slept in Lily's room, but it had been a mistake. Lily had realized it the moment they slid between the sheets and heard the huge old bed creak. They were both aware, too, of her father sleeping in the room on their left and the housekeeper in her room on their right. Lily could hear them moving about, so obviously they could hear her and Patrick. But these were not their only problems. The room smelt overpoweringly of camphor, the window resisted Patrick's efforts to open it and in trying he had knocked over a vase of flowers. Guiltily, like two naughty children, they had mopped up the spilt water with a towel. When at last they climbed back into bed Patrick said, 'I think I shall die of camphor fumes,' and they hugged each other, laughing to hide their nervousness.

Lily knew nothing at all about love-making, having had no mother or older sister to consult, and she had looked to Patrick for a lead, only to discover that he knew little more than she did. After a few chaste kisses he had suggested that they wait until the next night. When that night also proved disappointing they delayed until the following night and then tried again on the fourth.

The failure of Patrick's body to respond to her own threw them both into a state of acute anxiety and ensured that their remaining three nights together were equally unsuccessful. Saddened, they had clung together in a welter of self-reproaches, assuring each other that in New York in the privacy of their own home, it would be different. But the home in New York had not materialized, and now they would be reunited half-way across America. There was very little privacy in a wagon where conversation was easily over-heard by passers by, so they would have to whisper and move carefully. She had occasionally heard muffled sounds of love-making as she passed Ella's wagon and had discreetly hurried on, but the men were not so considerate and she had blushed at the ribald comments offered by some of the more envious. Patrick would find that sort of thing difficult to cope with and so would she.

They were such innocents, she reflected with a sigh – so young and inexperienced in the ways of the world. Patrick's pale slim body had been a source of wonder to her, as her own had been to him. She loved him so desperately and longed to give herself to him. He, in his turn, worshipped her. To Patrick she was a 'beloved princess' and a 'beautiful goddess' – she smiled at the memory. A romantic, her father called him, a true romantic, and she could not argue with that for no description fitted him better. He read poetry to her, his face aglow, his eyes tender, his mouth shaping the words with a beguiling eagerness. He sang to her, his voice sweet and clear. He even brought her flowers, posies of violets tied with white ribbon. Her father, with all his reser-vations, had finally been charmed by him. Once he bought her a gaily coloured finch in a wicker cage and they had released it together in a nearby copse. Yes, she thought, with a rush of longing, her young husband had a romantic soul and a gentle sensitive heart, but these virtues made him vulnerable. Rejection, failure, even disappointment cut him to the heart and he suffered more than most. Lily longed to protect him from the harshness of life's realities. She had married a dreamer and it was up to her to make his dreams come true. If Patrick's dream was of Californian gold, she was willing to share it.

She looked up suddenly at the sound of hoofbeats and saw a man approaching on a roan mare. As soon as he reached her he swung himself out of the saddle and stood beside her. He looked about thirty and his face wore a lazy, good-humoured smile. He was short and plain, with small button brown eyes and a nose that looked as though it had been punched out of shape. His dark hair was tied back with a ribbon and he wore a gold ring in one ear. A whippet pranced beside the horse.

'Mrs Golightly?' he inquired, smiling cheerfully.

'Yes.' She stood up slowly.

'Daniel Miller at your service,' he told her, his tone half mocking.

His gaze was direct, even bold, thought Lily curiously. Whatever did he want with her?

'I have noticed you about,' she told him. 'At least, to be honest, it is your dog I noticed. There aren't too many whippets going to California.'

'You're English then, Mrs Golightly.' He regarded her humorously, but behind the banter she sensed something more. Admiration, perhaps, or was she flattering herself?

'Yes, I'm from Kent. That's in the south-east of England. Where are you from, Mr Miller?'

'Kentucky,' he told her, 'but I shan't be going back. I aim to set up shop in California.'

'As what?'

'Would you believe a bank manager?'

She laughed. 'Actually, no,' she said.

He picked her up on the word. 'Actually? I'll be damned!' He laughed. 'Well, *actually* I'm a no-good bum, but if I don't make bank manager I'll think of something else, don't you worry. I've always fancied myself as a storekeeper.' He considered the idea, his head on one side. 'Then again, I might open a saloon . . . or maybe a whorehouse.'

Lily's eyes widened with shock. She lowered them hastily as his laugh rang out.

'*Actually*, you're shocked,' he teased. 'My apologies, ma'am. I told you I was no good.'

Lily wondered what to say. She had no wish to encourage him in such an outrageous line of talk, but neither did she want to sound prim or prissy. This was America, she reminded herself, not England. She was in the middle of the prairie, not the middle of the parsonage drawing room. She decided to steer the conversation in a safer direction.

'I expect your dog's enjoying himself,' she said. 'Plenty of open spaces and lots of gophers to chase.'

'Not forgetting the bitches!' he said. 'Yes, I guess he's enjoying himself!'

Flustered, Lily remained silent. She was sure she was blushing and was annoyed with herself. No doubt Kate would have put him firmly in his place by now, but Lily was unused to dealing with men like Daniel Miller.

'Have I offended you again, ma'am?' he asked innocently. 'Perhaps we should talk about the weather – I'm told that's what they do in England.'

Lily laughed. 'I believe we do rather go on about it,' she admitted, 'but perhaps the weather is more temperamental in England. Less predictable. I don't know.'

He looked at her very steadily for a moment and then winked – a slow, impertinent, provocative wink – and shook his head approvingly.

'I've been watching you,' he said. 'I said to myself there goes a pretty girl. Pity she's wed.'

Again Lily found herself hesitating, confused. It was flattering to be admired and complimented, but in England a gentleman would never make such an approach to a married woman.

'I . . . Mr Miller . . . I don't think – ' she began.

He slapped his thigh. 'Damned if I haven't forgotten what I came for,' he said.

'Oh?' Intrigued, Lily forgot her confusion.

He grinned and took something from the saddle of his horse. 'For you and your friend,' he said. 'It's fresh meat.'

'*Fresh* meat?' cried Lily, amazed and delighted. 'But how on earth – '

'We went out this morning and got ourselves an antelope.'

'That was very clever,' said Lily.

He grinned. 'Not as clever as you might think,' he confessed. 'They're so curious, the pronghorn. We crawled up to them and then I waved a piece of rag. They came closer to see what it was and bang! The rest took off, but we'd got ourselves a nice little doe.'

Lily tried hard not to visualize it.

'Stew it or fry it,' he told her. 'It'll make good eating.'

Lily's delight was genuine. 'Mr Miller, you are so generous. Unless . . . but of course I must pay you for it. I couldn't just take it. I'm not short of money.'

'I should think not,' he said with a suggestive grin. 'A pretty young woman like you need never go short of money. You're *sitting* on a gold mine, ma'am. You don't need to go to California.'

It took a moment for the meaning of his remark to sink in and another few seconds for the shock to register in her eyes. He roared with laughter as Lily glared at him furiously.

'Mr Miller!' she cried. 'That remark was quite uncalled for and I must ask you to apologize. And here, take back your meat. It would choke me!'

She held out the paper package containing the meat, but he stepped back out of reach.

'Ma'am, that was a *compliment*,' he protested. 'Where I come from . . .'

Lily drew herself up to her full height and her eyes were cold. 'I'm afraid we don't come from the same place,' she said. 'Where *I* come from a gentleman would never refer to . . . that is, he would never mention – ' She swallowed hard, unable to find suitable words.

Daniel Miller was now looking very innocent and contrite, yet she suspected that he was enjoying her discomfiture.

'There, take back your wretched antelope!' she insisted. 'Or I'll throw it at your feet.'

'My dog'll enjoy it, then, 'stead of you two ladies.'

He seemed quite unconcerned and Lily hesitated. They had

139

not tasted fresh meat for weeks and fond as she was of dogs, she did not relish the idea of giving Daniel Miller's whippet the luxury of fresh antelope meat.

Daniel Miller was shaking his head admiringly. 'I do like to see a pretty woman in a tantrum.' He grinned and suddenly Lily began to see the funny side of it.

'I'm *not* in a tantrum,' she said, struggling to keep her face straight.

'Ma'am, you're beautiful,' he told her. 'I apologize most heartily and I hope you'll forgive my rude American ways. I'm not one of your English gentlemen, but my heart's in the right place.'

'Well, Mr Miller – ' Lily began, but then her dignity deserted her and she began to laugh. Soon she was laughing hysterically and holding her sides while he laughed with her.

'Oh! Mr Miller! I've got a stitch!' she wailed. 'And you're to blame.'

He watched her with a broad grin on his face and Lily thought that he had the most wicked smile she had ever seen. Suddenly he swung himself back on to his horse and raised a hand to his hat in salute.

'It's been a pleasure meeting you, *Mrs* Golightly,' he told her. 'Enjoy your antelope.'

He was gone in a spurt of dust from the horse's hooves, with his dog leaping after him, barking shrilly.

Slowly Lily unwrapped the paper and saw two large steaks.

'*Actually*, Mr Miller,' she whispered, 'for fresh meat I think I could forgive you anything!'

To Lily's surprise, however, Kate greeted Daniel Miller's gift with horror.

'Mr Miller?' she repeated. 'Not *Daniel* Miller?'

'The same! Why?' Lily stared at her.

'But he's . . .' Kate bit her lip, looking at the meat which was firm and red and delicately veined with fat.

'He's what?' asked Lily.

Kate looked from Lily to the meat and back again.

'Amos says he's a really rotten apple,' she said reluctantly. If she told Lily what Amos had said to her about Daniel

140

Miller, she was certain Lily would refuse to eat the meat and Kate was already imagining a succulent antelope stew.

'What was he like?' she asked tentatively. 'Did he – that is, was he polite?'

'He seemed nice enough,' said Lily carefully. She was sure that if Kate knew what had passed between them she would be shocked. 'He's a bit of a rough diamond, but I don't think there's any real harm in him. Do you?'

They both looked at the meat and Kate rolled her eyes. 'I don't care if there is!' she cried. 'Antelope meat doesn't grow on trees. Blow Amos! Let's eat it. Are the animals tethered?'

'All present and correct.' Lily saluted briskly with a mocking smile. 'When shall we eat the antelope?'

'We could save the frijoles for tomorrow,' Kate suggested. 'I've already heated it up, but we could heat it up again.'

'Let's make absolute pigs of ourselves,' proposed Lily. 'Let's eat the frijoles now and cook the antelope and eat it later. Who's to know?'

Surprised, Kate looked at her through narrowed eyes. 'You are in a funny mood, Lily,' she said. 'What exactly happened out there between you and Daniel Miller?'

'Nothing,' replied Lily innocently. 'He just gave me the meat.'

'Just like that? You mean, he didn't make any . . . well, suggestions to you? He wasn't cheeky or anything? Didn't try to kiss you?'

Lily laughed. 'Kiss me? Certainly not,' she said.

'Well, he's certainly brought a sparkle to your eyes,' commented Kate suspiciously, not sure whether to be amused or jealous.

'He just made me laugh,' said Lily, 'that's all. I feel years younger.'

Kate's eyes widened. 'You *did* kiss him!' she cried. 'Ooh, I bet you did?'

'I did *not!*'

'Would you tell me if you did?'

'Of course not,' said Lily and they both began to laugh.

They decided after some discussion to eat the frijoles and

prepare the antelope stew for the following day. The fresh meat was soon cut up and went into a pan with a few slices of dried apple, a handful of beans, several sprigs of wild garlic and some peppercorns.

Later when the fragrant smell of the stew promised a rare delight next day, Kate looked at Lily.

'Well, if you *did* let him kiss you,' she said, 'you have my permission to let him do it again!'

*

The wayside graves had become a feature of the overland trail, the first appearing a few miles west of Independence — an isolated boulder or simple wooden cross to be remarked upon by the living as they trudged past. As the miles passed, so the number of graves increased. Small graves for the children: 'Sadie Cullen, died cholera, aged six'; larger ones for the adults. Some were dug with care and lovingly marked 'J. M. Cowper from Iowa, 21 years. Beloved son. Asleep for ever.' One grave contained a father and son who had both died of cholera. Another beside the Big Blue River read simply: 'B. A. Dround May 7'. The graves were to be found on both sides of the trail, grim reminders of the frailty of man. Many of them showed signs of haste and were very shallow, with the soil thrown back so carelessly that predators had already been at work. The inscriptions were pencilled on wooden crosses, but the small boulders bore carefully scratched wording. The companies moved unknowingly over some graves which had been deliberately sited where the feet of men and beasts and the wheels of the wagons would flatten and compact the earth, making it less likely to be discovered by the coyotes.

Lily read them all. At first they frightened and depressed her. Later they blurred together in her mind and their impact was somewhat dulled. Familiarity bred not contempt but helpless acceptance, yet the warning remained. 'Take nothing for granted', they seemed to say. 'This is the way of it.' Lily read the inscriptions and thought 'Poor man', or 'Poor child', and passed them by.

However, soon after they started to move on the twelfth

of June Lily, walking on the right side of the team, saw another grave. Her eyes registered the wording on the boulder, but her brain did not: 'Patrick Golightly. Aged 25. From England. Beloved friend. Died May 21 1849.'

She stopped suddenly, walked on again and stopped a second time. She was trembling from head to foot. Patrick Golightly? Confused, she tried to remember what she knew of *her* Patrick Golightly. *Her* Patrick was still alive and he would be twenty-six on the third of August. As she stood there her team passed her, then the wagon rolled by and after a short interval the next team appeared beside her. The man with the lead mule spoke to her and although she heard him quite clearly, she could not understand what he said. She still stared straight ahead, but now she could no longer see. A great darkness enveloped her and her lungs refused to function properly. Patrick Golightly? A name on a boulder? A name on a *grave?* She was aware of a great pounding in her chest and dropping her whip she put both hands to her heart, afraid that it would burst out of her body. The pounding, lack of air and sightlessness were making her dizzy. She was going to faint. Maybe she was going to die.

'I'm dying,' she whispered and was glad.

It seemed for ever that she waited for the end to come. Then slowly, painfully, her heartbeat slowed and her vision returned. Three men on horseback passed her and then another wagon.

'Oh, Patrick,' she said dully and at last she turned and walked back the few yards along the trail, her feet heavy, every step a tremendous effort. Her strength was failing and she doubted if she would ever reach the dreadful place.

When she did, her brain registered the usual details. The grave had been carefully made, obviously by caring hands. The mound was neatly shaped, the soil well compacted, the inscription legible and the message concise.

Lily dropped to her knees, her face rigid with horror. She wanted to utter his name, but her lips were frozen. Only the voice within her seemed capable of speech. 'He's dead. *Dead.* Patrick Golightly – *my* Patrick – is dead!'

For a moment or two she knelt there unable to move,

143

listening to the terrible keening cry of her inner voice which told her something she did not want to hear. The old man's words returned. 'I smelt death,' he had said. Panic flared briefly. But she could not, *would* not believe it. Her beloved Patrick was not lying in this grave, she *knew* he wasn't. It was all a cruel joke. It *must* be, and yet . . .

A long scream issued from her startled throat as the nightmare closed in. Wildly she dug into the dry soil, flinging it to one side, while dimly conscious of running footsteps and voices. She would prove to herself that whoever lay in the earth, it was not her husband. Feverishly she dug on and then suddenly rough hands took hold of her and tried to pull her back. Rage gave her astonishing strength, however, and she fought them off. The hole deepened and her fingers touched something soft. A blanket! Yes, they buried people in blankets. She remembered the burial on the island in the middle of the river – the body over which she had spoken the Lord's prayer. They had wrapped him in a blanket!

'It's not Patrick!' she screamed. 'It's not my husband!'

Then Kate was beside her. 'Lily, stop it! You mustn't! Oh, Lily, please don't!'

Lily struggled wildly as more and more hands reached out to restrain her. Then she heard a man's voice: 'Here, let me deal with her.'

She caught a glimpse of Daniel Miller and struggled to her feet, striking out wildly at him, but he slapped the side of her face and she crumpled, gasping with shock. Before she could fall, his arms were round her, holding her gently and as he lifted her from the graveside her last memory before she fainted was of his button-brown eyes.

*

When Lily recovered consciousness, she was lying beside their own wagon surrounded by a small crowd of people who stared down at her. Kate was beside her, holding her hand and urging her to wake up. Daniel Miller sat on his haunches nearby, watching her. There was a blanket over her and someone was holding a leather bottle to her lips.

She was aware of water trickling from the corner of her mouth.

'Lily!' cried Kate. 'Oh, thank the Lord! You're not dead.'

At her words, Lily felt a prickle of fear at the back of her mind. Something awful had happened. What was it?

The doctor said, 'I'll give her a sleeping draught. She'll need to sleep.'

'Kate . . .' said Lily and then the realization struck her. It was *Patrick* who was dead. She had seen Patrick's grave. 'Kate,' she stammered. 'It was Patrick. The name on the stone. It said Patrick Golightly from England. Oh God, Kate – '

Kate's arms went round her. 'I'm sorry, Lily.' She began to cry. 'I don't know what to say. My poor Lily! I wish I could say it wasn't true. I wish . . . oh God, Lily, you'll just have to be brave.'

They clung together; Kate was in tears and Lily envied her. She too wanted to cry, but her eyes remained stubbornly dry. She looked round her and her eyes met Daniel Miller's.

'Is he really dead?' she asked him. 'My husband – '

'Yes,' he said evenly, 'your husband is dead. There can't be two Patrick Golightlys, not both from England.'

'No.' She found the conversation incredible. They were talking about *Patrick*.

The doctor was pouring medicine from a bottle into a spoon.

'Drink this,' he said, but she shook her head.

Daniel said, 'Drink it. The doctor knows best and you've had a bad shock.'

Meekly she swallowed it. Then she heard herself say, 'Don't cry, Kate. Tears won't bring him back!'

'I'm crying for you, not him,' said Kate. 'For *you*. Stuck here in this wild country looking for a husband who . . . who's dead and gone.' She began to sob again, but at that moment Matt Wallis rode up to discover the reason for the delay. Daniel explained what had happened and Matt at once slid from his horse and knelt beside Lily. 'I'm so sorry,' he said.'

Lily looked at him dazedly. 'There can't be two Patrick

Golightlys,' she said with an unconscious echo of Daniel's words. 'Can there?'

'No,' he agreed. 'I think you must accept that the worst has happened.'

She nodded without answering and he stood up and looked enquiringly at the doctor who inclined his head. 'Yes, I've given her a sleeping draught.'

'Good.' Matt turned to Daniel. 'Was the grave sufficient?'

'Yes, it was. No problem there.'

'Then we must move on.'

Kate scrambled to her feet, shocked by his apparent callousness. 'Move on?' she cried, her tears forgotten in her indignation. 'So soon? But she's only just found him – his grave, I mean. Surely we could wait a while. I mean, why are we going on if her husband's dead?'

Matt looked at Lily. 'Are you going on?' he asked.

'I don't know.'

'She doesn't know yet,' said Kate. 'She needs time to think.'

'Then we'll move on until she makes up her mind. You can turn back at any time, but I can't hold up the train unnecessarily for someone who wasn't even in our company. Days count. *Hours* may count. It's my responsibility.'

'But her husband's dead!' Kate almost screamed at him.

Matt shrugged. 'What can we do? We can't bring him back to life. If I could, I would.' Suddenly he held out his hands towards Lily. 'Let me help you up, Mrs Golightly. We have to go on.'

'No,' whispered Lily. 'I won't leave him.'

'How can you stay with him?'

She shook her head helplessly but Matt's expression was unrelenting as he leaned down to take hold of her hands. 'We have to move on,' he repeated. 'I'm sorry.'

To everyone's surprise Lily allowed herself to be pulled to her feet. She stood facing him and for a long moment stared into his eyes. At last, in a voice that was no more than a whisper, she said, 'You're a very hard man, Captain Wallis.'

'I have to be hard,' he told her. 'You have to be brave. We each have a cross to bear.'

As he rode away, Hester stepped forward.

'I'll care for them,' she told the doctor. 'Change the order of the wagons so that we're next to them and we'll give an eye.'

The doctor thanked her and promised to look in later if he could manage it. Hester and Kate helped Lily to her feet and half carried her to the wagon. By the time she was tucked up in her bed, the sleeping draught was beginning to take effect, but perversely she fought against oblivion. Hester left her in Kate's care while she went to see how Charlie was getting on with arrangements to change their position in the wagon train.

Kate squeezed her hand. 'We'll go back home, Lily,' she said. 'There's nothing to keep us here now. We'll go back to England.'

Lily stared up at her drowsily. 'But Patrick's here,' she protested.

'Patrick here? Oh, Lily, but he's . . .' She could not bring herself to say 'dead' so substituted, 'not really here.'

'He is,' Lily insisted. 'He'll always be here.'

'But what about your father?' said Kate. '*He's* in England. You can go home to your father. I'll come back with you, Lily. I'll get you home.'

'You're very kind,' murmured Lily. She closed her eyes, then opened them again. 'I don't want to sleep, Kate. I don't want to dream. I'm so afraid.'

'Afraid of what?'

'That I'll dream he's still alive and then I'll wake up and have to remember . . .' Her eyes closed once more and she sighed deeply.

Kate said softly. 'Go to sleep, Lily. I'll stay right here, I swear it.'

'Oh Kate . . .' Lily murmured.

A few moments later her head tilted to one side and Kate saw that sleep had claimed her.

'Patrick Golightly'! muttered Kate. 'How could you let yourself die, leaving your poor wife all alone in a strange country?' She regarded her sleeping companion with pity and then shook her head slowly. 'Just look at us,' she whispered. 'You with no husband and me with a baby on the way.

147

They've let us down right and proper. Blooming men! They really are the very devil!'

*

The following evening Amos and Gabby sat round their camp-fire, talking desultorily before turning in for the night, while Bart was taking his spell on guard duty which would not end until dawn. The members of the company did a full night's duty every four nights. Amos had done the previous duty and Gabby would be next.

One of the mules had been rustled by Indians the night before and when the theft came to light soon after dawn, Bart, Gabby and six other men had ridden in search of it. They found a hastily abandoned camp site where a fire still smouldered and decided reluctantly that it would be pointless to pursue the thieves any further. Tonight those on duty would be more vigilant than usual.

As the two men discussed the loss of the mule, Gabby was still regretting the decision to turn back.

'I was just itching for a chance,' he told Amos for the fourth time that evening. 'I want to shoot me an Indian. I want an Indian's scalp!'

'They might have had yours!' said Amos. 'They're mean as hell.'

'Not mean enough for me,' boasted Gabby, who had enjoyed the expedition enormously. 'I'd like to get one right between the eyes.' He held up an imaginary rifle, squinted along it and pulled the trigger. 'Right between his mean little eyes.' He shrugged. 'Me and Bart, both. But the others wouldn't have it, they wouldn't go after them. Afraid of what Wallis would say.' He scowled. 'Wallis doesn't own you, I told them. You're big boys now and you can think for yourselves. But they wouldn't hear of it. Chicken shit, that lot!' He shook his head disgustedly and raised his imaginary rifle again. 'Bang! Right between the eyes! That Indian wouldn't live to rustle another mule if I'd had my way.'

Amos, growing tired of the subject, shook the coffee-pot

148

and said, 'Do you want to share what's left? There's not much.'

'No, you have it. Damned Indian! We could have got that mule back, but they wouldn't agree. It's Wallis this and Wallis that with them. Hell, we all own a stake, I told them. He doesn't make the rules, we all do.'

Amos poured the last of the coffee into his mug and eyed it with distaste. 'Someone has to carry the buck,' he observed. 'Someone with a bit of know-how. The Western Hopers are Wallis's responsibility. You can't get away from that and he's doing a fair job of it.'

'Is he?' Gabby argued.

'Isn't he? He's got us this far.'

Gabby snorted. '*This* far!' he repeated. 'We haven't covered a quarter of it yet. We've hardly started. And this is the easy bit, Goddammit! If he's pussy-footing with the Indians now, what'll it be like when we meet the Sioux?'

'*If* we meet them. They say they're keeping their distance because of the cholera.'

'Don't believe all you hear,' Gabby warned him. 'I reckon they tell us what they want us to hear and nothing more. Wallis is cagey. He likes to throw his weight around, but – '

'I trust him,' declared Amos. 'You've got to trust somebody.'

Gabby was silent. 'If he'd just let us pick off a couple of Indians,' he said at last.

Amos shook his head thoughtfully. 'We don't want trouble,' he pointed out. 'Not *real* trouble. There's hundreds of 'em out there. You know it and I know it. Wallis knows what he's doing.'

'Chicken shit!' said Gabby.

Amos bridled. 'Meaning me?'

Gabby thought better of it. 'Meaning them,' he qualified. 'They were just plain scared – Sammy Vent and Abe Nolly and that guy with the big ears.'

'Gerry Kappel?'

Gabby nodded, but at that moment Kate appeared round the end of the wagon and both men jumped to their feet to greet her.

149

'How is she?' Amos asked of Lily as all three sat down again around what remained of the fire. In its failing light they could see that Kate was worried.

'Not good,' she told them, drawing up her knees and wrapping her skirt around them, 'but then you can't expect anything else, can you? The doctor says it's the shock.'

'It would be,' said Amos. 'Finding his grave like that. Poor Lily.'

Kate nodded. 'She's gone all sort of quiet and she stares. Doesn't seem to hear. It's almost creepy.'

Amos frowned. 'What's wrong with staring?'

'I don't know,' Kate confessed. 'I just get a funny feeling when she looks at me. It's as if she doesn't see me – as if she's seeing something else. As if she's not really here. I know that sounds daft, but – '

'It does,' said Amos. 'You don't mean she's gone a bit funny in the head, do you?'

'Not funny exactly,' said Kate. 'Just queer and kind of dreamy. I expect it's the stuff the doctor's given her. Poor old Lily! What a thing to happen. I'm sure I don't know what's to become of us and that's the truth.'

Amos looked at her in sudden alarm. 'You don't think . . . Hell! you're not going back, are you? You *can't* do that, Kate.'

Kate shrugged her shoulders expressively. 'We can and we just might do that,' she said. 'What's to keep us in America now Lily's husband's dead and gone?'

'But not *you*,' Amos insisted. 'You'll go on to California, won't you?'

'Don't ask me!' said Kate. 'I only came with Lily to get away from being sent back to the – ' She checked herself, not wanting to say 'workhouse'. Companion to a parson's daughter was one thing. A workhouse girl was quite another.

It occurred to Gabby suddenly that now Lily was a widow and in different circumstances, she might well look around for another husband. He had admired her since their first meeting and thought her by far the most attractive of the two girls, even if she was a little prissy about manners. She had made it clear that she didn't like smelly feet, unwashed hands, too much drink or belching after meals. She could be very frosty if the conversation took a bawdy turn, but she was English and that might explain it. Lily was certainly trim and pretty and he supposed she could cook.

'Does she *say* she's going back?' asked Gabby, dismayed by the prospect.

Kate considered his question. 'Not in so many words,' she said at last. 'She doesn't say she's going, but she doesn't say she's staying either. First off she said she couldn't leave him – his body, that is – but now she just looks dreamy and doesn't say much at all. They'd only been married a few weeks, isn't that a wicked shame? One week together and then he was off to America. What sort of marriage is that? Funny sort of husband, if you ask me. He goes off looking for gold and she's supposed to twiddle her thumbs till he comes back. I know what I'd have said!'

'One week?' echoed Gabby, impressed in spite of himself. Good grief, the girl was almost a virgin. 'Reckon she'll wed again?' he asked but Kate rounded on him, her eyes flashing.

'Gabby Smith! Am I hearing aright?' she demanded. 'Her husband not cold in his grave and you talk about remarrying! They may not have been together much, but she must have loved him or they'd never have got wed in the first place.'

Amos said, 'Look, Kate, if Lily wants to go back to England *you* can still come on to California. We'd look after you, wouldn't we, Gabby? We wouldn't let you come to any harm.'

Kate rewarded him with a dazzling smile, but then shook her head regretfully. 'If she wants to go back, I'll have to go with her,' she said. 'I can't let her make that terrible journey all on her own. If she goes, I go, but we'd best wait and see.' She sighed. 'She hasn't eaten anything all day. Hester does what she can to coax her, but she won't have it. She's a real brick, Hester is – one in a million.'

'You and that Ella get along well,' Amos said. 'Thick as thieves, you are.' It annoyed him a little that Ella and Kate spent so much time together, because it meant there were fewer occasions when he could find Kate alone.

Kate grinned. 'And why not?, she asked. 'We need to be, with you men around!'

'Look' Amos countered, 'your trouble is you don't know which side your bread's buttered! When it comes to the point, a man's got a lot to offer.' He gave her a provocative look.

'Like what?' cried Kate, rising to his bait. 'What've *you* got to offer, Amos Carp?'

'Wouldn't you like to know!' he said and Gabby laughed loudly.

'No, I wouldn't,' responded Kate. 'I like being with Ella. We just have a talk and a laugh and she's not always bragging like some I could mention.'

'Meaning us?' asked Gabby.

'How did you guess!'

'But we've got something to brag *about!*' Gabby grinned. 'You'll have to ask Amos to show you some time.'

'Maybe I don't want to see it,' said Kate.

Amos and Gabby exchanged a meaningful look and Gabby said, 'You'll have to see it some day, Kate, 'less you mean to stay an old maid.'

Kate's good humour faded abruptly. Why on earth was she playing the innocent with them, she asked herself? They would all know eventually that she was pregnant and then she would look such a fraud. Quickly she stood up and brushed down the back of her skirt.

'I can't stay here chattering with all of you,' she said. 'I promised Hester I wouldn't be long. She wants to get back to her family and I said I'd take over watching Lily.'

'Watching her?'

'Yes, the doctor said not to let her out of our sight,' she lowered her voice, 'in case she does herself in. You know?'

'Jesus!' said Gabby, visibly shaken. 'She wouldn't, would she? I thought she was religious. Isn't her pa a preacher?'

'So what?' said Kate. 'She's still lost her husband and it takes people funny ways. The doctor said it would be better if she could cry instead of bottling it all up inside, but she doesn't. Poor Lily!'

'Give her our best regards,' said Amos. 'Remember?'

'Our *love* and best wishes,' Gabby amended.

Kate smiled. They really were very nice young men, she thought wistfully.

'I'll tell her,' she promised.

*

The two men talked for a while after Kate left and then Amos yawned and said, 'Time to hit the hay,' and Gabby agreed. They took off boots and jackets, climbed into the wagon half-dressed and rolled themselves in their blankets. The sounds of camp life persisted around them, a constant reminder that they were hundreds of miles from civilization. A coyote howled and was answered by another, causing mules and oxen to shift uneasily. A shot rang out, but caused Amos no alarm since Wallis's suggestion earlier in the week that an occasional random shot deterred both Indians and wild animals. The wind had dropped during the afternoon to allow low black clouds to roll in and now a light spattering of rain fell briefly on the fabric of the wagon. He liked to hear it because it watered the grass and ensured feed for the animals, and without it they would never reach California. Reports were already coming in from backtrackers that further along the trail they had encountered such severe shortages of water and feed that some of the animals had died.

Amos listened eagerly to all reports of the hazards to be expected. If the truth were told, he was a little disappointed with the adventure so far. The high plains had not lived up to his expectations. His own life had not held many excitements and, like most of his friends, he had read the various published accounts of life on the trail west with youthful enthusiasm, never imagining that he might one day be given the perfect excuse to abandon his life as a teacher and sample its heady delights for himself. According to all he had heard, life beyond the frontier towns was fraught with dangers – from the forces of nature to attacks by savage Indians. He had vaguely imagined shoot-outs with hostile Indians, droughts, storms, stampedes, bears, snakes and buffalo hunts. He had expected the opportunity to prove his courage and resourcefulness, both to himself and others, but so far – apart from last night's sortie in search of the stolen mule – all he had experienced was monotony, sore feet, badly cooked food, a choking dust and time to think.

The dream which occupied most of his thinking time was not original, in fact it was shared by thousands of other gold seekers. It was a vision of a man up to his knees in river water, his back bent, a round pan in his hands. He saw himself examining the washed gravel and watched as his fingers reached in to pick out the gold. He saw it go in to the leather pouch which was already bulging with gold and then watched as he made his way back home at the end of the day's labour. At this point, the dream became less precise. Rumour had it that the prospectors lived in makeshift shacks with a minimum of home comforts and that because of this, many men went in search of consolation and in so doing parted with a lot of their gold. Amos had gambled light-heartedly on the river boats – a little monte and faro, nothing serious – but he had no desire to part with any of his hard-earned gold. Why try to win money and risk losing it when he could amass a small fortune by diligent effort in the gold streams? He could foresee only one way in which he might possibly be persuaded to part with his gold and that involved women. Presumably there would be whores in Sacramento, and a man could easily lose his head.

It seemed only sensible to consider taking a wife. True, a wife cost money, but she would earn her keep by washing his clothes and providing him with a hot nourishing meal at the end of the day. After weeks on the trail, such simple pleasures had begun to assume the proportions of luxury and Amos had been seriously considering Kate Lester. He had believed, however, that he had plenty of time – the journey would take four or five months and he was in no hurry to commit himself – but now suddenly it seemed possible that the two girls would be turning back and if they did, his chance would be gone. He might find it hard to replace Kate and with so few women going to California they would be able to pick and choose a husband from hundreds of suitors. Yes, a wife would be a distinct asset and Amos knew he must make up his mind before it was too late. If Kate agreed to marry him, she could not be expected to accompany Lily on the journey back to England. Poor Lily would then have to fend for herself, but that was not his problem, he felt sure that Captain Wallis would make proper provision for her.

Suddenly, as he stared up into the darkness, another terrible thought occurred to him. Suppose Gabby or Bart were thinking along the same lines? Suppose that at this very minute Gabby was making plans to propose to Kate. He went hot and cold at the mere thought of such duplicity and listened, frowning, to Gabby's breathing – but it was shallow and stertorous, he noted thankfully. So Gabby was asleep, he did not breathe like that when he was awake.

He scratched at a fleabite with mounting unease. Suppose that first thing in the morning Gabby went to Kate . . . his eyes widened. Bart! Bart could go to her before either he or Gabby were astir, because Bart was on guard duty and would be wide awake – he might be planning his proposal even as Amos lay thinking about it! He sat up, greatly agitated. Would Kate be asleep yet, he wondered. Perhaps she too was lying awake, maybe hoping that she need not go back to England; hoping that Amos would propose. Or Bart or Gabby! Damnation! He swallowed hard and wondered how his parents would receive the news that he was going to marry an English servant girl – a girl they had never met and about whom they knew nothing. They would not be at all pleased, he reflected, but surely when they saw her she would charm them? She was not beautiful like Lily, but she wasn't ugly either, and her hair was a pretty colour. He wondered how she would compare with the wives of the other teachers at his school, but then remembered that if he found enough gold he would never have to teach again.

'Damnation!' he muttered. 'What the hell! I'll go and ask her.'

He slid out of bed, pulled on his boots and put on his jacket. Then he ran his fingers through his hair to tidy it and thanked God it was a dark night. Whatever happened, he must not wake Gabby!

With infinite care, he made his way around the line of wagons until he reached Kate's and then called in a loud whisper, 'Kate! It's me, Amos. Are you awake?'

To his relief, her tousled head appeared almost immediately.

'Amos Carp?' she hissed. 'What on earth do you want at this hour?'

'I must talk to you,' he whispered. 'Come on down here, but don't wake Lily.'

'But I'm not dressed!' she protested, 'and it's spitting with rain.'

'Bring a blanket, then, I won't look, but hurry.'

A minute later they were huddled together beside the large rear wheel on the sheltered side of the wagon, two dim shapes in the darkness.

'Kate, I've got to ask you something,' he began nervously.

'But why *now?*' she demanded crossly. 'My hair goes all frizzy in the damp. Frizzier than usual.'

He put a finger on her lips to silence her and felt the exploratory tip of her moist tongue. The sweet sensation which this produced in him drove out the few suitable phrases he had prepared and he snatched his finger away and grabbed hold of her arms instead.

'Don't talk, Kate! Just listen,' he urged. 'I've been thinking that you and I should ... no, I mean I've always had the greatest respect for you, Kate, not to say affection. Look, Kate, I don't want you to go back to England with Lily. I want you to stay here with me!'

'With you?' Kate was thunderstruck. 'But – '

'*Listen*, Kate. Don't talk. I want us to stay together always. I want you to be my girl – no, to be my *wife*. There's a parson in the next wagon train and he could marry us. I'd make you happy, Kate, and we'll be rich, I promise you. I'll work hard and find lots of gold and then the world's our oyster. What do you say, Kate?'

He waited longer than he had expected and Kate's answer when it came was surprisingly cautious.

'You mean you want to marry me?' she whispered.

'I just said so, didn't I?'

'Oh, Amos!'

He waited again, puzzled by her tone, and an awful suspicion seized him. Someone had already asked her! She was going to marry someone else. He was too late.

'What is it?' he stammered. 'Don't you like me? I thought we got along fine. I thought – '

'But Amos, you don't know anything about me,' she stammered. 'If you knew me better, you might not want to marry me.'

Bewildered, he tried to see her expression but it was too dark.

'There's someone else?' he asked. 'Is it Gabby or Bart? Have you given him a definite answer?'

'It's no one else.'

'Not Daniel Miller! Kate! Tell me it's not him!'

'Of course not. It's nobody else, Amos. It's just me. Oh, Amos, I'd love to marry you but I'm not sure I can.' Her tone was anguished. 'I can't explain, but I don't think I'm the right girl for you.'

Anxiety made him irritable. 'That's for me to decide, not you,' he declared, forgetting to whisper.

'Hush!' she reminded him. 'Keep your voice down. 'You'll wake Lily.'

'To hell with Lily!' he snapped and then, as she recoiled, added hastily, 'Sorry! Sorry! I didn't mean that, honest I didn't, but you got me all at sixes and sevens. I want to marry you and you say you want to, but you can't. What the hell's that supposed to mean? Do you love me or not?'

'I think I do,' said Kate. 'Yes, I do love you, Amos, but . . .' She took a deep breath. 'There's something happened in my past that I'm not very proud of, and I put off telling you because I know it will make a difference to what you think about me. I was going to get round to it some time – to telling you, I mean – but now there's no point. I'd better go back to England with Lily and then you can go on thinking well of me. Remember me as you think I am. D'you see, Amos?'

'No, I don't.' He was sweating. 'Kate, I love you and I want to marry you and to hell with what you did back in

157

England. This is America. Whatever you did, it won't make any difference. You're just Kate and I love you. You don't know all my past. You might not approve. I might be a murderer!'

'There you are, then,' said Kate. 'That *would* make a difference. I'd see you in a different light then. I wouldn't want to marry a murderer.'

'But I *haven't* murdered anyone.'

'No, but I . . .' she sighed deeply. 'I *have* done something. I wish you'd believe me, Amos. It won't be the same if I tell you; you won't want to marry me.'

He stared at her. 'You've been to jail!' he cried suddenly. 'That's it, isn't it? You stole something from your employer and went to jail. No one would employ you after that, so you decided to leave the country. Am I right, Kate? Because if I am you can tell me. I swear to you, it won't make any difference. What happened before we met is over and done with.'

He pulled her into his arms and kissed her in spite of her obvious reluctance. 'You worry too much, that's your trouble,' he told her. 'Look, if I love you and you love me, then – '

'But do you *really* love me?' she asked him. 'Really and truly?'

'I do, Kate.'

'Swear it on the bible?'

'I *swear* it, Kate,' he assured her. 'I *truly* love you and I *truly* want to marry you, and if what you did is so terrible you needn't tell me. I don't have to know because it doesn't matter, Kate. I don't give a damn about your past – it's over. Just say "Yes".'

To his surprise she began to cry.

'Don't, Kate!' he begged. 'Listen – just say "Yes" and everything will work out fine, I swear to you.' He had a sudden inspiration. 'Look, if it makes you feel any better, I'm not so wonderful. I've done things . . .' He hesitated, unable to think of anything.

She stopped crying and stared at him. 'But you're a

teacher,' she protested. 'You can't have done anything too bad.'

Desperately Amos racked his brains to think of anything unsavoury he had ever done.

'Well, I have,' he told her. 'I've never told anyone, so no one knows, but I – ' In desperation he decided to take a leaf out of her book. 'I don't want to tell you because it's too awful and if I tell you, you won't say "Yes".'

'I'm not saying "Yes" anyway,' Kate reminded him, her lips trembling, 'but I don't believe you. You're just making it up so as I'll feel better. Oh, Amos, I'm sorry, but – '

'I stole something,' Amos invented wildly, 'from my pa. Yes, I stole from my own father! I'll tell *you*, Kate, but I've never told a soul and you must never tell anyone else. I stole a lot of money and . . . and he thought it was the neighbours' son who was always hanging round our place and he . . . he accused him and he denied it and our parents had this terrible quarrel – '

Kate was so obviously intrigued by the story that Amos warmed to it. He *had* to convince her and the best way he could do that was by convincing himself. He could quite easily imagine how disastrous it would have been.

'We'd been friends for years, us and the Jeffersons,' he told her. Well, that part was true anyway. 'Poor Uncle Ted. I called them uncle and aunt, the way children do, because I'd known them all my life. And Jay, that is Jason, was my best friend. We grew up together. Yes, poor Jason. It must have been terrible for him. He guessed it must have been me because he knew it wasn't him. And I was supposed to be his friend!'

Amos allowed his expression to change to one of deep gloom, although he doubted if Kate could see it properly in the dark. 'So you see,' he shrugged, 'I'm not very proud of myself.'

Kate, it seemed, was convinced at last. 'But why did you do it?' she asked gently. 'Why did you need all that money? How old were you? Not that I *mind*,' she added hastily, 'but I just want to know. To understand.'

159

Damnation! She was never satisfied! Amos sighed deeply and tried to remember why he had done this terrible thing.

'I owed a lot of money,' he said after a pause. 'I'd been gambling. I was only sixteen and my pa would have whipped me if he'd found out.' He remembered, as he said this, that when he played monte on the *Michigan* it was the first time in his life he had ever gambled! 'It comes to be a habit,' he said. 'I thought I'd stopped it, but then on the steamer I had the urge again and I lost a lot of money.'

'But you won it all back,' said Kate. 'You said you did.'

He shrugged. 'This time I was luckier.'

'So what happened?' asked Kate curiously. 'About your parents and the neighbours?'

'They moved house,' said Amos. 'The neighbours did, not my parents. Never spoke to us again. It was awful.' That was partly true. The Jeffersons *had* moved away, though for quite a different reason, and they never did actually speak again although they wrote plenty of letters.

Kate considered this in silence. 'And don't they know now?' she asked. 'Didn't you ever tell them?'

'No, never. I was too ashamed.'

It occurred to him that if he were not careful he might make his past worse than hers. How ironic if she turned him down because of *his* spurious misdeeds!

But Kate put out a hand and patted his arm. 'Poor old Amos,' she said. 'I know how rotten you must feel, but it wasn't so terrible. I mean, if you were only a boy of sixteen that's really only a child. Why don't you tell them? They'd forgive you. And you could write to the Jeffersons and confess. Say how sorry you are and put everything right. You could put it all right – it's not too late.'

Amos counted to ten. Damn her! She was shaking hands with the skeleton in his cupboard. 'That's not all,' he said recklessly. 'There's more. That's just how it all started.'

'Don't tell me,' cried Kate. 'I don't want to hear any more.'

'Then say you'll marry me. We're neither of us perfect – far from it – but I honestly love you, Kate. I can't live without you!'

As she still hesitated, he had another inspired thought.

'You're going to turn me down,' he cried. 'Just like the other one! I should never have trusted you. Never trust a woman, they say, and I reckon it's true!'

'Other one? Which other one? Other woman, do you mean?'

He nodded his head. 'Annie,' he said. Annie was his mother's name. 'I was engaged to her, but when I told her she broke it off. *She* said it wouldn't make any difference, but it did.'

'But I thought you said you'd never told a soul,' said Kate.

Hell and damnation, thought Amos, beginning to lose patience.

'Not a soul but *her*,' he said. 'I'm never going to live it down; it will ruin my life!'

'Of course it won't,' Kate began.

'Then say you'll marry me,' Amos insisted. 'Right now! Without another word. Say you'll marry me. We'll both forgive and forget. The past's over and done with and we'll never mention it again. Say you'll marry me, Kate. Say you will.'

It seemed an eternity, but she finally said, 'All right, then, I will!'

Chapter Eight

After Kate had returned to bed, Lily lay dreaming. In the dream she stood beside a well and looked down. Or was it a well? It was deep, seven or eight feet down, the sides were smooth and the corners were crisply cut. There were no spade marks, she noted. It was like a grave. Wells were round, thought Lily, and very deep and at the bottom water gleamed. This well was rectangular and not too deep and no water gleamed. Instead she saw a patterned blanket. It was a grave, not a well.

It was Patrick's grave, only it was not beside the well-worn trail in America's west – it was in the middle of a graveyard surrounded by gravestones. Behind her a church loomed and there was a bell tolling mournfully. It was a funeral, but there were no mourners except for Lily who stood alone beside the deep hole and looked down at the blanket which would not keep still. It moved jerkily as though someone, or some*thing*, was trying to get out. Lily tried to say, 'You can't get out, Patrick' but her lips would not move and so she said nothing. Patrick must stay inside the blanket because he was dead of the cholera and this was his grave.

Lily fell to her knees and watched the moving blanket. Was he really dead? The dead did not move, so perhaps he was alive. Or had died and been resurrected. 'I am the resurrection.' A shadow fell across the yawning grave and Lily raised her head to see her father, unsmiling, standing opposite. He held out his hands to her across the grave, but

Lily could not move. She could not lift her own hands. She could not reach out and be comforted by the touch of her father's arms. Then he spoke and although she did not hear any words, she read his soundless lips. 'Patrick is dead, Lily.' She found her own voice and cried, 'But he's moving, Papa. Shouldn't we help him?'

Her father shook his head. He seemed much taller than she remembered and very thin. Then he was holding a small boy by the hand and she recognized Maurice Dent. The little boy looked at her with trembling lips and said, 'He's dead of the cholera.'

Lily asked, 'Are you practising your scales, Maurice?'

'Yes, Mrs Golightly.'

'Every day?'

'Yes, Mrs Golightly.'

Lily smiled at him then and said, 'I'm a widow, Maurice. I have no husband. He is buried in this grave, wrapped in a blanket.'

The small boy nodded and repeated 'I practise every day,' and then he and her father turned and walked away from her hand in hand, wending an erratic course around the hundreds of gravestones that surrounded them on all sides as far as the eye could see. Lily heard a familiar voice say, 'Help me! I'm not dead!' and recognized Patrick's voice. She looked down into the grave and saw that he was alive, he had got an arm free and now he reached up to her for help. She leaned over and grasped his hand but he pulled her down, down. She was falling . . .

Lily awoke from the nightmare to find herself drenched with perspiration and shaking uncontrollably. She knew it was a fantasy, a figment of her imagination, yet she almost wished it were true. She could still feel the firm pressure of Patrick's hand as it grasped hers. Wonderingly, she put her hand to her lips and kissed it.

'Patrick, I love you,' she whispered. 'I'm so sorry you're dead.'

She felt a terrible, hopeless yearning for the feel of his arms around her and the touch of his lips on hers. Remorse filled her. She had left him in that lonely spot without even a 'Goodbye' – without a flower, without so much as a prayer. She had abandoned him and now his poor body lay in the uncaring earth as though it were of no consequence at all; every day the wagons rolled past and strangers stared at the hasty inscription. She could not bear it, she must go back, she decided, and put matters right, for if *she* did not bother no one else would. Patrick Golightly was only a name to them – one more gold seeker gone to an early grave. To her, though, he had been a reason for living, a dearly loved husband.

'Patrick, I love you,' she repeated softly. 'I cannot just walk away. I'll come back and pay my last respects.'

She decided she would gather a few wild flowers for his grave and she would say a few prayers. Yes, he must have a burial service no matter how simple. Reaching a decision made her feel stronger.

'I won't be long, Kate,' she whispered and wriggled out of her makeshift bed without disturbing her sleeping companion.

She was so glad to have something positive to do that she could not wait to dress properly, but set off along the trail towards the east where the sun was lightening the sky. Her hair was tousled, she wore only her nightdress and her feet were bare.

The shapes of the wagons were softened by the early morning mist and between them she glimpsed the cattle, their breath rising visibly in the cool air. A dog curled beside a wagon wheel slept on unaware of her presence. Dead fires showed in circles of grey ash where last night the weary groups had gathered to eat their suppers.

Lily tripped, regained her balance and stumbled on. She did not want to consider her young husband in his present state, so she forced her mind back to their brief honeymoon, but those memories gave her no pleasure. Only she and Patrick knew how disastrous that one short week had been, and now he had taken his share of the memories to the grave.

'I'm so sorry,' she said aloud. 'I didn't want it to be like that. I didn't know how to help you.'

An unconsummated marriage was a terrible disappointment, but Lily had been so sure that when they were reunited in New York the problem would be solved. She had been clinging to that, for she desperately wanted to make Patrick happy and she had given a great deal of thought to the ways in which she might help him when finally they shared a bed again. The letter in which he announced his decision to go to California had hurt her more than she would admit, even to herself, and now she wanted to come to terms with it. Patrick was dead and she had not been a wife to him in the fullest sense of the word. They would never again be anything to each other and in Lily's confused mind her regret was overlaid with bitterness. As she walked towards his grave, she tried to rationalize her growing suspicions and face up to the truth.

'Perhaps he didn't want to try again,' she thought, 'and *that's* why he went to California. If so, then that's why he's dead. Maybe he was afraid of failing again? Poor Patrick.' She drew a long, shuddering sigh and stopped briefly to take stock of her position on the trail. She had passed the last of the Western Hope wagons but a long way ahead, maybe two miles away to the east, she could see the wagons of the following company drawn up in the familiar ellipse. The Michigan Pioneers, they called themselves, or so Amos had said. They were a larger company than the Hopers own, with nearly two hundred members, no women allowed and no plans to return home. They would all settle in California when they had found their share of the gold and only then would the womenfolk come out to join them.

Lily trudged on, shivering slightly but perversely enjoying her discomfort. If Patrick's grave was a hundred miles away, she would walk on and on until she found it. She no longer cared. Patrick was dead and nothing mattered any more. Their future together and the children she had hoped to give him had been her main reason for living and now they no longer existed.

The track dipped slightly and the ground had held the recent rain. Lily's bare feet slipped frequently on the mud, but somehow she managed to remain upright. Looking ahead she saw that for a few miles there were no wagons, no dogs, no cattle. No need to move quietly, for no one would hear her.

'Patrick,' she said aloud, 'why *did* you come on this crazy expedition? Did you do it just to escape our problems? Didn't you know how hurt I'd be? Didn't you care? I wanted so much to be a real wife to you. You knew that, Patrick, so why did you go? You and your wretched gold! Now you're dead and I can never please you the way I wanted to. Oh, Patrick Golightly! Don't you care that you've broken my heart?'

Half-way between the Western Hope wagons and the Michigan Pioneers she stopped again, and for a moment her despair gave way to awe as she became aware for the first time of the beauty of the surroundings. The prairie, wreathed in mist, was mysterious in the early morning light; the domed sky stretched darkly, streaked in the east with pale yellow where the rim of the sun, emerging above the horizon, glowed like a golden arc, bright with the promise of another day. Nearer at hand wild flowers grew among the tall grasses and Lily recognized prairie peas and wild gooseberries and here and there the nodding head of a sunflower. She felt small and insubstantial and was strangely comforted.

She began to walk on, unaware of her appearance, oblivious to her discomfort and believing herself quite alone, so that she was horribly startled when a human shape materialized beside her apparently from nowhere and she found herself face to face with a young Indian brave.

Lily uttered a sharp cry of fear, but immediately recovered and for a moment they regarded each other with unveiled curiosity. He saw a white woman, flimsily dressed, walking barefoot, her hair dishevelled. She saw a young man with three feathers knotted into the top of his glossy black hair. He wore a necklace of small animals' teeth, a pair of fringed buckskin trousers and beaded moccasins, a bow was slung over his shoulder and a quiver full of arrows lay across his back. His face, beneath the few daubs of paint, had a pinched look and Lily could see his ribs. He stood immobile about a yard away from her, but to her surprise she no longer felt threatened and was entirely unafraid. He spoke to her in his own language and she was sorry that she could not understand him. She shook her head and held out her hands, palms upward, in a gesture of incomprehension.

He took a step towards her and with his right hand plucked imaginary food from his left and conveyed it to his mouth. Having repeated this several times, he then said, 'Food.'

'I'm sorry, I have no food,' she said slowly, expanding her answer with a firm shake of the head.

He took another step towards her and Lily was immediately aware of a slightly rank smell.

He repeated his mime and said, 'Food! You – give – food.'

Again she held out empty hands to convince him that she had no food to give, but after a moment's hesitation he pulled the tooth necklace over his head and offered it to her.

'You – give – food,' he repeated carefully.

'No food,' Lily insisted, again showing her empty hands.

He put a hand to his belly and then pointed to the distance. Then he held out his left hand to indicate two children of different heights.

Lily smiled. 'Your children?' she asked.

He repeated the actions and then rubbed his stomach, pointed and said, 'You give food!'

Lily thought she understood. 'Food for your children?' she said, but he continued to stare. 'I have no food,' she said. 'I'm truly sorry.'

She began to walk on. He would have to beg from one of the wagons, she thought, suddenly weary. If she had food she would give it to him, but he could not know that and she could never explain. To her surprise, he ran after her, caught hold of her hand and thrust the necklace into it.

Perplexed, Lily stopped again. 'No food,' she said. She tried to return the necklace, but he would not accept it. She pointed back to the Western Hope wagons and said, 'Food', then she pointed ahead to the Michigan Pioneers and said, 'Food. You go.'

As she resumed her walk, he fell in beside her, moving with an easy loping stride. Lily wanted him to go away and leave her alone, but she did not know how to make herself understood unless perhaps she pushed him forcibly and she had no wish to do that. She might hurt his feelings; she might make him angry. What was it the Americans called the Indians? Hostiles! He seemed harmless, but she must not risk antagonizing him. They walked together thus for about a quarter of a mile and neither spoke again. Lily still held the necklace in her hand, hoping that he would not interpret her acceptance of it as a promise of food.

Suddenly she heard hoofbeats behind them and turned nervously, expecting to see another Indian. If they were going to kill her, so be it, she thought, still surprisingly calm. She would make no protest if that was to be her fate. At least she would be with Patrick again. Looking at the Indian beside her, she said, 'I don't care if you kill me,' although she knew he would not understand, but then the approaching rider drew nearer and Lily recognized Bart Smith and guessed that he had come to take her back to the camp. Now she would never reach Patrick's grave.

Remembering the necklace, she made a last effort to return it to the young brave; she expected him to refuse again, but this time he took it, smiled at her for the first time and reached up to drop the necklace neatly over her head. As he raised his hands Bart shouted something and two shots rang out. To Lily's horror, the Indian clutched at his chest with a look of disbelief and sank slowly to his knees. He looked up at Lily with terror in his eyes, opened his mouth in mute appeal and then toppled forward.

Lily stared down at his crumpled form and then up at Bart, who now urged his horse forward and reined in his horse. As he sprang down he shouted. 'Jesus! I've got me an Indian!' Then he turned to Lily, who was now trembling. 'Are you all right?' he asked solicitously. 'I saw him go for you. I reckon I turned up in the nick of time. He didn't hurt you, did he?'

He ran forward and stood astride the inert body of the young brave as Lily, shaking with repressed anger, cried, 'You stupid, brainless — oh, Bart! Don't you see? You've *killed* him! Of all the heartless, callous, *wicked* . . .'

He looked at her in utter astonishment. 'Lily! What's

gotten into you? It's only an Indian! I couldn't let him go for you.'

Tears welled up in her eyes, but furiously she blinked them back and knelt beside the fallen man who seconds earlier had been walking beside her asking for food. Gently, fearfully, she turned the crumpled body over, ignoring the smell which she now realized was oil with which his whole body was greased. His black eyes stared up lifelessly into hers and frantically she took hold of his wrist to feel for a pulse. There was nothing.

'You've killed him, Bart,' she repeated in a choked voice. 'Oh how could you! He's dead, I'm sure of it.'

'Hell, ma'am!' Bart protested indignantly. 'What else could I do? He was going to scalp you, you know that? Another second and I'd have been too late.'

He knelt beside her, wrinkling his nose at the smell. Lily looked at him, then indicated the necklace which was now round her neck. 'He was giving me *this*,' she cried. 'He was *not* scalping me. Don't you understand? Look, he isn't even holding a knife. There's his knife, tucked into his belt. How could he scalp me without a knife? You've killed him for nothing and he's got a wife and two children. Bart, you've *killed* a man.'

'But I did it for *you*, Goddamn it!' Bart glared at her, unrepentant. 'I though he was going to scalp you or something. Jesus, Lily, you know what Indians are like. How was I to know?'

Suddenly, as she bent over the prostrate Indian, Lily's tears began to fall. They fell on to his face and she wiped them gently away with her fingers as more fell. She was crying for the Indian, but she was also crying for her husband dead of the cholera and for herself, abandoned in a strange country. Somehow she was crying for the whole misery of the human predicament. So much of her pent-up emotions were suddenly released that her eyes seemed quite inadequate for the quantity of scalding tears that burst through them.

Bart watched her sulkily, making no move to comfort her.

'What can we *do*?' she sobbed at last. 'We can't just leave him here.'

169

'Well, we sure as hell can't take him with us!' snapped Bart.

He was mortified by Lily's refusal to appreciate his timely arrival and his neat shooting. 'And don't say we have to bury him.'

'But why not?' Lily struggled to compose herself. 'I should think that's the least we could do.'

'Because Indians don't bury their dead, that's why not,' he told her, his tone triumphant. 'They like it simple. They sling 'em up in the trees, wrapped in animal skins and such-like, with all their personal belongings. They're not Christians, Lily, they don't want hymns and prayers.'

She was appalled. 'But . . . but what happens to them?' she asked.

He shrugged. 'I guess they rot away. Or the birds eat them. Who cares? If that's what they want to do, it's up to them. So don't go expecting me to dig a grave, 'cos I won't. You're sure he *is* dead,' he asked. 'I mean, are you sure?'

'Yes,' said Lily. 'His heart isn't beating. Poor man! He was just asking for food, he didn't mean any harm, but . . .' She stood up and looked into Bart's sullen eyes. 'You didn't know that, Bart and I'm sorry I spoke the way I did. If he *had* been attacking me, I would have owed you my life and I would have been very grateful.'

She sighed deeply and fresh tears threatened. 'Not that it would matter.'

Bart shrugged. 'Tears won't help,' he said, 'and it's nobody's fault. I mean, we didn't know where you were and Kate got in a state because she woke up and found you missing. She thought you might be on your way back to your husband's grave, and as I was still on guard duty I offered to come after you. Was she right?'

Lily nodded. She leaned forward and gently closed the dead man's eyes.

'It won't help,' he told her, 'to go to your husband's grave, I mean. It's miles back and when you get there you can't do anything. Death is . . . well – ' He shrugged and looked at the Indian. 'However it comes, it's for ever, Lily. We just have to get along without them. It's tough but true.' He hesitated. 'We'd best hide the body in case they come looking for him and take revenge on the wagon trains.'

'Bart!' Lily was horrified. 'Do you think they might?'

He shrugged, pursing his lips. 'I wouldn't like to say, but I don't aim to hang around and find out.' He pointed. 'There's a bit of a dip over there – a hollow. We could drag him over – .'

'We'll carry him,' Lily amended firmly. 'He doesn't deserve to be dragged.' Seeing Bart's mouth tighten, she added, 'If you won't help me, I'll do it myself.'

Bart groaned. 'I keep telling you, ma'am, he's an Indian. And what's more, he's a *dead* Indian. What does he care?'

'He's not "just an Indian", he's a man,' Lily corrected him. 'He's a man and *I* care. He's entitled to some respect. We carry him, Bart. *Please.*'

'Suit yourself,' Bart said, his voice heavy with resignation. 'We'll *carry* him to that dip then and cover him over with grass and stuff.' He leant down and took hold of the man's arms. 'You get his feet, ma'am. He looks kind of skinny, he won't be too heavy.'

'He was just hungry,' Lily said again. She took hold of the Indian's legs below the knee.

'It's the buffalo,' Bart told her. 'They say they're moving south and most of the Indians will have followed them. Pity this one didn't. They rely on the buffalo for just about everything. Wallis was saying that they use every bit of the animal – they don't just eat the meat. Take the horns, for instance, they turn them into cups to drink out of and they use them in their head-dresses.'

The limp body was heavier than it looked and carrying it awkwardly they staggered towards its proposed resting place. 'And the hooves,' Bart went on, 'why, they make glue, and the hair is for stuffing pillows and making rope and suchlike. They even use the muscles, though I can't recall what for. The Indians have to follow the buffalo, they can't live without them.'

Lily paid him no attention. She was looking at the buckskin trousers which the young brave wore, seeing the work which had gone into making them. His squaw, she thought, has stitched them lovingly and now she is caring for their children, unaware that her husband is dead, killed by a stupid mistake. Still, he died quickly – a sudden, *clean* death without much pain. Unlike her own Patrick who must have died a painful lingering death, fully conscious of his approaching fate.

As a parson's daughter, Lily had believed herself accustomed to death. She had attended many funerals and had done her best to comfort the bereaved, but back in England death had been a civilized affair in which the dying were treated with proper respect and all possible care, and their bodies were buried with solemn words, sweet music and flowers. Here people died horribly and unexpectedly while an indifferent world gave scarcely a passing glance. People who died here were nothing more than a nuisance to be set on one side and forgotten as quickly as possible. To Lily's tender heart, this was unbearable.

As they lowered the Indian into the hollow, she wondered fleetingly what her father would say if he could see her now and smiled ruefully as she imagined his reaction. Bart left her to straighten out the body and went in search of brushwood with which to camouflage it. Lily arranged the Indian as though he were in his coffin, with his hands folded across his chest, then kissed him lightly on the forehead and whispered, 'That's from your wife and children.'

She sat back on her heels, feeling more helpless than ever before in her whole life.

'Please forgive me,' she whispered. Then, fearful of the state of his soul if he was not discovered and given an Indian 'burial', she uttered a hasty prayer as Bart came back with armfuls of greenery. Together they hid the body and then stood for a moment looking down at their handiwork.

'You will report it, won't you?' asked Lily.

Bart hesitated. 'Maybe the less said the better,' he suggested.

'Oh, but Bart – '

He gave her a resentful look. 'It's me that'll get blamed,' he pointed out, 'not you. And if you hadn't taken off like you did, I wouldn't have shot him.'

172

Lily stared at him, appalled by the implications of the situation. Bart had killed the Indian, but it was *her* fault.

'Maybe I should tell Mr Wallis,' she began.

'He's going to blame me whoever tells him.'

'Yes,' said Lily, 'I see that.'

Suddenly she was very tired. Her brain hardly functioned and she could see no way out of the dilemma. Seeing her confusion, Bart said quickly, 'So that's settled. We say nothing and hope.'

'Oh Bart, I don't know – '

'I do and I'm telling you – we say nothing.'

'But if the Indians attack?'

'They might do that anyway, even if they don't find him.'

Lily nodded. 'But I hate to just walk away and leave him like that,' she said. 'I suppose they *will* find him.'

'They'll keep looking,' said Bart, 'and they'll find him, don't you fret.' He shrugged. 'Tough on him but . . . thats life, I guess.'

'Or death,' said Lily sadly.

'So what now?' Bart asked, his tone unfriendly. Try as he could, he felt no sympathy for the waif-like creature who stood beside him. He had killed an Indian and Lily had ruined his big moment with all her stupid fuss. If it hadn't been for Lily insisting that the Indian was harmless, he could have gone back to camp as a hero. She should have stayed at home in England where she belonged, he thought bitterly.

Scowling, he said, 'You going to walk on or ride back to the camp behind me? Suit yourself, I'm in no mood to argue.'

Lily hesitated. She felt weak with shock and grief and all her strength seemed to have deserted her. The Indian's death had brought home to her the finality of her own loss. Like the young brave, Patrick was dead and there was nothing she could do for him except pray for his soul. She lifted her head and looked at Bart.

'I'll come back with you,' she told him.

*

173

Dearest Papa,

I thought the last letter I wrote to you was difficult, but this one is even harder for me. I have such sad news and I know it will grieve you. My poor Patrick is dead after so brief a life. I can hardly believe it. I found his grave beside the trail and there is no doubt about it. He died of cholera, such a terrible way to die.

But I must reassure you that I am recovering from the shock and you must *on no account* worry on my behalf. As you see, I am at Fort Kearny, the military outpost at the fork of the Platte, and I shall go no further. It almost seems as though God has intervened to bring me home to you again and if that is His will, I am resigned to it. Although our reunion will be dearly bought, I will take great comfort in the fact that you and I will be together again.

But, Oh Papa, it would break your heart to see so many poor souls laid to rest with hardly time for a prayer.

I will speak to Captain Wallis and arrange somehow to return to New York. From there I will travel back to England. At least we will be together.

When I think how little time Patrick and I shared, my heart aches. I feel certain we could have been happy, but now all that is over.

People have been kind to me, but the company will be moving on along the next part of the journey towards Fort Laramie and I will wait here to begin the long trek home. Now I shall be just another backtracker and that sounds so sad. Maybe you will not understand, Papa, but it is the sense of failure.

Be content, Papa, that I pray night and morning and still find time to read my bible and find it a great comfort as you always taught me. I try not to feel too sorry for myself because others have lost dear ones, too. My great regret is that I could not be with Patrick when he died, to offer what comfort I could.

But I know how this news will hurt you and I do not

wish to add to your burden. Be of good cheer and trust in God as I do. I will see you again before many months are past.

Meanwhile, I remain your affectionate but grieving daughter

Lily.

Matt Wallis looked up as the Englishwoman approached. Women! They were more trouble than they were worth. He wished he had not agreed to take them, but he had been soft and now they were just one more headache. This one had already delayed them by the discovery of her husband's death. He knew what it was she wanted to talk about – he had seen it coming – but when she approached him a few days earlier he had asked her to wait until they reached Fort Kearny. Now they had reached it and the company was resting for twenty-four hours, so it was time to talk to her. She ducked into the tent, her face pale and drawn.

'Every inch the bereaved widow,' he thought.

'Mrs Golightly.' He shook her proffered hand. The English were so obsessed with these little courtesies. Impatiently he indicated the small trunk that doubled as a seat. The tent served as an office and, apart from the trunk, contained one folding canvas chair and a rickety folding table which had seen better days.

'I expect you can guess why I'm here,' she began.

A typical parson's daughter, he thought, yet there was something about the smooth black hair, candid blue eyes and small resolute mouth that touched him. In spite of her precise manner he sensed a vulnerability and found himself wondering about her. What sort of wife had she been to her dead husband? He could not imagine that passion played a large part in her personality. Very different from Miss Lester, who had a decidedly roving eye – but then she was single, so perhaps it was an unfair comparison.

Lily repeated her comment and he hastily relinquished his inquisitive line of thought.

'You want to go back east,' he said. 'I understand. There's

175

nothing to keep you here now that your husband is dead. It's been tough on you; I'm sorry, but these things happen.'

She nodded, her knees neatly together, her hands folded in her lap, saying nothing.

Prim, he thought.

'Just as well we haven't travelled too far,' he went on. 'I take it your companion will be going back with you. I'll arrange a refund of your stake money and you can – '

'Mr – that is, *Captain* Wallis,' she interrupted. 'That is the problem. Miss Lester is *not* returning with me because she's going to marry one of the men.'

He brought his fist down on to the table with a bang.

'Begging your pardon, ma'am,' he exclaimed, 'but who the hell is she marrying?'

She looked startled. 'Amos Carp. He used to be a teacher,' she said.

'I know him.' He shook his head in obvious displeasure. 'As if I don't have enough problems! Who's marrying them?'

He saw that his outburst had offended her for now her voice was cold. 'A minister from the company up ahead. At least, that's the plan.'

'Damnation!' he exclaimed.

'I really don't see why – ' she began.

'I wouldn't expect you to, ma'am,' he interrupted her. 'Nobody does. Let's just say that it's going to be hard enough to get sixty people over to California if they all have their minds on the job in hand. You haven't seen the half of it yet, believe me. It will take every inch of my know-how and every ounce of their courage to make it to the other side.'

Her voice was frosty now. 'Presumably you chose to take the company across?' she said.

The attack took him by surprise. 'You could say that,' he countered.

'Then don't blame us if you're not enjoying the experience,' she retorted.

There was an uncomfortable silence. 'Anyway, I think it best if I turn back now,' Lily said at last. 'I'll need a horse and a pack-mule-'

'You'll need a *wagon*, Mrs Golightly,' he corrected, 'and

someone to travel with. Your best bet is to wait here for a family of backtrackers.'

'But we only have one wagon,' she protested, 'and if I take it, Kate – that is, Miss Lester – will have nowhere to sleep.'

'Can't she mess in with the Cooper family?' he suggested. She's friendly with the daughter, isn't she? Until she marries, that is.'

'But then where will they go when they're married?'

'That's not your problem,' he told her curtly. 'It's mine. You will be on your way home to England by then and long past caring.' His tone was harsher than he intended. 'And please understand, Mrs Golightly, that once you leave this company you're no longer my responsibility. You buy out Miss Lester's share of the wagon – I hope you can afford to – and then we'll give you enough provisions to see you back to Independence. After that, worry about yourself and I'll worry about Mr and Mrs Carp. Does that sound reasonable?' There was a hint of sarcasm in his voice which Lily chose to ignore.

'I suppose so,' she said.

'You *suppose* so? What the hell does that mean?'

The small mouth tightened and again the blue eyes flashed. 'I mean it sounds fine for me,' she said, 'but I'd be callous not to care what happened to Kate.'

'Does she care what happens to you?' he demanded. 'She could come back with you if she wanted, but she fancies herself as a married lady so she's prepared to let you go home alone.'

Lily made no answer.

'Is that settled, then?' he asked. 'We shall move out of here tomorrow morning early, and you will wait here at the fort until a suitable family turns up on their way home. They'll be only too glad to take you along, there's safety in numbers.'

'Captain Wallis,' she began, 'there's something else – at least, I feel I owe it to you to tell you . . .'

She broke off and his curiosity was aroused by the sudden change in her manner. She looked almost *guilty*, he thought, surprised.

'It's been on my conscience,' she told him, 'but I couldn't tell you before because it involved someone else.'

She was obviously finding it difficult.

'So . . .' he prompted, wondering what she could possibly have to confess.

He listened in astonishment as haltingly she recounted how someone she would not name had mistakenly killed an Indian in her defence and how together they had hidden the body. When she came to the end of her story, he shook his head.

'I should have been told,' he said.

'I wanted to tell you,' she replied miserably.

All her earlier composure had vanished, he noted, and he felt a sudden sympathy for her which he fought down.

'It was crazy,' he said, 'but we must be thankful there were no repercussions. It could have been very serious.'

'It was an accident,' she assured him earnestly. 'He acted in my defence. If anyone is to blame, it's me.'

'I'm fully aware of that.'

Her face flamed at the sting in his voice and again he was reluctantly moved to compassion.

'You should have told me,' he repeated.

'I am truly sorry,' she said. 'It's been a terrible weight on my mind.'

Her eyes, looking into his, were dark with misery and he suddenly wanted to horsewhip the impetuous young man who had added to her troubles.

'I'd like you to tell me the name – ' he began.

'No!' She jumped to her feet in agitation. 'Oh, please don't press me. I agreed to say nothing and already I've broken my word. I feel so bad about that.'

'A conscience is a luxury,' he told her. 'You should learn to live without one.'

Lily stared at him and he expected a sharp reply, but it seemed that momentarily her spirit had been crushed and inexplicably he was sorry for that too.

'Why are you telling me now?' he asked. 'You're leaving – you could have said nothing.'

She hesitated. 'I wanted to be honest with you,' she said.

'I didn't want us to part with a lie — at least, I thought . . .' She stopped and shrugged helplessly.

'Let's say no more about it,' he said, almost gruffly.

After a moment she held out her hand and he grasped it briefly.

'I'm sorry I've proved such an unwelcome burden to you, Captain Wallis,' she told him. 'I've no doubt you will be heartily glad to be rid of me but I must thank you, nevertheless, for your leadership this far. Whatever you think of me, I have to say that I think the Western Hopers are very lucky to have you as their leader. I hope with all my heart that you all arrive safely in California. It won't be your fault if they don't. My prayers will go with you.'

Before he could answer, she turned without a smile and left the tent.

'Damnation!' he muttered, annoyed with himself for allowing her to rile him. He prided himself on the ability to keep his feelings under control, but something in her manner provoked him. He had been discourteous to her, he reflected, and that too was something he regretted. Her intentions were good, so why did he have so little patience with her problems? He sighed heavily. Straining across the table with unfocused eyes, he tried to analyse his feelings. She was turning back. Was *that* what disturbed him? The thought that one of his company was backing out? He shook his head. No, she was not even a full member, only a temporary one. So was *that* it, he wondered. Or was it simply because she had been looking forward to joining her husband's company?

'No!' he said aloud.

He would be glad to be rid of her, he told himself, and it was a pity Miss Lester wasn't going with her. With an effort he pushed the matter to the back of his mind, telling himself thankfully that he had more important things to think about.

*

The next morning dawned bright and clear. While a bugle called the soldiers to the parade ground for inspection, the Western Hopers prepared to move on and Lily and Kate clung together in a final embrace.

179

'Are you sure you'll be all right, Lily?' Kate asked. 'I feel awful not coming with you. I ought to be, I know. After all you did for me, the least I could do –'

'I didn't do anything,' interposed Lily. 'Look, you're going to marry Amos and that's all that matters now. Think about Amos. Think about your life together and when you get to California and you dig up your first nugget, think of me!' She tried to smile, but failed miserably.

'Oh Lily! I wish you'd change your mind.'

Lily shook her head. 'I can't go to California without Patrick,' she said. 'It's not the same now. But Kate . . .' She hesitated.

'What is it? Oh!' She looked at Lily sheepishly. 'I know what you're going to say – about the baby. Honestly, Lily, I *will* tell Amos.'

'You must, Kate,' urged Lily. 'And it's only fair to tell him *before* you get married. Oh, I wish I could be there to throw rice.'

Kate grinned. 'You haven't got any rice!' she pointed out.

Lily smiled faintly. 'Well, to throw something,' she said. 'Please tell him, Kate – and *soon*. He'll understand. Amos is a really nice man, you're very lucky.'

Kate sniffed hard. 'I would never have met him, Lily, if it hadn't been for you letting me come with you. And I'm head over heels about him, Lily, really I am. And he swears he loves me – but they all say that!'

'I'm sure he does,' Lily assured her.

There were shouts from the road ahead and Wallis rode up, checking that all the wagons were ready to move out.

Kate gave Lily a final hug and then Kate's place was taken by Hester Cooper, who gave Lily a quick peck on the cheek.

'God be with you, child,' she said. 'I hope you're doing the right thing. Don't fret about Kate, she'll be fine with us – company for Ella and -- ' she lowered her voice, 'we'll see her through when her time comes.'

'Thank you. I know she'll be in good hands.'

Ella shook Lily's hand very formally and said, 'Goodbye, Lily. I'm sorry about everything, but at least your pa will be pleased to see you again.'

'I know,' Lily nodded. 'You just look after yourselves. I've given Kate my address in England and she's promised to write and tell me when you reach California. If you all get rich, you can come to England and visit us. We'd make you very welcome.'

Further along the trail the first wagon began to roll. Behind them on the parade ground the shouts of the drill sergeant ceased abruptly as the men fell out and a few soldiers drifted across to watch them go. Dust rose from the hooves of the animals and the wheels of the wagons and Lily waved as the Coopers' wagon passed her – Hester driving the mules, her husband beside her on the driving seat. Behind them came Jess, Ella and Kate. Ella carried Will on her hip and she raised his small hand in a farewell wave.

Tears blurred Lily's eyes as Adam Best passed her with his pack on his back. He looked weary in spite of the day's rest, but he smiled cheerfully at Lily and shouted, 'Hop up on my back-pack, ma'am. I'll *carry* you to California!'

Amos, Bart and Gabby were last to pass her and as they too went by Lily put her hands over her face to hide the extent of her desolation.

When she uncovered them, last-minute doubts began to assail her. Did she really want to turn back? Earlier she had felt so sure of the rightness of her decision, but now she hesitated again. Panic gripped her and, gathering up her skirts, she began to run after the receding wagons, faster and faster, fighting down the impulse to call, 'Wait for me!' Everyone she knew was in that wagon train and when they had gone she would be alone among strangers. She ran for a hundred yards or more before slowing to a halt.

'Lily Golightly!' she told herself. 'You're behaving like a child. Let them go!'

With a supreme effort, she turned her back on them and saw that the Michigan Pioneers were now approaching the fort from the east. Behind would be another company and behind them yet another. Everyone was going to California, she thought wearily. What room was there for an English widow? She really must go home.

She stared round at the half-completed fort and wondered

how long it would be her home. Suppose no one decided to turn back – she might be here for weeks. The prospect was not an appealing one. The newly established fort was no more than a collection of rough buildings without even a stockade to protect it. Lily let her gaze wander to the few adobe structures which had so far been compeleted: a store-house, stables and quarters for the officers. The other ranks were housed in a sprawl of tents around the area which served as a parade ground. Soldiers still worked on a large building, making a roof of poles which they covered with brushwood.

Even as she watched, another bugle call rang out, but its significance was lost on her.

'That's the sick call, ma'am.'

She turned to find a young soldier beside her. He was tall and thin and looked about twenty-five or -six; his hair was brown and he had grey eyes.

'Every bugle call means something different,' he explained. 'They measure out the soldier's day – first reveille, then boots and saddle, then it's the mess call, drill call – damned bugle!' He shook his head. 'You get so you hate the sound of it,' he told her. 'You can't wait for retreat call and extinguish lights.'

'Retreat?' Lily queried. 'Isn't that a battle call?'

A faint smile crossed his face. 'No, ma'am, it's not that kind of retreat. It marks the end of the working day! Who'd be a soldier, eh?' His tone was morose.

Lily hesitated. 'Don't you like the Army?' she asked.

'Like it, ma'am? Hell no! I wanted to be a soldier like my Pa but . . .' he shrugged. 'I guess it's not all I expected.'

His uniform consisted of blue wool trousers worn outside his boots and a darker blue jacket, the latter piped down the front with yellow 'lace' and fastened with a single row of brass buttons. The high collar was also trimmed with yellow, as were the epaulettes. A single white leather strap crossed the jacket and another wider strap was round his waist. The dark brown cap was pushed back at a rakish angle and the top three buttons of his tunic were undone. His left hand rested on the hilt of a sabre which reached almost to the ground. Yellow chevrons on his sleeves suggested to Lily that maybe he was a junior officer and his next words confirmed this fact.

'First Lieutenant Boyd Tanner, 2nd Dragoons, at your service, ma'am,' he said suddenly.

Lily held out a hand as she introduced herself, but his right arm had lifted in a half-mocking salute.

'There's just no action here,' he went on. 'No action and precious little training. A bit of shooting pratice would make a change from digging ditches and felling timber. If we ever get to tussle with the Indians, I reckon we'll have forgotten how to shoot. I spent four years at West Point and I'm ambitious. Promotion's slow, but I expected that. I didn't object to this posting but I didn't anticipate this.' He waved a disparaging hand. 'Cleaning a carbine is not the same as firing it and one day we shall need to do just that.'

He sighed deeply and looked so unhappy that Lily said, 'Can't you leave the Army?'

'I could buy my way out if I could afford it, or I could desert,' he told her. 'Plenty of men do, but I've got a wife and child to support. There's no way out for me.'

'But where are they – your wife and child?'

He jerked his head towards the tents. 'It was adequate married quarters when I enlisted, but now it's a tent . . .' He shrugged and his face brightened. 'Mae doesn't seem to mind it, though. Mae's my wife. Women are funny like that. I guess a tent's fine for the summer, but the winter will be another story. They reckon we'll have built the new quarters by then, but I'm not so sure. If the Indians and gold seekers give us time . . .' He smiled to soften his words. 'Meaning no disrespect, ma'am, but setting up a fort takes time and seems like every day there's a new distraction. Not that I blame them, ma'am – the gold seekers, I mean. I'd like to be one of them. I'd like to go to California and find myself some gold. We all would!'

While they had been talking a queue of soldiers had formed outside a nearby tent and now Lily's companion gestured towards it.

'Hospital tent,' he said. 'Any excuse at all to be relieved

duties for a day: scalded hand, festering ant-bite, strained muscle. They'll get to lie on their bunks for a few hours and dream of home and pretty women and decent food!'

Lily smiled in an effort to dispel his gloom. 'In that order?' she asked.

His mouth twisted wryly. 'I guess so,' he said.

He waved his hand suddenly and smiled and Lily turned to see a young woman hurrying towards them, her expression at once eager and cheerful. She was small and plump, neatly dressed in a pale blue jacket and skirt to which a few ruffles of lace had been added at the cuffs and hem. To Lily's surprise, she moved straight up to them and clasped Lily's hands.

'You must be Mrs Golightly!' she exclaimed. 'You poor, poor thing! We heard all about it. And Boyd is just letting you stand in the sun without a friend in the world. Boyd! How could you?'

She spoke with a distinctive drawl and Lily guessed that she might be from one of the southern states.

'We were just talking,' Lily began. 'Your husband was telling me about – '

Mae laughed. 'About Army life? I thought so. Don't you go believing a word of it! I'm Mae Tanner and you will just come along with me and have a glass of my cold maple beer and eat your fill of buck wheat cakes. Why, you look half-starved and I'm sure I'm not surprised. I'd starve if anything happened to Boyd.'

She dragged the unresisting Lily across the parade ground, leaving her husband to return to his duties.

'We shouldn't be going around here,' Mae told Lily, 'as it's kind of a special place, but the officers have gone back inside so there's no one to see us.' She stopped by the flagpole and shaded her eyes as she looked up at the red, white and blue flag with obvious affection. 'Isn't that just the prettiest sight?' she demanded without waiting for an answer. 'The American flag. The United States for ever! Oh, you mustn't heed Boyd. He's lusting after gold, like all the others. He just loved the Army before Mr Marshall found his nuggets. Now all the soldiers are dissatisfied with their lot, poor

184

things, but they'll get over it. I told my husband, "You stick with the devil you know and don't mix with the devil you don't." ' She laughed prettily. 'Why, most of those fools rushing off to California . . . Oh!' She clapped a hand to her mouth in mock dismay. 'Just listen to me! I never do think before I speak – Boyd's always telling me. And your poor husband gone to an early grave! I didn't mean *he* was a fool. That was just so sad, him coming all the way from England and you following him. When I heard, I said to Boyd, "That's so sad!" You know how it is, word gets round. I said to myself, "That poor thing, left all alone in a strange place." I felt for you. I really did. You come on in now.'

She stooped and went into one of the small wall tents and Lily followed, rather overwhelmed by the woman's brisk manner but grateful that her unbroken chatter was keeping her own sad thoughts at bay.

Although fairly large, the tent was very cramped. A double bed was screened off by a length of cotton sheeting dyed to a soft pink colour.

'Beet juice,' Mae told Lily proudly. 'I did it myself. Boyd says I could make a real nice home from a hole in a tree!'

The rest of their home was equally ingenious. The dresser was a trunk set on end, with temporary shelves fitted inside it to hold the white china tea service; the table was made of planks laid across two kegs; an upturned crate supported a tin jug and matching wash-bowl which Lily guessed were government issue. There was a small iron stove in the middle of the tent and a brightly coloured sampler worked in cross-stitch was pinned to the canvas "wall".

'We're not really supposed to do that,' Mae confided. 'It lets the rain come in through the canvas, but it comes in anyway if it rains real hard. My sister worked it for me before I came out here.' She pointed to two hand-made stools with grey seats. 'I sweet-talked the quartermaster into parting with an old blanket and cut out the best bits. Stuffed them with prairie grass. Don't they look pretty? Why, even the Colonel's wife admired them. Have you met her yet? She's very big, with a very loud laugh. She's older than she looks, too, they say she colours her hair with sage tea, but I wouldn't know for sure. I really envy you your hair, Mrs Golightly. I always did want to be a raven-haired beauty – my mama swears I told her so when I was a little-bitty thing of six years old. Someone asked me what I wanted to be when I grew up and that's what I said. A raven-haired beauty! 'Stead of which I'm mousey and I guess I always will be.'

Lily tried to think of something flattering to say about mousey hair, but Mae gave her no time.

'Still, I do like to keep it nice. Boyd says all men admire shiny hair on a woman. I make up my very own shampoo, you know that, and I don't think any woman on this fort has shinier hair than I do. Whisky and castor oil scented with lavender – I make up a bottle-full at a time and I just give it a shake each time I want to use it.'

She paused breathlessly, one hand to her heart.

'But now you must admire my chubby little boy – fast asleep, bless him. Why, he's no trouble at all and four months old tomorrow.' She drew aside the sheeting to reveal a crudely made wooden cot, each leg of which stood in a tin can full of water.

'Keeps the little old ants away,' Mae told Lily. 'If it's not ants it's fleas, and if it's not fleas it's mosquitoes. You know, those little devils bite Boyd but they don't touch me. Isn't he a pet?'

They both looked at the sleeping boy, a plump child with white-gold hair and a pale waxy complexion.

'And you've no baby, either,' Mae commiserated. 'Unless . . . ?' She left the question unfinished.

'No,' said Lily, taking her meaning. 'I'm afraid not.'

'Oh, you poor thing,' cried Mae. 'No man and no baby! You must be feeling low, but things'll get better. That's what I always tell Boyd. If they're bad, they just have to get better.'

'He's a lovely baby,' Lily told her. 'Really beautiful.'

'Isn't he just?' Mae agreed. 'You'll have one by and by, you'll see. You'll marry again – you'll have to. Every woman needs a man and a family, it's human nature, isn't it?'

Lily sat down while Mae busied herself setting plates and mugs on the table, producing cakes from a tin box and pouring the promised maple beer from a brown earthenware jug.

'Made it myself,' she said, referring to the beer. 'You can have the receipt if you like. It's just boiling water, maple molasses and essence of spruce. You add yeast as it cools, and it's ready to drink in just a few days. The Colonel's wife gave the recipe to my friend and she gave it to me, bless her. Try it. Isn't it just delicious?'

Lily nodded and drank and ate gratefully, surprised to discover a hunger she had not suspected.

Mae was regarding her keenly, hands on her hips, her face thoughtful.

'Pity you can't stay on here a few months,' she said. 'You'd soon find another husband here. No disrespect to your dead husband, the poor thing, but a woman should be married. It's what we're born for, isn't it? You'd like Army life. It's tough in some ways, but the wives are real close and we help each other out.' Her voice grew earnest. 'The thing about the Army is the feeling that you *belong*. Gives you a safe, warm feeling. Now there's Sergeant Will Hann, the poor man. His wife, Mary, died in childbirth and the child died at three months – just before we knew we were being posted out here. Poor Mary! I can see her now when she heard the news. Fort Kearny? Never heard of it. Well, none of us had. You'd like Will Hann. Or there's Corporal Riley. He's a bit on the wild side, but his heart's in the right place. All he *needs* is a good woman. Good-looking, too!' She rolled her eyes. 'He's got lovely blue eyes! That's Corporal Riley.'

Lily finished her third cake, took another mouthful of beer and wondered when she had last eaten.

'It's kind of you,' she protested, 'but I think I must go back to England. My father is a widower and it almost broke his heart when I left home.' She sighed. 'I don't think I should consider marrying again just yet.'

Mae laughed suddenly. 'I just love the way you talk,' she said. 'It's so English – just how I imagined it! Oh yes, your poor husband. Cholera is a dreadful way to go . . . oh!' She clapped a hand to her mouth for the second time. 'Listen to me. Boyd's right, I must learn to think before I speak.'

187

'It doesn't matter,' said Lily, deciding that she must not outstay her welcome. 'I ought to see the fort commander and arrange some sleeping quarters. I did hear that there's a boarding house nearby.'

To her surprise Mae shook her head emphatically.

'I doubt you'll be taken in there,' she told Lily. 'They're Mormons and they don't care for the gold seekers. It's a real strange thing, but the Mormons and the Indians seem to get along fine and the military and the gold seekers get along, but there's no cross-over, if you get my meaning. Has your company had any trouble with the Indians?'

Lily thought guiltily about her own particular disaster, but answered that so far they had been lucky.

'Well, you just hope it stays that way,' Mae warned. 'They do have some very nasty habits. I guess you know they scalp their victims and sometimes they chop off their fingers.' She shuddered. 'But they say the squaws make good wives for white men. Some of the trappers have taken squaws and the children are real pretty, some of them. Raven-haired.' She sighed. 'Live and let live, I say, but Boyd is a soldier and he has to think like a dragoon. But those Indians are so clever. They can live off the land if they have to. Why, they know what roots to eat. They make a dough from acorns and earthworms! Me, I call that real clever. I wouldn't fancy eating it, mind, but it's clever!' She broke off reluctantly as her husband entered the tent.

'I hate to interrupt two ladies who are *talking*,' he grinned, 'but I thought Mrs Golightly would maybe be interested in that gentleman who's been in the sick bay. He's heading back east and I wondered – '

Mae clapped her hands. 'Oh, that's right!' she cried. 'Now why didn't I think of that? The poor man's been so ill with dysentery, but I did hear he was recovering. Lost his partner on the way out here – died of cholera.'

'He was English,' Boyd began, but his wife broke in again.

'Oh, that's right. He was. That cholera has a lot to answer for. I never could see why the good Lord invented diseases. What's his name, Boyd?

'Simms,' said Boyd. 'Harry Simms, I think it is.'

Suddenly Lily's brain made a startling connection. 'Simms?' she stammered. 'Was it *Henry* Simms? Oh, it surely can't be – and yet there can't be so many Americans travelling with English partners.'

Boyd frowned. 'Henry? Yes, that's it. Do you know him, then?'

'Not exactly,' cried Lily, a flash of excitement staining her cheeks as she jumped to her feet. 'But if it's *Henry* Simms – my husband was travelling with a Henry Simms and it might be the same man! Oh, Mr Tanner, please do tell me where I can find him? I must find out at once. It would be *so* wonderful; he could tell me all about Patrick.'

Boyd took her outside and pointed across the parade ground to a solitary figure on the far side, standing among the newly planted cottonwood trees.

'That's him,' he told her and Mae came out of the tent in time to see Lily flying across the bleached grass, calling back her apologies as she went.

'She's a real nice woman,' Mae observed to her husband, 'but she had so little to say for herself. I hardly got a word out of her. I guess it's because she's English.'

And Boyd, wise man that he was, agreed with her without so much as a smile.

Lily ran across the courtyard, dodging a water-barrel rolled by a soldier and narrowly missing a sergeant who was leading a fractious horse.

'Watch out, ma'am!' he shouted irritably, but Lily scarcely heard him.

'Excuse me!' she called. 'Mr Simms!'

The man turned in surprise. He was very thin with lank blond hair, and his face was haggard. In his eyes Lily saw the defeated look which she had seen so often in the faces of those who turned back.

'I'm Lily Golightly,' she told him breathlessly.

He looked puzzled. 'Ma'am?'

'I'm Lily,' she repeated. 'Mrs Lily Golightly. Patrick's wife!'

He frowned uncertainly. 'Mrs Golightly? But how – ?' His eyes widened with shock. 'You should be in New York.'

189

'Well, I'm not in New York. I'm here!' Lily insisted. 'I was following him. I meant to catch up with you at Buffalo and come to California, and then I . . .' She blinked hard and took a deep breath. He was staring at her, dumbfounded. 'I didn't want to be left behind,' she said. 'I married Patrick and I wanted to be with him. I was going to surprise him.'

She saw the sudden change of expression in his eyes and realized that he could not know she had seen Patrick's grave. To put him out of his agony she said softly, 'I know he's dead, Mr Simms. I saw his grave.'

His blue eyes registered relief, compassion and then pain. 'I buried him deep, ma'am,' he assured her. 'No coyotes going to dig him up. You must believe me – I did all I could. The doctor, too. I'm real sorry, ma'am. He was a good friend. I only knew him a few months, but it felt like we'd been friends all our lives. I guess it's like that between some people.'

'You knew him almost as long as I did,' Lily told him. 'In a way you probably knew him better than I, sharing this life on the trail the way you did. Mr Simms, I envy you.'

He smiled wryly. 'And I think I know *you*, Mrs Golightly,' he said. 'Patrick talked about you so much – when he wasn't talking about gold, that is! I envied him having such a wonderful wife and I looked forward to meeting you, but I never thought it would be like this.'

'I think Patrick would be pleased that we have met.'

'I like to think so. He used to say that if only you had a sister she'd do fine for me. He wanted to find me a wife.'

Lily smiled. 'It's really incredible,' she said, 'meeting you like this. I was talking to one of the Army wives and her husband came in and spoke about you. When I heard your name . . . well, they say God moves in a mysterious way.'

He shook his head incredulously. 'It's strange,' he said. 'When you said you were Lily Golightly, I couldn't believe it, thinking that you were in New York. Patrick sent you a letter before he died and I wrote too, to tell you how it happened. I sent it to the apartment Patrick had rented for you.'

'I shall have to read it when I get back to New York,' she

told him. 'And thank you for all you did for Patrick.' She sighed deeply. 'One week, Mr Simms – that's all the marriage we had. I had such high hopes and so many plans.' She shook her head. 'And now it's all over.'

There was a silence, then Lily went on, 'It was a miracle that *you* didn't catch the cholera too. You might both have died.'

Henry nodded. 'Your husband was very brave,' he said. 'Would you like me to tell you about it – that is, if you can bear it? I've got coffee on the fire. I'm camped right there now that I've left the sick bay.' He pointed to a small tent beside which a horse grazed.

Lily nodded and they walked across together.

'I owe you an apology,' she told him. 'I was so upset when I knew that Patrick planned to go to California and I was so sure it was your fault, I thought you must have persuaded him against his better judgement. Then when I spoke to the Golightlys, they told me that Patrick had persuaded *you*. Do you feel any bitterness, Mr Simms? Fate's been rather unkind to you.'

'No,' he said. 'In spite of everything, I'm glad I tried it. It's been quite an experience, you know that? I don't regret anything except Patrick's death. Maybe I'm sorry for myself, but I'm a whole lot sorrier for him. He was so keen to do it – to find gold – and so sure that we would.' He laughed briefly. 'He never doubted for a moment. To Patrick, California was the promised land.'

They reached the tent beside which a small fire burned dully, a blackened kettle resting in the embers. Henry busied himself wiping the mug clean for Lily's use and making up the fire.

'My mother would be amazed if she could see how domesticated I've become,' he laughed. 'I shall make someone a good wife one of these days!'

He produced a small log from inside the tent for Lily to sit on, and then squatted beside her, pouring the coffee.

'My own recipe,' he grinned. 'Water, coffee and sugar all boiled up together in the kettle. I hope it's not too sweet?'

Lily took the cheap tin mug and stared at it. It was white, with a red rim.

'What's the matter?' he asked.

'Was this the mug Patrick drank from?'

His eyes darkened. 'Could have been.' He raised his own identical mug. 'You can have it. I kept his watch for you and a few personal belongings, but I buried him in his clothes. I was going to bring the odds and ends when I called on you. He had a bible too.'

Lily smiled briefly. 'I gave him that before he left for America. Did he read it? He promised me he would.'

Henry had learned to lie. 'Oh, he read it. Most nights.'

She nodded, satisfied.

While she sipped the hot sweet brew, Henry told her quietly about Patrick's illness and death. Even though he tried to omit any details which he thought might distress her too much, she listened with growing horror and when she could bear it no longer she wept long and bitterly while he waited patiently and in silence for her to recover.

Then he changed the subject and told her with some humour about his first meeting with Patrick in the office, about their friendship and their decision to go in search of gold together.

'He had a way with words, your husband,' Henry said. 'I used to say it was the Irish in him, but he always claimed to be English. "With a name like Patrick? You've kissed the blarney stone," I told him.'

He was relieved to see Lily smile.

'His parents were as English as they come,' she assured him.

Henry laughed. 'It's a wonder the whole office didn't head for California!' he went on. 'Patrick used to hold forth whenever he got the chance – which was whenever his uncle was out of the way! You'd have thought, to hear him, that they were shovelling up nuggets by the pailful! Rich beyond the dreams of avarice. That's what he used to say. "We'll be rich beyond the dreams of avarice." Poor Patrick.'

He sighed, staring into the fire, then glanced up at Lily.

'Patrick was so proud of you,' he said. 'When he wasn't

talking about gold, he was talking about his Lily. We used to pull his leg a bit.'

'He told me about that in his letters.'

'I take it your father wasn't too keen on the marriage? Patrick said you had to persuade him to agree.'

Lily smiled. 'Did he tell you how we met?' she asked him. 'We bumped into each other, *literally*, in a downpour of rain, both running with our heads down. He was so apologetic, but it was my fault as much as his. I suffered a huge bump on my forehead which came up immediately, like an egg. He insisted on accompanying me home to explain and, of course, Papa asked him in. Patrick always believed that it was Fate. He fell in love with me – '

'And you with him.'

She hesitated fractionally and then said, 'Yes. At least, I didn't know I had, but Patrick finally convinced me – and then I did!'

'I can imagine!' smiled Henry.

'He was waiting for a letter from his uncle,' said Lily, 'to tell him to set sail for New York. Patrick's father and Albert Golightly were brothers. They had been estranged for years over a family quarrel, but then when Patrick's parents were dead, Albert wrote offering to take him into the firm. It was very kind and generous of him. How did you feel when you were told about the English nephew coming over?' she asked curiously.

Henry rolled his eyes expressively. 'We didn't think much of that idea,' he admitted. 'You can imagine. Uncle's pet! That's how we viewed him but when he arrived, as I said, we liked him. I guess we jossed him, but most people liked him. Anyway, you were telling me how you met.'

'Oh – well, it was all a mad sort of scramble,' Lily told him. 'Patrick had to persuade me to marry him and I had to persuade Papa to allow me to marry him – much against his better judgement. Poor Papa! I had known Patrick for such a short time. Papa thought it was much too hurried, but at last we persuaded him.'

'And you've no regrets.' It was not a question.

'Not really,' answered Lily after a moment's hesitation.

'It was what Patrick wanted and we had such a romantic courtship, although it was all so dreadfully rushed. Patrick saw the world through rose-coloured spectacles. We didn't really know each other at all, but he convinced me that was unimportant. He said we would have all our lives in which to get to know each other – and when you're in love nothing else matters, does it? Patrick did say *you* were recovering from a "heartache", she ended gently.

For a moment his expression hardened. 'Let's just say that it didn't last,' he said. 'I was a fool. The lady had a husband, but she said she loved us both and I wanted to believe it. But I got over it . . . Patrick saw to that. He talked to me about gold and I'm as greedy as the next man!'

'Is that partly why you gave up your job to go with him?' Lily asked. 'Because of the lady, I mean.'

He frowned, considering the suggestion. 'Maybe,' he said, 'although I didn't realize it at the time. It had just about ended when I met Patrick. Yes, maybe I wanted to get away from the whole sorry mess.'

'Life plays some strange tricks,' Lily observed. 'Like throwing us together here. I'm glad I met you, Mr Simms. It helps to know about my husband and about the way his life ended.'

'I was going to visit you in New York,' he assured her, 'when I got home. I would have told you all about it then, but maybe this way's better. Maybe out here in this wilderness is the right place for you to hear about it.'

'If only he could be here with us,' said Lily sadly and then they were both silent for a long time.

Lily broke the silence at last by saying, 'And now you're going back home? One of the soldiers told me. I am, too. I was with the Western Hope Miners, but I've bought my way out. Captain Wallis was reasonable about it – glad to get rid of me, I suspect. I was going to wait here for a family to travel back with, but I have my own wagon.'

She hesitated. 'The young lieutenant suggested that we could go back together, but I don't know – just the two of us?'

'I don't see why not,' Henry responded eagerly. 'I think

Patrick would approve and he'd know I would do my best to look after you. I guess tongues would wag, but who cares? Do you want to think it over?'

'I don't think so,' said Lily. 'It might be days before a family comes along and by then we could be on our way back to civilization. I must say the thought of a bath and a feather mattress and a change of diet is very tempting.'

'You can get a shower of sorts here,' he told her. 'The dragoons have rigged up a couple and they let us use them.'

Lily stood up. 'How marvellous! Just show me where,' she said with a smile.

He grinned at her alacrity. 'So are we going back together? Is that settled?' he asked.

'I think so. Yes, it is!'

'And we travel east tomorrow?'

'We do.'

'Shall I tell the camp commandant that we'll both be going?'

'Yes, please.'

He pointed out a ramshackle structure of poles and canvas. 'Apparently the military have only been here a matter of months,' he told her. 'That's why it's all so primitive. By the end of the year, they reckon it will look a lot more permanent.'

'I'm thankful I won't be here to see it,' said Lily and held out her hand. 'I'm so glad we found each other,' she said. 'I'll see you in the morning at daylight.'

'My pleasure, ma'am.' He clasped her hand and then looked down at it. 'Patrick said you had dainty hands,' he observed.

The moment lengthened until self-consciously Lily withdrew her hand, 'I heard you've been ill with dysentery,' she said. 'Are you sure you are well enough to travel tomorrow? You don't look very fit and I wouldn't want to rush you. Another day or two won't make that much difference, I have nothing to go back to.'

'I'm fitter than I look, ma'am,' he said with a smile.

'Are you eating properly? I shall cook tonight and you're welcome to share it.'

'I'd like to do that, but why not use my fire? I'll keep it in and it will save you searching for firewood.'

'Thank you. I'll be back later then, after I've had my shower.'

As Lily walked away, she was not conscious of the slight lightening in her step but she was aware, deep in her heart, that for the first time since Patrick's death the nightmare was receding. Tomorrow she was going home.

*

That night she slept badly and her frequent dreams were confused and unhappy . . .

The water was very warm and deep and tall reeds grew in it, waving their feather tops like banners against the blue sky. Lily swam as hard as she could, but made no progress through the water. Patrick's voice, whispering somewhere ahead of her, urged her on.

'I'm here, Lily. I'm here. Don't leave me,' and then the reeds closed overhead to form a tunnel and she swam through the tunnel, making slow headway, urged on by his voice whispering amongst the reeds. 'Lily, Lily! Stay with me,' and then the blue sky darkened into night and the reeds pressed closer so that she could no longer swim. She stood up and found the water was only knee-deep and began to force a pathway through the reeds which tried to close around her. They grew taller and became the trees of a forest, while somewhere ahead the voice still whispered, 'Don't leave me, Lily.'

'I won't. I promise,' she told him. 'I'll stay, Patrick. Oh, Patrick, where are you?' And then the voice became a bright light dancing through the trees, elusive and uncaring, and as she struggled toward it brambles scratched her bare arms and she saw to her horror that she was naked – but still she plunged on through the trees, fighting down her terror. Then she saw Patrick and screamed, for he was waiting in the clearing – his clothes and hair earthy from his stay in the grave, his eyes staring sightlessly, his mouth slack, his hands outstretched.

'Patrick,' she whispered and was afraid of him until two

196

large tears fell from his eyes and then her heart was full of compassion.

'Are you dead, Patrick?' she asked and he nodded sadly. His lips remained motionless, but the voice repeated, 'Stay with me, Lily. I didn't mean to die.'

As she reached out to touch his hands, he began to change, disintegrating slowly and horribly until he was no more than a mound of earth on the ground and Lily, kneeling to gather it in her hands, found that it gleamed with specks of gold . . .

As she awoke the dream began to slip away. Tears streamed down her face and she sobbed helplessly for a long time. When she had stopped, she scrambled out from the blankets and knelt on the mattress in her nightdress, her hands pressed closely together, her eyes closed.

'Dear Father in Heaven, please help me,' she prayed. 'Show me what to do. Guide me, I beg You, because I'm lost. I don't belong here and yet I'm not sure I want to go home. I put my faith in You, but I don't feel Your presence and without You I am nobody. I'm trying to be strong, but I'm weary and confused and if You don't help me nobody will. Maybe I should go home to Papa, but something tells me I should stay. Won't You give me a sign? Show me the way I should go? Just help me this once and I will try never to bother You again.'

After a long pause she added 'Amen', and then waited.

Outside she heard the distant call of a coyote and an answering cry from somewhere much nearer. Horses whinnied uneasily and a dog growled. Somewhere a cock crowed and she realized it must be nearly dawn. She could hear the footsteps of one of the soldiers whose spell of night duty was nearing its end, and somewhere a canvas flapped in the rising breeze. She thought about the sleeping fort and the soldiers like Boyd Tanner who would rouse up unwillingly at the first bugle call to splash themselves with cold water and wriggle into their uniforms, buttoning jackets with uncooperative fingers, straightening caps and buckling on belts for the early morning's inspection. The fort would spring into life and Mr Simms would be preparing to leave.

'You have about ten minutes to make up your mind, Lily

Golightly,' she told herself fiercely. 'Maybe God is not going to help you. If not, you must make your own decision and stand by the consequences. You either go on or you go back. Only two choices, so it's really very simple'.

Desperately she closed her eyes and tried to listen to her inner voice. She waited for a flash of inspiration, but none was forthcoming Then she began to think of Patrick and his eager, touching faith in California. Could she turn her back on all his dreams? Death had robbed Patrick of his chances, but she was still alive and maybe she could make his dreams come true. She opened her eyes again.

'That's it, then,' she said, surprised. 'I must tell Mr Simms that I'm going on. He must go back alone.'

Without allowing herself time to reconsider, she pulled on her boots, wrapped herself in a blanket and hurried across the courtyard to Henry Simms' tent.

'Mr Simms, are you awake?' she hissed. 'It's me, Lily Golightly. I must talk to you.'

To her surprise he opened the tent-flap immediately. His blue eyes were alert, though his hair was still tousled. She thought he looked at her anxiously.

'Mrs Golightly, I was coming over to see you,' he said. He came out of the tent and Lily saw that he was already fully dressed. 'Look, I don't know how to say this,' he began, 'I want you to understand that it's nothing personal against you, but I've changed my mind and decided to go on.'

Lily's eyes widened. 'But so have I!' she cried. 'I'm going on to California – that's what I came to tell you!'

For a moment they stared at each other in disbelief, then on both faces a look of relief replaced the earlier apprehension.

Lily's eyes shone. 'Then we might as well go *on* together.'
'Why not?'

'Mr Simms!' she cried. Impulsively she threw her arms round his neck and kissed him and as his arms went round her in a hug of delight, the blanket slipped from her shoulders and she stood in her nightdress. However, Lily, was too excited to be troubled by such a breach of propriety and for a moment they clung together, their hearts too full for words.

198

When at last they drew apart, they looked at each other and Henry held up an imaginary glass of champagne. 'To California!' he said. Lily copied him and the imaginary glasses touched. They were going on.

Chapter Nine

With Fort Kearny eighteen miles behind them, the following day found the Western Hopers on the move once more. The sun shone from a cloudless sky and promised a hot day. Kate stumbled along with head bent, surveying her dusty cracked boots with disfavour.

'The seventeenth of June,' she said wearily, 'and we're not even half-way to California! I must have been mad to come on this crackpot expedition. Too blooming headstrong, that's my trouble. My ma always said I was headstrong and she's right. "You never stop to think, Kate. Your head will never save your legs." That's what she used to tell me. Ooh, I used to get so mad!'

Hester, walking opposite her, tapped the haunches of the leading mule and said, 'Get along now.'

She gave Kate a quick glance, her eyes narrowed. Usually Hester rode in the wagon from where she drove the mules, while the two girls walked. Today she had sent Ella on an errand to give herself the chance of a talk with Kate, and Charlie was perched in the driver's seat out of hearing.

Kate went on, 'I should have listened to Lily. She told me I shouldn't come, but I wouldn't take no for an answer and now look where it's got me! My back aches, I've got blisters on my heels and my lungs are full of this stinking dust. I must have been mad. *Mad!*'

'Look on the bright side,' Hester suggested. 'You *have* found yourself a husband – you wouldn't have met Amos if you'd stayed in England. Soon as he can find that preacher, you'll be wed.'

Kate twisted her mouth. '*When*,' she said. 'The preacher seems to have vanished into thin air!'

'Still, you've got yourself a nice young man,' repeated Hester. 'Kind, thoughtful, *honest*.'

Kate did not miss the emphasis which Hester laid on the word and looked up sharply.

'Meaning what?' she asked defensively.

Hester shrugged. 'Meaning that if he's honest with you, shouldn't you be honest with him?'

Colour flamed in Kate's cheeks and with her stick she struck out furiously at the inoffensive mule who, startled, tossed his head and laid back his ears.

'It's none of your business!' cried Kate. 'I *am* going to tell him in my own good time. I was going to tell him today – I don't need you nagging me.'

Hester snorted. 'Leaving it a bit late, aren't you? He's going to look a real fool. Who else knows?'

'Only Lily.'

'And the doctor?'

'How does he know?' Kate demanded. 'I never told him.'

'Then you should have. You ought to be looking after yourself and the baby.'

'I'm fine,' Kate said sullenly, 'and I don't need looking after. Nobody's ever looked after me before, so I don't reckon they'll start now.'

'Your husband should look after you,' Hester persisted. 'When's it due?'

'I'm not sure,' Kate admitted. 'Maybe around September . . . or October. We'll be in California by the time it's born.'

Hester shook her head. 'Well, if you want my advice, you'll tell that young man as soon as possible. You're only storing up trouble if you don't.'

Kate was silent for some time, but then she looked up and all her defiance had crumbled.

'He'll throw me over,' she said tremulously. 'I know he will, and it's so nice being "promised". He's so kind, like

201

you said, and I can't bear it if he throws me over – but he will. *I know it.* Sure as eggs is eggs! It's too good to last.'

Two tears rolled down her face and she wiped them away with the back of her hand, sniffing loudly.

'Maybe so,' said Hester, 'but you've still got to tell him. And don't expect miracles, Kate. He's a fine young man, but you've treated him very badly by not telling him before and nothing can alter that. If I was him I'd send you packing – and if I was his mother, I'd expect him to do just that. You've only got yourself to blame, but that's something you have to learn in this world.'

'That's right!' said Kate. 'Make me feel worse! Rub it in. I thought you were on my side, but now I know better.'

'Right's right,' Hester told her sternly, 'and you must tell him the truth and hope for the best. Perhaps he'll surprise us.' They walked on thoughtfully, the mules moving between them.

'I'll kill myself!' Kate burst out suddenly. 'If he throws me over, I'll kill myself. That'll teach him. Then he'll know!'

'Don't talk so wild,' said Hester, quite unmoved by this outburst. 'You'll do no such thing and you know it, so don't try to frighten him with that sort of talk.' She scratched at an itch on the back of her neck. 'Who was the father?' she asked, her curiosity getting the better of her. 'Married man?'

Kate tossed her head. 'No, he was *not* married,' she said. 'He was a policeman, if you must know. He said that getting married so young would ruin his chances of promotion and his mother would never forgive us.'

'Hmm!'

'He was ever so handsome,' Kate said wistfully. 'It could be a handsome baby, but I bet it won't be. I bet it'll take after me.'

'You'll have to wait and see,' said Hester. 'Meantime you ought to eat a bit more and drink some milk.'

'I used to,' said Kate, 'when I got it from the folks with the goat, but then their cow fell sick so now they need all the goat's milk. But it must be all right; I feel it kick sometimes.' She sniffed again and wiped her nose on her sleeve. 'Anyway, I don't want a baby,' she said. 'I hate babies.'

202

'You should have thought of that a bit earlier then,' Hester told her. 'Are you keeping well?'

'I suppose so. I never think about it.'

Hester snorted at Kate's lack-lustre tone. 'It's no good taking that attitude,' she said sharply. 'We've all got our worries, so don't expect everyone to fall over backwards just because you've got yourself in the family way. If Amos does marry you, you think yourself *very* lucky and you make it up to him every way you can. It's a lot for a man to take on, and it's more than you deserve if you ask me.'

'I'm not asking you,' responded Kate sullenly. 'You just keep going on about it.'

'Well, someone's got to make you see reason,' said Hester, 'so it might as well be me. Now, you tell Amos before the sun goes down or I might tell him myself!'

Kate whirled to face her. 'You wouldn't dare!' she gasped.

'Try me,' said Hester, unperturbed.

'Why, you – !' Kate was speechless. 'You wicked old bat!'

'But you said *you* was going to tell him,' Hester reminded her, 'so why get so upset?'

'I am!'

'Well, now's your chance,' said Hester triumphantly. ''Cos here he comes.'

With a shock, Kate turned to see Amos riding towards them. He carried a bunch of wild flowers and greeted the two women cheerfully with a mock salute. Springing down to stand beside Kate, he handed over the posy with a flourish.

'Flowers for the fair!' he said and kissed her. She mumbled something and he suddenly became aware of the tension between her and Hester.

'What's going on?' he asked, disappointed that his romantic gesture had not been properly appreciated.

'Nothing,' replied Kate quickly.

At the same time Hester said, 'Women's talk. Not for the ears of young men.'

He looked from one to the other, then shrugged. 'I won't ask, then,' he said. 'Do you like the flowers, Kate?'

'They're lovely,' answered Kate, avoiding his eyes.

'I've got some news,' he told her, 'about a preacher.

There's definitely one in the train *behind* this one – the Michigan Pioneers. Hollis said it might be easier to fall back, rather than rush on to try and catch up the parson in the train ahead of us. I said I'd ask you what you thought.'

There was a long silence and then Hester clutched at her stomach and groaned.

'I've got the skitters today, something awful,' she invented. 'Real bad, it is! I'll have a word with the doc about it in case I'm taking the wrong physic.'

Kate, immediately recognizing her ploy, tried to delay her departure by asking what physic she was taking, but Hester was not to be diverted.

'Never you mind,' she said. 'That's between me and my gut. Now, if you'll excuse me – '

Left alone with Amos, Kate groaned inwardly, cursing Hester. She had intended to find the right time to talk to Amos, but now she had been precipitated into it and she felt resentful. Surely Hester would not *really* tell Amos? Kate hesitated. Suppose she did? It would all sound so much worse – and maybe there *never* would be a right time to tell him. As he slipped his arm round her waist, she felt herself stiffen.

'What's the matter with you?' he asked, his voice concerned. 'What's Hester been saying? She's upset you, hasn't she?'

'She's been telling me what I must and mustn't do,' said Kate bitterly. 'Meddling old fool!'

He stared at her in surprise. 'I thought you liked her,' he said. 'I thought you said you were like one of the family.'

'Perhaps that's the trouble,' said Kate. 'She treats me like a daughter and thinks she can order me about.'

She took another swipe at the long-suffering mule and Amos said, 'You *are* in a state. Do you want to tell me what it is? If she's upset you, I'll have a word with her. I'm not having her bother you.'

'No!' cried Kate. 'What she said was right.' She took a deep breath. 'I've got something to tell you, Amos, which you won't like – it's about before I met you – '

'I don't want to hear it,' he told her. 'I thought we'd settled all that. No dragging up the past – it's forgotten.'

'This can't ever be forgotten,' said Kate. 'It's about me and another man. Can't you guess?'

'No, I can't,' he replied, 'and lay off that mule.'

'It keeps treading on my feet,' said Kate.

'It does not,' he protested. 'You keep whacking it for no good reason.'

'That's right. Argue with me!'

He looked at her in exasperation. 'Kate,' he said, 'I don't understand it. You're not usually like this. You said you *liked* the animals. Whatever is wrong with you?'

Kate struck the mule another and final blow and then she hurled the stick away and cried, 'I'm having a baby, *that's* what's the matter!' and folded her arms tightly over her chest, waiting for the worst to happen. She walked on, her eyes unnaturally bright, her head thrown back.

Amos stumbled along beside her in shocked silence.

'Well, say something, for Christ's sake!' Kate told him. 'Or didn't you hear? I am going to have a baby!'

'I heard the first time,' he whispered.

'Nice news, isn't it?' Kate went on recklessly. Because she could not soften the blow, some devil within her made her add insult to injury. She *knew* with a quiet desperation that Amos would leave her and she did not want to cry. If she could feel angry enough, she could watch him go and shout, 'Good riddance!' She opened her mouth and sucked in a great gulp of air.

'Well, say what you've got to say,' she demanded. 'Get it over with. I don't care.'

'A baby!' he repeated. 'Jesus Christ!' He stumbled again as though all the strength had left his legs, but Kate hardened her heart. He was going to break *her* heart so she might as well break his, she thought illogically.

'Why didn't you tell me?' he gasped. 'You should have told me.'

'I'm telling you now,' she said. She caught hold of the mule's halter and tugged at it; the animal jerked its head uneasily and grunted, but she hung on grimly.

Amos glanced sideways and saw what she was doing. 'I've told you – let it be,' he said.

Kate clung on tenaciously as the mule tried to free itself from her grasp. She was pulling its head sideways so that the other mules were forced to deviate slightly from the trail, while behind them the wagon creaked protestingly and Charlie yelled at her from the driving seat.

Amos caught hold of her wrist and tugged her violently away.

'I said "Let them be"!' he cried. 'They're just dumb animals. What the hell's the matter with you? It's not their fault if you've made a fool of yourself.'

'Oh, so you think I'm a fool? Thanks very much!' Kate rubbed her wrist, which was smarting from his vice-like grip.

'Yes, I do. Don't you?'

'No,' she said. 'I didn't want to be this way.'

'You must have said "Yes"!'

'Must I?'

His eyes widened. 'Didn't you?'

'Mind your own business, Amos Carp,' she told him angrily. 'You're as bad as Hester.'

He turned towards her. 'Ah, so *that's* what you were talking about.'

Kate looked at him with mounting fury. He was going to leave her, she knew it with a sickening certainty, yet still she could not bring herself to behave properly. She ought to admit that she was ashamed; she ought to apologize for having kept the truth from him; she ought to admit her fault and ask his forgiveness, but she could not do any of these things. She could only taunt and abuse him so that when he went she could convince herself that she was glad to see the back of him.

She had taken a quick look at his stricken face and her conscience smote her. He was suffering and she was making no effort to help him. She was genuinely fond of him and hated to see him so white and shaken, yet what else could she do? If she tried to comfort him, he would repulse her and then she would suffer more. And she had suffered long enough, she told herself fiercely, recalling her humiliation at the hands of the pompous policeman and her subsequent treatment at the hands of Mrs Harrington and the Golightlys.

Only Lily had been compassionate and now Lily had gone back home.

Kate thought bitterly of the child within her and told it silently, 'If only you knew the trouble you've caused me.' Life was so unfair.

And now, she thought, she had got Amos on her conscience along with everything else. It was too much! There he was tottering along beside her wondering whether or not he ought to do the decent thing and stand by her. She sighed heavily. The sun, blazing down on the back of her neck, was making her hot and sticky. Still, it made a change. They'd had a lot of rain.

Looking at Amos she saw his anguished expression and couldn't bear it any longer.

'Look,' she said wearily. 'Just sod off, will you?'

He turned to stare at her in disbelief, shocked as much by her language as by her peremptory dismissal.

'Go on,' she said with a dismissive wave of her hand. 'I don't need you or anyone else. Don't bother with the "Goodbye" speech. Just leave me alone!'

Still he stared at her open-mouthed, his eyes full of the reproach she could not endure.

'Well, go *on*, can't you!' she shouted. 'This is your chance – why don't you take it? I'm not the first girl to have a baby on the wrong side of the blanket.'

For a long minute they stared at each other like two dogs bristling for a fight, then he turned and swung himself up into the saddle.

Kate looked up at him, white-faced. 'So that's it, is it?' she asked. 'It's over between us.'

'You're right it is!' he said. 'No woman's going to make a fool out of me. Oh boy, I take my hat off to you, Kate – you certainly fooled me.'

'Oh, hark at you!' she cried. 'Acting all hard-done-by and innocent. You're not exactly perfect, are you? Stealing money from your own father and letting someone else take the blame! Oh yes, I remember. I should have known the sort of man you are,' she rushed on. 'I should have guessed you'd never stand by me. All that hogwash about love! You've

207

never loved anyone but yourself, Amos Carp, if you want my opinion.'

He began to protest that he had never really stolen the money.

'Oh no!' she cried. '*Course* you didn't. And I'm not really having a baby. Couple of blooming saints, aren't we? Well, I reckon I'm better off without you, Amos Carp. At least I only got myself into trouble – you dropped your best friend in the soup!'

'I didn't really – ' be began again.

'And no more did I!' she taunted, patting her abdomen. 'This here's a balloon!'

They glared at each other until she screamed, 'For God's sake, get out of my sight!'

Amos kicked his heels into his horse's sides and wrenched at the reins and the unfortunate animal sprang forward with a whinny of protest.

'They're just dumb animals!' Kate shouted after him. 'Remember?'

He clattered away along the trail in a cloud of dust and Kate trudged on, sick with disappointment. 'What did you expect?' she asked herself bitterly. 'Hearts and flowers? Hester was right. No decent man's going to want me.'

She put out a hand and patted the mule. 'I'm sorry,' she said. 'You're a nice old thing and I didn't mean to hurt you. I don't mean to hurt anybody, but somehow I just do.'

She blinked back the tears and addressed the baby. 'It's all your fault,' she told it shakily, 'but we'll get by somehow.' She wished she could believe this, but the doubts crowded in. How exactly would they get to California – if they ever did? The prospects were daunting and Kate was under no illusion about the future. Nothing ever came easy in her experience, which meant that if they were going to survive she would have to find a way of earning money. Of course she hoped to find gold, but if she didn't – what then? And how could she spend all day searching the rocks and gullies for gold is she had a baby to look after? She knew from bitter experience that babies were time-consuming and could not be ignored. And even if she did have time to search for gold, she might be one of the unlucky ones and find the other stuff – pyrites or whatever they called it. That would be just her rotten luck. She sighed. Perhaps someone in California would want a maid who was good with freckle waters and complexion pastes. But would they want a maid with a baby? It seemed most unlikely. Some girls, of course, sold their babies to rich women who could not have any of their own, but Kate didn't know any rich women.

'We're stuck with each other,' she told the baby grimly.

The child kicked feebly in her womb, but Kate could not say whether in approval or dismay. 'Something'll turn up.' And she patted the mule again and whispered into its ear that to make up she would give it an extra handful of food when the going got rough.

*

Later when Hester returned, she was surprised to find Kate dry-eyed. Before she could ask what had happened, Kate said, 'You'll be glad to know that the wedding is off.' Her voice was hard. 'And I suppose the reason why is all over the company by now. But I don't care, see? You can all go hang!'

'Now, Kate,' Hester began, 'you don't have to take that tone with me. You had to tell him some time and today was as good as any.'

Kate glared at her. 'Don't you "Now, Kate" me,' she cried. 'I don't care what you or anyone else thinks of me. I done wrong and I'm stuck with a baby, and that's all there is to it. If I've got to be on my own, then so be it, so don't waste your pity on me, Hester Cooper, because I don't want it!' She tossed her head defiantly. 'I'll get by without your help or anyone else's. I don't need Amos Carp or any other man, come to that, because men make me sick, if you must know. They just make me sick!' She swallowed hard. 'All they think about is themselves and what they can get from a woman, so don't you go giving me any more lectures about Amos Carp, thank you very much. I'm better off without him!' Her voice shook. 'Some people have no backbone, no stomach for a fight.'

209

'Now that's a silly way to talk,' said Hester, taken aback by Kate's attitude. She felt aggrieved that the girl was not more abject in the face of this reversal. Kate was a nice enough girl – Hester meant her no ill-will – but deep down it galled her to think that after behaving so badly with the young policeman, she might have made a better marriage than Ella who had only managed to ally herself to Jess Cash. Jess was a worker but he did not have the good looks of Amos Carp, who was also a teacher and as such respected by the community. Hester, conveniently forgetting the circumstances of Ella's hasty wedding, felt that if Kate ended up as the wife of a teacher after the way she had behaved, then there was something very wrong somewhere. She did not put all these feelings into words, and would probably have denied them if anyone else had done so, but she felt much happier now that Kate was not going to 'outdo' Ella in the marriage stakes and she had been prepared to show great compassion for the girl. Now it seemed that Kate would not allow her this show of magnanimity.

'It may be silly talk,' said Kate, 'but that's the way I feel. And it just might interest you to know that Amos Carp is no angel either. His halo slipped years ago when he was sixteen – stole from his own father! Ah, that surprised you, didn't it? Wonderful Amos Carp's fallen off his pedestal, hasn't he?'

'I don't believe it!' exclaimed Hester.

'Well, it's the truth!' cried Kate. 'He told me himself. And what's more, he blamed it on his best friend and got *him* into trouble. Oh yes. Amos Carp – decent, *honest* Amos Carp – is not all he's cracked up to be. Ask him if you don't believe me. So maybe I'm better off without him. Who wants to be married to a blooming thief? I'm sure *I* don't!' She stopped to draw breath, then added, 'But don't worry, since you disapprove of me so heartily I shan't bother you any longer. I shall take my things and find myself another place – I'll go and see Captain Wallis right now.'

If this last remark surprised Hester, it surprised Kate even more, because she had not intended to make such a rash gesture. The words had sprung to her lips, however, and

210

now she could not take them back so she tightened her mouth and straightened her back. 'So you'll be well-rid of me,' she told Hester, enjoying the older woman's obvious dismay. 'Don't bother to pretend you're not glad. A girl like me – a *fallen woman* – must be a great embarrassment to you.'

Hester stammered, 'But, Kate, I never meant you should – I mean, where will you go?'

'Who knows?' said Kate airily. 'But I'll find somewhere – somewhere where I'm not made to feel like dregs in a teacup!'

Before she could lose her resolve, she flounced to the back of the wagon and pulled herself up into it, snatching up her few belongings and wrapping them in a shawl. At that moment Ella returned and stared as Kate climbed down from the wagon, her face pale but determined.

'Kate?' asked Ella. 'What are you doing? Where are you going?'

Kate glared at her. 'Best ask your ma,' she told her. 'She'll tell you all about it. I'll just say goodbye.'

Ella's mouth fell open. 'Goodbye?' she began, 'but why . . . where – '

'She's acting real silly,' put in Hester, recovering quickly. 'Real silly!'

Ella frowned. 'I just saw Amos,' she said, 'riding like a mad thing. Face like thunder. I called out to him, but he wouldn't answer. Have you and him had a row, Kate?'

'You'll have to ask *her*,' said Kate with a jerk of her thumb in Hester's direction. 'It's all her doing. I'm off.'

'But Kate, please – ' begged Ella. 'What's all her doing?'

'It's not my doing – ' Hester began.

'Oh yes it is!' snapped Kate furiously. 'You and your high and mighty airs. Holier than thou! That's what my ma would have called you. So blooming righteous – you're too good to be true. Couldn't wait to see me go down, could you? Well, I hope you're satisfied. If I fall flat on my face, you'll be the first to cheer. Oh, I know your sort, Hester Cooper. Well, I don't want help from folks like you. It would choke me!' She turned to Ella. 'I pity you, having a ma like that. I really pity you!'

Ella's face crumpled. 'Oh Kate, please don't be like this. Just tell me what's happened.'

'I told you – ask *her!*'

'But, Kate –' She put a restraining hand on Kate's arm, but Kate pushed her away and hurried away towards the head of the column.

Hester said loudly, 'Let her go. She'll be back.'

Kate heard and hardened her heart. Now Ella would be upset, she thought, and would quarrel with her mother. Serve them both right!

She hated Hester for being right and now she hated Ella for being married. Unreasonably, she also hated Lily for having turned her back on the whole business.

'You can all go to hell!' she told them fiercely. 'You can all rot.'

Kate marched on, feeling like a martyr, her pathetic bundle tucked under one arm; she ignored the curious stares of people she passed, but she slowed down abruptly as she saw Daniel Miller ahead of her. He was leading his horse, which was lame, and he was alone – that was unusual, for he liked company and rarely lacked someone to talk to. Kate recalled what Amos had said about him. Now *that* really would upset Hester, she thought vindictively. That would show the old bag! Impulsively, she hurried to catch up with him and he turned when he heard her.

'Good morning, ma'am,' he said, smiling and raising his hat.

The word 'ma'am' warmed Kate's cold heart a little and she allowed her face to relax slightly into a semblance of a smile.

'Is it?' she said.

'Going someplace?' he asked, noticing the bundle under her arm.

'Looks like it, doesn't it?' She took a deep breath. 'I suppose you've already heard,' she said. 'Bad news travels fast.'

'I heard.' He grinned again. 'Lucky fellow, I said to myself. The policeman, I mean.'

'He didn't seem to think so,' retorted Kate bitterly.

'More fool him, then! Missed a treat, I should say.'

Kate swallowed hard. If he was too kind to her, she would start to cry and that would not do at all. Her new role of tough survivor hardly allowed for such weakness.

'I don't need him,' she declared. 'I don't need Amos Carp either. All I need is a way to earn some money and then I can do without a husband.'

Miller glanced at her. 'That's no problem,' he said, 'for a pretty girl like you. I could arrange it.'

They walked on and the full import of his words registered in Kate's jumbled thoughts.

She knew exactly what Daniel Miller had in mind, but in her present mood she did not care. Kate imagined Hester coming to her to beg forgiveness for casting her into a life of sin; then she would toss her head and say, 'It's too late now, Hester, you should have thought of that before you decided to meddle.' Everyone in the company would blame Hester and that thought gave Kate a small glow of comfort, She, Kate, would be pitied, but Hester would be shunned for the part she had played in Kate's downfall. Yes, she would let it be known that it was all Hester's fault.

'You'd make yourself a tidy little sum,' Miller told her. 'Set yourself up, and the baby too. Time you get to California, you'd be a rich woman.'

'A *rich* woman?' asked Kate dubiously. 'Rich? Are you serious?'

He grinned. 'Well, rich enough!'

She shifted her bundle to the other side and looked up at Miller's face.

'I don't know – ' she said. 'I mean, it's not really right.'

He laughed. 'Might as well be hung for a sheep as a lamb,' he suggested. 'I'd take good care of you – see everyone treated you with proper respect.'

Kate looked at him, astonished. 'Respect?' she echoed.

He nodded. 'Why not? Oldest profession in the world, remember. Nothing wrong in it. Look at Lady Hamilton.'

'Who's she?'

He shrugged. 'Lord Nelson's mistress,' he said. 'Nobody treated her with disrespect.'

'Didn't they?'

'Not on your life!'

'She was a *lady*?'

'Certainly.'

Kate sighed. It sounded very unlikely, but she was prepared to clutch at straws and was grateful to Daniel Miller for not treating her like an outcast.

'I don't know,' she said again. 'Sounds a bit funny; I'll have to think about it.'

Miller took the bundle from her. 'Let me carry that,' he offered.

Kate swallowed hard. He was being kind to her again. In spite of her past and the fact that she was pregnant and unmarried, he was being *kind*.

He grinned down at her. 'You could move in with me,' he said, 'as part of the arrangement. I'd protect you. It's not right for a lady to live alone – not in a wagon train with so many men. Specially a pretty one like you.'

'I don't feel very pretty,' Kate whispered.

'Take my word for it,' he told her. 'You're a very handsome woman, and properly handled you could make a lot of money between here and California. We could be a very successful partnership. The way I see it is this. You've got what the men want. I mean, what is the one thing they lack on this Goddamned expedition? Women! Poor devils – all they can do is eye the few married women and dream about it. Know what that backtracker told me a few days ago? Some of the men get so desperate, they go with squaws – or try to. One guy he knew was approached by a squaw, so he gave her the money and followed her away from the wagons. Out of sight, see. Just as he was getting his pants down, some of the braves turned up and she just ran to them, laughing. It was a set-up, you see.'

Kate frowned. 'A set-up? You mean – '

He nodded. 'Course it was. They knew he'd be too scared to do anything about it. Certain death with all those braves around, tomahawks at the ready. Oh, that's happened more than once. Our poor lads getting set up by Injuns. It's a crying shame when all they want is a bit of loving.' He gave

214

her a quick sideways glance and saw that his story was having the desired effect. 'Far from home and lonely, they'd give their right arms – most of them – for a few minutes with a woman. A pretty woman, that is.' He shook his head. 'Why women give it away beats me. If I was a young woman, you wouldn't find me giving it away for love. What good does that do? You gave it to your young policeman, didn't you? Was he grateful? Did he treat you with respect? Course he didn't!'

Kate sighed. 'He said he loved me,' she whispered. 'I thought he did.'

'And did he?'

'He couldn't have; none of them did when it came to the push. Not that there were many,' she added quickly. 'Just a few before the policeman.'

'And why ever not?' he said. 'A willing girl like you is bound to have lots of admirers, so why not make some money out of it? You women don't realize how lucky you are. Do you ever hear of men being paid for what they give a woman? Course you don't. But a pretty woman can ask a fair price for her favours and that's all it is really. Favours.'

Kate looked at him thoughtfully. Put like that, it was beginning to sound very reasonable. 'And I'd be with you?'

'You would,' he said. 'I'd beg, borrow or steal a wagon and set you up in it. Your own little home. I'd make it really smart and I'd sleep alongside in my tent. You'd have your callers and I'd be nearby to make sure you were treated with respect and all that. Any man did anything you didn't like, you could holler out and I'd be in that wagon like a shot and the man would be out on his ear! Sitting in the dust, wondering what hit him!'

Kate laughed and he went on, 'We'd go fifty-fifty on the money. I can't say fairer than that, can I?'

Still Kate hesitated. 'But when the baby comes – ' she said doubtfully. 'I wouldn't want the baby to know what I'd done.'

'How would it know?' demanded Daniel. 'You'd stop when the baby arrives – well, before then. You couldn't go on too long. By then you'll have all the money you need, so you can afford to stop. When we reach the gold fields, the company's going to split up and the men will be scattered. They're not going to tell anyone, are they?'

Another thought struck him. 'The beauty of it is,' he continued, 'that you can do what you like for the next few months and you can't get caught out like most single women. You've got the baby on the way, so nothing else can happen! It's foolproof as far as you're concerned. You think it over. If you say "No" that's the end of it. Saying "No" is a woman's privilege, whatever the question. But you can trust me, Kate. I'd never hurt a woman; I love them too much. If you say "No", we'll still be friends.'

'You won't be earning any money if I say "No",' Kate pointed out.

He laughed cheerfully. 'You don't think you're the only woman who's thought of this little money-spinner, do you? There'll be plenty more who'd appreciate a manager to help them get rich.'

'Not in this company,' said Kate. 'They're all married or else too old.'

'There you are, then,' exclaimed Daniel triumphantly. 'You're the lucky one. If you say "No" I'll probably move on to the company up ahead. I've been thinking about it for some time now – several young women there, I'm told. I'm not trying to talk you into anything you don't want to do,' he added ingenuously. 'I just thought it would help you out of a spot. It's not me that's having a baby and it's not me that needs money.'

Still Kate hesitated. 'What about you?' she asked after a long silence.

'What, you and me, d'you mean?'

She nodded.

He grinned. 'You wouldn't charge me, would you?' he asked.

'Why not? You're a man same as the others.'

'But I'm your *manager*. Your *protector!*'

It was Kate's turn to smile. 'I haven't said "Yes" yet,' she reminded him. 'But if I did say "Yes"?'

'Half-price, then,' he suggested.

'No,' said Kate, suddenly generous. 'I couldn't charge you. Not if you're really going to protect me like you say, and set me up and all.'

'I *will* protect you,' he told her. 'Cross my heart.'

There was another silence.

'If anyone dares say a wrong word to you,' he said, 'you tell me and I'll deal with them. I told you, I'll look after you.'

'Just until the baby's born.'

'Who knows?'

Kate sighed deeply, then turned suddenly and held out her hand.

'Mr Miller,' she said, 'it's a deal.'

They shook hands solemnly and as they walked on and Kate didn't know whether she was glad or sorry.

Chapter Ten

The land through which the company now travelled had undergone certain changes since their departure from Independence. The tall rich grasses of the eastern prairie were surrendering to the sage-brush – a plant which had previously appeared in isolated clumps but now grew more profusely and soon would dominate the landscape, stretching endlessly on all sides. The Western Hopers would grow tired of the interminable grey-green vista, but it flourished where nothing else would grow and when trodden underfoot its familiar aroma lingered briefly in the air. Trees so plentiful in Missouri now disappeared from the landscape except on the mud-banks in the middle of the river, where a few stunted cottonwoods and willows still survived.

The weather, too, altered significantly as they drew nearer to the deserts. The earlier rainstorms were growing less frequent and the temperature was rising along with the dust!

After leaving Fort Kearny, the Western Hope Miners followed the River Platte on its south bank. Ahead of them – as they knew from Wallis's weekly briefing – they had more than three hundred miles to go before they reached Fort Laramie, which was the second and probably the last military post which would offer them aid. After that, they would be thrown entirely on their own resources. From Fort Laramie the river divided into the North and South Platte and they would follow the northern branch along its southern bank and to reach it they would have to cross the southern branch of the river. Wallis planned to do this at a spot called Upper Ford.

Ella sat on the driving seat with the reins held loosely in her hands, oblivious to a bank of dark grey clouds on the western horizon and wishing that Kate was still friends with them. There were rumours that she was living with Daniel Miller, but Hester had forbidden her to make further inquiries and Kate herself had made no contact with any of them. Ella was depressed and resentful, blaming her mother entirely for Kate's defection. She had enjoyed exchanges of confidence with Kate and the fact that they were both expecting babies had been a bond, even though Ella's child would be born on the trail while Kate expected to be in California before hers was due.

This morning the interminable jolting of the wagon made Ella feel sick, but if she walked her back ached intolerably. She felt lethargic and generally sorry for herself and Jess was no help, with his frequent jokes about her ungainly shape and constant nightly demands for what he called his 'connigal rights'. But although she felt out of love with her husband and cross with her mother, the real cause of her depression was her son. Today Hester walked beside the mules with Will on her hip and as Ella watched them her secret fear surfaced again, black and terrifying. He was never going to grow up! Ella was convinced of it. He would get bigger and heavier but he would never walk, never talk, never feed himself. No one else would admit this; aware of the conspiracy of silence on the subject Ella felt that she alone faced up to the facts and she found the burden intolerable. Night and day she was haunted by the prospect of her son's future and the vision horrified her, for the time would come when she would not be able to carry him – it would be a physical impossibility. Then how would he get about? Would he become an invalid? Bedridden? The picture was unutterably depressing from her own viewpoint, but when she considered it from Will's it was disastrous.

'He's just a cabbage,' she whispered now, her heart heavy with dread. 'A poor little cabbage. No fun. No excitement. No nothing. What a life – if you can call it a life.'

Sometimes she wished he had never been born, although he had been such a beautiful baby – 'a golden boy', the midwife had called him – with smooth glossy skin, huge eyes and firm, well-shaped limbs.

She flicked the reins listlessly and watched her mother, Will and Jess as they moved along beside the mules.

'I hate you,' she muttered to Jess and her mother. 'Both of you! But not you, Will. Of course I don't hate you.'

Another major problem was Will's bodily functions, over which he had no control at all and Ella assumed he never would. She wondered vaguely if the doctor could give him anything to 'buck his ideas up', but almost at once acknowledged the futility of the idea. Will was never going to change, soon she would have another child to care for and the prospect looked bleak.

Jess turned his head suddenly. 'Wind's swung round,' he called. 'It's coming from the north-east. Reckon we're in for a storm.'

Apparently other people thought so too, for ahead of them Ella heard similar shouts and everyone began to prepare for it.

Ella reached behind her to the big wooden chest and pulled out the oilcloths which she handed out.

'I'd best have Will up here with me,' she called to her mother. 'Then if it gets bad, I'll put him inside.'

Hester handed him up and he sat blankly on the seat beside her, his head on one side, his eyes vacant.

'Oh, *Will*,' whispered Ella. 'I do love you, but oh Lord! I do wish you were different.'

As if to compensate for this disloyal thought, she put an arm round him and hugged him fiercely before fastening him into his straps so that he could not roll off the seat.

The dark clouds, driven by the wind, now began to race across the sky towards them, casting an unnatural gloom over the wagon train. The wind increased rapidly and then without any warning, large hailstones began to fall as a flash of lightning lit up the sky and was followed by a terrific crash of thunder. Shouts of astonishment at the hailstones changed very quickly to cries of alarm as the size of them increased to that of small eggs. The unprotected mules and oxen began to suffer cuts, bruises and bleeding and – horribly frightened – they instinctively turned their heads away from the storm, which made the wagons swerve violently and caused even more havoc.

'Get under, you two,' Hester screamed and Ella needed no second bidding. She unstrapped Will who cowered beside her, whimpering like a puppy, and dragged him over the back of the seat and under cover.

'It's all right, Will,' she comforted him. 'It's only a horrid old storm!'

The 'horrid old storm' raged on and Ella clung to the side of the rocking wagon as the mules plunged off the trail with Hester and Jess trying desperately to hold them back. Ella prayed that the wagon tongue would survive, but almost as she mouthed the words there was a crack as it splintered under the strain.

'Hell and damnation!' cried Jess as the desperate mules finally broke free and galloped away, heads down, in search of non-existent shelter from the punishing hailstones.

Without the mules, the wagon's erratic progress came to an abrupt halt and Hester and Jess scrambled back into it, cursing and complaining, gingerly feeling their heads and shoulders which had borne the brunt of the onslaught.

'God almighty!' cried Jess. 'That's the damnedest storm I've ever seen. Just listen to her!'

'Good job I had my bonnet on,' Hester told Ella. 'That saved me from the worst, but lordy, that hurt! I shouldn't care to be stoned to death if that's what it's like. I should reckon – '

Another crash from somewhere outside sent Jess scrambling to the back of the wagon to peer out.

'Jesus!' he said. 'Harper's wagon's been pulled clean over. I'd best give a hand soon as it eases up.'

'Where's Pa?' asked Ella.

'Don't ask me,' Hester snorted. 'Never where he's wanted, that's for sure. Said he was going up ahead to talk to Captain Wallis. Reckons that some of the men's getting lazy and not doing their guard duty. I dunno – maybe they are and maybe they're not, but he won't do no good tittle-tattling like that. Leave well alone, I told him, but "Duty's duty", he said, "and I do mine so they should do theirs".'

Taking off her bonnet, she felt her head. 'Lordy, my head's sore. I'm surprised it's not bleeding. My shoulders and back too — what a pounding, and it still hasn't let up. Will all right, is he?'

Ella hugged him. 'He's fine,' she said, 'but where've our mules gone?'

Hester shook her head. 'God knows! We'll have to go look for them when this lot's over. Hailstones like giant marbles, they are. Just listen to 'em — it's a wonder they don't come through the canvas.'

They sat and marvelled as the hail continued to drum on the wagon's cover and beat a dull tattoo on the unresisting prairie.

'It'll flatten what grass there is,' said Ella.

Hester made no answer and Ella ventured, 'I wonder how Kate's getting on in all this? I wish she was here.'

'Well, she's not,' snapped Hester, 'and she's only herself to blame. No one sent her away, it was her own decision. Hussy, that's what she is. Getting involved with a man like Miller — I don't know what got into her, silly girl!'

'You do know,' flared Ella. 'You *nagged* her into it and all because of Amos. You know you did. Now I've got no one to talk to.'

'I merely told her a few home truths,' said Hester, 'so don't go picking an argument with me because I'm not in the mood for it. If she wants to become a byword, that's her business.'

'Just let me *ask* her to come back, Ma,' Ella pleaded. 'She might say yes.'

'No! You let her be. No one sent her away and she can come back any time she likes. No one's stopping her. But we're certainly not asking her — not with what she's doing.'

'You don't know what she's doing,' Ella argued. 'She may not be doing anything. Just your nasty mind.'

'My nasty mind, is it?' cried Hester. 'What, living alongside

222

Miller and most likely sleeping with him too. Everyone says so, so it's not just *my* nasty mind.'

'She may not be sleeping with him.'

'And pigs might fly!' said Hester. 'Probably sleeping with half the men in the company, if the truth be known.'

Ella gave her mother a spiteful look. 'Would Pa be in that half, d'you think?' she asked.

Hester's answer was to slap her face and Ella lapsed into an aggrieved silence.

She had never yet bested her mother in an argument, so as usual she retired into a deep sulk. As a child she had used this weapon very effectively and had frequently sulked for days at a time, until eventually one or other of her parents had been forced to appeal to her better nature with the promise of a bedtime story. Today, however, the sulk failed dismally.

'And take that look off your face, Ella Cash!' Hester snapped. 'Just you remember we're all in this together and there's no place for tantrums. Before long you'll have another kid and you'll be needing us more than we need you, so put a better face on things and don't let me hear any more about Kate Lester.'

For Hester, it was a long speech and Ella was surprised into silence.

When at last the hailstorm ended as abruptly as it had started, they all ventured out under a still lowering sky to assess the damage.

Confusion reigned. Many of the animals had broken free and were now scattered over a wide area. The oxen that remained were in a highly fretful state, their sad eyes rolling mournfully as blood ooozed from numerous small cuts and bruises along their backs. The mules were skittish and wild, kicking out spitefully in their distress. Two wagons had collided. Buckets, kettles and water barrels which normally hung on the outside of the wagons were now lying around on the ground. While their owners retrieved them, others rode off in search of their lost animals.

Wallis decided they would have to stop over for the whole day so that the damaged wagons could be repaired and lost animals recovered. The doctor was sent round to apply liniment where necessary, while the women brewed hot coffee to soothe everyone's ragged nerves.

Hester began to fill buckets and the kettle with the fallen hailstones, while Ella lifted Will down from the wagon. She talked to him until eventually Jess and her father came back with the runaway mules; then after several cups of coffee Jess and Charlie helped the blacksmith to replace the broken tongue with a new one from the store wagon. Hester melted the hailstones she had collected and used the water to do some washing, which she then hung up to dry on a makeshift line.

Seeing the row of undergarments, Ella found the homely sight reassuring and suddenly, for no other reason, she felt better and began to hum cheerfully under her breath.

*

Looking into the small mirror, Kate took a deep breath and then another and nervously smoothed her frizzy hair. She had brushed it so hard that it now stood out round her head like a ginger halo. Her throat was painfully dry and her eyes were bright with anxiety as Daniel held up the lantern and surveyed her, his head on one side, an approving gleam in his eyes.

'*Vairy* nice,' he said. 'You look a real treat, Kate. I'll wager there's not another woman on her way to California who could hold a candle to you. Don't shake your head at me, I mean that. You do look very tempting.'

Kate relaxed a little. Daniel Miller had a way with words and he made her feel like a queen. That was the strange part about it, she thought, grinning back at him. She had teamed up with Daniel only days ago, but already he had managed to restore her battered self-esteem. Here she was, waiting for her first client and feeling good about it. Or almost good. There were times when her conscience troubled her, but she had only to catch Daniel's eye and he would wink at her with that small quick movement of his head which made her feel as respectable as the next woman. His approval was all that she needed to convince herself of the rightness of what she was undertaking.

'D'you think he'll like me, then?' she asked, anticipating his answer.

'Like you?' Daniel slapped his thigh as though she had said something very witty. '*Like* you! He's going to *love* you, Kate. He's going to adore you. A young man always adores his first woman.'

Kate's eyes widened in alarm. 'His first woman. You mean I'm his – you mean – oh Lordy!'

Daniel grinned. 'Lucky man. What a way to start. You'll be hard to follow – you know that, Kate. Hard to follow.'

But Kate was worried. 'I won't know what to say,' she wailed. 'If he doesn't know how to, you know – well, how to go about it. What shall I say to him? Daniel, perhaps this isn't – '

Daniel laughed. 'You'll know,' he said. 'Remember, you're the best. What did I tell you last night? You are the very best, Kate, and I should know. I've had plenty of women – all the women I ever wanted. And you' – he jabbed a stubby finger into her ribs – 'you are the best. The *cream*. You said you'd trust me, didn't you?'

Kate nodded. 'I wish it was you tonight and not a stranger.'

'A *client*,' he corrected her. 'They're not strangers, they're clients, Kate.'

'Sorry, clients,' she amended, 'but I do wish – '

'Listen, Kate,' he told her. 'You'll do fine. You look really handsome in that nightdress and with your hair all fluffy, and I'll take the lantern with me – '

'You won't listen, will you?' she begged. 'You promised not to listen. If I thought you were listening, I'd be all embarrassed.'

'I *won't* listen. I'll go for a stroll around, but I won't go too far, so if you holler I'll come back at the double. But you won't need me. He's a nice young man and he's dying to give it a try. Only seventeen and never dipped his wick. He must be all of a tremble with excitement. You'll make him the happiest man in the whole company.'

Kate considered. 'Perhaps if he's so young we could charge him half-price,' she suggested.

'Half-price!' Daniel was scandalized. 'Certainly not! If you go dropping your charges, you'll never get rich. Leave the financial side of it to me. He'll pay me before he sets foot in the wagon, don't you fret, so you won't have to think about such sordid details. You just think about – ' He stopped. 'Hullo, I think that might be him!' He put his head through the opening of the wagon and nodded. 'It's him.' He pulled out his watch and glanced at it. 'Five minutes early! That's how keen he is. Now, give me a quick kiss and be a good girl. You go to it and earn a few bucks for that baby of yours.'

This reference to the child startled Kate and she clutched her abdomen.

'You're sure the – the client won't mind about this?' she asked. 'I mean, it does show a bit now. You're sure he – '

But Daniel had gone, taking the light with him and plunging her into darkness. Kate took another deep breath. She heard low voices and the clink of coins and her heart began to race. She blessed the darkness; if she was blushing, her client would never notice.

'The *cream*,' she told herself nervously. 'You are the *cream*, Kate Lester. You can make men happy.' Suddenly she was glad he was going to be young and innocent and inexperienced.

She put up both hands in a last vain bid to subdue her rebellious hair, then closed her eyes and breathed deeply.

'Good evening, ma'am.' The voice was almost squeaky with nerves.

Opening her eyes, Kate saw the dim outline of a young man kneeling at the foot of the 'bed'. Instinctively she pulled the bedclothes up around her, then remembered and let them fall back again.

'Good evening,' she said and was astonished to hear her own voice sounding quite normal. Daniel had told her to talk a little at first, unless the client showed signs of desperation in which case she was to 'go right ahead'. She began the little speech she had prepared earlier. 'What a storm that was,

226

this morning,' she said. 'Crikey! Hailstones like eggs. I do hope you wasn't too inconvenienced by it. So sudden, I could hardly believe my eyes.'

The young man stared at her, removed his hat but said nothing. Now that her eyes were getting accustomed to the darkness, she could see him more clearly by the light of the moon. He was sturdily built, with a round face and dark hair that hung thickly to his shoulders. His face was clean-shaven and he clutched his hat to his chest.

'Bit of luck, though,' she elaborated, 'the storm, that is, because it gave us all a bit of a break.'

Still on his knees, he edged towards her and said suddenly. 'In more ways than one.'

Kate looked blank. 'What?' she said.

'In more ways than one,' he repeated. 'A bit of a break.'

'Oh?' Kate was still mystified.

'A break,' he explained. 'The wagons got broke, leastways some of them did. Break. Broke.'

Light dawned and Kate beamed with relief. 'Oh yes! A break in more ways than one. That's very good, that is.'

He placed his hat on the trunk and wiped his forehead with his right sleeve. 'It sure as hell is a hot night,' he said.

'Yes.' He looked so young that Kate felt almost maternal. With an effort she resisted the urge to ask, 'Does you mother know you're here?'

'What's your name?' she asked instead. 'Daniel – I mean Mr Miller – wouldn't tell me. He says that it's best to let a man volunteer his name if he sees fit. Some men like to keep their names to themselves.'

'Jedediah!'

'What?'

'My name, ma'am. It's Jedediah Wilcox.'

'Oh. That's a nice name.'

'Kate is a pretty name too.'

'Is it?'

'I reckon so.'

'Thank you, Mr Wilcox.'

'You can call me Jed.'

'Thank you, Jed.'

Silence fell and she could see the Adam's apple move in his throat.

'Ma'am – '

'Yes.' Kate was suddenly rather hoarse.

He leaned forward. 'I've only got half an hour,' he whispered. 'Maybe we should start right in.'

'Who said that's all you've got?' she demanded indignantly. '*I* never said only half an hour. Did Mr Miller tell you that?'

'Yes, ma'am, he sure did. But I don't mind as long as we don't waste too much time. I'm real keen, ma'am, to – to – '

'I know,' said Kate hastily. 'Well, I'll speak to Mr Miller later, but you just forget about him. Half an hour, indeed!'

'Yes, ma'am. Should I take off my clothes?'

Kate hesitated. 'I suppose so,' she said. 'Or maybe just your boots and trousers.'

'Pants, ma'am.' He was struggling to pull off his right boot. 'We call them pants in this country.'

'Pants, then,' she said, 'and I suppose you could get into the bed.'

'Or we could lie on top of it,' he suggested hoarsely as the left boot came off. 'I want you to know I really appreciate this, ma'am, and my friend is all raring to go too, but not tonight. I think he's booked in for Thursday.'

'Oh, is he?' Kate tried to sound only mildly interested. 'Thursday, you say.'

'He likes to pretend he's a randy devil, ma'am, but I've beat him to it! Oh Lord, ma'am, you do smell sweet!' He dived towards her, his thin legs pale in the moonlight. Then he was snuggling down beside her, wrapping his arms round her, pulling up her nightdress. Kate thought it was rather like playing with a frisky, rather *precocious* puppy and she thought at one stage that she was going to laugh at his eager antics. Fortunately, she managed to keep a straight face and five minutes later she was as pleased as he was when he achieved his first triumph with small cries of rapture.

'Oh, ma'am!' he exclaimed, collapsing beside her, sweating and breathless. 'You're the most wonderful thing! You are!

You were so – so – Oh ma'am, that was really – Wowee! That was really – '

Kate took him into her arms and cuddled him as he babbled on and thought how nice it was to have given him so much pleasure. It was a good feeling to know she had made him so happy. She began to stroke his hair, but a few moments later she realized that he had stopped telling her how wonderful she was. Was he asleep? She stared down at him. He *was!* She smiled and went on stroking his hair. Daniel was right. He had told her that all men were different. 'Some need a long time,' he had said, 'and a lot of coaxing; some need a couple of minutes and won't give you so much as a "thank you"; some are too old and can't do it at all – they just need a bit of a cuddle and some kind words.' Daniel seemed to know an awful lot, she reflected, and not just about men and women. She wondered how far he had gone on his stroll and was tempted to call him in to look at their first satisfied client, sleeping peacefully in her arms.

Jedediah! What a terrible name. Like something out of the bible. 'And Jedediah begat' – only he wouldn't beget anything with her, because she was safe while her own child slept within her. 'You didn't mind, did you?' she asked the child silently. 'It's not going to be for long. Just until we get a bit of money. I hope you don't mind. You're my real baby. This is just a young man; he's just a lad really, like you.'

She thought she wouldn't mind having a grown-up son; it was just babies she hated.

After a while, Kate heard Daniel outside the wagon whistling under his breath. Then he banged several times on the wooden side and she kissed her client awake.

'Time to go, Jed,' she told him and was rewarded with a beatific smile of gratitude before he scrambled back into his clothes.

'I'll most likely come and see you again,' he told her earnestly, 'if that's all right with you. I'll kill me a few game-birds and sell 'em, I'll soon get the money.' He jammed his hat on his head and said, 'You were wonderful, ma'am. I'll tell my friends. Well, good night, ma'am.'

When he had gone, Kate tied her hair back into two

bunches and was smoothing down her nightdress when Daniel came in to hear all about it.

Kate was not telling much, however. 'I don't think I *should* tell,' she said primly. 'It's between my client and me – unless I have a problem, and then I'll ask your advice.' She looked up at him, grinning suddenly. 'But it went all right. He was fine. And it felt better than I expected. No, not that way! I mean, I thought I'd feel like a rotten apple, but I didn't.'

'Didn't I tell you!' Daniel crowed. 'You're a natural, Kate. You'll be talked about from here to California! No, no,' he amended quickly, seeing the sudden dismay on her face. 'I was only joking. Of course you won't be talked about. But you'll be *dreamed* about. How's that?'

'*Dreamed* about?' repeated Kate softly. 'Yes, I'd like to be dreamed about.'

She waited to see if *he* would ask to join her in bed.

'You'd best get to sleep,' he told her. 'Must get your beauty sleep.'

He threw her a kiss and left her and soon she heard him outside settling into his tent.

'You're a decent old stick, Daniel Miller,' she whispered.

Sliding down into bed, she wriggled about to find the most comfortable position on the scratchy hay-filled mattress.

'If I'm ever rich,' she thought, 'the first thing I'll buy is a real feather mattress.' Her eyes gleamed with anticipation at this heady prospect and then she fell to thinking about Jedediah and wondering about his friend.

*

Ten days later Matt Wallis sat under the darkening sky and surveyed his assembled company with mixed emotions. They sat around him on an assortment of trunks, saddles and rolled blankets, while the less pernickety sprawled on the well-trampled grass. They were all there except the youngest children who were in bed, two men who were sick and the four men on watch. Wallis saw from their faces that though many still regarded him with polite respect, many others looked disgruntled – and he noticed too that the number of men wearing the latter expression had increased since the previous meeting. Bart and Gabby Smith looked sullen, he thought; Daniel Miller watched him with his usual arrogance; Amos Carp looked resentful, as though the blame for Kate Lester's fall from grace might somehow be laid at *his* door.

'To hell with them all,' he thought wearily. Whatever had induced him to think another overland trek would be a good idea? He should have stayed at home. Profitable it was *not* – his own 'cut' would merely suffice to take him back east. Perhaps this last expedition was a mistake. He should have stayed in Virginia where he belonged and where he was appreciated. Still, he ought not to complain. As Mrs Golightly had reminded him so scathingly, he had chosen to take them across and he had known how it would be. That fact should make it easier, but somehow it didn't, because already the rules which had been agreed were being evaded by a combination of laziness and perverseness, while some of the men seemed to think they could manage the wagon train better than he could. Their original admiration was being eroded by the day-to-day strains of trail life and they now gave only grudging acceptance to the agreed rules. There was a general disappointment that their captain was not superhuman, as they had hoped.

He took out his watch, saw that it was eight o'clock and lifted a hand for silence.

'We'll make a start,' he said.

'The Coopers and Cashes aren't here,' someone called.

Wallis shrugged and nodded to a man called Marcus Lutts who had the unenviable task of recording, albeit briefly, the 'minutes' of each meeting. He stood up with alacrity and cleared his throat importantly, and Wallis thought wearily that for Lutts these meetings were the highlights of the adventure.

'June 25th 1849.' Marcus paused to smile round encouragingly, but dashed by the total lack of response, he went on, 'Item one. There is now a shortage of timber, since so much of the stores had to be used to repair tongues and wheels after the hailstorm. Captain Wallis said that since there is no standing timber, that is growing trees – '

Someone groaned and another called out, 'We do know what standing timber is!'

He pressed on hastily: 'Captain Wallis said that if anyone had anything to spare, it should be given to supplement the store.'

'And nothing has been,' Wallis broke in. 'There has to be something you can do without.'

'Such as?' cried a middle-aged man, his tone belligerent.

'Such as grandfather clocks, rocking-chairs, fancy cabinets, bedsteads and similar,' said Wallis, 'which you all cling to in the hope that you'll get it to California. You won't, take my word on it! Long before we get there, you'll have abandoned it. So hand it in now and we'll all get to California that much earlier.'

His words provoked an outburst of indignant conversation, but before anyone rose to challenge him on the subject Ella, Jess, Charlie and Hester arrived with muttered apologies for being late.

'I'm just saying,' Wallis repeated for the benefit of the latecomers, 'that we still have very little timber for repairs, so if you've any furniture you don't need, donate it to our rapidly dwindling store – or next time you break a tongue or an axle the blacksmith might have to say "No".'

He nodded to Lutts, who cleared his throat again and continued.

'Item two. It was agreed some time ago that the playing of mouth-organs, fiddles and the like should stop at eleven, so as not to inconvenience others, and there are complaints that this is *not* being observed.'

Someone muttered, 'Oh, for Pete's sake! Does it matter?'

Lutts' face reddened. 'Yes, it *does*,' he said, his voice squeaky with indignation. 'What's the good of agreeing something and then not abiding by the decision? That's the whole point of taking a vote.'

He again looked at Wallis for support, but before he could speak, Bart called out, 'What's it to be for disobeying – fifty lashes?' and there was a roar of laughter.

Only Wallis did not laugh. 'You have a point,' he told Bart coldly. 'If this company is to hold together there have

232

to be rules, same as there are back home. Back home, the law provides the punishments. Here, we'll have to provide our own if it ever becomes necessary. Not a happy thought, but if you can't all pull your weight and act responsibly –' His shrug was a thinly veiled threat and an uncomfortable silence followed.

This was broken by Lutts, who said, 'Well, that's the end of the minutes,' and hastily sat down.

Wallis stood up with a sheet of paper in his hand, his feet slightly apart.

'Two things on tonight's agenda,' he stated. 'Firstly, dogs not being properly controlled and secondly, Sunday travel. Mrs Cooper has raised the latter point and all I can say is that the needs of the animals take precedence over everything, including observance of the Sabbath. Without the animals, we're all lost. If there's not enough grass when we stop on a Saturday, we've got to move on the Sunday until we find some.'

There were a few shouts of dissent and he held up his hand. 'This question is *not* open to discussion and it's not going to be put to a vote. I know the route and I know the risks. You don't. If anyone feels that strongly about observing the Sabbath, you'd best drop out of the Western Hope Miners and wait for a company that *will* observe it. That's that. Now, the other point about dogs not being properly controlled. Mr Willcox? This was your point, I believe?'

A man stood up, his hat clutched to his chest. 'Me and my brother Ned's got an unsympathetic neighbour,' he began. 'I won't mention no names, but there's a dog in their wagon that's more trouble than a cartload of monkeys. Tips over my coffee, steals my pork and two days ago it frightened my team so they ran away and nearly had the wagon over.'

Daniel Miller called out, 'Shoot it!'

A surly man in his thirties leaped to his feet. 'Anyone shoots my dog, I'll shoot him!' he cried. 'That dog's going with me to California. That dog's the smartest animal that ever I saw. That dog's more to me than –'

Wallis said brusquely, 'Then keep it under control or *I'll*

233

shoot it. Now, a report on what's ahead.' The man blustered on for a moment but was eventually pulled down by his neighbour as Wallis continued, 'We are, as most of you know, on our way to Fort Laramie. You'll soon be able to pick out Laramie Peak in the distance. On the way to it we shall pass both Courthouse and Chimney Rocks – you'll have heard of them – and beyond them Scotts Bluff where there's a small trading post – or was last time I was in the area. Who can tell? We're still east of the Continental Divide; this side of it the rivers drain east, when we pass it they drain towards the Pacific. Incidentally, *when* we cross it you'll likely not even notice.'

He nodded to Lutts, who unrolled a large map with which they were all very familiar and Wallis stabbed at it with his forefinger.

'First we drop down into Ash Hollow here, here's Courthouse Rock and Chimney Rock, here's Scotts Bluff and then Fort Laramie. Any questions? No? Good.'

He had given no one time to voice a question and there was some laughter at his peremptory manner, but it was not entirely unkind.

He went on. 'Right, until we get to Laramie we've got the Platte River on our right. After Laramie, it will be the North Platte winding past the Laramie Range and after Fort Laramie we've also got a steady climb into the Black Hills.' He saw Kate whisper something to Daniel Miller. 'So called,' he said with a slight nod in her direction, 'because of the dark trees that grow there – pine and juniper – which trees, incidentally, are sacred to the Indians.'

Kate smiled her thanks and Wallis found himself once more remembering her companion. Recently, for some reason which he did not understand, he had regretted her departure. Did he *miss* the prim English woman? He thought of her now, seeing her dark hair, the pale face and smooth forehead. And such clear blue eyes. She had always looked so delicate, yet she had endured as much as anyone else and often with far less complaint. At the time of her going he had been glad to be rid of her, glad to relinquish responsibility for her, yet her image returned frequently as though to reproach him. He had left her alone at Fort Kearny to await companions for the journey back east – companions who might not treat her properly and who might not appreciate that, recently widowed, she was in need of comfort and reassurance. Damnation! Perhaps he should have put her in the temporary care of the military . . .

With a shock he realized that everyone was watching him curiously and he wondered how long he had allowed his thoughts to wander. He glanced quickly at Lutts.

'The Black Hills, Captain,' Lutts prompted. 'Pine and juniper trees.'

Wallis nodded. 'We'll soon be leaving the plains and the going will get rougher, so be prepared. I don't want any belly-aching. We haven't reached Fort Laramie yet. Any questions? No? Good! Right, last thing I want to say is that in ten days' time it'll be July 4th – '

'Nine days!' shouted Jess.

Wallis paused, then nodded. '*Nine* days,' he agreed. 'It'll be Independence Day and if you want to celebrate we'll stop at noon and take a half-day.' There were some cheers and whoops and desultory applause. 'I guess the committee will want to fix up some way to celebrate, so if anyone has any ideas – ?'

Several hands shot up and others, less patient, shouted out.

'Run up the American flag!'

'Fire a salute!'

'Let's have a hoe-down!'

The earlier bad feeling was immediately dispelled by the prospect of a celebration and there followed fifteen minutes of earnest and amicable consultation, at the end of which a programme of entertainment had been provisionally arranged. The meeting was then concluded and the assembly broke up, but it re-formed almost at once into smaller groups who talked for a while longer before drifting back to their respective wagons.

Wallis watched Kate's retreating back and wondered who would be tonight's lucky man. Word had spread and he understood that her services were in great demand. No doubt, he thought, the price was rising. He saw Daniel's arm go round her shoulders protectively and suddenly imagined himself walking beside Lily Golightly. Turning abruptly, he began to walk away from the camp, trampling a path through the sage-brush. Skirting the grazing oxen, he avoided a group of tethered mules and automatically averted his eyes from a man squatting with his trousers round his ankles.

So many men, he reflected, and only a handful of women. And, of course, it *had* to be Miller who master-minded the project. Daniel Miller would find a way to make money if he was shipwrecked alone on a desert island! And yet he didn't dislike the man. But how would he feel towards Miller if Kate was the widow and Lily the whore? His mouth twisted as though he were in pain. Jesus Christ, he'd kill him! No, that was foolish talk. Lily Golightly was on her way back to New York and from there she would then return to her own family in England, where presumably she would be safe from the Millers of this world.

He frowned, trying to recall any snippets of information about her. She had married her husband just before he left England, so they had had very little time together. He imagined her digging with her bare hands to unearth her buried husband and his throat contracted in sympathy. He saw her again as she explained that she was turning back — her eyes vivid in her white face, her small mouth framing the words carefully, afraid of saying the wrong thing or of losing her fragile self-control.

'Hell!' he said aloud. 'I should never have left her like that.'

He stopped to relight a half-smoked cheroot and lingered, hands on hips, to survey the surrounding prairie. Wherever he looked, it stretched for miles, the green grass and grey sage-brush both warmed into amber by the sun which hung low and large in a sky streaked with trailing clouds. The high plains. How eager they all were to be through it. How little anyone cared for its wild beauty . . .

Wallis pulled himself up sharply.

'You're getting maudlin,' he told himself irritably. 'It's that damned woman. She's getting to you. Forget her. Women aren't for you.'

He had told himself this for the past nine years and had always been able to believe it. Even now the memories were agonizingly sharp. He had made his way into the western wilderness in an attempt to escape the past, and after nine years the wild country and the solitude had wrought their miracle and today he could no longer remember his wife's face with any real clarity. The bitterness was fading also.

'Rest in peace, damn you,' he muttered grudgingly.

Overhead a buzzard wheeled and out of the corner of his eye he saw a quick movement as a small animal scurried for cover.

There was at the same time a burst of laughter and a few isolated rifle shots which he recognized as target practice. He wished they could come upon a buffalo herd; it would give the men the chance they had been waiting for to show their prowess. The action would also help to get rid of the hostilities which were growing within the company. Hardly surprising, really, with so many strangers thrown together haphazardly. The presence of a few more women might have checked the bawdy language and careless manners that were creeping in, but then again they might have aroused jealousies. It was a moot point.

He recalled with nostalgia the years he had spent alone in the hills, fishing the streams, eating wild berries, hunting elk and buffalo as well as the dainty pronghorn and deer. He had trapped beaver and traded the pelts for coffee and sugar. The Indians had, for the most part, left him severely alone on the occasions when their paths crossed. He had explored the Colorado River and then turned, following the Green River to the foot of Bitter-root Range. By that time he was a changed man – the country did that to any man who surrendered himself to it. He returned to Virginia, but was not ready for the security of life on the farm. Instead he had volunteered to lead a company of emigrants to Oregon. That same year James Marshall had found gold in John Sutter's mill-race and a new rush west had begun. Guides and leaders were needed to escort the enthusiastic innocents from one side of the continent to the other. Such men were easy to find, but good men were more rare and Matt Wallis knew, without conceit, that he was one of the few.

Chapter Eleven

The next morning Matt Wallis's prayers were answered, for the camp was awoken just before four by an excited shout.

'Buffalo to the east!'

The company – most having slept in their clothes – responded with roars of delight and, reaching for their firearms, they sprang down from their wagons, eager to share in the excitement of the long-awaited buffalo hunt. Unfortunately, only a limited number of men had horses or ponies suitable for the chase, and these men were now watched with deep envy as they saddled up.

The buffalo herd was a comparatively small one consisting of perhaps a hundred beasts who were grazing with apparent unconcern about a mile away. As they moved slowly forward with their heads down, they gave the Western Hopers a first-class opportunity to study them. Silhouetted against the rising sun, each beast showed the distinctive buffalo outline – slim, smooth flanks and heavy shoulders covered with thick brown hair which extended over the head. The bulls stood over five feet high at the shoulder, but there were cows and calves among the herd.

Hester, her arms folded, watched tight-lipped as her husband talked with the man in the following wagon, offering him the earth for the use of his pony. She made no effort to hide her satisfaction when Charlie returned disappointed.

'Course he's not going to let you have it,' she told him. 'I could have told you that, Charlie Cooper. A buffalo hunt's what they've all been waiting for. Why should he give you the chance?'

'But he's too old,' Charlie grumbled. 'Damned old fool! He must be forty if he's a day.'

'And you're nearing fifty!' she cried. 'You both ought to have more sense. Fine mess we'll be in if you get yourself killed and all for a bit of sport.'

Behind them Ella climbed heavily out of the wagon and then lifted Will down on to her hip; together they watched the first few hunters roar off in the direction of the buffalo. More men followed, whooping and yelling in their eagerness, foolishly alerting the herd which turned inquiringly towards the approaching horses.

'God almighty, that's Jess!' shouted Ella, clutching Hester's arm and pointing. 'What the hell's he doing out there? Where'd he get that horse from? Damn and blast him! And there's Amos Carp right behind him – and that dreadful Daniel Miller.'

By this time the whole company had ranged itself alongside the wagons, eyes straining towards the disappearing hunters.

'They'll scare 'em clean away, young idiots!' grumbled Charlie. 'No more sense than jackasses, most of 'em! No more sense than they were born with. Damned greenhorns!'

As if to prove his point, the buffaloes took fright at last and hunters and hunted blurred, dwindling into the distance in a cloud of dust and a rumble of hoofbeats.

'Well,' said Hester, 'guess that's the last we shall see of them for some time. We'd best get breakfast on the go. I just hope to God they keep their wits about them.'

'Just wait until I get my hands on Jess,' cried Ella.

Charlie shook his head wistfully. 'There's something about buffalo,' he said. 'Stirs your blood.'

'Doesn't stir mine,' snapped Hester. 'Staying in one piece and getting to California is what stirs mine. Finding gold and getting a bit of luxury – that's what stirs my blood. You've spent your whole life riding round steers, Charlie, so what's special about buffalo?'

Ignoring his muttered answer, she set off with a gunnysack in search of fuel and Ella, with Will beside her, prepared to milk the cow.

The buffalo, meanwhile, were instinctively leading their pursuers over the worst terrain, where the ground was rough and pitted with gopher holes and the sage-brush was dense enough to be hazardous. At last, inevitably, one of the horses stumbled and a cry went up from its rider who was flung headlong to the ground; but no one stopped to help him as they all raced on, firing indiscriminately toward the retreating buffalo but all so eager to make the first hit that they could not be bothered to take proper aim. The herd was moving fast about three hundred yards ahead of them when, without warning, some of them wheeled abruptly and headed back towards their attackers in a body. The hunters, taken by surprise, hestitated as the buffalo thundered towards them. A shot rang out, followed by a cry of pain and rage, one of the men clutched a bleeding ear and screamed that he had missed almost certain death by less than an inch.

In the following confusion, a warning shout went unheeded and a furiously charging buffalo bull drove his horns into the soft belly of Amos Carp's horse. The terrified animal, crazy with pain, threw up his head and Amos was thrown backwards on to the ground. At once the buffalo turned towards him while the wounded horse stumbled in an effort to retain its balance and then staggered away. Amos, panic-stricken, scrambled to a kneeling position as the enraged buffalo bore down on him. He flung himself sideways at the very last moment, just as Daniel Miller bore down on them, guiding his horse with his knees. He steadied the rifle and fired twice at the buffalo, wounding him in the flank and slowing his charge. Two more bullets from another rifle brought the huge beast crashing to his knees, where he was quickly and triumphantly dispatched. The rest of the buffalo galloped away to regroup and no one seemed inclined to follow them. One of the Harpers hauled Amos, mercifully uninjured, up behind him and then set off in pursuit of the injured horse who was now running eastwards in the company of five or six buffalo.

It had all ended so quickly, but the men were in a seventh

heaven of delight. They gathered to slap each other on the back, exchange experiences and congratulate each other on their one dead buffalo. Within minutes, they were skinning it and the tail had been cut off as a memento and awarded to Daniel Miller, who had saved Amos's life by his shooting and was the hero of the hour.

They now had the problem of getting the meat back and it was decided that two men would share a horse, the spare mount being used as pack animal. Nothing would be wasted. The best meat would be broiled or cooked on a spit; the liver would be eaten raw; offal and bones, boiled in a kettle, would make excellent soup. Some might even roast the intestines. It was all fresh meat and would be greatly appreciated.

When the hide had been removed and flesh cut from the bones, the men still hesitated, reluctant to relinquish what was left to the coyotes and birds of prey. They stood round looking down at the bloody skeleton, while the man with the bleeding ear argued passionately with the man who had nearly killed him.

Amos said, 'What about the tongue? We've forgotten the tongue,' and that, too, had to be removed and added to the unappetizing pile of raw meat and offal which, wrapped in the hide, was already laid over the saddle of the pack-horse.

It was only when they were remounting and preparing to leave that someone realized Jess Cash was missing.

'Jesus!' exclaimed Amos. 'What happened to him? Where did he go?'

They looked at each other sheepishly, ashamed at their oversight.

'We'd best go find him,' said Amos, but as they all began to turn their horses, Daniel Miller held up a hand.

'No need for all of us to go,' he said. 'Some can go back with the meat. He can't be far away. I'll stay for one.' He turned to Amos, who was still sharing a horse. 'You two had best go, and take that injured horse with you, though I reckon he'll have to be shot.'

No one else volunteered to join the search party, so they drew straws. There was some grumbling on the part of the four who drew short straws, and they watched the more

242

fortunate men ride off towards the camp with ill-concealed envy.

In fact they were not delayed too long for Jess was found in a hollow, unconscious and with a badly broken leg. He regained consciousness as soon as they tried to lift him on to the saddle, screamed with pain and lost consciousness again. He was unable to ride, so they left one man with him and rode back to camp to fetch the doctor, who returned with them bringing an improvised stretcher and a bottle of whisky. By the time the leg was roughly splinted, Jess had drunk most of the whisky and was in an alcoholic stupor.

Everyone in the camp ate fresh meat that night amid great rejoicing, but their delight was somewhat tempered by the high cost of the enterprise. The wounded horse had been put out of its misery; one man had a bleeding ear and Jess had a broken leg. It was hard to say whether man or buffalo had triumphed, but in years to come the men concerned would take their grandchildren on to their knees and tell how they hunted buffalo across the plains.

*

Fort Laramie had had a chequered history. Once it had been a wooden stockade known as Fort William, but later on adobe building had replaced it. Known as Fort John, that had served as a trading post for bear pelts and antelope hides and Indians and white men had coexisted in the area with very little friction. With the coming of the emigrants to Oregon, the relationship had grown less friendly as the Indians became aware that the passage of large numbers of white men through their territories was not in their interest. The threat to their traditional way of life brought occasional outbursts of hostility and it was thought that a military fort on the site of Fort John would be advisable. The Army accordingly purchased it early in 1849 and it was therefore even less well established than Fort Kearny. There was no stockade, merely a group of half-finished buildings set to the north of the Laramie River with the old fort between the new one and the water. Already a large frame building was going up to house the officers, but work had stopped on these on July 4th because celebrations were under way for Independence Day.

Wallis's company had reached the fort late the previous night after a long and determined ride during which they covered twenty-three miles in sixteen hours of travel.

They were camped a few hundred yards south of the fort and now all was bustle and excitement as they too made preparations for the festivities which were due to start later in the afternoon. Wallis had warned that they would be on the trail promptly at 4.30 a.m. on the fifth of July regardless of the telling effects of over-indulgence, and everyone had agreed solemnly on the need for moderation though very few, if any, intended to practise it.

The catering had naturally been left to the women and Hester had made soda bread and was now making a large number of fried cakes. Arrangements had been made for Ella's apple pies and Agnes Harper's johnny-cakes to be baked in one of the fort's ovens. Some of the brandy from the company's medical stores had been appropriated as the main ingredient in a punch and there would be 'cider' made from dried apples and wild gooseberries. Daniel Miller had produced a few gallons of 'Indian whisky' made from corn whisky, tobacco, red peppers and water. He had refined it with a pinch or two of black gunpowder and those few privileged to test it in advance gave it top marks.

Will sat on the grass beside his grandmother, his mouth open, his eyes unfocused as she tried unsuccessfully to interest him in her cooking.

'So in goes the water, into the flour,' she told him, 'and we mix it all up with a fork – and then we make a lovely squashy dough like this – and we sprinkle some flour – now where's my old rolling-pin gone? Have you hidden it, Will, you young monkey?' She smiled at him, raising her voice. 'Ah, here it is, hiding from me. Naughty old rolling-pin!' She laughed loudly to encourage him, but his expression did not alter. 'Now for the fun! I'm going to roll out this squashy old dough, pull it into lumps and flatten it into balls.'

As he continued unaware of the proceedings, she tutted to herself as she put a knob of lard into the largest skillet. While

244

it heated up over the fire, she mopped her perspiring face and tried not to think about her grandson's blank future.

When the fat was hot enough, she dropped ten balls of dough into it.

'If only we had some currants, we could pop them in too,' she said, 'but we haven't, so we can't. They smell good, don't they? Eh, Will? Are you listening to Grandma? Or if we had some cherries – but we haven't. Yes, they smell good. Mustn't burn them, must we? Can't have a party with burnt cakes, can we?'

Five minutes later she was turning over the cakes when Gabby Smith strolled up, his hands deep in the pockets of a buckskin jacket which he had just bought from one of the Indians.

Hester glanced up and whistled approvingly. 'Quite a dandy, Mr Smith,' she grinned. 'Those Indians certainly know how to use hide. Look, Will. Look at the pretty beads and the lacing. That's real pretty, isn't it?'

Seeing the pity in Gabby's eyes, Hester flew to Will's defence.

'He'll pick up,' she said sharply. 'There's no need to look at him that way. Some kids are slower than others, that's all.'

'Sure he will,' agreed Gabby hastily. 'I just came by to ask after Jess.'

Hester's eyes darkened and she shook her head. Lowering her voice, she said, '*I* don't think he's much better, Mr Smith. The doctor's trying, but the leg's still very swollen and paining him most of the time. Don't look right to me. Poor Jess – never was a good patient. Cut his hand real bad once on a billhook and wouldn't let no one near it. Blood dripping everywhere, it was, and Ella hollering like a stuck pig. You'd have thought it was *her* hand got cut instead of his. Then when we got it bandaged, he wouldn't have it off to be looked at. Weeks and weeks that bandage stayed on. Ella says he was feverish in the night – wandering in his mind – but he was OK again by this morning. Damned fool thing to do – chase after buffalo. Plenty of single men was only too willing. A married man's got responsibilities and Jess should have thought of his wife and kids. Now he's got himself laid up, he's cursing and grumbling, but he's only himself to blame. If you've a few minutes to spare, you might have a few words with him. Cheers him up to have a bit of conversation.'

'That's why I came by,' Gabby told her. 'I'll leave you to your cooking. Smells good – I'm looking forward to the shindig. There's going to be dancing. Will you save one for me?'

Hester stared at him, surprised by the compliment, then her face broke into a smile. 'Why, that's mighty nice of you, Mr Smith,' she said. 'Be pleased to.'

She watched him climb up into the wagon and then turned to Will.

'That's Mr Smith, Will. Real nice manners he's got. Oops! The cakes are done. Now, you watch Grandma get them out of the pan – watch close, mind.'

While she cooked, she went on talking to her unresponsive grandson, but Gabby's invitation to dance had brought back a favourite memory of herself aged eleven in a blue hand-me-down dress with a daisy as a buttonhole, dancing with her Uncle Fred – such a dashing young uncle. She had believed herself the focus of every eye with her long hair swinging and her skirts billowing. Then at fourteen, she was kissed for the first time by a cousin. Nothing dashing about him, for he was dying of consumption, although no one knew it at the time and Hester had thought him pale and interesting. And then her wedding day with a borrowed sunbonnet with new red ribbons and a blue shawl knitted by her mother. She had walked out of the clapboard church with Charlie Cooper – a bride at seventeen and with young Ella already on the way.

Hester sighed. She had been personable then, with a reasonable skin, well-shaped fingernails and thick hair that still had colour in it. *And* could she dance! She never would stop dancing while there was someone to play the fiddle and Charlie's eyes had been so full of admiration and desire that the other men had teased him. Not that he didn't still desire her – he did, and a sight too often! The trouble was that she no longer desired *him*. But in those far-off days before they married, when he was the hired hand, they had stolen out at nights to meet in the barn. There they had tickled and teased and done all manner of things, until their desires finally led them astray and her father found out and gave Charlie a hiding he had never forgotten.

Hester smiled at Will. 'They were good days, Will,' she said.

She looked up as Ella came back from the fort with her four pies on a large tray, face flushed with excitement.

'The soldiers were ever so kind,' she told Hester, 'and all giving me the eye and making remarks and winking.' She tried not to show how pleased she was by their attention. 'How's the fried cakes coming along? They look good. And how's Will? Has he been good?'

'Course he has,' said Hester in a slightly disapproving tone, 'and Gabby just came by to see your husband.'

She laid a little emphasis on the last two words.

Ella, reminded of the sick husband, hastily adjusted her expression. 'Oh, that's good,' she said. 'Jess likes a bit of company. Well, I must put these under the wagon in the shade to cool off.'

'Best cover them first,' suggested Hester. 'Use a cloth; it'll keep the dust off. They look fine. You've done well, Ella. And look out for Mr Miller's dog – that animal will eat anything he can find!'

Ella made no answer and Hester glanced at her daughter's face. 'What is it?' she asked intuitively.

'Nothing.' Ella set down the pies on the makeshift table.

'It's something,' said Hester. 'Spit it out.'

Ella drew a deep breath. 'Well, it's this dancing,' she began. 'There'll be that many fellers with only fellers to dance with, and not many womenfolk, and Jess is laid up . . .' She looked appealingly at Hester. 'I was wondering, would it be *right* for me to dance?'

'There's the baby,' Hester reminded her.

'I'd dance carefully,' pleaded Ella. 'Just a few dances?'

'Ask Jess then,' said Hester. 'I reckon he'll say "Yes".'

Ella scowled. 'I do wish he hadn't gone after those stupid buffalo,' she began.

'Nothing stupid about them,' stated Hester. 'It's the ones that go chasing after them – *they're* the stupid ones.'

'They had to get meat,' Ella protested. 'You didn't mind eating it; you said you enjoyed it.'

'They didn't have to go off like lunatics,' Hester insisted. 'They didn't have to risk their lives. They should have had more sense – gone at it sensibly instead of charging in like that, firing off their guns like a lot of silly kids. They went after those buffalo for *fun*, Ella. They'll never admit it, but you know it and so do I. Someone could have gotten killed and it could have been Jess.'

Ella bent down to pick up Will and immediately wrinkled her nose. 'Oh, Will! You're smelly again. *When* are you going to learn?'

'All in good time,' said Hester.

Ella tossed her head irritably. 'I reckon *now* would be a good time,' she declared as she went off to clean up her son.

*

That afternoon, promptly at four o'clock, the entire company of the Western Hopers gathered within the circle of the wagons. The American flag flew from a broom-handle fixed above one of the wagons and the men were drawn up in three ranks facing it. They held an assortment of firearms and had smartened up as best they could with clothes well brushed, hair slicked back. Some had even trimmed their beards. Jess was propped up alongside them, but two other men, stricken with cholera, were too ill to attend and had reluctantly been left in their wagons. The women and children in their Sunday clothes stood in a small group and watched proudly as the ceremony began.

Bart Smith had been chosen to make a short speech, so after a brief and rather discordant bugle call he stepped up on to an upturned packing case and read aloud the 'few words' he had laboured over for the past two days.

'Greetings, fellow members of the Western Hope Miners,' he began, separating his words carefully. 'This is a proud

248

moment for all of us, for we are all members not only of the Western Hope Miners, but of the United States of America.'

There were a few ragged cheers, but he went on, 'Today is the Fourth of July, which we call Independence Day. We are independent because others died for us. They died that we might be free to make decisions and to shape our own destinies. We remember them with gratitude.' He took a deep breath. 'Ours is a great country and a great nation and we are proud to call ourselves Americans. We are proud to celebrate this great day and I now call upon my fellow members to salute the United States of America.'

He stepped down to enthusiastic applause and took his place at the end of the front rank. At a word of command from Matt Wallis, the front rank then aimed a collection of rifles and pistols at the sky. On the second command, they fired. The same procedure was followed by the second and third ranks. Then Bart stepped up again on to the 'dais'. He was recovering from his earlier nervousness and beginning to enjoy himself.

'And now a final volley – to the gold in California!' he cried. A ragged but deafening volley shattered the air as they all fired together and a great cheer went up from the assembled company followed by much excited hugging and back-slapping.

Miller called out, 'Let's drink a toast!'

Then ranks were broken as the men rushed for their mugs and queued patiently for either punch or whisky – both proved surprisingly good and the latter unexpectedly potent. When everyone had been served, Amos raised his mug.

Someone struck up a tune on the fiddle and within minutes most of them were dancing. Charlie danced with Hester, Amos danced with Ella and on the far side of the circle, Daniel danced with Kate. The rest of the men partnered each other, boisterously flinging their arms and legs about and whooping noisily, intent on enjoying themselves. They were determined to forget the hardships and deprivations they had suffered so far and the hazards which were still to come. Today they were going to have fun and relax with good food and drink. A mood of general goodwill swept through the company, and personal animosities were mostly forgotten as the time passed and more than one handshake put an end to an old grudge. A mouth-organ eventually took over from the fiddle and a flute joined the mouth-organ. Hours passed and still the party atmosphere continued because no one would allow it to end.

Jess Cash watched it all through a haze of misery and fear. His leg ached abominably, his head was thumping, he had no appetite and so ate very little – just a slice of pie to please Ella. He had drunk too much and his eyes were blurred. He knew from his own pain and the doctor's anxious face that his leg was not mending nor likely to. It was broken in three places between knee and ankle and he dreaded the moment when he would hear the word 'gangrene' and later, inevitably, the word 'amputation'. When that word was uttered, he knew that his *real* problems would start because he had made up his mind to refuse. He did not intend to spend the rest of his life as a cripple – he would rather die. Jess knew that most probably that was the choice he would have to make, and had made up his mind to choose death.

Ella would want him to lose the leg and live, so would the Coopers, and there would be angry scenes and bitter recriminations. There was going to be a showdown, he knew, but he didn't care. He would resist all their pleadings and his life would come to an end. As a boy, he had felt a deep repugnance for mutilation of any kind; he hated to see a lizard teased until it shed its tail, nor could he bring himself to pull the wings off flies as the other boys did. When his father's dog lost a leg in a trap, it was weeks before he could even look at it without an uneasy churning of his stomach.

He had gone to school with a crippled boy named Luke Spinney and Jess could still recall the unreasonable loathing he felt for him – a loathing that was part fear and part disgust. Some of the boys had teased Luke, while others appointed themselves his protectors. Jess had ignored him, physically revulsed by the boy's uneven gait and irritated by his clumsy manoeuvrings with the wooden crutch. He had not wanted to reject the boy, but his revulsion outweighed any compassion he felt for him and he had breathed a sigh of relief when Luke finally left the school.

Now it was his own turn to face those dreadful humiliations and his whole being recoiled from the dreadful prospect. No, Jess told himself again and again, he could *never* agree to the amputation of his leg. He would lie in his grave complete. His gaze wandered aimlessly until he saw Hester 'dancing' with Will in her arms and another more familiar misery overwhelmed him. All he had achieved in his life was that sad little boy – and God alone knew what Ella's next child would be. Another Will, perhaps. Oh, please God, not another Will! He sighed again and comforted himself that by the time Ella's child was born he would be dead and need not see it. He need never confront another disappointment or face up to another failure; he would be well out of it all. A new thought surfaced suddenly like a bright light in the darkness of his mind; if the rotten leg did not kill him fast enough, he would kill himself. He would find a way; a bullet in the brain would be quick and certain!

He glanced up to find Ella beside him, a look of concern on her face. She sat down, hands crossed over her swollen abdomen.

'How you feeling, Jess?' she asked. Her face was flushed with the exertion of the dance and her eyes sparkled. Jess looked at her in surprise. He had forgotten that she could be almost pretty.

'Oh, I'm great!' he answered. 'On top of the world. Never been better in my life!'

She ignored the sarcasm, determined not to let him spoil her pleasure. 'Can I get you anything? More pie or punch, or d'you want to try some johnny-cake?'

'I said I'm fine.' His tone was thick with a resentment he could not hide. It was so bloody unfair that she was whole and well and enjoying herself. 'You shouldn't dance so much, the way you are,' he added.

'I didn't dance much,' she protested.

'Then why you puffing?'

'I'm not. I'm just breathing heavy – 'cos I'm hot. It's the punch, you know alcohol makes me hot.'

'Then don't drink it.'

'But it's the Fourth of July!' she tossed her head. 'I've got to celebrate, haven't I, same as everybody else?'

'I'm not celebrating,' he said bitterly and she gave him a quick look. 'What have I got to celebrate with this stinking leg?'

'It doesn't stink,' she argued.

'It will,' he insisted.

Ella preferred to change the subject. 'Did you see Will dancing?' she asked. 'He's having a fine time, bless him. Ma's dancing with him.'

Jess looked at her. 'He never has a fine time,' he said. 'You know he doesn't. He never has any sort of a time, that kid.'

All the animation fled from her face as she silently acknowledged the truth of his statement.

Jess went on, perversely determined to put an end to her brief escape into happiness. 'He's most likely scared of all the noise,' he said, 'and you all whisking him round like that. Most likely making him feel dizzy or sick – '

'Stop it, Jess!' Ella cried, putting her hands over her ears. 'I don't want to hear all that. Not now, not ever. Why do you do it, Jess? Why do you want to make me cry? It's not my fault he's the way he is.'

At once he regretted his cruelty but it was too late, the harm was done. He sat silent and ashamed, his face sullen and despairing as tears welled up in her eyes. No one, he thought, would miss him when he was gone. No one would care. They would all go through the motions and cry over his grave and then they would forget him. Ella would remember his callousness and might even be glad and then, with so many men to choose from, she would marry again. Hell and damnation! There was no way he could win.

'He looks cheerful,' said Ella, struggling with her tears, not wanting to spoil her face. 'He's kind of smiling.' She mopped her eyes and blew her nose loudly.

'He never smiles,' said Jess. 'You know that as well as I do.' He hated her for her prospect of life and happiness. 'He'd be better off dead,' he added.

She didn't answer immediately and then she turned large,

tear-filled eyes towards him – eyes that were full of unspoken grief.

'I know,' she whispered. 'I've always known. Oh, Jess! What can we do? Ma says God has a special corner in His heart for children like Will, but – '

He broke in harshly. 'Your ma talks through the back of her hat!'

'Oh hush, Jess. Here she comes!'

Hester arrived with Will, whom she settled in Ella's lap before lowering herself to the ground beside them.

'My oh my!' she gasped, one hand to her heart. 'That was some dance, wasn't it, Will? He makes a real good partner, you know that? I'm that puffed. Danced off my feet.'

Jess and Ella regarded her stonily.

'Well?' she demanded. 'What's got into you two? Nothing to say for yourselves?' She peered into Ella's face. 'You been crying?'

'No, Ma. Give it a rest,' said Ella, her mouth tightening.

'You sure you're all right?' Hester persisted. 'Maybe you shouldn't dance any more. You don't want to shake the poor kid out before its time.'

'I won't, Ma. Leave me alone, will you?'

Jess said dully, 'He doesn't like dancing. It scares him, most likely.'

A terrible blackness had entered his soul with Ella's confession about their son. She had never before admitted to feeling that way and now Jess found the knowledge unbearable and hated her for that moment of candour. With terrible clarity he saw Will in twenty years' time – a useless, helpless lump in the shape of a man.

'Will wasn't scared,' Hester argued. 'He likes to dance, all kids do.'

Jess hated her, too, for her stupid complacency and her determination to look on the bright side. There *was* no bright side.

'Probably scared him witless,' Jess insisted and watched with a flicker of satisfaction as the faces of mother and daughter crumpled unhappily. He made up his mind at that moment that when it was time for him to die, he would somehow take Will with him into oblivion.

*

Two weeks after leaving Fort Kearny and two days after Independence Day, Lily and Henry reached Chimney Rock, the famous landmark which towered over two hundred feet into the air above its steep broad base. They stood beside the wagon and together stared up at the rock; a dozen or more men from the Michigan Pioneers were already clambering over the lower part, intent on climbing higher than any of the earlier travellers who had inscribed their names on the rock's worn sides.

'Just like a giant chimney,' Henry agreed, but Lily thought it looked like a finger pointing skyward.

Henry grinned. 'Fancy a climb?' he asked. 'Carve your name for posterity?'

Lily smiled back. 'I don't think I've got any energy to spare,' she said, 'but if you want to go, I'll watch you. I'll be glad just to sit and rest.'

He handed her the reins of the pack-mule and his horse. 'What shall I write?' he asked. 'Something romantic? "H. S. loves L. G." with a heart and a bleeding arrow?'

'I shouldn't,' she laughed. 'It would take much too long. Just our initials would do.'

'Not the date?' he queried.

'Oh yes, that too.'

She settled herself on a large piece of rock and watched him start to climb. Hundreds of earlier climbers had made holds for feet and hands, so it was not too difficult. As Henry went up, others were passing him on the way down.

'H. S. loves L. G.,' repeated Lily, amused and a little flattered.

Over the last fortnight, after the initial diffidence had worn off, an easy camaraderie had developed between them. Lily looked on Henry Simms as the brother she had always wanted, and it did not occur to her that his feelings towards her were anything more than brotherly. He had teased her once or twice with references to 'undying admiration' and

254

'untimely affections', but he always spoke so humorously that she treated them as the jokes they obviously seemed. He had a way of smiling with his head on one side and eyes half-closed so that she could never see his full expression.

Lily had learned a lot about him since their first meeting and she liked much of what she knew. He was honest and well-intentioned, with a warm romantic heart, but he was sensitive and quick to take offence. Once or twice his temper had flared briefly, but each time he had it quickly under control. On balance, she enjoyed his company and thought herself lucky to have found him. With Henry beside her she had no fears about the rest of the journey to California.

Whether it was Fate which had thrown them together, as he had suggested, she did not know, but Henry's appearance in her life had been most timely and, feeling sure Patrick would approve their friendship, she was reasonably content.

Shading her eyes from the sun, she looked for him and saw his lanky figure, already dwarfed by the height of the rock. A member of the Michigan Pioneers slithered down the last ten feet of the rock's base, dusted himself down and walked towards her. She did not know his name, but she recognized him by sight because for the past two days she and Henry had ridden alongside his company. He was tall and gaunt and his clothes were too big for him. Like hers, his face was blotched by mosquito bites and even as he spoke, he slapped at the back of his neck. His skin, too, was covered with the inevitable layer of brown dust, his clothes were patched and he wore a floppy hat well faded by the sun. Lily guessed him to be in his early forties – much older than most of the gold seekers.

'Darned mozzies!' he said. 'I'll be glad when we reach the mountains. I'd rather be knee-deep in snow than eaten alive by insects.' He chuckled as he drew nearer. 'I see they've been dining off you as well?'

Lily nodded. 'I gave up counting the bites days ago,' she said. 'I try to resign myself, but I must admit they try my patience.'

'English, are you?' he asked.

'Yes.'

'What's an English lady doing in these parts?'

'I'm going to California,' Lily told him. 'Just like you.'

'What, all alone?' His surprise was obvious.

She shook her head. 'I'm travelling with a companion,' she said, 'I was planning to join my husband, but he died of cholera.'

He tutted sympathetically. 'Too many fine souls gone that way,' he said. 'I reckon their ghosts will haunt this trail. Six gone in our company – three in the first two weeks. You not with a company?'

Lily explained briefly how she and Henry came to be travelling together, then it was her turn to slap at a mosquito which had settled on the back of her hand.

'What *use* are mosquitoes?' he demanded, sitting down beside her. 'That's what I want to know. Why did the good Lord make 'em in the first place, except to drive folks mad?'

'I don't know,' said Lily. She waved to Henry, who was now scrambling up the sloping middle section of the rock.

The man glanced up at him and also raised a hand in greeting.

'That him?' he asked. 'That your "companion"?'

Lily thought she detected disapproval in his voice.

'He's a very good friend. I don't know what I'd do without him,' she declared.

'A good friend. I see.' He nodded. 'Well, we all need good friends on this caper, ma'am, so you hang on to him. What's his name again?'

'Henry Simms.'

'I think I noticed him yesterday,' he said. 'Wasn't it him that was asking around about oxen limping or some such?'

'That's right,' said Lily, pointing to the sick oxen. That's the one. It's poor old Duffy, he seems to be having trouble with his left foreleg. It's not too bad, but . . .'

He watched the animal for a moment with narrowed eyes. 'It'll only get worse,' he assured her. 'My mate says hot tar and resin's the stuff. You smear it into all the cracks in the hoof. Worth a try, I guess. Got an answer for everything, my mate.'

'Hot tar and resin,' said Lily. 'I'll tell Henry. Thank you.'

256

She swatted another mosquito and asked, 'How are the Michigan Pioneers faring, Mr – ?'

'Tapp, ma'am. Nathaniel Phineas Tapp.'

'Mr Tapp. I'm Lily Golightly.' She held out her hand, but he merely touched his hat. 'The Michigan Pioneers, ma'am? Why, I reckon we're no worse off than the next. Bit of squabbling, but nothing too serious. Yankees baiting the Southerners on account of their slaves.'

'I've heard all the arguments' said Lily, 'but I know in my heart that it can't be right for a man or woman to be held as a slave.'

'Oh, it's not right, ma'am' he agreed. 'Make no mistake about that.' He shook his head emphatically. 'It's wrong, but those slave owners ain't never going to admit it. To them no slaves means no cotton, and that means no money. The whole of the South depends on it. Take away the slave labour and you've ruined them with a capital "R". Facing ruin scares a man, you can understand that.'

'I know, but still . . .'

'Trouble is, it just crept up on them. First it was just a few slaves, then gradually the numbers grew until now the slaves probably outnumber the free men. That's a thought to rock you back on your heels, ma'am; that sure is a thought. Still, that's for other folks to worry about. I'm going West away from it all and I've got worries enough of my own and likely to have more. I guess that's enough about politics, ma'am. Religion and politics – I try to steer clear of them. A man can get his head knocked off talking religion and politics.'

Lily took this strong hint and asked him what he thought of the management of his company.

He grinned. 'Well now, we change our committee more often than we change our socks but we're making out, I guess. We've got a reasonable leader and that's what counts. You should join us, they'd take you on.'

Lily shook her head and smiled. 'We must press on,' she told him. 'Henry is very impatient. He must be everywhere yesterday!'

They both turned to gaze once more at Chimney Rock.

'Where's he got to?' he asked. 'Not fell off and broke his neck, I hope – oh, begging your pardon, ma'am! I was forgetting your sad loss – cholera you said.'

She nodded and he shook his head.

'A sad thing to lie on this lonely trail,' he said. 'I've seen some sights that would turn your hair grey. Bodies dug up by the coyotes and half-ate. Put in too shallow, you see, and they smell them. And another just dumped in a little hollow with not a stitch on and the buzzards having a rare feast. Must have had his clothes stole. It hardens folks, this life.'

Lily had gone pale but he blundered on, unaware of her distress.

'And I'll tell you something else, ma'am.' He leaned forward and lowered his voice conspiratorially. 'Not all the graves is what they're supposed to be. Oh no! Folks is burying what they can't carry and making 'em look like graves. They reckon when they've made it rich they'll come back and dig the stuff up again. I seen it with my own eyes not three days ago. Woman by the name of Porritt had a writing-box that'd been in her family for generations – or so she said, boastful like. Too heavy to take further, so she wraps it in a blanket – cuddling it like a baby she was, with tears in her eyes. Her husband dug a grave and in it went with a bit of a headstone. "Here lies Martha Briggs. Died of cholera, etc., etc." ' He tutted disapprovingly to himself. 'Says they'll be back for it by and by. "Stuff and nonsense," I told her. "When you get the gold you'll buy a new writing-box," but no! She would have it they'd be back. Like one of the family, she told me, that box. Those were her very words: "That old box is like one of the family, Mr Tapp." When I heard that, I reckoned I'd heard everything!'

Lily smiled, 'Poor woman,' she said.

He snorted derisively. 'Plumb stupid, I call it,' he said. 'There's such a thing as priorities. We're going to need shovels and pans, good food and even better luck. That's what we're going to need in California. We won't need writing-boxes. One of the family! Humph! I've never heard such a crazy thing in all my life.'

Several more members of Mr Tapp's company came down

the rock to join them and eventually they all said 'Goodbye' and left Lily alone with her thoughts. She considered Henry Simms again; Mr Tapp probably believed that the relationship between them was more than it was. She tried to imagine herself falling in love with him, but hastily abandoned the attempt. Patrick had only just gone to his grave, she reminded herself guiltily, and already she was thinking about another man. It was quite unpardonable.

'I'm sorry, Patrick,' she whispered. 'Please forgive me. It's just that this country is so wild and a woman alone is so vulnerable . . .'

No. That was hypocritical, she decided. There might be other women travelling alone – widowed, like herself, since leaving Independence. If she was ever to consider Henry Simms as a possible husband, it would be because she found him attractive as a man and for no other reason.

'Be honest, Lily Golightly,' she told herself.

If she was totally honest, she discovered, she did find him attractive.

'Oh, Patrick,' she murmured. 'I *do* like him very much. Not that any man would ever take your place. But, if I am to finish this journey and then search for gold, there is safety in numbers. I do need a travelling companion.'

Sternly she pulled herself up again.

'No, Lily', she muttered. 'That is dishonest too. You can join up with the Coopers again if all you need is safety in numbers.'

She felt disloyal and angry with herself for voicing such thoughts, but the truth was that she had looked forward to married life. Like most women, she wanted to share her life with a man she loved and she had longed to rejoin Patrick so that she could make him a good wife. *Caring* for a family of her own – that was what she had planned to do with her life and that was still what she wanted. That was a woman's role and all her upbringing had been directed to that end. Instead she found herself leading a hazardous and extremely uncomfortable life with no man of her own.

Suddenly she jumped to her feet, thoroughly ashamed of herself.

'Lily Golightly!' she muttered. 'You should count your blessings. You don't have Ella's problems, or Kate's. You are perfectly fit, you have a pleasant companion and you *chose* to go on with this journey. Think yourself lucky and stop feeling sorry for yourself. As for Henry Simms . . .' she faltered a little, then went on, 'he's a very nice man and you have absolutely no claim on him.'

She smoothed her skirts and shook off the worst of the dust. When she looked for Henry on Chimney Rock she could not distinguish him from any of the other figures silhouetted against the setting sun, so she gave up and decided to go back to the wagon and organize some food. She tethered all the animals where the grass was plentiful, made a fire and put some salt pork into the pan.

'Hot tar and resin,' she muttered to herself. 'I must remember to tell Henry. If we lost any of the oxen – it just doesn't bear thinking about!'

She left the pork to its own devices and anxiously subjected the four oxen to a closer than usual scrutiny, patting them affectionately and making encouraging noises as she did so. Would they last the journey? They were beginning to look jaded and already their bones showed through their rough coats. With a worried frown, she turned her attention to Henry's horse which was listless, its coat (and no doubt its lungs) thick with the dust from which neither beasts nor men could escape.

Once they passed Fort Laramie, she knew the grass would gradually disappear along the trail and they would have to cut hay when and where they could find it. Supposing they didn't find any? Supposing the animals starved to death! Already in the last week they had passed several dead animals: a mule with a broken hind-leg which had been shot through the head; two emaciated oxen and also a bloated cow which had died of something nameless. Lily shuddered and made a determined effort to put aside such dreary thoughts. The animals *would* survive and they would reach California. Anything else was quite unthinkable.

Chapter Twelve

Two days' good travelling brought Lily and Henry to Scotts Bluff, and in the western end of the valley they found the fur-trading post owned by the legendary Robidoux who lived there with his Indian wife and half-breed children. Originally established for trade with the Indians who brought in furs, it now doubled as a small but useful staging post for the gold seekers and hundreds of messages from people who had already passed through were pinned to the walls of the store.

The tyre on one of the rear wheels of Lily's wagon was working loose – the heat had shrunk the wooden wheel – and they decided to have it repaired by the blacksmith in Robidoux's smithy before they moved on. They both watched as the iron tyre was removed and a strip of willow nailed on to the outside rim of the wheel to enlarge it. The tyre was then heated to expand it and hammered back on to the wheel. Cold water thrown over the hot metal cooled it and it shrank, fitting closely round the wheel once more.

Members of the Michigan Pioneers then arrived to have various wagons repaired and strengthened before they tackled the mountains which lay ahead, and which everyone knew would test their vehicles to the full.

Lily and Henry, eager to make up for lost time, pressed on alone and after another three days' ride they reached Fort Laramie where they caught up with another company called the Indiana Hawks and where a letter from England awaited Lily. She was dismayed to recognize Mrs Spencer's hand-

writing on the envelope and stared at Henry, her eyes wide
with apprehension.

'It's Mrs Spencer's writing,' she whispered. 'Why hasn't
Papa written? I daren't open it. Oh, Henry! If anything's
happened to my father, I'll never forgive myself.'

He laid a finger gently on her lips. 'Read it, Lily,' he told
her. 'You're only putting off the evil hour and it may not be
so bad. You are such a worrier. Take a deep breath and then
open it and read it.'

'I can't!' she cried, her face pale. 'Oh, Henry, I *know*
something's happened to Papa!'

He shrugged. 'Lily, I know how you feel, but what difference will it make when you open it? The contents will be
just the same. Do be sensible.'

After a further hesitation, Lily nodded and made her way
outside into the sunshine. She sat down on a convenient log,
oblivious of the soldiers who stared at her curiously, and
opened the letter with trembling fingers. It contained four
sheets of paper closely covered with a neat handwriting:

My dearest Lily,
    There is no cause for alarm. I had a slight fall in the
garden yesterday and my right wrist is somewhat sprained,
so that I may not easily take up a pen. I am therefore
dictating this letter to Mrs Spencer, who has kindly agreed
to act as my secretary until my hand is recovered.

Lily breathed a long sigh of relief and glancing heavenwards,
murmured a heartfelt 'Thank you!' before reading on.

    Your letter dated 7 March came this morning and I
thank the Lord for your safe arrival in America. I put my
faith in Him and He has not failed me. Your account of
life at sea does nothing to reassure me about such a
hazardous mode of travel, and I fear I will never willingly
undertake such an ordeal, but trust that you and Patrick
will one day visit me in England as you promised. Not that
at present I am kindly disposed towards your husband. I
am bound to say, Lily, that I can *never* condone such

irresponsible conduct on his part. Rushing off at a moment's notice to search for gold is not the behaviour I expect of a son-in-law and I am deeply shocked and disappointed in him. By the time this reaches you I don't doubt that you will already be reunited, and I intend that you show him this letter so that he can fully appreciate my disapproval. I almost find it in my heart to wish I had not sanctioned your marriage – as you will recall, I was not happy about the fact that you hardly knew each other. I blame myself for not standing out against your tears, Lily. I allowed you to make a hasty marriage and the trust I put in Patrick was sadly misplaced.

'Oh, Papa!' whispered Lily. 'Don't blame him. He's paid for his rashness with his life!'

I am even more surprised at your decision to follow him on this mad escapade, but my feelings on the matter can be of no consequence for by the time you receive this letter you will be half-way to California.

Lily looked at the date at the top of the letter and saw that it had been posted in England on the eighth of March – weeks before Patrick's death.

Doubtless my reproofs will fall on deaf ears, but my heart is heavy for you both and I shall pray day and night for your continued safety. I shall also scan the newspapers for details of life 'on the trail' as they call it. I believe the climate to be changeable, so please take care of your health. Do not overtax your strength; take care that your bedding is *well aired* – a mirror held briefly between the sheets will moist over if they are damp. Eat *well* and *regularly* and do be careful of the river water which should be *filtered* if at all *unclean*.

Lily could not resist a smile. If only he knew! If he had the slightest inkling of the rough life she was leading! 'Oh Papa! I love you,' she whispered.

She tried to calculate whether or not he might now have received her letter telling him of Patrick's death. She *must* find time and energy to write to him again, although she doubted if a description of her present situation would bring him much consolation. The letter continued:

If you do have trouble with your digestion, I am told that Dr Zoril's Cure-All Medicine is of inestimable value and that a moderate dose of gunpowder has a most cooling effect in cases of fever. Mrs Spencer's sister recommends a lump of asafoetida worn on a string round the neck as a certain guard against spasms. You have never been robust, Lily, and Patrick *must* safeguard your health at all times if he and I are ever again to be fully reconciled. Miss Perring, who inquires after you most kindly whenever we meet, also advises that mustard plasters spread over the abdomen, calves of the leg and soles of the feet will bring speedy relief to the discomforts of the dread cholera.

Lily laid down the letter and allowed herself to think about Miss Perring sitting at the piano beside young Maurice. And Mrs Spencer pottering about in the morning room with a feather duster while her father bent over his desk, busy with his Sunday sermon. It seemed quite incredible that such civilized society still existed and she smiled briefly. There were still places in the world where people sat on comfortable chairs, changed their clothes regularly, sang duets in the evening and ate their food from china plates with a selection of silver cutlery. She sighed happily, she had almost forgotten such luxuries.

Turning over the page, she continued the rambling letter, thinking that Mrs Spencer must have been heartily glad when it was finished.

My dear child, I must not go on in this morbid way, for I would not have this letter depress you even though yours has thrown me into a state of great agitation, but I shall be myself again before too long. Mrs Dent says that your young Maurice is making good progress with his lessons and that Miss Perring is pleased with him. Miss Lyons has succeeded with the Sunday school in your place and I have persuaded her to stay on permanently, so do not worry on that score. She asks to be remembered to you. Poor Mrs Burke has had a mild seizure, but the doctor hopes she will make a full recovery. Meanwhile her sister is running the shop.

Mrs Spencer sends her love and good wishes and is knitting you a thick shawl, which she plans to send to you in the hopes it may reach you before you cross the mountains which I suspect from a perusal of my map will prove cold and inhospitable, so do purchase *stout footwear*, Lily. Cold wet feet can chill the entire body.

Now Mrs Spencer tells me she has a headache and that I have said quite enough. I am anxious to commit this letter to the post, so that you will receive it as soon as possible.

God bless you, my dears. Take care of each other and put yourselves always in God's hands. We include you both in our prayers every Sunday during morning service, so you are well represented!

I am mainly well and have painted some fruit on the old pewter plate. It has turned out rather well and pleases me immensely.

My prayers go with you,

Your affectionate Papa.

Lily glanced up, blinking back tears, as Henry's shadow fell across her.

'Is everything well?' he asked.

'Yes, quite well,' she told him. 'Take no notice of me; it's just hearing from him after all these months. He's so concerned for me.'

'And why didn't *he* write?'

'He's hurt his wrist. Nothing serious.'

'So now you're happy again?'

'Yes.' As if to disprove her words, more tears gathered. 'I'm not crying,' she said shakily. 'I'm just . . . I'm suddenly missing him for the first time. If I could only put my arms round him . . .'

Henry nodded. 'Does he know about Patrick?' he inquired.

'No, that was in my third letter. I wish I hadn't told him but I had to.'

'You did right.'

'Did I?' she wiped her eyes and drew a deep breath. 'What about your parents, Henry? Do you write to them?'

'I will do,' he grinned. 'I hate writing letters.'

'Oh, you *should*,' she insisted. 'They'll be so worried. Will you tell me about them some time?'

He looked surprised. 'If you like.'

'I do like,' she said. 'I would like to know about your family – you don't say much about them.'

He shrugged lightly. 'I have two parents – a mother and a father – '

Lily laughed. 'You're quite incorrigible, Henry,' she said, 'but I – '

In great confusion, she stopped, her face burning with embarrassment and shock. Then she turned away hastily, making a great show of folding her letter and replacing it in the envelope.

She had almost said, 'I do love you.'

*

The following day, soon after they all moved out, a large herd of buffalo was spotted and a well-organized hunting party from the Indiana Hawks went after them. Henry went with them and they brought down four bulls and returned with much needed meat. Soon, however, they would be in mountain country and there would be no buffalo. They would have to rely on game birds, nuts, berries, jack-rabbits and whatever provisions they had with them. The buffalo meat, cut from the carcass, had been distributed as fairly as possible among the members of the company; Henry had been allowed to buy three and a half pounds and had also been given instructions on how to prepare 'jerky'.

Under his watchful eye Lily cut the meat along the grain, forming it into thin strips. It could be dried over the fire, he

266

told her, but that would mean removing the kettle and Henry liked a constant supply of strong black coffee, so Lily draped the meat over a low bush so that it would dry in the heat of the sun.

'It reminds me of catkins hanging there,' she told Henry. 'It's the way the meat hangs over the twigs!' Seeing his puzzled expression, she explained, 'In England, catkins grow on a hazel tree – they're long and yellow and so delicate. When the catkins appear, you know winter is almost over and spring is on the way. My aunt used to call them lambs' tails. Don't you have catkins in this country?'

He shook his head. 'I couldn't say,' he confessed. 'I don't know much about trees, I'm a city boy.'

She thought he looked at her strangely and waited for him to speak, but when he did not she said. 'And pussy willow. They're fluffy and silver and *they* look like tiny rabbit-tails.'

'Pussy willow?'

She nodded. 'And then we get the blackthorn and hawthorn – '

Puzzled by his manner, she hesitated again and then continued.

'Blackthorn has white flowers,' she told him. 'Hawthorn's a sort of dark pink. It has orange berries in the autumn – that's your fall.' She broke off uneasily. 'Henry, have you got bad news?' she asked. 'You look as though . . .'

'No, it's not bad news. Do I look like it's bad news? I guess it's good news. Lily – '

He looked around. Lily had walked about forty yards to find a suitable bush for the jerky, so they were on their own.

'Hell!' he muttered and thrust his thumbs into the waist-band of his trousers. His collarless shirt was open at the neck and the sun had burned a mahogany vee-shape on his smooth, hairless chest. His wide-brimmed hat cast a shadow over his eyes, hiding his expression.

'Look, Lily,' he said at last. 'I'm no fancy talker like Patrick, but I would do my best for you, I swear it. I'll work all the hours God sends and you won't want for anything. And I like kids!'

267

Lily stared at him. 'Henry?' she stammered, 'are you asking me to – '

He rushed on. 'I don't care for my own company and I had meant to settle down as soon as I got myself sorted out. But it seems that we've been thrown together and we're travelling together and people will talk.'

'Oh Henry!' said Lily.

He *was* proposing! She was taken by surprise and shocked to find that she longed to say 'Yes'. But of course it was out of the question. Quite impossible, in fact.

'Lily, I don't reckon Patrick would mind,' he said, reading her thoughts. 'We got on so well, him and me, and he wouldn't want you to stay on your own.'

'Henry, *please*,' begged Lily, casting around in her mind for the right words.

'No, hear me out,' he insisted. 'If you're going to stay in this country, Lily, you've got to have a man of your own – and if you don't marry me, you'll marry someone else. Sooner or later you'll marry again, probably sooner. You *will*, Lily. So why not me? Better the devil you know than the devil you don't know!' He tried to laugh and failed. 'Lily, please say yes.'

Lily played for time, still fighting her instinct to say just that. She tried to imagine the letter she would write to her father, telling him of her marriage to Patrick's friend a few weeks after Patrick's death. No, it was preposterous. Sadly it was quite out of the question, she must be mad to even consider the idea. She took a deep breath and unconsciously squared her shoulders.

'I'm sorry, Henry,' she said, 'but I can't think of remarrying so soon after Patrick's death, though I do thank you for your proposal. I'm very flattered and it's not that I have anything against you personally. Please don't think that.'

'Then you do like me enough to marry me?'

'I like you very much,' she told him, 'but – '

'Then you could love me, Lily.'

'Maybe. Yes, probably,' she admitted cautiously, 'but not

268

now, Henry. It wouldn't be right. It would be so disrespectful to Patrick, don't you think? And really I hardly know you.'

With a heavy heart she saw his mouth set in a stubborn line.

'How long did you know Patrick?' he asked. 'The way I heard, it was a whirlwind courtship.'

'It was,' Lily admitted.

'And you were blissfully happy. Everything was just fine. Perfect, in fact. Patrick told me himself.'

Lily avoided his eyes. 'Henry, we weren't together long enough to *know* if it would be perfect,' she said, striving for truth but unwilling to undermine Patrick's glowing version of their relationship. 'We only had a week together before Patrick left England.'

'And how many *hours* did you spend in each other's company *before* you were married?' he demanded. 'Not many – not as many as you've spent in *my* company! We've been together all day every day ever since we met! I know what I'm talking about.'

As he took her hands she thought how young he looked. She longed to make him happy with a simple 'Yes'. It would be so easy and would solve so many problems, but she could not do it. Her upbringing cried out against such a rash step. Once before, when swept away by her first experience of love and by Patrick's entreaties, she had allowed herself to believe that marriages were made in heaven. Now she knew that marriage was not merely the fulfilment of a romantic dream, but a relationship between two people which could prove unexpectedly difficult.

'When I married Patrick,' she said quietly, 'I didn't know him at all. Papa was right, we really should have waited. It *was* too soon – much too rushed. We were both impulsive and irresponsible. Poor Papa, he was absolutely right.'

Henry was looking at her in disbelief. 'But you were so *happy*,' he said. 'It was all so *perfect*. How can you say that?'

'We were happy,' agreed Lily, 'but we married in haste. I was in love for the first time in my life and I thought that was enough. It might have worked out – I like to believe it would have done – but living together happily ever after isn't as easy as you might imagine. I loved Patrick, but I didn't *know* him at all. We didn't give ourselves time to get to know each other. I'm wise enough now to realize that it could have been a terrible mistake. No wonder Papa was so reluctant to give his consent.'

'But Patrick told me – ' he stopped.

'It doesn't matter now,' Lily said quickly, 'and I'm not saying I regret it, don't think that. I loved Patrick very much. I wanted to marry him and I'm glad that I did, even though our time together was so short, but I don't want to rush headlong into another marriage. It wouldn't be fair on either of us. It's not that I don't admire and respect you, Henry, because I do and I think I half love you – I'm certainly very fond of you – but it's all too soon. If you asked me in six months' time . . .'

'Six *months!*' Henry was horrified. 'But Lily, we'll be in California long before then. What happens when we get there? Do you go wandering off on your own?'

'I don't know,' she confessed. 'All I know is that I'm going to California because I can't bear to go back east. I don't know what I'm going to do when we reach the gold fields.'

'But aren't you still going to be with me?' he asked. 'I imagined we'd be together.'

'Most likely we will be, Henry.'

He seized eagerly on this admission. 'Then folks will talk,' he told her. 'A man and a woman unmarried and without a chaperone! If you half love me and I love you . . .' He broke off in confusion. 'Oh, Jesus, Lily, did I forget to say that? Did I *say* that I loved you? Is that it? Because I do, believe me!'

'I do believe you, Henry.'

'Lily!' He sighed deeply, still holding her hands. 'I guess I've made a mess of this, but I do love you. I've loved you since I first set eyes on you. Maybe even before that! Maybe Patrick taught me to love you. Who cares? I simply want to look after you, I want to work for you and I want us to have a family. Maybe we'll buy a farm or build a store – oh Jesus, Lily, please don't cry.'

'Please, Henry,' whispered Lily, 'I can't marry you or

anyone else. I've only just lost my husband and I don't think I would ever feel good about it. Give me some time, Henry. I want to stay with you and I think I could love you, but I must have time.'

'Will you marry me if I ask you in three months' time?'

She shook her head. 'No, Henry, not even that. I'm saying I *might*. There's no one else in my life.'

He was looking slightly more cheerful, she noticed thankfully.

'Lily, suppose another woman steps in,' he suggested with an attempt at humour, 'and steals me away? You'd lose me then.'

'I should be very sorry,' she said, smiling.

'You wouldn't fight her for me?'

Lily knew how hard her rejection must be for him and guessed that his humour was a way of hiding the hurt. She laughed. 'I think I might,' she told him.

Suddenly he pulled her into his arms and held her so tightly that she could hardly breathe.

'I love you, Lily,' he said urgently. 'We could make it together, I know we could. I could teach you to love me. The way I see it, it was *meant* to happen. Remember that it was Patrick brought us together? He wouldn't want you to wander about California all alone.'

He released her just as suddenly and pleaded, 'You won't say "Yes" to anyone else, will you?'

'I won't.' She smiled. 'You have first refusal, Henry.'

At last he laughed and the sound tugged at her heart. She *did* want a man of her own. She wanted to make someone happy and she thought it might as well be Henry Simms, but she was no longer the carefree, impulsive girl Patrick had married in such haste. In the intervening months she had grown up. The 'Lily' whom Patrick had known and loved had disappeared for ever.

*

The Western Hopers' progress continued haphazardly with an irritating number of minor delays – the inevitable wagon repairs, numerous strayed animals and a flare-up between

271

two groups of men which threatened to become violent if not resolved. They had passed Horseshoe and La Bonte, two shallow creeks which they had easily forded. The rocks had changed abruptly from a milky brown to a deeper red, against which the blue vetch and lupins and yellow sunflowers made striking contrast. There was good water in the creeks, grass for the animals, and the trees lining the watersides gave wood for the fires. Sage-brush had come into its own and stretched as far as the eye could see in all directions, while over everything the sky loomed a deep blue and the sun shone relentlessly. They reached La Prele Creek on the eleventh of July and Wallis planned to cross on to the north side of the Platte when they reached Deer Creek, which in his estimation would be the thirteenth. These hopes were dashed by a small deputation which sought him out immediately after the evening meal: young Doctor Bonner and Hester and Charlie Cooper. Wallis took one look at their faces and guessed the worst. He rose to his feet, muttered a greeting and asked what was wrong, then listened grimly while the doctor informed him that Jess Cash's leg was already gangrenous and must be taken off at the knee. The problem was that Jess refused to agree to the operation. Neither Ella's tears nor her parents' threats could persuade him to have the leg removed. Assured that he would die if the gangrene spread further into his body, he insisted that he would take his chance.

Wallis asked the doctor bluntly what Cash's chance of survival was if he *did* have the operation under the difficult and unhygienic conditions of trail life.

The doctor spread his hands helplessly. 'There are so many things to consider,' he hedged. 'How strong is his constitution? How will he react to the shock? Can we keep the wound clean? Will he develop a fever?'

'I don't reckon we'll hold him down if he don't *want* to be held down,' Charlie put in.

Hester said, 'I reckon we should let the doc take the leg, with or without Jess's permission. After all, we'd be saving his life and he'll thank us for it later on. He's just scared and who can blame him? I'd be scared.'

'Jess is *not* scared,' Charlie argued. 'He just don't want to be a cripple.'

'He's scared of being a cripple then,' said Hester.

Doctor Bonner and Wallis exchanged exasperated looks and Wallis asked, 'How do you intend to go about it then, if he won't cooperate?'

'Give him a lot of alcohol,' explained the doctor. 'Laudanum's going to make him vomit and alcohol's the only alternative. It'll dull the pain for long enough, but we'll have to tie him down, I'm afraid. I don't care to work like this, Captain, but I see no other way. By the time he comes round, it'll be all over.'

'There'll be hell to pay then,' said Charlie. 'I don't like it at all.'

'You'd rather let him die then, would you?' demanded Hester. 'I'll remember that in case it's ever you with a gammy leg.' She sighed heavily. 'Damned buffalos,' she said. 'He brought it on himself. Now he's got to take the consequences.'

Wallis unfolded his arms and glanced at the doctor uncertainly. 'Could we get a paper signed by somebody?' he asked. 'Next of kin, maybe. Authorizing you, so to speak – just to avoid any trouble later. Puts you in an awkward situation otherwise.'

The doctor looked doubtfully at Hester and Charlie and the latter shook his head violently.

'You then, Mrs Cooper?' asked the doctor. 'Or his wife, perhaps?'

'Not Ella,' said Hester firmly. 'She's got enough to worry about. I'll sign it, it's for his own good and if he doesn't bother to thank me, I guess I'll survive.'

Wallis nodded. 'That's agreed, then,' he said. 'How long will all this take, doc? I want to cross the river at Deer Creek tomorrow. We're falling behind schedule already.'

The doctor considered for a moment. 'A day should see him through the worst of it, but no less. Shock can be a killer and he'll need time to recover. I'd like to say two days, but I – '

'Out of the question,' Wallis snapped. 'A day's all he can

have and I give that grudgingly. If we don't cross the mountains in time, we'll get caught in the snow and we could all die.'

'If there are complications – ' the doctor began.

'If there's complications, you and his family will have to stay behind with him,' said Wallis tersely. 'I'm leading a wagon train, not running a hospital. One day, doc – that's all you can have.'

'So be it,' said the doctor. 'We'll operate as early in the morning as we can.'

Charlie shook his head. 'He's not going to like it one little bit,' he muttered dolefully, but Hester tossed her head.

'He's not going to like being dead!' she cried. 'Now you just keep your trap shut, Charlie, and don't go warning him. We've got Ella to think about, and Will, not to mention another baby on the way.'

The doctor said, 'We'll need two bottles of brandy to keep him under,' and Wallis took them from the locked chest where the medicines were stored.

As he watched them leave, he sighed. Doctor Bonner looked barely old enough to have left medical school. Was he really experienced enough to amputate a man's leg?

'Rather him than me,' he muttered, referring to the unfortunate Jess Cash.

He was resentful of the enforced delay, for the North Platte River was already swollen with rains and he was not looking forward to the crossing. Fed by melting snow from higher up, the water would be freezing and the cattle and horses would resist it. The current would be strong and the water deep. A raft which was top-heavy with wagons could easily be overturned and animals swept away. He was anxious to have the crossing behind him, but now this wretched Cash boy was going to hold them up. His job was to get as many people as possible to California and every day lost lessened their chances of getting there. He suspected that Jess Cash would not survive the operation, and in his eyes that made the hold-up unnecessary. Still, the members of his company trusted him; they might not all *like* him, but they believed in his integrity. If he was to keep their respect, he

274

must be seen to be fair and humane. They could ill afford to lose a day but, as the doctor so often said, 'So be it.'

*

Jess slept fitfully, in constant pain from his injured leg and tortured by dark thoughts. When Ella woke in the early hours and suggested a brandy, he took no persuading but propped himself up on one elbow and drank it down in one gulp.

'Where did you get it?' he asked, reaching for the bottle.

Ella pretended an unwillingness to part with it. 'Take it easy,' she said. 'It won't last ten minutes if I give you the bottle. That cost money, that did.'

'So how did you get it?'

'Pa and Mr Harper did a deal,' she lied. 'Mr Harper's got a sick ox and Pa doctored it for him.'

Jess winced with pain and held out his hand. 'For Christ's sake, Ella,' he said, 'give it here.'

Ella hesitated, then handed it to him. 'Don't you drink it too fast,' she warned. 'Pa said it was to last you.'

'I don't give a damn about your Pa, Ella!'

He put the brandy to his lips and gulped greedily at the fiery liquid, gasping appreciatively.

'Christ, that's bloody good!' he exclaimed.

'You go steady on it,' Ella insisted, feeling pleased with her performance. 'Pa will blame me if you drink it too fast!'

'He should have this leg! Then he'd drink it fast. There are times when I think your father is –' He grimaced suddenly and leaned down to clutch at his leg and Ella watched him.

'Leg hurting?' she inquired.

'What d'you think!'

'I was only asking.'

'Well, don't!' He drank again and Ella noted with satisfaction that a third of the brandy had already gone.

'Give that bottle back,' she said. 'You're swilling it down like it was water.'

'I got to pee,' he said and Ella handed him the empty bottle which the doctor had provided for that purpose.

275

She went outside to empty it and when she came back he was lying back on the pillow with his eyes shut. Already his breathing was changing. Ella knew the signs; she had frequently seen him the worse for drink with bloodshot eyes, a flushed puffy face and slack jaw.

'How you feeling?' she asked.

'I'm gonna be fine,' he muttered, holding the empty bottle to his chest with both hands.

Ella crossed her fingers. It was almost going too well. 'I expect the doctor'll be here soon,' she said casually.

Jess breathed heavily for a moment before answering, then he muttered, 'I don't need him. I'm fine.'

His fingers, clutching the brandy bottle, were white with tension and Ella felt a moment's compassion. She wondered what would happen when he woke up and found his leg sawn off, but then remembered that he had brought it on himself and hardened her heart again while her own self-pity surfaced. She had wanted romance and love and excitement, and all she had was a useless child and now a crippled husband. She didn't think she deserved such a raw deal.

Ella looked at her husband's fingers as they clasped the bottle and thought how they had thrilled her in those far-off days of forbidden courtship. Then she had thought them wonderful fingers, slim and provocative, fingers that could thrill her body and unlock her passions. Now they looked ugly and a deep sigh escaped her.

'Damn you, Jess Cash,' she thought bitterly and began to dress.

Then she climbed down and went in search of Doctor Bonner. She surprised *him* taking a swig of something and he looked up sheepishly, wiping his mouth on his sleeve.

'I've never done an amputation before,' he confided, 'but don't you worry, I've watched plenty and assisted at two. We took an arm off once, below the elbow. Bled like a pig before we could cauterize it.'

Ella felt an unpleasant coldness in her back. 'What happened to him?' she asked, dreading the answer.

'Died of shock two days later,' he admitted, 'but he was older than your husband – nearly sixty, he was. Lived two days and then he was gone. Just sudden and quiet, no fuss. Speaking to me one minute, he was, and then he sort of sighed and closed his eyes. His wife died a month later to the day. That often happens, so they say – partly shock, partly a desire to be with the loved one. You want to be there while I operate?'

Ella's face paled. 'No,' she said, 'I couldn't. I'd faint. Not with expecting the baby and everything.'

'It doesn't matter,' he answered. 'Your mother's volunteered. No, you take your son and go somewhere – find someone to talk to.'

Ella thought longingly of Kate, but they had not spoken since Kate's fall from grace.

The doctor straightened his back and reached for his bag. 'Well, best get it over with,' he said, with an attempt at confidence which did not deceive her for a moment.

Ella went in search of Will, who had spent the last few nights with Hester and Charlie in a borrowed tent. Charlie was drinking coffee and wiping the last of the bacon fat from his tin plate.

'Well?' demanded Hester.

'He's drunk it all,' announced Ella.

'Good!' said Hester. 'Now Will, here's your ma come to fetch you. Give her a nice smile.' She told Ella, 'He's been a very good boy.'

Ella was feeling sorry for herself.

'Did he wet the bed?' she asked, knowing that he had. He always did.

'Yes, but he – '

'What's he done that's good, then?'

Hester bridled defensively. 'Well, he hasn't done anything bad,' she protested. 'Not that he meant to do, anyway. He can't help it, you know that, so don't start picking on him, Ella. The kid's not to blame because his father's losing a leg.'

'I never said he was.'

Remorsefully she pulled Will into her arms and rocked him. Once she had thought how wonderful it would be to see her son growing to manhood – handsome, appreciating her cooking, possibly helping her occasionally around the house.

Hester glanced at Charlie. 'You coming with me or not?' she asked. 'The doc can't start without us.'

She had put on a clean apron made of bleached sacking and she looked calm and capable. Charlie got to his feet grumbling under his breath and followed her in the direction of Jess's wagon.

After they had gone, Ella gave them ten minutes and then followed, Will on her hip. She stood outside the area where a trestle table had been set up between two wagons, the open ends covered with rough sheeting to ensure a minimum of privacy. A small crowd had gathered and people were listening with avid interest to the commotion within the 'surgery' where Hester, Charlie and the doctor were trying to tie Jess down to the table. Until they could immobilise him, the doctor could not proceed with the operation and vital minutes passed.

Ella heard Jess shouting obscenities, but she recognized the slurred speech and knew that the brandy had taken effect.

After much shouting and cursing, it fell quiet and the crowd assumed that the patient had finally been subdued. They heard the doctor say, 'Open his mouth. Force some more down. I can't stop once I get started, and he's going to need more to put him right out.'

There were more obscenities which were abruptly choked off, then a frenzied spluttering and Hester's voice said, 'Don't choke him to death, you stupid old fool!' and Charlie responded, 'Quit nagging. I'm doing the best I can.'

Outside Ella was the focus of all the attention. She felt her cheeks flame, but no one passed comment.

There was a short interval during which they heard Jess mutter and the doctor answer him soothingly. The crowd outside grew bigger, then suddenly there was a terrible scream and Ella fell to her knees with Will in her arms and pressed her face against his plump, yielding body. The sawing began, erratic and higher-pitched than anyone expected, and the screams continued without let-up. Charlie rushed out from behind the sheeting, white and visibly shaking, and

278

vomited against the wheel of the nearest wagon. He refused to go back, but Amos Carp volunteered to take his place and disappeared inside. Then the sawing stopped abruptly, the doctor cursed and it began again, continuing for several more minutes.

'He's a butcher!' whispered Charlie brokenly, sitting on a barrel with his head between his knees. 'Hacking away with that saw. Never seen anything like it in my whole damned life!' He drank whisky gratefully from a proffered flask. 'Shaking like a leaf, the doc was! Can't hardly hold the saw!' He shook his head. 'Jesus Christ! I never seen anything like it before and never want to again!'

He looked round with watering eyes, his chest heaving. 'Turned me over it did – all that blood and bits of pink bone everywhere. And the leg! Horrible! Not to mention the smell! Ugh!'

Talking about it brought back unwelcome memories and his shuddering listeners moved back quickly as he vomited again.

Twenty minutes later it was all over and Jess was sleeping off the brandy, oblivious of the heavily bandaged stump of his right leg. He was still strapped to the table and would remain so for another hour or so while the doctor hovered uneasily beside him, prepared for any emergency. Later they would carry him back to his own wagon and the makeshift 'surgery' would be dismantled.

The young doctor was highly praised for his part in the drama and when he had recovered from his fright, he was able to see the ordeal as first-class experience. If his patient survived, his reputation as a surgeon was made and if he did not find gold he would make his fortune from a career in medicine. All in all, he was pleased with the day's work and secretly congratulated himself on a job well done.

Chapter Thirteen

Ella was wiping Will's face with a damp cloth when a shadow fell across them both and she looked up to see Kate smiling uncertainly at her.

'Kate!' Ella stood up slowly and they regarded each other curiously.

Ella was tousled and harassed, her hair tied back into a scrawny bunch with a scrap of ribbon. Kate was wearing a clean gown of dark blue silk (which bulged noticeably below the waistline) and her hair was brushed up on top of her head. There was also, Ella was sure, a trace of powder on her face and her lips were unnaturally red.

'How is he?' Kate asked. 'Jess, I mean.'

Ella hoisted Will on to her hip.

'He's still alive,' she said. 'It'll be a few days before the doctor can say one way or the other. He's on a light diet – nothing but milk – and he hates that.'

'It must be terrible,' sympathized Kate. 'I had to come and ask. I slipped past your ma.'

'Oh, her!' Ella shrugged. 'Take no notice of her. She's just . . . you know . . .'

Kate nodded. 'I didn't know if you'd speak to me?'

'Why not? I've missed you.'

Kate's relief was obvious. 'How's Will?'

'Fine.' Ella hesitated, then blurted out, 'How are *you* making out?'

'Fine.'

'Is it — I mean, people are saying that . . . I mean, what's it *like*, Kate?'

'Fine,' Kate repeated. 'Daniel's really good to me and so are the men.'

'Good to you?' Ella was fascinated. 'How d'you mean, Kate?'

Kate was gaining confidence from Ella's reaction and she paused to smoothe her gown. 'They treat me like a lady,' she explained, 'and they call me "ma'am" and take off their hats. I'm making a lot of money, Ella. I'll have enough to care for this.' She laid a hand across her bulging stomach.

Ella regarded her wistfully. 'I'm glad for you,' she said.

'Anyone treats me rough,' went on Kate, 'Daniel would kill him.'

'Kill him? Honest?'

'Honest Injun!'

They both laughed and then Kate looked round nervously. 'I must be going,' she said. 'I just wanted to ask about Jess. I do hope he pulls through.'

'If he doesn't,' said Ella, greatly daring, 'I'll know where to come if I want a job.'

Kate giggled. 'Daniel *would* be pleased! I think he'd like one of those harem things they have in Arabia. He'd make a bloomin' fortune! He *gave* me this dress — bought it off the Harpers for me. It's real silk!'

'It's lovely, Kate.' Ella fingered the material enviously.

There was a short silence and then Kate asked, 'Ella, what are they all saying — about me, I mean?'

'Not much,' replied Ella. 'It's only the women and there aren't many. The men don't say much — leastways I've never heard them.'

'And your ma?'

'She's sorry you went off like that.'

Kate lowered her voice. 'And Amos Carp?'

Ella rolled her eyes. 'Buttons his lips and looks moody!' she said and they both laughed.

'And all because of a bloomin' policeman!' said Kate. 'Sad, really, but you have to laugh.'

281

Suddenly they heard Hester's voice calling to Ella and they both looked round guiltily.

Kate spoke quickly. 'Well, I'm friends if you are, Ella, and if you can sneak off any time and you want to see me, you'll find me easy enough.'

'I'll try,' promised Ella.

Kate gave her a crooked grin. 'I'm not busy daytimes!' she said and they both laughed again.

'I'd best go back,' said Ella, 'and see how Jess is. Ma's been marvellous – in there all the time, holding his hand and helping the doc. Pa couldn't take it.'

'Give him my kind regards,' asked Kate, 'when your ma's not listening.' She leaned forward to kiss Will's blond head. 'He's handsome, your Will,' she said kindly. 'He may not say much, but I bet he's thinking.'

Ella nodded and then impulsively held out her free arm and the two girls hugged awkwardly.

And then Kate was gone with quick strides, holding the precious silk skirt high to avoid the worst of the sage-brush, her ginger hair glinting in the sunshine.

Ella kissed Will. 'Yes, you *are* handsome,' she told him with a rush of tenderness, 'and you *are* thinking, aren't you?'

She craned her head to see his expression, which was as vacant as ever, but her meeting with Kate had strengthened her in a way she did not understand and as she made her way back to her stricken husband, she held her head just a little higher and the world did not seem quite so grey.

*

Lily and Henry finally caught up with the Western Hopers as they prepared to cross the Platte at Deer Creek. Twenty miles further along the Mormons had established a fee-paying ferry service and for some time had been making a great deal of money from the business. They charged three dollars to take a wagon across and fifty cents extra for each person. The Western Hopers would willingly have paid for the service, but the single Mormon ferry-boat could not deal with the demand fast enough. Word had filtered back to the Western Hopers that a succession of companies was already halted between Deer Creek and the Mormon ferry, awaiting their turn to cross. They decided to ferry over their own wagons and set about exploring the best ways to do this. Some groups combined efforts, cut down cottonwood trees and built their own rafts. Others took the wheels off their wagons, caulked the wooden bases and prepared to float them across. The River Platte, in some places two miles wide, was at this point no more than two hundred yards across, but it was still a risky undertaking and no one underestimated the very real dangers.

The Smiths, the Harpers and the Cashes joined forces to build a raft. They had chopped down and trimmed the timber and were lashing it together with ropes when the arrival of another wagon made them look up. There was an immediate cheer of delight and disbelief.

'Lily Golightly!'

'By all that's wonderful!'

Lily was touched by the welcome and a little flustered, too, when Bart Smith dropped the rope he was holding to lift her off the ground and swing her around.

Work on the raft stopped abruptly as they all gathered round, eager to hear how she came to be at Deer Creek instead of half-way back to Independence. By way of explanation, Lily indicated Henry Simms who dismounted from his horse and stood beside her.

'This is Mr Simms,' Lily told them. 'He was travelling with my husband before his death and looked after him. We met by chance at Fort Kearny and decided to go back together. Then – well . . .' She laughed and glanced at Henry.

'We couldn't do it,' he said simply. 'We decided we had to go on.'

Lily added, 'California tugs at the heartstrings.'

'It certainly does!' cried Amos.

Charlie said, 'Well, I'm mighty glad to see you again, Lily. You'd best let Captain Wallis know you're back. Hester and Ella are doing a bit of washing in the creek; they'll be pretty set up to see you again.'

Lily was puzzled. 'And Kate?' she asked.

There was an awkward moment and no one knew how to

answer. Amos turned away to continue lashing the trees together and Charlie scratched his head.

'I guess she'll be pleased, too,' he said reluctantly, 'but she's . . . well, she's changed a bit since you left.'

'Changed?' echoed Lily.

Charlie shook his head. 'It's a queer old business,' he said vaguely, 'but we've troubles of our own.' Lowering his voice, he told Lily and Henry about Jess's leg. 'He's been real quiet since he sobered up,' he confided. '*Too* quiet. Never raised his voice, never raged, nothing. Just this damned quiet and a real funny look in his eyes, as if he's gone off his rocker. Not that he has,' he added quickly. 'Leastways, the doc don't reckon he has. Shock, he calls it, but I think there's more to it. Creepy, it is, the way he looks. But there, Hester won't have it. Says I'm imagining things.' He shook his head.

'Poor Jess,' said Lily. 'Should I call in on him later, or would that make things worse?'

Charlie shrugged. 'Can't do no harm,' he said and with another shake of his head went back to his work on the raft.

Lily and Henry had agreed that they would not actually rejoin the company, as Henry believed they could travel more quickly if they went on alone, but he offered to help with the raft and the offer was promptly accepted. Lily went in search of Captain Wallis and found him helping an elderly man and his son, who were tying ropes to their caulked wagon in order to guide it across the water.

As Lily called his name, he turned and for a moment the expression on his face startled her. As she looked into his eyes, she was conscious briefly of a turmoil within him and something she could not define – a harshness, perhaps, which burned darkly in his eyes. The intensity of his look disturbed her, but then the moment passed and his face assumed an expression of polite surprise.

'Mrs Golightly,' he said. 'This is an unexpected pleasure.'

Lily smiled uncertainly. 'I changed my mind, Captain Wallis. A woman's privilege! I'm travelling on to California with a Mr Simms who was – '

Again she saw a flash of that other emotion in his eyes and faltered.

'Who was what?' he prompted.

'Who was my husband's companion before he died. I met him at Fort Kearny just after you all left. We've decided to travel on until possibly we can rejoin his old company – the Brown Bears.'

'Becher's outfit?'

'That's right.'

'But you'll honour us with your company in the meantime, is that it?'

His tone was mildly sarcastic and Lily bridled. '*If* you will allow us to do so,' she said.

She could not understand the change in his manner. He had always been courteous to her and Kate before she had decided to return to New York. Did he perhaps despise her for her decision and rate her a coward? Somehow the idea was not convincing.

As he still did not answer, she added, 'But if you'd rather we moved on, we will.'

'That won't be necessary,' he said. 'You are quite welcome. How are you travelling? This is a bad crossing, probably the worst of the whole trip. The current is deceptively fast and strong.'

'I still have the wagon,' she told him. 'Mr Simms is on a horse with a pack-mule. We shall cross with the Coopers. Henry is – '

She saw the slightly raised eyebrows at her use of the Christian name, but resisted the impulse to explain their relationship. It was none of his business, she thought.

' – already helping them with the construction of their raft,' she finished.

'If I can be of service . . .' He made it sound like a necessary politeness.

'Thank you, Captain,' said Lily and after a long moment he turned back to his task.

Lily began to walk away, her thoughts whirling. Whatever had she done to antagonize him? Suddenly a new thought struck her and she turned back. 'Captain Wallis, where can I find Kate Lester – or is she Mrs Carp now?'

Glancing back he said, 'Look for Mr Miller,' and then resumed his work.

'Mr *Miller?*' said Lily, but before she could query his information, she heard a familiar voice.

'Lily! Over here!'

She spun round and saw Kate hurrying towards her. In spite of her bulk, she was managing to look very grand wearing a dress Lily had never seen, and with her hair piled up under a straw hat which was lavishly decorated with ribbons and flowers.

'Kate!' she gasped and then the two girls were hugging each other like the lost friends they were.

'Why Kate, you look so different!' exclaimed Lily.

'Lily, I thought I'd never see you again!' cried Kate.

'Kate, how are you? You must be well, you look so – so *grand!* What's been happening while I've been away?'

Kate's eyes darkened. 'We'll talk about me later,' she said hastily. 'You tell me what you're doing here – I thought you were going back to New York?'

Quickly Lily explained yet again about her meeting with Henry Simms and their decision to carry on to the gold fields.

'So here we are,' she concluded. 'It's not terribly exciting. Now tell me your news, Kate.'

Kate's self-possession wavered momentarily. 'You'll be shocked,' she said, 'but I suppose you've got to know.'

'Kate!' Lily frowned. 'Is it so terrible? Captain Wallis mentioned Daniel Miller.'

Kate swallowed. 'It is fairly terrible. Oh Lily, promise me you'll still be my friend. Not like some I could mention. Promise me, Lily.'

'Of *course* I will.'

To Lily's astonishment, Kate closed her eyes and began to gabble almost incoherently, anxious to get it over as quickly as possible.

'I'm Daniel Miller's woman now, because when I told Amos about the baby he threw me over, the rotten pig! And Hester Cooper was rotten to me too, so I walked out on the whole blooming lot of them and Ella's not supposed to talk to me, but now she does, and I'm earning a lot of money –

286

that is we are, Daniel and me, and it was him who bought me this dress and in his eyes I'm a real lady.' She paused, breathless, then added defiantly, 'It's not as bad as what people think it is, and whatever they say I don't blooming well care! So there!'

'Amos threw you over?' said Lily, who had grasped that much. 'Oh, poor Kate, and I was imagining you married and – '

Kate tossed her head. 'I'm *not* your poor Kate!' she said. 'So you needn't feel sorry for me, Lily Golightly. Not you nor anyone else! I don't care that much – ' she snapped her fingers, 'for Amos Carp, because I'll be rich one day *and* I won't have to go grubbing for gold, standing up to my knees in freezing water and the sun beating down on my back and living in a tent in the middle of nowhere. I'm going to rent a proper house, and eat proper food and – oh Lily, it *is* all right, what I'm doing. It really is!'

Lily stared at her, uncomprehending. 'But what *are* you doing, Kate?' she asked. 'Have you married Daniel Miller? Is that it? That's not so terrible. I'm sure he's a nice man at heart.'

Kate rolled her eyes despairingly. 'He *is* a nice man, Lily, but I haven't married him. I *work* for him.'

'Doing what?'

Kate groaned. 'Strewth, Lily, you really don't know, do you? Your sort never do. Well, you've got to know some time, 'cause if I don't tell you there's plenty who'll be only too pleased.' She took a deep breath. 'I sell my favours, Lily. That's what I do.'

Lily's eyes grew round with the beginning of comprehension and the dawning of horror.

'Your *favours!*' she whispered. 'You don't mean you . . . oh, Kate! You *can't* mean what I'm thinking.'

'Well, I do!' Kate's tone was aggressive. 'And you can stick your nose in the air as much as you like, Lily Golightly, I don't *care*.' Her voice trembled, but her eyes flashed. 'Because we can't all be the pampered few, Daniel says, and we don't all have fathers who dote on us and servants and a carriage to drive around in. Some of us have to make our own way

287

and me and Daniel's like that. Anyway, Daniel says it's the oldest profession in the world and if I think like a lady then I *am* a lady and – oh, Lily . . .' Her voice wavered. 'Don't look at me like that! I can't bear it!'

Kate's face crumpled and her stiff demeanour softened as she began to cry and Lily put her arms round her to comfort her.

'I'm sorry, Kate,' she whispered. 'I didn't mean to look like anything. I know I've had advantages and you haven't. Please don't cry, Kate. Of course I don't want you to do what you do, but I blame myself. I should never have left you here on your own; I should have insisted that you came home with me. Oh, Kate, do you really know what you're doing? How will it all end? You can't do . . . this for ever and one day you'll be too old. What then?'

Kate's eyes gleamed triumphantly through her tears. 'Ah well, I've thought of that,' she told Lily. 'I shall sell toilet waters. I shall use all these recipes I learned at Mrs Harrington's – freckle remover and stuff like that. There'll be more women in California by then, bound to be, and they'll all want to pretty themselves up. Oh, I've got it all figured out, Lily. I'm not as daft as you might think.'

Lily was silent, impressed in spite of her misgivings. 'I was so sure Amos would look after you,' she said helplessly.

'Amos Carp!' cried Kate. 'Don't talk to me about him. I hate him, I really do. He made me feel so cheap and common . . .' Her tears came faster at the memory. 'But Daniel was so kind. You'll never know, Lily, how much it meant to me to have him say nice things. He *appreciates* me, Lily, he really does. Nobody else gives a damn – '

'I do, Kate. You know I do.'

'Yes, but you weren't here, were you?' said Kate rather illogically. She freed herself from Lily's arms, found a handkerchief and spluttered into it. 'It's no good caring if you're miles away. I needed somebody *here*. I needed somebody on my side.' She gasped for breath and dabbed at her eyes. 'Now I suppose I look a terrible fright,' she smiled wanly. 'That's your fault, Lily Golightly. Making me feel bad again.'

288

'I'm sorry,' said Lily contritely, 'but I don't know what to say.'

'Then don't say anything for it won't make any difference. I shan't change my ways, Lily, just 'cause you're back, so don't start preaching at me. I know you're a parson's daughter and you can't help that, but don't start on me, Lily – I won't put up with it.' She sniffed. 'Either we're friends or we're not, but I'm not changing my ways for you or anyone else. Daniel's been good to me and I'm staying with him as long as he'll have me.'

'Of course we're friends,' Lily told her, 'And I will try not to preach but – oh, Kate . . .'

'Don't "Oh, Kate" me!' cried Kate furiously. 'It's none of your business. I tell you I'm staying with Daniel and I'm not giving up what I do.' Her reddened eyes stared into Lily's. 'To tell the truth, Lily, I quite like it!'

Lily's expression was so incredulous that Kate burst out laughing.

'Oh, Lily, your face! Look, it's not that terrible, what I'm doing. A woman has to make the best of what she's got. If I had a beautiful voice I'd earn a living by singing – be an opera star or something. If I could paint, I'd be an artist. Well, I can't do anything like that but I can . . . well, you know what I mean!' Seeing that Lily's expression had not changed she added, 'Well, that's what Daniel says and that's what I believe. Oh, speak of the devil!'

At that moment Daniel himself appeared, the same wicked look in his eyes that Lily remembered.

'Aha!' he said with a grin. 'The charming Mrs Golightly! Has Kate been converting you? There's plenty of demand and I can easily handle . . .'

Lily tried to look severe, but she knew he was mocking her.

'I don't wish to talk about it, Mr Miller,' she replied. 'It's none of my business. Now if you'll excuse me, I must get back to Henry and see if I can help them with the raft.'

His eyes gleamed. 'Yes, I met your new beau,' he commented.

'Beau?' echoed Kate, surprised. 'You didn't say anything about a beau, Lily.'

Lily fought down her irritation. It would never do to let this wretched man know he had annoyed her.

'Mr Simms is a travelling companion,' she said firmly. 'That is all.'

Daniel smiled. 'Why, so are me and Kate,' he said. 'Real cosy, isn't it?'

If looks could kill, he would have been fatally wounded by Lily's expression, but still she struggled to appear unruffled.

'I would not call our arrangement cosy,' she replied. 'More like sensible and convenient. Now I must be going.' She gave Kate a hug and walked quickly away.

'I do like a woman with spirit,' Daniel said loudly, but she pretended not to hear.

Lily's thoughts were chaotic as she made her way back to rejoin the others. Kate could not possibly mean what she said, she told herself. That awful Mr Miller must have some kind of hold over her. Perhaps she should talk to her again and try to persuade her to give it up, but . . . Doubts crept in. By interfering she might conceivably make matters worse. How on earth had Hester let such a thing happen? Lily made up her mind to talk to Hester. And the *impudence* of that Daniel Miller! He really was the most infuriating man. It would give her great pleasure to put him firmly in his place, she decided, although she also admitted that to deal with a man like Miller would not be easy.

Perhaps she should leave well alone. Perhaps, as Kate had said, it was none of her business. And Kate had said she liked it! The more Lily thought about it, the more convinced she became that Kate did not want her help. Kate, it seemed, had her future mapped out, which was more than could be said of Lily. Perhaps, thought Lily, *she* should be asking Kate for advice! She sighed deeply; she had enough troubles of her own – she would concentrate on these and leave Kate to her own devices.

*

The raft took to the water just after three-thirty. Eleven of the other wagons had already crossed the river successfully and the mood of the company was optimistic. Wallis inspected the Coopers' raft and declared it sound, and then examined the way in which the wagons were lashed on to it. The Coopers' and Lily's smaller wagon were going over together and all the mules and Henry's horse would swim alongside. A second trip would be made to bring Gabby and Bart's wagon, the oxen and the Coopers' cow.

Ropes had been attached to the four corners of the raft and Henry and Gabby were already on the far side of the river with two of these. They would pull from the far bank in an effort to keep the raft steady and prevent it going downstream if the animals decided to swim the wrong way.

It had been agreed that Jess, Will and Ella should cross with the first load and the rest would follow with the lighter load. Jess, still unnaturally silent, sat with his back against one of the wagon wheels, one arm through the spokes to steady himself. Will was on his lap. To balance the raft, Ella sat on the far side of the wagon.

When all was ready, the reluctant mules were driven into the icy water, dragging the raft behind them, while Hester, Charlie and Bart pushed it from behind. As soon as it was in the water, it floated and a great cheer went up from the crowd of spectators whose turn would soon come. Amos, on one of the horses, went alongside the swaying raft on Ella's side to help control the mules.

Shouts echoed back and forth across the two hundred yards of water.

'Straighten her up!'

'There's a list!'

'Watch out!'

'Get over, you stupid brutes!'

Ella, terrified of water, closed her eyes and clung on to the wheel with both hands, her lips moving in an urgent prayer.

'How you doing, Ella?' shouted Jess.

'I'm fine,' she called back. 'How's Will?'

'He's fine.'

'Ella – I love you,' he called. 'You and Will.'

Impatient to resume her prayers for their safety, Ella did

not stop to consider her husband's uncharacteristic remark. She did not even bother to answer it with an assurance of her own love for him. All her energies were focused on the need to hang on tightly and to direct God's attention to the raft and its cargo.

Jess blinked back the tears which filled his eyes and his arm tightened round Will's plump body. He was breathing deeply to steady his nerves, but still his body trembled violently with the burden of his intended action. The raft rocked and dipped, ropes strained and the wagons creaked as they made slow progress towards the fastest stretch of current in the middle of the river.

Jess watched the blue sky with its heavy scattering of white clouds and they looked so incredibly beautiful that he marvelled that he had never noticed it before. Then he looked down at the stump of his leg and the familiar loathing filled him. An ugly, mutilated stump of a leg – and he was an ugly, mutilated lump of a man. They had deceived him, all those people who professed to love him. They had debased him and made him hideous in his own eyes, but he would have the last word because he would make his own choice. In fact he had already made it.

He waited until they reached the most dangerous section of the crossing and then he kissed Will and, holding him tightly with both arms, rolled quickly over the side of the raft.

When the icy water closed round them the first involuntary gasps filled their lungs, but Jess still clung to Will. They went under the raft together, buffeted upwards against it by the eddying current and then Will was torn from his grasp. Jess's last thought was that at least he had put things right for his son and he gave in almost gratefully to the painful, bursting agony that was his death.

*

No one on the far side of the river knew how many people had been on the raft, so the sight of it arriving with only one passenger did not arouse any comment or curiosity. Eager hands reached out to steady it while the animals were brought to land. When Ella felt the raft bump against the river bank, she opened her eyes.

'We made it!' she cried with relief and looked under the wagons, through the intervening wheels, to share her relief with her husband and son. When she did not see them, she thought with only slight surprise that they must have been quick to get ashore. She scrambled to her feet and stepped from the raft to the safety of the once grassy bank which was now a mass of mud, churned up by the wheels and hooves of the many wagons and animals which had already passed over it.

'I'm glad that's over,' she told Henry. 'I had my heart in my mouth all the way across.' She looked around her. 'Where's Jess got to? And Will?'

No one knew. She turned to Amos, but he was urging the mules out of the water. A small glow of panic flared within her as she turned to Gabby.

'My husband and Will?' she said. 'I don't see them.'

'When did they cross?' he asked.

'With me!' she cried. 'We crossed together!' The panic was taking shape. 'I don't see them,' she repeated, trying not to think what she *was* thinking, trying to stay calm. 'They must have got off before me. You must have seen them.' Her voice sounded high and thin. Then his eyes met hers, she saw his expression change and knew that suddenly he was sharing her fear. He looked quickly round, then spoke urgently to several other men who all, unbelievably, shook their heads. Ella's clenched hands went to her heart, protectively.

'You *must* have seen them!' she insisted. 'They were there, on the raft on the other side of the wagons. They were *there!*' She pointed a trembling finger. 'They *were*, he spoke to me – ' Her voice rose to a scream as she recalled Jess's last words to her. 'Oh, Jesus! They were there, I tell you. Oh, God! They must be – they can't be – God almighty!'

She could see the alarm in his eyes as he put a hand on her arm; she also saw something else which terrified her as she recognized it as compassion.

'Take it easy!' he told her soothingly. 'We don't know

yet.' He raised his voice and shouted, 'Anyone seen Jess Cash and the boy?'

Ella wanted her mother, but she was on the far side of the river.

'Ma!' she screamed. 'Ma! They've gone! They've drowned. I know they have. Jess did it. He drowned them. Oh Jesus, he's drowned them!'

Amos Carp came up to them and took the trembling woman into his arms. Over her head he spoke urgently to Gabby. 'Are you sure? How could it have happened? I heard nothing – not a shout, not a splash. Do you really think . . .'

Ella raised her face which was chalky-white and haggard. 'He meant to do it,' she whispered. 'He meant them to die. I should have thought, but I didn't. He said goodbye – it was a kind of goodbye . . .'

'When?' asked Amos. 'When did he say goodbye?'

'He didn't say it in so many words – ' She spoke jerkily, as if the words were being wrenched from her against her will. 'He said he loved me – and Will – he said he loved us. He never said things like that. I should have known. Oh, Jesus!' She turned shocked eyes towards Amos. 'I want my ma, Amos. I want my ma!' she began to cry. 'I want Will. I want my poor little boy. How could he do this? How *could* he kill my poor little boy . . . ?'

Amos patted her back awkwardly as she swayed towards him, tears streaming down her face, her body shaking.

'We don't know that,' he told her. 'It must have been an accident; he wouldn't do that.'

'But he did!' she sobbed. 'I know it, inside me. I *know* it. Don't you see? That's why he said it – that he loved us. Oh, Ma!'

'She'll be crossing shortly,' said Amos. 'She won't be long.' To Gabby he mouthed, 'Is the doctor across yet?'

Gabby nodded. 'I'll fetch him,' he said. 'Just let her cry it out. Christ, what a mess!'

*

It was established later that Jess could not swim and agreed that neither he nor Will could possibly have survived. Will

294

and Jess were officially declared dead and that evening Captain Wallis, his face grim but inscrutable, read a short memorial service for them. There were no bodies to bury, so there could be no real grave, but a crude headstone was erected with a short inscription:

Jess Cash and beloved son Will.
Drowned. RIP.

This was followed by the date.

Ella, supported by her mother and Lily, stared down at it in a daze of grief, while her fingers twisted aimlessly in the folds of her skirt.

Later that night, her mother shared the bed with her and they talked as the doctor's sleeping draught failed to take effect.

Hester, holding her daughter in her arms, tried desperately to bring her some comfort.

'Who knows what made him do it, Ella?' she said. 'Maybe we've misjudged him. Maybe it was God's will. Maybe God spoke to him, the way it says in the Bible. God knows everything and maybe He could see that poor Will was going to have a tough life. Or a miserable one. He could have wondered how to save him from it and saw Jess as a way to do it. Like a kindness, Ella.'

'A kindness,' Ella argued dully. 'What's kind about taking my husband and my kid? You call that *kind*?'

'Kind for *him*, Ella,' Hester insisted. 'Kind for Will. Kinder than letting him go on like he was.'

'You said he'd be OK. You always said that.'

'I know I did, but that was to cheer you up, Ella, you know it was. We all realized he hadn't got much of a chance. It used to worry me sick sometimes; I felt so helpless.'

'He could have got better.'

'He never would have.'

'Oh, Ma!'

Ella wept again and her tears released the pent-up misery in Hester which she had struggled to hold back since learning of the tragedy. Mother and daughter surrendered themselves to the anguish of loss, crying for a long time until exhaustion claimed them and they had no tears left to shed.

Hester drew a long shuddering breath. 'It's God's will, Ella, I'm sure of it,' she said. 'You just cling on to that notion and you'll come through. You've got another baby to think about, remember. Maybe a little girl. I guess that's God's will, too. See, He didn't want to leave you all alone, so He's left you with Jess's baby. He's worked it all out, Ella. I know I never spoke much about God and all that, but He's got to be up there somewhere and He must know what He's doing.'

'You reckon?' Ella asked hopefully, blowing her nose hard.

'I reckon.' Hester sighed deeply. 'Somehow we've all got to go on and we can if we make up our minds to it. We have to look forward to California and the new baby and being rich and everything. Look at Lily – she lost her husband and she didn't give up. You go have a talk with her tomorrow. She'll help you, Lily will.'

There was a long silence and then Ella asked, 'He was happy, wasn't he, Ma? Will, I mean.'

'Course he was. Happy as pigs in muck, but he just couldn't show it. Hadn't learned how to smile, but he had no worries and we all loved him. He knew that. Babies are happy and that's what he was all his life – a baby, in spite of his size. And Jess was happy – you made them both happy.'

'I hope so,' responded Ella. After another long pause, she said drowsily, 'D'you think it takes long to drown?'

'Certainly not,' Hester said firmly. 'Quickest way to go, I'd say. All over in a few seconds. I hope I drown when my turn comes.'

'Ma – '

'What is it?'

'You do love me, don't you?'

'Course I do, you're my little girl. Now go to sleep.'

'I want to pee,' Ella said.

'No one's stopping you.'

Ella sat up and reached for her shawl. 'Stay awake till I get back,' she asked.

'Make it quick, then.'

'There's snakes.'

'There's no snakes. Get on with it.'

Ella climbed out of the wagon and was back within minutes. She wriggled back under the blankets gratefully and said, 'There's lots of stars. It's a real pretty night.'

'Mm.'

'Ma –'

'What now?'

'Nothing.'

'Go to sleep, Ella, there's a good girl.'

Chapter Fourteen

The travellers soon discovered that the terrain on the other side of the North Platte was quite as inhospitable as Wallis had promised, and as the rainfall lessened the dust triumphed. At last the true value of the draught animals was properly appreciated, as the few who had neglected their beasts now paid for their short-sightedness when the weeks of unremitting effort brought more than one exhausted animal to its knees. They had survived the prolonged and gruelling conditions across the prairies, where at least the grass was in reasonable supply and water readily available, but now the trail was rising steadily, grass was harder to find among the sage-brush and water was frequently in short supply. Many of the oxen had nothing else to offer and no amount of bullying or coaxing could persuade them to get up again.

Fortunately for the Western Hopers, Wallis had been strict with regard to the care of the animals and their casualties were fewer than they might otherwise have been, but the bodies of the oxen from companies up ahead littered the trail as a dire warning. Whenever grass *was* found, the animals were grazed and some grass was cut and stored against the days when feed-stuff would be unobtainable.

At first the countryside became more rugged with outcrops of slaty rock, and a few spindly conifers appeared here and there, but later another problem presented itself which posed a further hazard for the unhappy cattle. The standing pools which served as watering places contained poisonous alkalis and three oxen who drank from them were quickly in a state of collapse, and had to be force-fed with fat salt pork to neutralize the effect of the alkali. For one beast this came too late and the unfortunate animal died.

The trail, now fourteen miles or so from the river, soon entered a hostile desert-like region which stretched for nearly fifty miles, but when at last the Western Hopers put that behind them they found themselves in the comparative heaven of the Sweetwater Valley. Here they carved their initials on the smooth brown surface of Independence Rock and then pressed on doggedly towards the long-awaited South Pass which would tell them they were half-way to California.

During these weeks the various loads had to be lightened again and more personal and family treasures were left by the wayside by tearful owners. Wallis did not woo them with false promises, but reminded them daily that the worst was *not* over and that the second half of the journey west would be infinitely more difficult and dangerous than the first half. They had steeper paths to negotiate and fewer animals now remained to haul the wagons. Only the most vital equipment could be carried, as they could only travel at the speed of the slowest. If they wanted to reach California while there was still gold to be found, everyone had to make sacrifices for the general good. The point was taken, albeit unwillingly, and as the abandoned treasures went over the side their owners consoled themselves with the assurance that when they reached the gold fields they would earn enough money to replace their goods ten times over.

When they did reach South Pass it was already the thirtieth of July and there was no time to stop and celebrate, so the company moved on and two days later came to a stream known as Dry Sandy where the trail split into two. Wallis explained that the southerly trail would take them past Salt Lake City, the new community set up by the Mormons two years earlier. This south trail was the long route to the gold fields, but there *was* civilization and a chance to rest animals and people. The alternative was Sublettes Cut-Off, a trail which would lead them more directly towards their ultimate goal but would cross a succession of mountain ranges running from north to south; they would, therefore, be forced to carry all the water they needed and the going would be harder than ever. But 'No', Wallis told them firmly, they would *not* be taking a vote on it. They were going to take the cut-off and there would be no argument. Of course there *were* arguments – many members of the company longed for a little luxury and others argued for a more democratic decision. Wallis was adamant however and, grumbling but resigned, the Western Hopers agreed to press on.

For the next ten days they hauled their protesting bodies and creaking wagons up steep rocky paths and lowered them, still protesting, into equally steep gullies. They unloaded and reloaded wagons and combined teams where necessary. Two oxen collapsed under the constant strain and had to be shot. One of the mules broke free and fell to its death. Tempers frayed and friendships faltered, but somehow they struggled on and on the thirteenth of August they reached the valley of Bear River where Wallis allowed them a whole day in which to recoup their energies and relax in the first pleasant surroundings they had experienced for weeks. The valley was idyllic by comparison with the discomforts of the previous weeks. The river ran swift and clear and was full of trout and the dazed animals grazed thankfully in lush grass. Game birds were plentiful and the men shot ducks, plover and even a large goose while birds sang overhead as the women and children gathered wild berries. A whole day's rest! It was so wonderful *not* to be on the move, and a brief visit by a number of friendly Snake Indians added the spice of excitement to the holiday.

Lily and Kate planned to bathe in the river and Lily decided to invite Ella to join them. Since the loss of her husband and child, Ella had been withdrawn and uncommunicative and all efforts to rouse her had failed. Her eyes wore a haunted look and on the rare occasions when she did speak, her tone was flat and her words monosyllabic.

Lily found her seated on a blanket beside the fire, staring into the flames, her arms wrapped around her knees. Hester, a few yards away, was patching one of Charlie's shirts.

300

'Ella? It's me, Lily.' Looking down at her, Lily smiled cheerfully. 'Do you feel like a dip in the river? Kate and I thought we'd bathe and then do our washing. Some of the men have been in and they say it's not too cold.'

Ella gave no sign that she had heard and Lily crouched beside her, trying to win her attention.

'It would do you good, Ella,' she said. 'Make you feel fresher. Do come with us.'

Ella did not turn towards her, but she gave an almost imperceptible shake of her head which Lily pretended not to notice.

She put an arm around Ella's shoulders. 'I know you're grieving, Ella,' she told her gently. 'I lost my husband, too, remember, but life goes on. It *has* to Ella, believe me.'

Ella's answer was a deep, ragged sigh which shook her whole frame, but still she said nothing.

'Please, Ella,' begged Lily, 'let us help you. You have so many friends and we *can* help you if you'll let us. I felt like you, desperate and lonely, but everyone rallied round to help me get over it. You never really get over losing someone you love, but you *must* make the effort, Ella, to make a new life. And the horror won't go away by itself, you must *make* it go. You've got to pick up the pieces, Ella, and struggle on.'

Ella's lips moved at last. 'Jess didn't,' she said flatly.

Lily hesitated, unable to deny it. 'Jess was wrong,' she replied. 'He wouldn't give it a chance. He could have survived losing his leg, just as I survived losing Patrick and you'll survive your loss. It hasn't been easy for me, but I've come to terms with it. You can, too, Ella – I promise you.'

At last Ella turned her head and Lily was appalled by the depths of misery she saw in her eyes.

'He killed Will,' said Ella. 'He *murdered* him.'

'Oh, no, Ella,' cried Lily. 'You mustn't see it like that.' Glancing up, Lily saw that Hester was watching her and the older woman gave a slight nod to show that she approved. Ella was *talking* again.

'He did,' said Ella tonelessly. 'He murdered my little boy.'

'Only because he thought it was for the best, Ella,' Lily told her gently. 'You know how Will was, how he found

301

everything so difficult. He always would have done, Ella. We all know that. I think poor Jess wanted to save Will from a difficult life. *We* know it's not right, but in Jess's eyes it *was*.'

Ella shook her head slowly and repeated, 'He drowned him. He drowned Will in the river.'

Lily hesitated, having second thoughts about the wisdom of bringing so much grief to the surface. Perhaps Ella needed more time in which to grieve; more time in which to come to terms with the dreadful circumstances of her loss. The deliberate death of a husband *and* a son was a tremendous blow. How could one person be expected to deal with so much sorrow? Should they expect Ella to recover from such a tragedy in the space of a few short weeks?

Uncertain, Lily glanced towards Hester who nodded vigorously, telling her to continue, so she took hold of one of Ella's hands.

'Come to the river with us, Ella,' she urged. 'You'll feel better if you do. We're all tired and dirty and a good splash in the water would do us good. If you don't feel better afterwards, I'll eat my hat!'

Another long sigh was the only answer, but impulsively Lily stood up, took Ella's hands in her own and pulled her to her feet.

'We are going to bathe in the river!' she declared with mock severity, 'and I won't hear another word.'

Ella stared at her, red-rimmed eyes framed by tousled hair. When Lily realized that she was not going to resist, she called out to Hester with exaggerated cheerfulness. 'Any washing to be done? We girls are going to enjoy the river while we can.'

Quickly, Hester bundled up a few garments – taking care to include none which had belonged to Will or Jess – and pushed them into Lily's hands with a wink and a whispered, 'Thanks, Lily.'

Lily, an arm round Ella's waist, led her to a sheltered spot on the river bank where Kate was furiously shaking dust from her clothes. Ella looked at the sparkling river without interest but she made no protest when Kate and Lily, with much gentle teasing, coaxed her out of her clothes.

Apparently oblivious of her nakedness, she watched as Kate and Lily took off their own garments.

'Ugh!' cried Kate, holding her faded blue skirt to her nose. 'This skirt really *stinks!* All that blooming dung, mud and sweat, not to mention splashes from the skillet. It's so stiff with dirt it could stand up on its own.'

To prove it, she balanced the skirt on the grass, but it crumpled slowly into a heap.

'Typical,' laughed Lily. 'Right, who'll be last in the water?'

'Not me!' cried Kate and she threw up her arms, jumped into the river and began to thrash around, screaming ecstatically and splashing water over herself.

'It's lovely!' she cried. 'It's cold but lovely! What's up with you two? Come on in. I tell you it's lovely. Lov-er-ly! Whoops! I think I trod on a fish! No, honest! I did! Come on, Ella. I *dare* you to! Come on, Lily. If you don't get a move on, I'll come out there and pull you both in. You're windy!'

Lily smiled at Ella. 'Do you hear that?' she asked. 'Windy, she called us. Here, give me your hand and we'll go in together. It's not deep – see, Kate's only up to her knees.'

With infinite patience, she urged Ella down the grassy bank and into the water. It was certainly not as warm as the men had pretended, but it was wonderfully refreshing and the hot sun shone down on them. When they were all in the river, Lily sank down gratefully and let the smooth cold water wash away the accumulation of dust and grime. They shared a small piece of home-made soap and Lily and Kate took it in turn to soap themselves and wash their hair. Ella stood knee-keep in the water and watched them, but made no effort to wash herself, so Kate and Lily washed her – making a joke of it all, pretending great hilarity in an attempt to provoke a positive reaction. They had just finished washing her hair when Hester put in an appearance, a bundle under one arm.

'That water looks good,' she cried, hands on her hips, 'but you're never going to put on those dirty clothes again.'

'No,' cried Lily, 'we're going to wash them all.'

'And what will you be wearing then?' Hester demanded.

Lily clapped a hand to her mouth and Kate giggled. 'I didn't think of that!' Lily confessed. 'Oh dear!'

'That's what I thought,' said Hester with a grin. 'I've brought Ella's Sunday best. Here.' She laid it on the grass. 'Should I get yours and Kate's?'

'Please,' said Lily and they gave instructions as to where their own spare clothes were to be found. When she had gone, Lily and Kate exchanged surprised looks.

'She's coming round,' Lily told Kate. 'She's fetching *your* dress as well as mine.'

'Looks like I'm forgiven!' grinned Kate, and Lily could see how pleased she was to be accepted once more.

Half an hour later the four women sat round Hester's fire, sipping coffee and eating flap-jacks. Lily, Hester and Kate talked animatedly, but Ella had relapsed once more into silence. A short distance away, the clean clothes were spread on the sage-brush to dry.

Henry had made some leather 'boots' for Lily's oxen to preserve their tender hooves from the gravels and sands which were beginning to cause them so much distress, and with Charlie's help was fitting them over the feet of the wondering animals. From the river bank came the sounds of laughter and a continual splashing as the men washed their clothes and swam. Elsewhere, a man was singing to a fiddle and someone was dancing on a wooden board to a boisterous chant and the rhythmic clapping of an appreciative audience. Hammers rang on metal as various repairs were carried out and horses, mules and oxen added their contented voices to the motley sounds that filled the air.

Matt Wallis, strolling unobserved amongst his company, felt a rare moment of satisfaction. These were his people; he had brought them this far and for the time being, most of them were content. His feelings were heightened by the brief and unexpected glimpse he had caught earlier of the three women bathing in the river. His eyes had dwelt on them only briefly, but he had firmly acknowledged what he had known for some time past, that if he ever took another wife it would be Lily Golightly.

*

304

Later that evening an impromptu hoe-down was organized, but as Ella was not in a dancing mood and Kate was not feeling too well, Lily, Hester and Mrs Harper were the only women taking an active part in the proceedings. Mr and Mrs Harper retired to their wagon soon after nine, as they always did in preparation for the early rise the next morning. The men valued the opportunity to hold a woman in their arms and knowing this, Lily and Hester accepted offers from young and old until Henry complained to Lily that she had only partnered him twice and it surely must be his turn again! She laughingly agreed and they danced a particularly lively reel until the music speeded up impossibly and all the dancers retired laughing from the 'floor', admitting defeat.

'I'm quite exhausted!' Lily declared, mopping perspiration from her glowing face.

'I'll get you a drink,' Henry offered. 'I could do with something myself. My throat's as dry as the proverbial bone. Give me your mug.'

Thoughtfully Lily watched him go, one hand to her heaving side as she gulped air into her depleted lungs. She had given up trying to convince herself that what she felt for him was no more than sisterly affection, but was it love? She did not feel, as she had with Patrick, that unless they were together every moment of the day her life was being wasted, nor did thoughts of him dominate her waking moments. The ecstasies and agonies of first love were conspicuous by their absence . . . and yet perhaps she loved him. He had spoken to her of love and she did not doubt his feelings towards her. Perhaps one day they would be man and wife and the idea gave her a feeling of security, but she regretted the lack of the vital spark which she had believed so necessary. Maybe, she told herself, it marked the difference between being in love and loving. Patrick had burst across her heavens like a fiery comet, but Henry was a familiar star.

Lily watched him making his way through the crowd, his long lean body clad in a dark blue cotton shirt and trousers tucked into his boots. She sighed involuntarily. Perhaps the passion of first love would never come again. If that were so, then she must settle without complaint for this new kind of love. Henry Simms was an honest man and would make her a good husband. She had tried to imagine the two of them as lovers, but the image had never quite materialized. Her failure with Patrick troubled her and she found herself wondering once more if *she* had been to blame and if so, how. Would the same problem arise again? Would Henry Simms be able to make love to her, she wondered, and if not, how would they produce a family? The thought of being childless saddened her and she pushed it resolutely out of her mind. She must not anticipate such difficulties; it was not 'seemly'. She was as ignorant about sex as a well-brought-up woman was supposed to be, she reminded herself. Her husband would take the initiative – that was his rightful role . . .

A voice beside her made her jump guiltily. 'Mrs Golightly, may I have a word with you, please?'

Before she could protest Matt Wallis had taken her arm and was leading her away from the circle of people. Glancing up into his face, she saw that he looked stern and wondered uneasily what she had done to deserve his attention.

'What is it?' she asked.

'I wondered,' he said, 'if you still mean to move on with Mr Simms. You did tell me you intended to rejoin the Brown Bears, Mr Simms' original company, but that was more than a month ago.'

So that was it. Lily relaxed.

'We had intended to,' she answered, 'but one of the Brown Bears' company passed us going home one day last week, and he reckoned the rest of his company were more than a week ahead of us and making very good time. We don't know now if we would ever catch up with them, so we haven't actually decided what to do.'

'You certainly won't catch them up if you travel with the wagon,' he told her, 'but Mr Simms might manage it alone on horseback with only the pack-mule to worry about.'

His face was expressionless as he looked at her and Lily stared at him. 'Go on *without* me, you mean? Oh, but I don't think – that is, we had intended to stay together.'

'Is that really wise?' he asked.

'Is it *un*wise?' She was flustered.

'With respect, ma'am,' he said, 'I think it is more suitable for a respectable widow to travel with the security of a company. A woman travelling alone with a man who is not her husband is bound to provoke a certain amount of curiosity and unfavourable comment.'

Lily stammered, 'Unfavourable comment? I don't think there is any inpropriety . . .' She hesitated. No, he *was* right. There *was* impropriety and she would be a fool to pretend otherwise.

'Believe me, I only have your welfare at heart,' he assured her. 'A young widow – '

Lily drew herself up to her full height in an effort to hide her humiliation. 'Captain Wallis,' she said coldly, 'I must confess you may be right. Perhaps we are bringing your company into disrepute. Is that what you mean? Because if so, I assure you we shall both move on as soon as possible!'

Captain Wallis appeared quite unmoved by this pompous speech. 'I did *not* mean anything of the kind,' he replied. 'I'm sure we can survive a little gossip. I am just asking if your intentions are the same as they were, and trying to give you a little advice.'

'I don't need your advice, Captain Wallis.' She sounded almost shrill now and cursed her own stupidity; she was over-reacting and she knew it.

'Then please forget it,' he said. 'I shan't mention it again. What I said about Mr Simms can stand, though. He will make much better time without you and you will be better off with us. I would take responsibility for your safety.'

'You?' asked Lily, startled.

He looked directly into her eyes. 'I would be glad to,' he said evenly.

'Oh, I see,' Lily said doubtfully.

To her surprise, he lowered his voice. 'Do you?' he asked. Lily became aware of a subtle change in his manner.

'Mrs Golightly, I respect you,' he said. 'I . . . *care* about you. You don't need anyone else – don't you *see*?'

'Captain Wallis – ' Lily began, but without any warning he pulled her suddenly towards him and his lips came down

307

hard on to hers. His arms held her in a fierce grip from which she could not hope to escape, but then just as suddenly he released her and she stumbled and almost fell.

She saw at once how completely he regretted his action.

'Christ! That was stupid,' he said. 'I don't know why . . .' He broke off, completely at a loss to explain his actions. 'I owe you an apology.'

'There is nothing to forgive,' stammered Lily.

Through her own confusion she recognized his and saw the anger mingled with regret in his eyes, but there was something more which she failed to identify.

'It was unforgivable,' he insisted. 'Crazy!' He shook his head, mortified by the situation in which he found himself.

For a few moments Lily glimpsed the real man behind the stern façade which he usually presented to those around him. She had never seen him make a wrong move and had accepted his sometimes brusque manner and inflexible character at face value. Now she was seeing a different Matt Wallis – a more human man had emerged briefly and this man was capable of error and regret and could suffer just as much as anyone else from his mistakes. Lily felt a rush of sympathy for him.

'Please,' she begged, 'let's forget it. I'm sure you intended no disrespect.'

He looked as though he was going to speak again, but hesitated and then with a slight nod swung away from her and strode off across the grass.

Lily covered her face with her hands and drew a deep breath, her thoughts confused and guilty. This man who meant nothing to her had somehow kindled within her a spark which was an entirely new experience. His unexpected and unwelcome kiss had caused a flicker of physical desire; the feeling was unfamiliar but immediately recognizable and Lily was shocked at the thought that her body could respond in that way to a man like Matt Wallis when it had never responded so to Patrick. Slowly, she lowered her hands and drew another deep breath. There was so much to learn about love and passion and she was only a beginner. Should she be pleased that her body showed such promise or ashamed that it had betrayed her? And had he felt a similar arousal, she wondered. Was that the indefinable emotion she had glimpsed in his eyes? Dismayed, she wondered how she would be able to face him when they next met and decided to pretend it had never happened.

Slowly she made her way back to the circle and smiled at Henry who stood waiting for her, the promised drink in his hand, but even as she smiled at him her heart raced with the memory of that stolen kiss.

The company moved on at four the next morning, the fourteenth of August. Lily walked beside one of the oxen and Henry walked alongside the other, leading his horse. The pack-mule, tied to the rear of the wagon, plodded along behind them with its head down, the load swaying precariously with every roll of its gaunt body. Above them the sky was still dark and a few stars lingered. The chill night air persisted and Lily wore a thick shawl to keep out the cold. The damp air settling on the sandy soil of the trail had formed a brittle crust, but the wagons and animals ahead of them had crushed it and the familiar gritty dust was already rising into the air, so that most of the company wore kerchiefs or scarves tied over mouth and nose. As usual, the early morning mood of the company was one of resigned fortitude, but the day's rest had helped their morale and there were fewer arguments than usual and even a few cheerful remarks.

Henry and Lily walked in silence for the best part of a mile before Lily pulled the kerchief from her face to speak to him.

'Henry, do you want to travel on alone?' she asked abruptly. 'I wouldn't mind too much if you did.'

He pulled down his own scarf and gave her a quick sideways glance. 'Alone? Why should I?'

'I just wondered. You could go faster without me and the wagon.'

'I know. I've thought about that.'

Her heart lurched uncomfortably. 'And what did you decide?'

'Nothing,' he grinned. 'I didn't want to leave you, if you

must know. California's a big place and if I went on without you I don't reckon we could be sure of finding each other again.'

Lily's relief was almost tangible. 'I'm glad,' she said, 'but do you think we'll all get there in time? Will there be any gold left when we arrive?'

'I guess so, they say there's enough for everyone. We'll have to hope so.' His eyes narrowed slightly. 'Do you want me to go on alone, then?'

'Of course not,' said Lily. 'I like us being together, but if it meant you coming all this way for nothing . . .'

He shrugged. 'If we don't find the gold, at least we've found each other,' he told her. 'But we *will* find it, I know we will. I feel lucky!'

Lily glanced at him across the curved horns of the oxen and thought how reassuring it was to have him so near.

'All these questions,' observed Henry casually. 'Was it something Wallis said? I saw him talking to you yesterday evening. Has he put these ideas into your head?'

Lily kept her eyes fixed on the trail ahead of her. 'Sort of,' she admitted. 'I think he feels I'm holding you back.'

Henry gave a short, mirthless laugh. 'How *considerate* of him!' he said. 'Wants you all to himself, I suppose, with no competition.'

Taken aback by this shrewd assessment of the facts, Lily could only shake her head. The news that Henry had been watching them the previous night made her uneasy. Surely he had not seen that kiss? She certainly hoped not.

'What makes you say that?' she inquired.

'I've noticed the way he looks at you.' He walked on in silence for some time and then asked, 'Why didn't you tell me last night what he'd suggested?'

'I don't really know,' replied Lily. 'I suppose I was afraid you *would* want to go on without me. I wasn't going to mention it at all, but then I changed my mind. I didn't mean to be deceitful.'

'I know,' he said. 'I'm sorry; I'm just jealous, I guess.'

'You needn't be, Henry,' Lily assured him. 'There's no one

310

in this whole company who could hold a candle to you – not in my eyes, anyway.'

After another long pause he said, 'I do wish you'd marry me, Lily. It would be so much more sensible.'

In spite of herself, the word 'sensible' sent a chill into Lily's heart. Was that how Henry saw their proposed union – as *sensible*? It sounded so dull.

'I'm sure I will marry you, Henry,' she said. 'I just want some time, as I told you.'

'You mean you *are* going to marry me?' he cried. 'You *mean* that, Lily?'

'I think I do.'

Her reply seemed to take him by surprise. 'You really mean that you love me?'

She hesitated. 'I'm very fond of you Henry, and I think I will learn to love you.'

He gave a whoop of excitement and his joy was infectious. Lily smiled back at him as he snatched off his hat and threw it into the air. When he had jammed it on again, he cried, 'Oh Hell, I don't believe this! You're going to marry me? Are we betrothed, then? Is that it?'

Now that Lily had committed herself she had a rush of doubts, but it was too late. 'I don't know,' she said. 'I suppose I'm "spoken for".' She hesitated. 'But . . .'

'But what?'

'Could we keep it to ourselves for a while, Henry? Because of Patrick.'

He was obviously disappointed. 'If that's the way you want it,' he said reluctantly.

Lily hardened her heart. 'Just for a little longer,' she begged.

'And then we'll be married?'

'I suppose so.'

'You keep saying you "suppose so",' he protested. 'Hell, Lily! I can't make you out!' Abruptly he urged his horse into a trot and led it round in front of the oxen, making them flick their ears and roll their eyes in alarm. Lily put a hand on the head of the nearest animal and murmured soothingly to it as Henry took his place beside her.

He put an arm round her shoulders experimentally and then kissed the side of her face.

'Hey, we're going to be wed!' he teased. 'Imagine that. You'll be Mrs Henry Simms! I'm getting myself a wife. My folks'll be pole-axed!'

Lily's eyes widened. 'Your folks! I'd forgotten all about your family! Oh dear, Henry, it will be a bit of a shock for them, won't it? Do break it to them gently or they'll never forgive us.'

'They'll be overjoyed,' he assured her. 'An English daughter-in-law – that'll set the tongues wagging. Maybe I'll write them a letter at long last.'

'Henry! Haven't you written to them yet?'

He shook his head, looking entirely unrepentant. 'They know I hate to write,' he said. 'They know I'll be fine.'

'*How* do they, Henry?' Lily protested. 'It could easily have been you that died of cholera instead of Patrick. For all they know, you might be dead and buried. Oh, you really should have written to them.'

To her surprise, this short homily made him laugh. 'Listen to that!' he cried. 'You're nagging me already! Just like a real wife.'

'Henry!' Lily regarded him crossly. 'I am not nagging and anyway nagging is not "wifely". Men can nag, too.'

'But women do it best,' he said slyly. 'My pa reckons they're the experts.'

'Then I don't care much for your father's opinion,' Lily retorted.

He grinned again. 'So you don't like your pa-in-law!' he said. 'Not a good start to married bliss!'

'Marriage is *not* bliss!' cried Lily and then bit her lip in vexation. What she had said could only be interpreted as disloyalty to Patrick and she had not intended that. Henry must not think that her marriage to Patrick had been unhappy. That was far from the truth.

But he was looking at her strangely. 'Patrick thought it was,' he told her. 'He praised it daily as a wonderful institution and urged me to find a wife as soon as possible.'

'And yet he set off for California without me,' cried Lily

before she could stop herself, 'after only one week of married "bliss".' She drew in a long breath.

Henry's teasing tone had vanished as he said quietly, 'I did wonder about that. I wondered if I would be able to leave *my* new bride for nearly a year, but it wasn't my place to ask questions.'

'No.' She glanced up at him and her eyes were troubled. 'It doesn't matter now. I shouldn't have spoken the way I did and I'm sorry. I don't want to talk about it too much but . . . I think we were both unprepared for married life. Maybe if we'd had longer together . . .' She shrugged. 'Not that we weren't happy, we were.'

He nodded. 'I'm glad, Lily, for both of you.'

'It's just that being starry-eyed is no way to go into marriage,' she told him earnestly. 'Papa was right. He said we would come down to earth with a bang and of course we did. If only my aunt had lived, I might have been better prepared. Being a wife isn't easy.' She smiled at him. 'I don't suppose being a husband is easy, either.'

'I'm very keen to find out,' he assured her and they both relaxed into laughter.

Henry put an arm round her wiast. 'Look, Lily,' he said, 'I take your meaning, but I do think we'll make out together. I'll do everything in my power to make you happy and if we strike it rich in the gold fields, so much the better. We'll be happy *and* rich. If not, we'll just be happy. What d'you say, Lily? Does it sound too terrible?'

Lily slid an arm round his lean back and shook her head. 'It sounds rather good,' she told him, pulling him closer.

He stopped walking and bent to kiss the top of her head, but his horse and the oxen moved on inexorably, tugging them apart again, and he grumbled in mock exasperation. 'How's a fellow supposed to do his courting?' he demanded. 'Courting on the Californian trail isn't easy.'

Lily laughed. 'If love can survive this, it can survive anything! And you will write to your parents, won't you, Henry?'

He put a hand on his heart. 'I promise,' he said. 'Now stop nagging, wife-to-be!'

They walked on for some time in a more comfortable silence until Henry remarked suddenly, 'But he's right — Wallis, I mean. We *could* make much better time without the wagon. Suppose we both rode? Do you think you could bear it? We could trade the wagon for another horse and mule and we might cut the time by a third or even a half.'

Lily frowned. 'I don't know,' she said slowly. 'Maybe I could, but where would I sleep? In a tent?'

Henry rolled his eyes. 'In *my* tent?'

'Certainly not, Henry!'

'You could if we were — '

'But we're *not* married yet,' she laughed. 'You must remember I'm a parson's daughter. Do stop it and be serious, Henry. Could I bear it in a tent? I don't know. Are there snakes and suchlike? I'm not very brave about such things.'

'There must be rattlers, but I've never seen one. Honest Injun!'

'Leave the Indians out of this, Henry.' She trudged on, her eyes closed. 'I'm trying to imagine it. Yes, I think I could get used to it if I had to. Would it really make so much difference to the time?'

He nodded. 'You know how frequently men pass us, going ahead — some without even a pack-mule. They don't lumber themselves down with anything that's not vital. A bed's not essential and neither is a covered wagon. If it rains, you wear your oilcloths and a broad-brimmed hat. I'll get you a man's hat.' He was rapidly becoming enamoured of the idea. 'All we really need is a blanket, a rubber sheet, a few cooking pots — '

'Food,' put in Lily.

'I'd shoot what we need.'

'But flour and — '

'We'd take some and buy the rest as we go along. Bedding, food, rifle and plenty of ammunition — '

'The Indians, Henry! What about the Indians?'

'They won't harm us. We won't be all alone, remember; we'll only be travelling independently and we're bound to be passing other companies most of the time. We'll have the best of both worlds, Lily, and we'll beat most of them to the gold! However much gold there is, it can't last for ever. It's got to run out some time.'

'I've just remembered,' said Lily, dismayed. 'I've never ridden a horse!'

Henry laughed. 'You just sit on and hold tight. You can't go wrong!'

'I could fall off.'

'Of course you won't.'

Lily's heart was beating a little too fast for comfort as Henry continued. It was all so sudden and she wanted time to think about it, but one look at Henry's excited face was enough to tell her that she would not have that time.

'We'd make out fine in the gold fields, Lily,' he was saying. 'Just the two of us. I could pan and you could cook and some of the time you could give me a hand. We don't need anyone else. I know what they say about teaming up – four or five to a claim – but that way you have to split your gold four or five ways. Our way, we'd get to keep it all. Oh, Lily, I feel so lucky! I've got this hunch that we're going to be two of the lucky ones. Someone has to find the stuff, Lily. Why not us? If only we can get there while there's still time to find the right spot and stake our claim!' His eyes glinted and he ran his fingers through his hair until it stood up untidily in blond spikes. 'It's going to be us, Lily! I feel it in my bones. What d'you say? Shall we give them all the slip and go it alone?'

Gazing into his eager blue eyes, Lily found all her doubts melting away in the heat of his enthusiasm and realized suddenly that she was nodding her head.

'You will?' cried Henry. 'Oh Lily, you're twice the girl I thought you were, d'you know that? And I thought you were really something before! Lily Golightly, I love you. We'll do it!'

He flung down the reins and threw his arms around her. Lily found herself returning his bear-hug with equal enthusiasm.

'Tomorrow, then!' he said. 'We'll go tomorrow. Just you and me, Lily. You won't regret it, I promise you. Lily Golightly, I *adore* you!'

315

He took her hand and dragged her along in pursuit of his horse who had ambled on, indifferent to his owner's erratic behaviour.

'I'll go and see about trading the wagon,' he told her breathlessly, 'and you can tell Wallis we're leaving – that'll take the smile off his face!' He laughed, relishing the thought of it. 'And we'll set out before first light while they're all yoking up the animals and preparing their wagons. We'll fly off, free as a couple of birds!'

The last of Lily's doubts were vanishing and she, too, was filled with a wonderful excitement. The dreary weeks of trail life were over. No more petty squabbles, no more delays, no more restrictions for the good of the majority. They would travel light, in full control of their own destinies, paying for their own mistakes and dependent on no one. She felt a great surge of confidence. They could do it together. She would put the past behind her and look to the future. Tomorrow was a new day and the world looked suddenly bright.

Chapter Fifteen

Kate frowned into the mirror and fingered a small spot on her chin.

'Go away!' she muttered and reaching for her powder — obtained for her by Daniel in yet another of his mysterious 'deals' — she applied it vigorously. Not that he would see it in the dark, she reassured herself, but she knew it was there. Tonight she wanted to look her best, because her client was none other than Bart Smith and she was anxious to make a good impression. Then, hopefully, he would confide in his brother Gabby that she was wonderful. Gabby was very friendly with Amos Carp and Kate was relying on Gabby to pass on the 'confidence' to him. Then Amos would know just how foolish he had been to reject her. Kate allowed herself a few moments of wishful thinking as she imagined Amos approaching her to ask again for her hand in marriage, and she smiled gently at herself in the mirror.

'I'm sorry, Amos,' she told him. 'I don't want to be a married woman. See? I want to go on as I am — I can do just what I like and I've no husband to moan at me if his dinner's not on the table and no screaming kids to — oh, blow it!'

The cheerful vision faded abruptly because, of course, she *did* have a 'kid' to consider and her present way of living could not continue much longer. A baby would complicate life. She still had not had the courage to discuss the baby with Daniel. He knew it was coming and yet he talked about the future as though they would still be together. Did he

mean to find a nursemaid? Someone who would care for the
child overnight while she was working, or did he imagine
the child would sleep all the time, because if so he would be
sadly disillusioned. Kate had no illusions where babies were
concerned; in her experience they were noisy, smelly, permanently hungry and utterly time-consuming. If, however, they
could pay someone to care for the child then that would
come out of her earnings – and then there would be precious
little left and she could not expect Daniel to contribute to
the child's upkeep. It was a problem. Maybe she *should*
accept Amos if he changed his mind and proposed . . . but
he never would.

When Daniel had first asked her to take Bart as a client
she had been reluctant, but he had soon persuaded her,
pointing out that good news travels fast. She recalled the
first time she had seen Bart on board the *Michigan*. Amos
had told her his name and had pretended that he had 'had
enough of petticoats' and wasn't looking for a wife! But Bart
had hinted otherwise.

'Who cares!' said Kate aloud. 'I'm not looking for a
husband.'

She stuck out her tongue and then sighed. If *only* she
wasn't expecting a baby! She wanted to stay with Daniel
Miller. If only she hadn't encouraged Constable Ernest
Bailey, but it was too late now.

'I don't even like babies,' she told her reflection. 'They're
horrible!'

But if ever she did manage to find a husband, babies would
be her lot. She really would prefer to go on as she was, with
Daniel Miller 'protecting' her and everyone queuing up for
her favours. It gave her a wonderful sense of power.

'I'm somebody,' she said, adjusting the frills on her chemise
and straightening the ribbon.

She turned as Daniel peered into the wagon. 'All set?' he
asked in a loud whisper. 'He's out here, cooling his heels,
nervous as a kitten.'

'How do I look?' she asked.

'Very ladylike.'

318

That answer always pleased her. 'I'm ready then.' She put a hand to her back and grimaced.

'What's up?' he asked.

'Nothing. Bit of pain, that's all. It's gone now. You're sure I look good?'

'Never better. You're a real queen, Kate. Good Queen Kate, that's what we'll have to call you!'

He winked and blew her a kiss and was gone. Kate, waiting, hummed nervously under her breath. A candle gleamed dully – she had decided that a little light was better than complete darkness.

'Bart Smith,' she muttered. Once he had said that she looked very like the sort of girl he wanted to marry.

'Only thinner!' she thought. 'And not with a baby on the way!'

Another sharp pain made her wince. Damnation! She rubbed her back awkwardly, but then a sound made her look up and she saw Bart climbing into the wagon.

He took off his hat and made an elaborate bow. 'Good evening, Miss Lester.'

'Good evening, sir,' she replied, with the same hint of mockery.

'It was nice of you to say I could come,' he said. 'I thought you'd say "No".'

Kate smiled brightly. 'Your money's as good as anyone else's,' she said in her most businesslike tone.

'I guess so.'

'There's a cushion to your right,' she told him. 'Make yourself comfortable.'

'Oh. Thanks.' He sat down awkwardly, and rested his hat on his knees.

'How's Gabby?' asked Kate.

'Doing fine.'

'That's good – and you look well.'

'I'm doing real fine.'

'So am I,' she said sharply.

'Are you, Kate?' he asked. 'I did wonder – I mean, we all wondered – that is, we hoped that Miller – '

'*Mr* Miller,' Kate corrected him.

'Sorry, Mr Miller . . .' He stopped, embarrassed.

Kate did not help him, but watched as he began to turn his hat round and round, straightening the battered brim with nervous fingers.

At last he looked up. 'Well, we're more than half-way there,' he remarked.

'What?'

'To California, I mean.'

'Yes, we are.'

'There was a long pause.'

'Sure is something to write home about, this trip!'

'Sure is,' agreed Kate.

'It can change a man's life,' he said.

Kate nodded. It can change a woman's life a whole lot faster, she thought, but she let that pass.

'Kate . . .'

She waited. Was he going to make small talk all night? She was disappointed in him.

'Oh God, Kate, you do look pretty!' he stammered. 'Sitting there with all them frills and stuff and your hair shining.' He threw down his hat and began to tug at his left boot, then stopped and said, 'May I?'

'Go ahead.'

Another pain shot through her and Kate bit her lip hastily to suppress an involuntary gasp of pain.

His boots were off and he was pulling off his jacket. Kate wondered uneasily about the unfamiliar pain. It couldn't be the baby's time – that was several months away – yet there was a strange urgency about it.

'What's up?' he asked.

'Nothing,' said Kate. 'Why do you ask that?'

'You're frowning.'

'I didn't mean to.' She rearranged her features hastily.

He pulled down his braces and began to tug his shirt over his head. 'Yes,' he said, swallowing nervously, 'you look real pretty, Kate. Amos was a fool to let you go – a pretty girl like you.'

Kate said hopefully, 'He doesn't think so.'

'I reckon he does, Kate.'

'Did he say so?' she asked. 'I mean, did he actually say that he wished he hadn't – God almighty!' She clutched at her back and her mouth opened in a loud groan.

'Kate?' he looked at her, startled.

'It's nothing!' she gasped. 'At least, it is something. A bit of a pain. It's gone now, but it took me by surprise.'

After a moment he asked, 'Have you had it before?'

'No – but it's nothing.'

Kate could see that his earlier excitement had been somewhat dashed and she tried to think of a way to restore his confidence. A shock, she knew, could easily dampen a man's ardour. As he began to unbutton his trousers, she said, 'This life seems to suit you. You're looking very fit. I saw you back at Deer Creek with Gabby, felling that tree.'

He brightened. 'Did you? I didn't see you, leastways – '

He broke off as Kate doubled up, both hands clutching her abdomen, her eyes wide with fright and pain.

'It's the baby,' she cried. 'It must be! Oh, Bart, it *hurts!*'

'The baby?' he gasped. 'Are you sure?'

'No,' said Kate, 'but I think it is. What else would it be?'

'Peritonitis?'

'Oh, thanks very much. You can die of that.'

'You can die in – oh, sorry, Kate. I didn't mean that.'

'I know.'

'Hell, Kate, does it have to come *now?* I was so looking forward to – '

Kate rolled her eyes. 'Hang on, I'll ask it to wait. I'll explain how inconvenient it is!'

Without taking his eyes from her face, he was reaching for his shirt. 'Do you mean it? It's coming now?'

She nodded breathlessly.

'I'd best be going,' he said, panic in his voice. 'I'll fetch someone. You'll be fine, don't worry.'

He buttoned his trousers with fingers that trembled, his eyes fixed fearfully on Kate.

'Keep calm,' she told him. 'It won't come that quick, they never do, but that really hurt. Like a knife it was. A whole bundle of knives, stabbing right through me. Why can't men have the kids? It's not fair.'

She felt strangely composed. So this was it. The end of her life with Daniel. The end of being 'Queen Kate'. She sighed. The baby was coming. Either it was well before time, or her arithmetic was not all it should be – or it wasn't Constable Bailey's child!

Dispassionately, she watched Bart pull on his boots and shirt and finally his jacket.

'I'm sorry about – you know what,' she told him. 'You must tell Daniel – Mr Miller, I mean – and ask him to give you your money back.'

He snatched up his hat. 'Who shall I tell about the baby?' he asked. 'The doctor?'

Kate shook her head, but before she could answer another pain gripped her and in spite of herself she cried out as she doubled up once more and perspiration broke out on her skin.

'Tell Lily,' she gasped. 'Ask her to come. Say it's the baby – and Bart, I'm really sorry – that you're disappointed.'

'Forget it,' he said with an attempt at gallantry. 'You just look after yourself. Soon you'll have a baby to bounce on your knee.'

She managed to smile. 'Maybe if it's a boy I'll call it Bart,' she said and lay back exhausted against the pillow. When she opened her eyes again he had gone.

'Now then, baby,' she told it firmly, 'I know you're in a hurry to get out, but it's not much fun out here so you might as well take your time. You don't have to hurt me like that, do you? Go easy, can't you?'

Another pain made her scream and she was filled with a terrible foreboding. She had seen women in labour – her mother, a neighbour and, later, a woman in the workhouse. Some had it easy and some had it bad. She was going to be one of the unlucky ones. Oh God! How she hated babies!

*

Lily had just rolled herself into her blanket and settled into her new tent when Bart arrived, breathless and agitated. She put her head out and he told her in loud frantic whispers that Kate had gone into labour.

'I'll go at once,' she told him and withdrew to pull on the rest of her clothes. She wondered whether to disturb Henry with the news, but decided against it. There was no sound from his tent, so it seemed probable that he was already asleep.

She emerged from her tent to find Bart waiting for her.

'She's in terrible pain,' he told her hoarsely as they hurried towards Kate's wagon. 'Really groaning. It turned my stomach just to hear her. I wanted to fetch the doctor, but she said to fetch you instead.'

'Lucky you happened to be passing,' Lily remarked innocently, 'but you can go back to bed now, if you like. I don't think there's anything you can do for her.'

'Should I fetch the doctor?'

'I don't think so, if Kate said it wasn't necessary.'

'Do you know how the – I mean, she *is* having a baby . . .'

Lily put a hand on his arm. 'She told me herself that she knows all about it. I know nothing at all, but at least I can sit with her. You go back to bed.'

She climbed up into Kate's wagon in time to hear another deep groan.

'I'm here, Kate,' she called softly. 'Bart told me you're having the baby.'

There was no answer until Kate was able to straighten up once more.

'Strewth, Lily!' she said, gulping for breath. 'It hurts like hell! I hope it doesn't take too long. Blasted kids! I never did want any.'

'Can I get you anything? A drink of water? Is there something I can do?' Lily knelt beside her and put a hand on her forehead, feeling worse than useless. She had no idea what to expect and wished Kate had agreed to call in the doctor, for her face was running with perspiration.

'You're very hot,' Lily said nervously.

Kate managed a crooked grin. 'You'd be hot if you was getting these pains,' she told her. 'But don't be scared, Lily. I'm not an invalid. I'm all right in between the pains. I could do my knitting if I had any; it's just that when it comes I have to grit my teeth a bit.'

'Perhaps the doctor should come, or Hester?'

'Oh no, not Hester, Lily. She'll only fuss. I'd rather talk to you for a bit because you're off again tomorrow.'

Lily smiled. 'Tell me the truth, Kate,' she joked. 'You just want to show off your baby before I go! You've done this on purpose.'

Another pain gripped Kate just then and she gave a thin scream. Lily wondered if she would ever have the courage to go through such an ordeal. Once, as a young girl, she had waited outside the house of two of her father's parishioners while he paid a visit. The woman inside had been screaming almost without pause and Lily had wondered anxiously what was happening to her. Later her father came out and she was surprised to see tears in his eyes.

'God has seen fit to take them both,' he told her and she had nodded solemnly without comprehension. A Mr and Mrs Hodd lived in the house and Lily assumed from her father's remark that they were both dead. Later she saw Mr Hodd alive and well in the village shop and thought it very odd. Now, years later, she understood.

Lily fussed with the blankets while she wondered what to do next. 'Shouldn't there be hot water?' she suggested. 'And towels and things?'

Kate shrugged. 'It'll be hours yet,' she said.

Lily was horrified. Hours of those terrible pains! How could anyone bear such a prospect?

'Some coffee then?' she asked. 'I think I should get a fire going, Kate. It won't take long and I'll only be outside.'

Kate sighed. 'If you must,' she agreed.

As Lily was about to climb down, she asked, 'What did Bart say about him and me?'

'Nothing. He said he was passing and heard you call out. What should he have said?'

'I just wondered.' Kate grinned wickedly. 'He was here on business, you see. What Daniel calls one of my gentlemen callers.'

'I don't want to hear about it,' said Lily.

Kate laughed at her frosty tone. 'My very best client,' she

said wistfully. 'The very last one and he didn't make it. Poor lad. I do hope he got his money back. I must ask – '

The next pain was so excruciating that she screamed again and Daniel Miller's voice shouted, 'Bart Smith! If you've hurt a hair of her head – ' as he clambered into the wagon.

'Where is he?' he demanded. 'I'll kill him, so help me God! What did he do to you, Kate?' He was scrambling towards her, ignoring Lily, his face full of concern.

Kate raised a haggard face. 'It wasn't him. He didn't do nothing, honest. It's the baby, Daniel. It's coming early.'

'The baby?' Daniel repeated. '*Your* baby?'

Kate managed to laugh. 'Well, I'm not having anyone else's,' she told him. 'These pains just started and he wasn't anywhere near me. You'll have to give him his money back, Daniel. That's only fair'

'I will,' he said as he sat down abruptly. 'The baby! Why didn't you send for me or the doctor?'

'I sent for Lily. She's going to get a fire going for some coffee.'

'I could do with some,' he said. 'The baby! Jesus, Kate, you said there were weeks yet.'

'I thought there were.' She closed her eyes, breathing deeply.

'The baby!'

Kate's eyes snapped open. 'For Christ's sake stop saying "the baby". It's coming and that's all there is to it. I'm sorry if I've upset all your plans, but I can't hang on to it for ever and it seems like now's the time. Now, if that's all you have to offer, then hop it because having a kid's no bed of roses and I'm – aah!'

This time the scream was literally torn from her and Daniel watched, horrified, as the pain engulfed her.

'Christ almighty!' she gasped weakly when at last it subsided. 'Fetch Hester for me, Daniel, and the doctor. I can't stand much more of this.'

'And some whisky!' cried Daniel, pulling himself together. 'I'll get you some whisky. Kill the pain!'

He dived back into the darkness outside and Kate fell back

against the pillows, one trembling hand to her head, the other clutching the source of the pain. She gave Lily a crooked grin.

'Constable Ernest Bailey,' she whispered, 'or whoever it was – I hate his blooming guts!'

*

Kate's labour was much too quick and very severe. At a quarter-past one the following morning she gave birth to a small but healthy boy, but by that time she was unable even to acknowledge him and slipped at once into an exhausted sleep, while Lily wrapped the boy in a piece of clean sheeting and the doctor swallowed his fifth cup of coffee.

'Is Kate going to be all right?' Lily asked, holding the baby awkwardly in her arms. Hester had returned to bed about an hour earlier at her insistence.

He hesitated. 'I don't know,' he replied. 'She looks tough enough but she's had a difficult time. Very difficult. There was some tearing and she's lost some blood. She's also badly shocked and utterly exhausted. I'm afraid she'll want nursing for a week or two. Luckily she's got you.'

It was Lily's turn to hesitate. 'She hasn't got me for long,' she explained. 'I'm leaving tomorrow – or rather, today. Mr Simms and I are riding on.'

'Hmn!' He pursed his lips unhappily. 'Who else is there?' he asked. 'She certainly can't manage alone.'

'I don't know,' said Lily. 'Maybe Hester Cooper would lend a hand.'

The doctor shook his head. 'She's in no fit state,' he said, 'and I don't think we should ask her; it wouldn't be fair. All that trouble with her own family, I reckon she's got enough on her hands already without taking on any more.'

The baby whimpered and Lily held it closer, murmuring soothingly.

'I'll talk to Mr Simms,' she said, 'and we could maybe delay our start for a day or two.' She looked up at the doctor. 'What about the baby? Shouldn't it have some food? Doesn't it have to be fed? I'm afraid I know very little about babies.'

He smiled briefly. 'You'll learn,' he said. 'It won't need feeding until tomorrow. We can feed it goat's milk if we have to – depends how well the mother is in the morning. She might be able to feed it herself. Just put it down to sleep somewhere where it can't roll or be smothered, and try to get some rest yourself.'

'Sleep here, you mean?'

'Of course.'

Lily frowned. 'We ought to tell Mr Miller,' she said.

'That man!' The doctor was obviously not impressed.

'And I should warn Mr Simms that I won't be ready to leave. He'll be getting up early.'

The doctor took out his watch and snapped open the lid. 'It's nearly two o'clock now,' he told her. 'I'll stay here and settle the child while you pop along and break the news.'

*

Henry's reception of Lily's news was even less enthusiastic than she had feared it would be. He was most unwilling to delay their departure and argued that they should go ahead with their plans. Lily sympathized, but tried to convince him that another twenty-four hours could not make that much difference.

'I can't just leave her with that baby to care for,' she told him. 'I've just seen what she went through, Henry; it was sheer torment for her and she's in a very weak state.'

'But she's not your responsibility!' His mouth was setting in a stubborn line. 'Let Miller look after her; he's been keen enough to manage her all these weeks.'

Lily lowered her eyes. 'I think it was understood between them that it was only until the baby came. Kate knew that.'

'More fool her, then. She should have stayed respectable. What about Mrs Cooper?'

'The doctor thinks she's got enough problems with Ella, and he's right.'

'But for heaven's sake, Lily! If you had stuck to your plan to go back east, who'd look after her then? It wouldn't be you, that's for sure, and they wouldn't just write her off and let her die. Wallis would find someone.'

She looked into his face and her heart sank as she saw his bitter disappointment. 'I know how you feel and I'm sorry,

Henry,' she told him, 'but I can't go with you this morning. If you will wait another twenty-four hours . . .'

'Twenty-four hours.' He latched on to the words. 'Will she make a miraculous recovery in twenty-four hours? Are you sure of that? Or will it be another twenty-four hours after that? Or a week?'

'I don't know,' Lily said sharply. 'I can't foresee the future any more than you can.' She put a hand to her head, which was beginning to ache. The night's experience had been harrowing for her too, and she was tired and worried. 'All I know is that Kate is my friend and she needs me and I can't let her down.'

His jaw tightened and Lily felt a knot of misery forming deep inside her.

'You'd rather let *me* down!' he accused. 'I'm supposed to be the man you love, or had you forgotten?'

'No, Henry,' said Lily. 'I hadn't forgotten and I haven't said I don't love you. I've only asked you to wait another day.'

'Right!' he said. 'You've got it – one more day it is. But not two days, Lily. I'll wait one more day and then I'm leaving. You'll have to choose between me and your fine friend Kate.'

Tears pricked at Lily's eyelids. 'She's not a "fine friend",' she protested. 'She's just a friend who needs me.'

'*I* need you, for Christ's sake,' he shouted. 'I *love* you! She doesn't. She wasn't prepared to give up her big chance to travel back to New York with you when your husband died. She chose Amos Carp – and much good that did her! She had to choose and she chose the man she loved. Why can't you?'

'I don't know why,' said Lily, struggling to keep back the tears.

All she wanted was to be taken into his arms and kissed. She wanted to ride away with him and finish the journey to California. She wanted to say all that, but she felt too weary to think clearly, let alone put it into convincing words.

'I can't explain,' she told him. 'I know you're disappointed and I do love you, but I must get back to Kate. The doctor's waiting and I said I wouldn't be long.'

'Oh no!' he exclaimed bitterly. 'Mustn't let anyone down, must you? Don't let Kate down and don't let the doctor down. You're letting me down, though. I don't seem to come very high on your list.'

They gazed at each other, Lily white-faced and near to tears, Henry hurt and furious.

'I'm sorry,' said Lily again and she turned on her heel and began to walk away.

'Twenty-four hours!' he shouted. 'I mean it, Lily. You'll have to choose!'

Lily's heart was heavy. What a choice! A sick woman and a helpless child – or the man she loved. She did not really believe that Kate would make 'a miraculous recovery' in the next twenty-four hours. She also knew that Henry would not wait.

*

Lily, sharing the bed with Kate, managed to doze only fitfully for the remaining hours before the company roused up. Kate slept heavily but she cried out several times in her sleep, which fortunately did not wake the baby. Lily lived in fear of this, convinced that she would never be able to soothe it back to sleep. What did you do to calm babies? Sing? Rock them? Pat their backs? And why did they cry? Was it hunger or fear, or maybe the need for love and attention? When the pale dawn light crept into the sky, she left the bed and crouched beside the baby which lay wedged between two cushions. To her surprise the child was wide awake and seemed to be staring up into the arched roof of the wagon. His deep blue eyes were fringed with dark lashes and his head was crowned with a dark fluff of hair; his skin was rosy and his nose beautifully formed above the tiny mouth. The small hands were clenched, his fingers and thumbs so small that in spite of her nervousness Lily caught her breath in a gasp of delight. As she watched, spellbound, the fingers of one hand uncurled and she could see his fingernails, pink and transparent.

'Well now, little man,' she whispered. 'How are you today? And what are we going to call you, eh? You must have a name. We shall have to ask your mama when she wakes up.'

Tentatively, she put a finger into his outstretched hand and to her astonishment the fingers closed round it immediately in a grip that was surprisingly firm. She was at once enchanted and amazed at the intensity of her feelings towards him.

'I saw you come into the world,' she told him. 'You led your mama a fine dance. Oh yes, you did!'

The moment of his birth returned to her with striking clarity and she fought down a shudder at the memory of the nightmare. Would Kate forget all that pain when she awoke, she wondered. Did the joy of seeing and holding your own child banish such unpleasant memories?

'Wait until she sees you!' Lily told him. 'Her own little man. She's got a dear little son and you've got a very nice mama. Oh, I nearly forgot. This – ' she waved her hand to indicate the interior of the wagon – 'is your home and you're on your way to California.'

The baby seemed to respond to her voice and shifted his gaze a little. Could he focus his eyes, she wondered. The grip on her fingers had not relaxed.

'You're a very strong baby,' she told him, 'and you'll grow up to be a big strong man. How sad that your papa will never see you. He'd love you if he did, I'm sure of it.' She felt a wave of resentment towards Constable Bailey. How dare he father this lovely child and then callously abandon him to his fate?

She smiled down at the boy, unaware of time passing, unable to tear herself away from him. There was washing to be done, fuel to gather and breakfast to prepare, but she wanted to remain with the child whose presence was like a small miracle to her. Amidst all the dust, toil and sweat of the trail, this shining child had appeared and Lily was moved to the core of her being.

'I wish you were my son,' she whispered suddenly and knew as she uttered the words that even if she could bring herself to walk away from Kate, she could never walk away

330

from the baby. She would stay as long as he needed her. Henry would have to go on alone.

Kate was still asleep when the doctor arrived, but she woke soon after while he was examining the baby. She seemed distraught still and irritable and her face was flushed. When he spoke to her, she did not answer but turned over and hid her face in the pillow.

Lily and the doctor exchanged dismayed looks. The doctor wanted to examine Kate, but Kate clung frantically to the blankets and at last he gave up.

'You try talking to her,' he suggested and Lily took his place beside the bed.

'Kate,' she said softly. 'It's me, Lily. Don't hide from me, Kate. I want to talk to you. I want to tell you about your little boy. He's so beautiful, Kate. You'll adore him . . . Kate? The doctor wants to examine you. Let me pull the blankets away from your face. You'll make yourself so hot.'

However, none of her coaxing had the desired effect.

'What's the matter with her?' whispered Lily. 'Do many women behave like that?'

'I don't know,' he admitted. 'This was only my third delivery so I'm afraid I'm not an expert. She might be running a fever – she does seem rather confused – or it may be a reaction to last night. She did have a particularly painful time and it can cause problems. I have heard of a mother refusing her child – they blame the child for their pain.'

Lily shook her head. 'Kate's not the resentful kind. At least, I don't think she'd blame the baby – not if she saw him.'

He shrugged. 'The mind plays funny tricks,' he said, 'and I don't pretend to know all the answers. We'll leave her alone for another hour or so, she might sleep again and then wake up in a different mood. We can't force these things. I'll have a word with Mrs Cooper, to see if she has any bright ideas. Keep an eye on her and if you see any change for the worse, let me know at once. I shall probably be with the Harpers; the mother's very weak – it's her lungs, I'm afraid. She should never have come.'

Lily had one last question. 'Shouldn't we notify Captain

Wallis of the birth?' she asked and added with a faint smile, 'A new member of the Western Hope Miners!'

'I will,' he said.

Kate slept for nearly an hour, but it was a fretful, restless sleep. She began to toss and turn in the bed, muttering incoherently. When she did wake up, she was sweating and shivering and the doctor was forced to confirm the onset of fever. Lily's heart sank as she saw Kate's wild expression, and she was ridiculously grateful for the doctor's sleeping draught which sent her friend back into an uneasy slumber.

Hester called in briefly to admire the baby, but could offer no solutions. By this time it was past five o'clock and the company was ready to move on and Captain Wallis, although sympathetic, would not allow one wagon to hold up everyone else. Daniel Miller drove Kate's wagon and Henry, his face like thunder, rode alongside with Lily's horse and the pack-mules. Hester found a bottle and made a teat from the finger of a leather glove, and when the baby grew hungry Lily fed it with goat's milk; to her surprise it appeared satisfied and went straight back to sleep. Not long afterwards, however, it awoke screaming lustily and Hester was hastily sent for; she showed Lily how to hold the child against her shoulder so as to allow it to bring up the air it had swallowed – and peace reigned once more.

Later Ella came by to see the child, but she at once burst into tears for her own lost boy and Lily had to take her back to her family.

When the company stopped for the noon break Lily, Henry and Daniel Miller ate together, swallowing salt pork and beans and saying little. All the time at the back of Lily's mind the realization grew stronger with each passing hour: she would not be able to leave, Henry would go alone and she might never see him again. Perhaps when they all reached California, she could look for him – but there was no guarantee that she would find him. From all accounts, the gold fields were extensive and a man could disappear without trace. 'Oh Henry! Don't leave me,' she begged silently, but knew that to him it was a test of her love. She understood

332

that for Henry it was very simple. If she stayed with Kate, he would consider it a betrayal.

By the evening, Kate was much worse and had eaten nothing. Her temperature was 104 degrees and her pulse fluttered erratically. They could force no liquids between her clenched teeth and the doctor could do little to alleviate her suffering.

That night Henry came to Lily for her answer and they stood together outside the wagon where Kate slept and the child cried fitfully.

Henry's expression was anguished as he looked at her. 'I'm leaving at four in the morning,' he told her, 'and I want you to come with me, Lily. I believe I mean more to you than Kate or the child – '

'Of course you do,' Lily began, but he ignored the interruption.

'I've asked you if you love me and you say you do,' he went on 'I've asked you to marry me and you've said you will eventually. Now I'm asking you to stay with me.' He took her hand. 'Please say you will.'

Lily felt such an intense longing to say 'Yes' that for a moment she could not trust herself to speak, but at last she took a deep breath and uttered up a silent prayer for the right words.

'I can't leave them,' she said at last. 'I want to be with you, Henry, and I'm asking you to wait a little longer – maybe a week at the most. Kate may be quite recovered by then – she most probably will be.'

'Is that the doctor's verdict?'

Honesty compelled Lily to shake her head. 'But he could be wrong; he admits he's not familiar with the problem. Hester seems to think she could rally quite quickly if she put her mind to it – that all she needs to do is to pull herself together. But then she and Ella had their babies easily, apparently – like dropping a foal, Hester said.'

'You mean Hester thinks she's shamming?'

Lily's head jerked up. 'I did not say that,' she told him, 'and anyway, it's only Hester's opinion; she's not an expert either. That's the whole trouble, Henry. Nobody knows what to expect or what to do to help. If you could see her, Henry, you'd understand that she can't be left . . . and there's the baby, too. Oh, Henry, please give me a few more days. If I just knew she was improving, I'd feel better about leaving her.'

'But every day's delay means less chance of finding gold!' he insisted. 'I was talking to Wallis last night and he firmly believes that it's first come, first served.'

'But that doesn't mean we won't find any – just that we'll have to work harder for it,' Lily exclaimed. 'There are hundreds of people further back on the trail. You don't suggest they're all going to leave California empty-handed, do you? The papers said there's enough for everybody.'

'The papers!' he scoffed. 'All I know is that I want to get there as soon as possible and stake my claim. I've wasted enough time already, one way and another. Wallis says – '

'Damn Wallis!' interrupted Lily. 'Why do you set store by what Wallis says? He's bound to urge you to go, isn't he?'

'Is he?' Henry pounced on her slip, his eyes narrowed. 'Why should he do that?'

Lily was already regretting her careless words, having no desire to stir up trouble between the two men. 'Why, because . . .' she floundered, searching desperately for a convincing answer.

'Because what?' he asked levelly after a long silence.

Lily could only shake her head helplessly.

His eyes flashed. 'Because,' he said, 'he wants to have you all to himself. Is that what it is?'

Lily could not bear the look in his eyes. 'I can't speak for Captain Wallis – ' she began, but his expression had hardened.

'Maybe *that's* why you want to stay,' he said. 'Maybe Kate is just an excuse.'

Lily had intended to remain calm, but now she felt her composure deserting her.

'If you believe *that*,' she exclaimed, 'then you don't know me at all, Henry Simms, and obviously you don't love me!'

'I don't know what to believe,' he answered. 'It looks very

334

simple to me – you either come with me or you stay here with Kate and Wallis.'

Lily's control snapped and she slapped him across the side of his face.

'Don't you dare bring him into it,' she cried furiously, 'when you *know* I feel nothing for him! You're just trying to make me feel guilty when I've done nothing wrong – trying to make your action seem more reasonable.'

He caught hold of her wrist and held it fast. 'You feel nothing for him but he feels something for you, is that it?'

'I didn't say that . . .' She faltered into silence and wrenched her arm free.

They faced each other wretchedly and Lily swallowed hard. 'I'm truly sorry,' she said. 'I shouldn't have struck you. I apologize.'

'I provoked you,' he said.

'I don't want to hurt you, Henry. Please be reasonable,' she begged, laying a hand on his sleeve. 'One week, that's all I ask. Maybe less.'

Henry appeared not to hear. 'What *did* happen between you and Wallis that evening?' he asked slowly. 'Do you love me enough to tell me?'

Lily's heart sank like a stone and she felt all her hopes were drowning with it. Either way now she would lose. If she told him about the kiss and repeated the conversation, he would feel he had been deceived and would never believe she was staying only for Kate and the child. If she refused to tell him or told him a lie . . . 'No, a lie will not do', she said to herself sternly.

'What he said is of no importance,' she answered. 'What matters is that *I* tell you I love you. If you accept that I do, then Wallis's feelings for me – '

His voice was full of bitterness as he broke in, 'I *see!* So he spoke of his feelings for you!'

'Henry Simms!' she cried, terribly tempted to strike him again. 'If Ella were to fall in love with you, that wouldn't mean that you returned her feelings. You're being so unreasonable.'

'So he's *in love* with you,' he said flatly, looking as though

335

she *had* struck him. 'Why didn't you say so? That explains everything.'

Lily clenched her fists and prayed for patience.

'It explains nothing,' she insisted. 'You're twisting everything I say. Maybe he does find me attractive, maybe Amos Carp does. Or Daniel Miller or Charlie Cooper! Maybe I am attractive. You find me so. What does it matter as long as I love *you*? I want us to be together. Please give me a week with Kate and the baby.'

'I'll be leaving tomorrow,' Henry said. 'If you want to come with me – if you *love* me – be ready at four o'clock. If not, you'll just have to come looking for me. And if you don't find me . . .' He shrugged.

'I shall look for you,' promised Lily, 'and I'll keep looking until I find you. I promise you that, Henry.'

He gave her a long look that was full of bitterness and then walked away without a word.

Lily spent a miserable night. The baby woke frequently and refused to be comforted. Kate became increasingly restless and rambling and finally delirious, so that by three in the morning Lily felt compelled to send Daniel for the doctor. Kate's movements became more violent and she seemed to be delirious, frequently throwing up her arms to protect her face from something no one else could see. She begged them to 'take the baby away!' and insisted repeatedly that she hated it. In the end, Daniel and Lily had to hold her down in the bed while, in desperation, the doctor forced a sleeping draught between her unwilling lips. At four o'clock an exhausted Lily was feeding the baby with warmed goat's milk, Kate was sleeping again and Daniel was heating a pot of much-needed coffee on the fire outside.

Henry Simms rode out of camp alone and Lily didn't realize until much later that he had gone.

Chapter Sixteen

My dearest Papa,

I am shocked to discover that I have not written for more than a month and hope you will forgive me. I do not know when or how this letter will reach you, but I will send it to you at the first opportunity.

Firstly, to put your mind at rest, you must know I am well but very tired. For the past two weeks I have been nursing Kate Lester through a debilitating fever brought on by a difficult childbirth. She has now taken a turn for the better, but is very weak and so thin as to be hardly recognizable. Today she took a light broth and I thank God that her wits are also returned, although she still refuses to feed or even to see her baby – a beautiful boy, who thrives meanwhile on goat's milk which he takes through the finger of a glove! Meanwhile, I care for him; I do believe he knows me and I have quite fallen for his charms. You can imagine how much I love him.

We have travelled for nearly a month since leaving South Pass, which was roughly the half-way point, and have somehow negotiated the mountains between Sublettes Cut-Off (in England, I suppose we would call it a short cut) and Hudspeths Cut-Off, the latter only recently discovered and now adopted by some companies. It was strange to have no map references but to rely only on the tracks of a previous company.

Today we descended Steeple Rock to the north-east of the Great Salt Lake. Imagine, Papa, if you can. Kate had to be lifted out of the wagon and laid on the ground wrapped in blankets, while I waited a short distance away with the baby in my arms. (He still has no name, poor little man.) Ropes were then tied to the back of the wagon and chains put through the rear wheels to lock them so that they acted as a brake. Some men led the oxen down the steep and slippery path while others attempted to slow the wagon's descent with the ropes. This whole procedure was then repeated by all the other wagons with only one accident, and that not fatal – a wheel lost. Captain Wallis was very pleased.

So, Papa, we move on at a snail's pace towards our goal. Most of the time spirits are high, though several of the men chose to travel on alone. Mr Simms was one of them. You will recall he was Patrick's partner.

Ella's child is due any day now. She suffered a most terrible tragedy a few weeks ago when her husband and son were drowned, but is now as cheerful as can be expected and being courted by a gentleman named Gabriel Smith of whom I have also spoken.

Life is strange on this everlasting trail. We are so wrapped up in our own small community that we could easily believe that the rest of the world has ceased to exist. I suspect that California will bring us back to reality with a jolt. Do not think, Papa, that I am unprotected. The captain of our company, Matt Wallis, is very concerned about my welfare and I also have several good friends.

Tomorrow we make a start towards the Humboldt River, but it will take many weeks of arduous travel through arid country. The rains which fell so heavily in the east have deserted us and the mud has given way to dust and yet more dust. The sun is merciless, but there are rumours that soon we shall travel only by night which will be easier.

Enough now about my circumstances. I pray nightly for your continued good health and happiness. I think I have omitted to say that I received a letter from you which is greatly treasured. I read it again and again. I trust that your wrist is now recovered.

Give my kind regards to Mrs Spencer. I know she will take every care of you.

My thoughts are often with you in England. Pray for me, Papa.

Your affectionate daughter,
Lily.

She was sealing the letter when a shadow fell across it and she looked up to see Ella beaming down at her in a state of obvious excitement.

'Ella!' she said, scrambling to her feet. 'What's happened?'

'I want you to be first to know,' cried Ella breathlessly. 'Gabby and I are going to be wed! He asked me and I said "Yes" and I don't care what folks say, I'll have a father for this one,' she patted her abdomen, 'and I always did fancy Gabby. Ma says he's a real good man and Jess can't expect me to stay single and grieving for ever after what he did, and it's different here – not like it is back home. It's a hard world and I need a man, and Jess couldn't begrudge me a new husband after leaving me all alone with a baby on the way.'

She ran out of breath and wiped a gleam of perspiration from her face with the back of her hand.

So Ella would soon have another husband. Lily felt a pang of jealousy which she quickly stifled. This girl had a right to her happiness. She herself had had her chance and thrown it away.

'I think it's wonderful news,' she told Ella, smiling and taking her hand. 'I'm quite sure everyone will wish you both well and Hester is right. Gabby is a good man.'

Ella's face clouded slightly. 'Pa said it was too early after Jess dying, and poor Will and all that, but Ma says it's never too soon to forget sorrow and shake hands with joy.'

Lily stared at her in astonishment. Why was life so straight-forward for some people, she wondered enviously. The Hesters of this world with their homespun philosophy were sadly underestimated, she decided.

'She's right,' said Lily. 'You must have a father for the baby.'

'Gabby's going to get us a wagon and we shall live together until a preacher can make it proper. He said he wants to care for me and the baby. He doesn't care that it isn't his – not like someone I could mention. Poor Kate! If Amos Carp had been half the man Gabby is, she never would have done what she has.'

Lily nodded without comment. That was Kate's misfortune in a nutshell.

Ella went on, 'Ma don't reckon I should tell Kate yet awhile; it might upset her. How is she? I heard the worst was over, but Ma said I was to stay away until the fever was past.'

Lily's smile faded. 'Making progress,' she said, 'but she still won't have anything to do with the baby. She shuts her eyes if I try to show him to her – says she wasn't cut out to be a mother and she doesn't want to be one. The doctor says she'll come round in time, but I'm not so sure.'

They began to walk together in the direction of Kate's wagon and after a moment Ella gave Lily a sideways glance. 'I think Captain Wallis has a soft spot for you,' she remarked. 'Ma says so, too, and she reckons you could do a lot worse.'

Lily felt her face redden. 'I suppose he feels he has to keep an eye on me, a woman travelling alone.'

Ella was not deceived. 'It's more than that,' she insisted. 'Everyone says so.'

Lily was horrified. Were they all talking about her? 'Then everyone's wrong,' she stammered. 'And even if it was true, *I* certainly don't return his feelings.'

Ella sighed noisily. 'You'll never see Mr Simms again,' she said. 'Ma says – '

But Lily had swung round to face her. 'I don't want to hear what she says,' she retorted sharply. 'I don't like people discussing me behind my back.'

'But what else can we talk about?' asked Ella. 'There's the weather and there's the gold in California and there's folks. There's no harm in talking, Lily. Everyone likes you and they want to see you happy. We all thought you and Mr Simms were just right for each other, and you always seemed so happy together, and then he went off like that – well, we *were* surprised. Ma says he was wrong to leave you; any decent man would have waited. Must have been a shock for you.'

'It wasn't,' Lily protested. 'We agreed he should go on and I shall join him again when we get to California.'

'You hope,' said Ella. 'However will you find him? Ma says – '

Lily forced a smile. 'Don't let's talk about me any more,' she said. 'You're the one with the exciting news, Ella, and I really am pleased for you, but now I want to see to Kate so you'll have to excuse me. Mr Miller's been entertaining her to give me some time to myself.'

Ella's nose went up a little at the mention of Miller and her 'Goodbye' was briefer than it would otherwise have been.

However, Lily did not at once rejoin Kate in the wagon, but stood leaning thoughtfully against the back of it. Ella's announcement had stirred the emotions she had been trying so hard to suppress. Was it possible that Ella was right about Henry? The thought that she would never see him again was one which she had so far refused to consider, yet the chances of finding him in the wilderness that was California did seem rather remote. If only they had not parted so suddenly and on such terms. If only he could have given her some idea of where he might be found – even a vague idea of the area he might head for would have been better than nothing. But how could *he* know until he reached the gold fields? From all accounts the diggings were scattered over a vast area. The only name that was familiar to everyone was Sutter's Fort. Perhaps he would repent his anger and leave a letter for her there. She could certainly leave one there for him.

To blot out the memory of their quarrel, she had welcomed the extra work that Kate's illness and the baby made for her. Afraid to give herself time to think, she had thrown herself into her new role as nurse as well as cooking, washing and caring for the animals. Matt Wallis had not been the only person to remonstrate with her, or to suggest that she was 'overdoing things'. The doctor had also hinted that if she continued to exhaust her energies, he would soon have another patient on his hands.

She had also tried to forget Wallis's kiss, but now Ella's careless words jangled noisily in her mind: 'Ma reckons you could do a lot worse.' Lily had been well aware that Wallis was taking a personal interest in her welfare, but she had not realized that people were gossiping about the two of them. Still, as Ella had said, topics for conversation *were* limited and it was natural enough.

But suppose she did *not* find Henry again? At the back of her mind was the frightening possibility that Ella might be right. And suppose she found him only to be rejected? And what would happen to Kate and the baby if Lily *did* rejoin Henry? Whatever would she do in California all on her own? If, however, she stayed with Kate and the baby, how would they all live? There were very few women travelling to California alone and most of these had been widowed on the way. It was going to be a man's world. True, a married woman could care for her children while the husband worked the claim, but it was his labour that would produce the gold. Could two single women stake a claim and support themselves and a child on the proceeds? It seemed improbable, if not altogether impossible. And suppose Daniel Miller had a change of heart and took on Kate and the child? In that case, Lily would be entirely alone with very little money and only the vaguest idea of how to work a claim. Fear surfaced and she felt a moment's panic. Seen in the cold light of day, her predicament was difficult. Perhaps she *should* consider Matt Wallis as a possible suitor. But no! That would be unfair. She could not make use of him. Somehow she would have to organize her own salvation.

*

As Lily had written in her letter, the Western Hope Miners had passed Steeple Rock and were approaching the Humboldt River, but they had nearly a hundred miles still to go before they reached it. During the next four weeks the company pressed on through Goose Creek Valley and made its way through an extended area of marshy ground dotted with springs of hot water. The daytime temperature was so high that they altered their routine and travelled only at night when it was cooler, although progress was a little slower then and they could only average about fifteen miles each night.

Matt Wallis continued to take more than a passing interest in Lily's welfare. He consulted the doctor on several occasions, anxious about the state of her health. All the members of the company were showing signs of fatigue and strain, but Lily had the added burdens of Kate and the baby. He did suggest at one stage that she should return the baby to his unwilling mother and force Kate to care for him, but Lily was horrified by the suggestion and had refused point blank. Another suggestion that perhaps Hester or Ella might take the child from her for a few hours each day had met with the same determined 'No'. It was becoming obvious to Wallis, as it was to many others, that Lily was becoming much too attached to Kate's child. Wallis felt that she was making a mistake, but she had stubbornly ignored the few hints given to her by well-meaning people. Sooner or later he foresaw heartache, but his attempt to point this out to Lily had met with a sharp rejoinder.

The management of the company demanded so much of his time that he was unable to do more than keep a watchful eye on her. The presence of Indians in the area they were passing through was a source of constant irritation to him and one he could well have done without. The Digger Indians, as they were called, were a poor race living mainly on roots and berries, but although he pitied them their wretched existence he gave orders that they were not to be encouraged. Normally not sufficiently aggressive to be considered dangerous, they were nevertheless not to be trusted. When soft-hearted men *did* give them something, they immediately demanded more; when they met with a refusal, they frequently resorted to stealing and so a constant watch had to be kept on both provisions and livestock.

The animals were also proving a constant source of anxiety, for many more of the unfortunate beasts had reached the limits of their endurance and scarcely a day passed without the loss of an ox or a mule. Some of the larger wagons could not be pulled by fewer than six oxen and when one died there were two alternatives – either the wagon must be made lighter or another ox must be found to make up the numbers. This meant rearranging other teams, which led to ill-feeling, and occasionally the grumbling flared into open hostility.

On the first of September Matt Wallis sat in his tent, his elbows on his makeshift table (a plank laid over two trunks), his head resting in his hands. In a rare mood of depression, he was reviewing the past months and could find little comfort in his achievements. He had brought the company more than half-way across the continent with comparatively few casualties – seven deaths from cholera and the two drownings – but he had received little thanks. They drew daily nearer to their goal, but tempers grew shorter and complaints more numerous and today he wondered why on earth he had ever thought the members of the Western Hopers worth the effort. He should have put an end to his wanderings; he should have stayed at home. They were not aware of the qualities of his leadership, nor did they appreciate the fact that he had kept them together as a company which in itself was no mean feat. They had heard of several companies which had split into dissatisfied groups, each of which lacked the resources of a major unit and were thus made more vulnerable.

He lifted his hand, reached for a bottle of whisky and poured himself a large measure which he tossed back in three quick gulps. Whisky: he did not drink more than his fellow men, but tonight his mood was black and his view of past, present and future sadly jaundiced. For a few seconds he closed his eyes and savoured the comforting whisky as it burnt a fiery path down his throat to his stomach. Then he turned his attention to the list of remaining stores and shook his head.

The corn meal would have to be rationed and the dried apples had all gone. Salt pork had been finished over a week ago, but there was plenty of fresh game to be had if the men were not too tired or lazy to seek it out. Sage-hens, very like chickens, were plentiful and there were rabbits and marmots. If necessary, they could eat rattlesnakes, although he couldn't recommend it! No one need starve, but they might well have to tighten their belts before they reached California and a drastic change of diet might be unavoidable if they were to survive.

Wallis thought of Lily and sighed again. He wished he could do more to look after her, but she had made it clear in the nicest possible way that for the time being she preferred her independence, although she had promised to ask for his help if she needed it.

'Lily Golightly,' he murmured, 'I wish you *would* come lightly, into my arms and then my bed. Damn Henry Simms!'

He shook his head, appalled by his own words; he must be growing soft in his old age! He had told himself that he did not need a woman in his life and over the past years he had come to believe it. Now Lily Golightly was undermining his conviction and he did not know what to do about it. She had foolishly promised herself to Henry Simms and there was no persuading her that she had made a mistake. And if he did persuade her – what then? Did he want her as a wife, or was it only her body that had captured his imagination? He did not think so. Damnation! He had tried not to think about her, but it had proved quite impossible. How much longer could she go on, he wondered, without a breakdown? He remembered her as he had first seen her with that fine white skin, large clear eyes and smooth black hair plaited round her head. A typical English rose, he had thought: the genteel daughter of an English parson. Mrs Golightly, the newly-wed – prim and prissy, with her precise English vowels – following an English husband who had left her high and dry in a strange country while he went to look for gold. At that time she had been demure, fragile, trusting and eager for adventure. Today it was a very different story. Now her hair, tied back roughly, was dulled by the dust, her eyes were reddened and her lips parched by the heat. She was too thin and her naïve eagerness for adventure, long since satisfied, had changed into a grim determination to survive. Some of the spring had gone out of her step and she moved a little more slowly, reserving her strength; lines of fatigue marked her face.

He took another drink, this time straight from the bottle, and tried once more to focus his attention on the lists of stores. Beans had been jettisoned ten days earlier to lighten the stores wagon when one of the oxen collapsed. How many oxen had they lost so far – was it ten or eleven? No, more than that. Perhaps a dozen, plus four mules and two horses. Several more would not last out the week. Would they all get to California? Would he manage to get them over the Sierra Nevada, or would the snows close in and trap them? It was now September and already the nights were much colder; there had been a sharp frost the previous night and they would get sharper. He calculated that two more months should do it, but could the animals last that long? He was beginning to doubt it, although he kept his fears to himself.

A sudden commotion outside jerked him back to the present. He could hear a man's voice and a woman's scolding furiously and he frowned in disbelief. It sounded like Lily Golightly, but it was not like her to . . . Even as he rose to his feet, the tent-flap was tugged aside and Lily ducked uninvited inside, her face flushed, her distress apparent.

'Captain Wallis, this man is a monster. A *monster!*' she exploded. 'You must reason with him, for he won't listen to me. That poor dumb creature – after all it's done for him – he's treating it so cruelly! You must stop him; he ought to be horsewhipped.'

'Mrs Golightly, whatever – '

She went straight on, shaking with anger. 'He's scraping its bones with a knife! And he's twisted its tail – Captain Wallis, don't just stand there! The poor creature is *dying* and he's tormenting it without pity! At least it ought to be allowed to die in peace.'

Without waiting for any kind of answer, she darted outside again and Wallis heard her screaming at the unfortunate owner of the ox. There was the sound of a scuffle and the man cried, 'Mind your own business, you stupid English bitch!'

346

He went out to find Lily on her knees pummelling the man with all her strength while he did his best to protect himself from her fury. So, he thought, she can tap reserves of energy when she needs to!

'Don't you dare call me an English bitch!' screamed Lily. 'I'm English and proud of it! You are a cruel, wicked unfeeling American *lout* and if you touch that poor suffering animal again I'll kill you!'

'Get off me, I say!' yelled the man and Wallis leaned down and lifted Lily bodily into the air, her fists still flailing. He had never seen her like this before. It was a new and unexpected insight into her character, he reflected, hiding his amusement.

'She's crazy, that one!' the man told him, struggling to his feet and eyeing Lily warily. 'If she'd been a man, I'd have flattened her – '

'I'd like to flatten you!' cried Lily as Wallis stood between them, keeping them apart with outstretched arms.

'Look at the poor creature,' cried Lily, her anger giving way suddenly to pity. Her eyes filled with tears as she pointed to the ox which lay on its side where it had fallen. Its tongue was swollen, its eyes were glazed, its body heaved as its dust-filled lungs laboured.

Lily pulled herself free of Wallis's restraining hand and knelt beside it, her tears falling on to its head as she gently stroked its neck.

'Die in peace, poor old thing,' she whispered. 'I won't let him near you. You've done your best and brought him all this way. It's all over now.' She ran her fingers over its horns. 'You're a handsome beast,' she said softly. 'You've done well.'

The two men watched her for a few moments in astonishment and then the man looked up at Wallis. 'You can't let them lie down,' he said defensively. 'You've got to try to get them back on their feet – you know that.'

'I know,' said Wallis, 'but she's right, I'm afraid. This one's too far gone. It's going, Mr Hart, and there's nothing you can do.'

The man's face fell. 'But it *can't* die!' he wailed. 'It *can't*

347

I've only got three now. Where will I get another? My wagon can't be lightened any more and three oxen will never pull it. I'll never get to California! That damned ox has *got* to get up!'

In his anguish, he snatched off his hat and threw it down and then aimed a kick at the prostrate ox. Lily whirled in its defence and punched him with all her might and he lost his balance and fell backwards.

'Mrs Golightly!' said Wallis gently. 'Let the man be. Can't you see he's just plumb scared?'

'That's no excuse – ' she began hotly and then stopped, biting her lip.

The man lay where she had pushed him, then slowly he rolled over and lay face downwards in the dust, cradling his face in his arms and sobbing.

Lily put a hand to her face, moved by his despair and immediately contrite. She ran over and knelt beside him. 'I'm sorry,' she said, tugging and coaxing him into a sitting position. 'I'm truly sorry; I had no right.' With small soft movements she brushed away his tears and smoothed his tangled hair back from his eyes. Then with her own handkerchief she tried to stem the flow of his tears. 'Will you forgive me?' she begged. 'I *do* understand. We're all frightened. I'm sorry about the ox, but don't worry, Captain Wallis will think of something. He'll help you, he'll get us to California.'

She brushed the dust from the man's face and then helped him to his feet while Wallis walked away, unable to bear her tenderness. He went into his tent and reached for the whisky bottle; having pulled out the cork he stopped, considered and pushed it back, driving it home with the flat of his hand. Lily had said, 'He'll get us to California.'

If that was what Lily wanted, then that's what he would do! He tossed the bottle on to his bed. As he turned his full attention to the list of stores, his depression was already lifting.

'Two sacks of pilot bread, three of coffee . . .'

Chapter Seventeen

Two days later Ella's child, a little girl, was born dead. Ella's grief was complete and terrible and nothing anyone said could console her. She clung to the dead child for two hours, refusing to be parted from it, but later – at Gabby's insistence – she allowed the small grey body to be wrapped in a blanket and the pathetic bundle was laid to rest beside the trail like too many before it. Most of the company attended the simple burial service and Lily was among them. She listened to Matt Wallis as he read aloud from the prayer book and looked across at Ella who stood with Gabby's arm around her. Lily wondered what it was like to lose a baby, and her heart ached for the young girl who had started out for California with such high hopes. She had lost her husband and son and now she had lost a daughter who had lived for such a short time.

How would she herself feel if she lost *her* little boy – here she brought herself up sharply. He was not *her* boy, he was Kate's and she must never, *never* forget that. The child she looked after, and for whom she felt such love, was Kate's child and not hers. She knew she should not allow herself to care for the boy too deeply, but the longer she had sole charge of him the harder it would be when finally she had to give him up. If only Kate would soften towards him . . . but her attitude remained unchanged. Lily found it impossible to understand her friend's indifference, but if Kate did not want to care for the boy, Lily did and was more than happy to do so. All babies needed love and Kate's child was no exception. Suppose it was Kate's child who was being lowered into the cold hard earth – Lily's heart lurched with fright at the very idea. Nothing, she vowed inwardly, would harm *her* baby. She would protect him with – there! She had said it again! The boy was *Kate's* son. Tears filled her eyes and ran down her cheeks, but they were not only for Ella's little girl. They were for Lily, because the boy was not hers and never could be.

When the simple funeral was over, she began to make her way back to the wagon but was waylaid by Daniel Miller.

'A word in your ear, ma'am,' he began.

Lily gave him a sharp look. Something in his manner made her uneasy.

'I mustn't be long,' she said. 'I have to get back to – '

'I won't keep you long,' he assured her. 'It's about me and Kate.'

Lily allowed herself to be led away from the wagons where they could talk without being overheard.

'I've had a talk with her,' he said, 'and she wants to stick with me. She wants to carry on, the way we were – a team, if you like. I'm not the marrying kind, but nor is she – '

'Who says so?' Lily snapped. 'Did she say so?'

'She didn't say she wasn't,' he parried. 'Put it another way, then. She'd rather stick with me than chance her arm with another man. Some women are the wifely kind, others are . . . the other kind. Kate was enjoying herself before the kid came and she was good at it. Some women are natural – '

He stopped at the flash of anger in Lily's eyes and the word 'whore' died on his lips. 'Look, Lily, you may not approve – '

'I certainly don't,' said Lily. '*I* shall talk to her. Kate said it was just until the baby came.'

Miller's eyes rolled and he grinned disarmingly. 'It's a woman's privilege to change her mind,' he told her. 'I didn't force her. Honest Injun! Hand on heart!'

He laid his hand across his chest and bent his head reverently. Lily regarded him dispassionately. 'You mean you and Kate are going to carry on together until we reach California?' she asked. 'Or after that?'

'After that,' he told her. 'If you want it in plain English –
and you *are* English after all – we shall start up a whorehouse
in Sacramento. I'll find a couple more girls later on – '

Lily put her hands over her ears and she looked at him in
shocked disbelief.

'I don't want to hear any more!' she cried. 'I'm going to
Kate right now and – '

To her surprise, he caught hold of her arm. 'Wait,' he said
and something in his expression frightened her. She looked
into the brown eyes and waited with a cold feeling of dread.
Of course! The child! They were going to take the child. He
had agreed to take the child. Lily's senses swam as a blackness swept through her, paralysing her thoughts. As though
from a great distance, she heard his voice and snatches of
what he said registered in her mind.

' . . . doesn't want the boy – not a natural mother – a
better chance than we can give him . . .'

Desperately, Lily struggled to understand what she was
being told.

'You don't *want* him?' She cried and was suddenly wildly
hopeful. 'You mean, *I* can keep him? Is that what you mean?
Are you saying *I* can – oh God! Is that it?'

The compassion in his eyes terrified her. 'Ma'am, you can't
take on a baby,' he began, 'but Ella can. Ella has a man to
take care of her – '

'*Ella?*' Lily stared at him uncomprehendingly.

'Yes, ma'am. Kate's giving him to Ella.'

Lily clutched at his arm for support as the world seemed
to spin.

'You mean, *Ella's* going to have Kate's baby? Oh no! She
can't! I won't *allow* it!'

'It's for the best,' he insisted. 'The baby needs a proper
home, a family. We can't give it to him, but Ella's got a man
to – '

'So have I!' cried Lily desperately. 'I've got Henry Simms.'

Miller shook his head. 'He's gone, Lily. You know he has.
Ella's the best person to care for the baby. You must think
of the baby, and Ella's got milk.'

'Milk?' Lily looked at him blankly.

Miller nodded. 'She's had a baby, so she's got milk. She can feed Kate's baby with proper milk. Be sensible, Lily. It's ideal for him. Good milk, a mother and father, grandparents – a proper family.'

Lily swallowed, her eyes dark with pain as she searched for words that would express what was in her heart. They were going to take the boy away!

'But he *knows* me,' she stammered. 'He's used to me. He *loves* me, Mr Miller. It will upset him terribly if he goes to a stranger. Believe me, *I* can care for him if Kate doesn't want to keep him. I'll talk to her. I'll – ' She turned to run, but his hand tightened on her arm and suddenly suspicion flared through her and became certainty. He was keeping her talking while they took the child!

'Let me go!' she screamed, but the harder she struggled the tighter his fingers closed on her wrists.

'Ma'am, please be sensible,' he begged. 'It's all been decided. It's all been thrashed out.'

'Where was I?' Lily demanded. 'When did they decide?'

'Does it matter?' he said gently. 'Hester came to see Kate and put it to her. Kate agreed. Look, ma'am, it's all settled.'

Lily felt a great weariness creep into her limbs and she would have fallen if he had not supported her.

'Please, Mrs Golightly,' he urged. 'Try to see it from the boy's point of view. You want what's best for him, don't you?'

She nodded helplessly, but her eyes grew dull as the enormity of her loss struck home. They were taking the baby from her without so much as a 'by-your-leave'. They had conspired against her. She felt utterly betrayed. After all she had done for Kate! Now Ella would hold the little boy and comfort his tears. She would feed him with her own milk! The thought made Lily sick with envy. How could she ever bear it? And all these people, her so-called friends, had plotted together to break her heart.

Miller was watching her closely. 'It's best for the baby,' he said. 'And it's best for Ella. Don't you think she's suffered enough? Doesn't she deserve a child after all she's lost? Be honest.'

'Yes,' Lily whispered. 'She does.'

'There you are then,' he said triumphantly.

Lily looked at him. 'And you were sent to tell me – to keep me out of the way while . . . while they took him.' It was not a question but he nodded. 'Poor Mr Miller,' she said dully. 'Not very nice for you.'

'No, ma'am.'

'Why didn't Kate tell me herself?'

He shrugged.

'*Why?*' persisted Lily. 'After all we've been to each other. I thought we were friends. I've nursed her – I let Henry go without me . . .' With a fierce movement she freed her wrists and looked at him, bewildered and confused.

'I know,' he said. 'You've had a rotten deal.'

'You *don't* know,' cried Lily passionately. 'Oh no, Mr Miller, you *don't* know because you're an insensitive man and you don't know right from wrong. You've turned Kate from a nice girl into a . . .' She faltered. 'You've ruined her.'

'She's happy,' he stated. 'She's got pride in herself.'

'Pride? How can she have pride? She must be so ashamed.'

'No,' he answered. 'But you wouldn't understand. Look, Mrs Golightly, I don't want to fight with you . . .'

'Then don't,' she said and for a long moment she stared at him in silence. 'So I'm not needed any more,' she said at last. 'Then you can look after Kate.'

His face fell. 'Look after Kate? Me? Oh, but – '

She hardened her heart. 'Yes, I'll move out. I shall speak to Captain Wallis.'

'But I can't – I mean, Kate still needs nursing,' he said.

'You and Kate,' Lily reminded him. 'That's what you said. Then you nurse her. I'm finished with her – I'm finished with all of you.'

She was making a tremendous effort to retain her self-control. She wanted to run and scream and cry, she wanted to tear at Kate's frizzy red hair and pummel Ella's soft arms, she wanted to hurt them as much as they had hurt her, but she knew she dare not give rein to the rage that filled her. She was the daughter of an English clergyman and she would behave like one; she would not disgrace her father.

353

They regarded each other warily and Lily spoke first.

'What are you waiting for?' she demanded. 'You've done your part. Aren't you satisfied?'

He shrugged. 'It's for the best,' he said. 'You'll see it that way by and by.'

'I doubt it,' said Lily coldly. 'Well, go on – don't you have to report back?'

He had the grace to look ashamed and hesitated. 'Shall we walk back together?' he suggested.

Lily shook her head. 'You go on,' she said, her throat tight with misery. 'I've nothing to walk back to. Nothing at all.'

*

It seemed for ever that Lily stood there after Miller had left her. The whole world seemed to be crashing around her and she could not think of anything positive to do. She remained with her head bowed and hands clenched at her sides while a jumble of emotions churned through her. Patrick was dead, Henry had gone away and her so-called friends had cheated her of the only thing she had left to love – Kate's son. A deep grief welled up inside her and she felt sick and cold.

'Oh, Papa,' she whispered. 'Comfort me.'

If only she could be safe at home among people who loved her. What a luxury that would be!

'It serves you right,' she told herself. 'You were so headstrong, so sure that you were right. You gave Papa no peace until you got your own way. Now look at you!'

Suddenly the shock began to take effect and her legs gave way beneath her. She sank heavily to the ground and sat with her head and arms resting on her knees, abject and defeated and longing for oblivion.

Perhaps it was an hour later when Matt Wallis walked over and stood looking down at her slender figure which shook with the ferocity of her sobs.

'Get up, Mrs Golightly,' he said abruptly. 'Here, give me your hands.' She appeared not to hear him and in a louder tone he repeated, 'Get up, Mrs Golightly.'

At last she raised her head and the sight of her ravaged face shocked him. Her eyelids were puffed, her skin blotched, her eyes reddened by the volume of tears she had shed. He had never seen her proud spirit crushed before and for a moment he could think of nothing to say. When at last he did speak his voice was harder than he intended.

'That's enough. Tears don't change anything.'

She shook her head wordlessly and the misery in her eyes tugged at his heart.

'It's hard for you now,' he said, softening his voice with an effort, 'but it's best in the long run.'

'Don't say that,' she gasped. 'It's not true, I won't listen.' She put her hands over her ears and after a moment Matt dropped to one knee beside her.

'It's tough, I know – ' he began, but she interrupted him passionately.

'Tough!' she exclaimed. 'Is that what you think it is? Just "tough" – to lose everything in the world that matters – my poor Patrick, Henry and now my little boy. Yes, *my* little boy! He was all I had left to love. Tough, you call it, to have your friends deceive you – *mock* you.' Her momentary anger disappeared and her face crumpled again. When she spoke her tone was anguished. 'Oh no, Captain Wallis, it's not just tough.' Her shoulders shook as she covered her face with her hands. 'It simply breaks . . .' She gulped for air and finished brokenly, 'It simply breaks my heart.'

As her distress deepened, he felt obliged to put an arm awkwardly across her shoulders in a mute gesture of sympathy, but to his surprise she swayed suddenly towards him as though the last of her energy had been drained away. He found himself holding her in his arms, patting her shoulder from time to time and murmuring soothingly. His own emotions were confused, for it was a long time since he had held a woman and his instincts were to kiss her and stroke her hair, but Lily Golightly was not his woman and she was crying for her dead husband and Henry Simms.

Gradually he became aware that her grief was subsiding and he gave her a handkerchief and watched her shaky attempts to stem the last few tears. Then he stood up abruptly, reached down and pulled her to her feet. 'It would be easy to give up,' he said, 'but you can't do it because I won't let you. You have to go on, however hard it is.'

Lily regarded him dazedly. 'I just don't care . . .' she whispered.

'You have to care.' He put an arm round her shoulders and tried to turn her back towards the camp, but she stiffened at once.

'I don't want to go back,' she protested. 'I don't want to see anyone.'

'You mean you don't want to face them?' he told her. 'Why's that? You've nothing to be ashamed of.'

Lily sighed deeply. 'I feel so worthless,' she confessed. 'I've never felt that way before – not once in my whole life.'

'We all have to do what we think is right,' he said. 'You did what was right and that doesn't make you worthless. Come back now; you can't stay here.'

'I've nowhere to go,' whispered Lily. 'I won't go back with Kate. Nor Hester, nor any of them. I couldn't.'

He began to lead her back.

'I've made room for you in one of the store wagons,' he told her. 'It will be rather cramped, but at least you'll be on your own. My wagon is next to it, so you'll be safe enough.'

She said dully, 'I lost Henry Simms because of Kate and now – now she . . .'

'You'll find him again,' he assured her. 'I can't pretend I'm glad because I'm not, but you'll find him if you look hard enough.'

Lily's lips trembled. 'Maybe I won't look,' she said. 'Maybe I don't care any more.'

He turned to look into her eyes. 'You'll look and you'll find him,' he said, 'and I hope to God he deserves you.' Then he smiled. 'Right, head up, Mrs Golightly. We're going in, as they say in the Army.'

She smiled faintly and he bent to kiss her briefly on the forehead.

'Now,' he said. 'There'll be folk watching you to see how you've taken it. Do you need my arm around you?'

'No, thank you,' replied Lily after a moment's hesitation. 'I'll walk alone.'

The Humboldt River was a great disappointment, being both dirty and sluggish, but it was a river and they had to be thankful for small mercies.

On the twenty-third of September they reached a point where the trail divided into two, and both turned south and led through an area of desert which extended for forty miles. One led to the Truckee River and the other to the Carson. The Western Hopers were dismayed to meet a family who had turned back from the latter and who told terrible stories of both routes – of men and animals with tongues bloated by the heat, and sand so deep and soft that the wagons could not be moved through it.

After a hasty consultation, the company agreed to try a third and newer route known as Lassen's Cut-Off, which by all accounts would lead them to the mining camps in less than two hundred miles. They set out along the new pass with renewed enthusiasm.

The trail led them over the crusted surface of the Black Rock Desert, where two mules and five oxen died of heat and exhaustion. Shade temperatures were frequently above 90°F and water was desperately scarce. On October 3rd, however, they entered Little High Rock Canyon, so named because of its steep sides, where at least there was grass for the cattle.

Two days later they came in sight of the highest range of the Sierra Nevada. Lily, driving the stores wagon, stared at the snow-capped peaks and tried to imagine the far side where they would find the first of the 'diggings'. She exchanged a quiet smile with Wallis, who rode alongside; she had kept apart from her former friends since Ella's 'adoption' of Kate's son and had come to rely more and more on his company. When he was occupied elsewhere, as was frequently the case, she remained alone from choice. She had not seen Kate's baby since the day they took him away from her and she had begun to come to terms with the searing sense of loss. Although not seeing him was almost as bad as seeing him in another woman's arms, she dared not test her emotions further and thought it best to stay away.

As she drove the four gaunt oxen, she allowed herself to

think about Henry Simms and to wonder how he was faring. Any stranger overtaken on the trail caused her nerves to jangle with a mixture of hope and fear – the former that it might not be Henry, the latter in case it was and he had not forgiven her. Wallis had said she would find him again, but she was not so confident and prepared herself for a lonely future. If she did not find Henry Simms, she must be able to survive alone. She was reasonably intelligent and could surely earn her own living. Provisional plans buzzed in her head as hour by hour she trudged alongside the team. There would be children in California for her to teach; there would be groups of men she could cook for; doctors she might assist; stores which needed an assistant. She could sew and darn and she could wash clothes if necessary. If she starved it would be her own fault, she told herself. She had no ties and could move about at will, so she might join a group of prospectors or even go prospecting on her own. At times she felt apprehensive, but most of the time these tentative plans sustained her. Her health was holding up – so far. Apart from the inevitable headaches, blisters, exhaustion and occasional diarrhoea, she had nothing to complain of – unlike many of the others. Poor Mrs Harper had died, three of the men were very sick and another had a broken arm.

She watched Wallis out of the corner of her eye. His curly hair was dark with dust, but his beard was less straggly than many of the men who had given up caring about their appearance. He sat his horse lightly for so large a man and the white scar on his jaw showed up pale against his sunburned skin. He was a fine man, she reflected, and would make someone a good husband if that was what he wanted, but she found it hard to imagine someone so self-sufficient sharing a life of domesticity and wondered if he had ever been married. He never spoke of a wife or family, but he was a very private man.

She sighed. Another few weeks maybe and it would all be over. They would be *there*, in the land of opportunity. All these people who had shared so many hardships and dangers would go their separate ways. And she would go hers. Lily viewed the prospect with mixed feelings.

*

In the middle of October they crossed the summit of the Warner Range and Goose Lake lay ahead. Their path, however, lay southward. On the western slopes of the summit they were astonished to find that a military camp had been set up to give assistance to the emigrants. Wallis at once rode down to the camp and conferred at length with the unit, which was led by a man called Todd. When he returned, he called a meeting of the Western Hopers and they listened in gloomy silence as he recounted what he had learned.

'Apparently the snows could start at any time,' he told them, 'and when they do, we will be in serious trouble. I needn't spell it out to you; we all remember the Donner party and you'll know exactly what I mean.'

There were murmurs of assent for there was no one who had not heard of the tragedy. Even Lily knew the tragic story of the earlier emigrants who had only avoided starvation by eating their dead comrades.

'I'm not trying to frighten you,' Wallis continued, then gave a short laugh. 'No, dammit, I *am* trying to frighten you,' he said. '*I'm* frightened and you should be, too. We've been misled about this cut-off and Todd tells me we still have two hundred miles to go.'

There were horrified gasps and furious comment. The cut-off they had taken should have saved them days of travelling, but instead they had *lost* time. Wallis held up his hand for silence and reluctantly they quietened down to listen.

'I've talked to Todd, who is in command,' he informed them, 'and as most of you already know, they've given us some fresh beef so we'll all dine well tonight.'

A murmur of appreciation rewarded him, but his expression was grim.

'The point is this – they're expecting serious trouble. There are hundreds of people behind us on the trail and it looks as though some of them won't make it before the weather breaks. *We* might not make it. We don't really have enough oxen to pull our wagons. Our only hope, in Todd's opinion, is to split up for the rest of the journey and travel as fast as we can – that means abandoning a lot more stuff so that we

can all travel lighter and faster. It might even mean abandoning the wagons . . .'

A great outcry greeted this suggestion and for a while he
was silent, letting them have their say. When at last he could
again make himself heard, he resumed.

'Todd recommends that we all press on separately with
no more stops for sickness, no more Sabbaths, no more
delays for any reason. If we all travel together as one
company, we probably won't make it. Those who can take
horse and mule and pack in to the gold fields should do so
with all speed. Those who *must* take wagons must lighten
them. Any women and children who can ride horses and
have horses to ride, should do so. This is imperative. If
everyone who can make it on their own does so, there'll be
more help available for the sick and those stragglers who
otherwise will most certainly die. Anybody who doubts my
word is welcome to take a walk down into the camp and
talk to Todd. He'll tell you what I've just told you – but he
won't thank you for wasting more of his time.'

'What about you?' cried Mr Harper. 'Are you going on
on your own?'

'No, I'm not,' he replied. 'I shall travel with the slowest.
I'm paid to get you all to California and that's what I shall
do. But I won't mollycoddle those who are fit and able to
get in under their own steam. We shall have to abandon
everything which is not vital to our survival. Not just the
items you think you can spare – but *everything*. It's either
that or getting caught in the snows and freezing to death.
Take your pick, ladies and gentlemen!'

Bart Smith stood up. 'Amos and I lost our horses a week
ago,' he said, 'and the mule a month back. Do we have any
chance on foot with a back-pack?'

Wallis told him that they did. A large number of men
volunteered to join them and several groups were assembled
to attempt the last two hundred miles on foot. Another group
of sixteen men decided to share four horses and four mules,
riding and walking alternately. Of the remaining members,
some opted to manage with small wagons with four oxen to
pull them instead of eight. Others voted to carry on as they

were, but to lighten the loads; Kate and Daniel Miller were among this last group.

Eventually the only remaining members were the Coopers and Ella, Gabby Smith and Kate's son (now named Moses), Mr Harper and his sons and Lily and Wallis himself. It was finally agreed that Ella, Hester and the baby should ride in a wagon with whatever provisions they would need. All the rest would go on horseback.

'And if the horses die?' Charlie asked.

'We double up – two to a horse,' Wallis told him.

The provisions would be divided up the next mroning and everyone would go their own ways. The company would be formally disbanded and Wallis wished them all a safe journey.

'See you all in Sacramento!' cried Gabby with an attempt at cheerfulness, but although his cry was taken up by the rest of them, the mood was subdued and nobody relished the prospect which awaited them on the morrow. Despite all the hazards there had always been a sense of unity and with it a sense of belonging. Now there was nothing. It was every man for himself and many were fearful.

*

Early next morning the various parties moved off. Wallis's group was last to go, but they rolled out just after seven with Wallis and Lily riding up front, Hester and Ella in the stores wagon which was pulled by four mules and the other riders bringing up the rear. Their route lay southward along the Pit River, which wound its way amidst a rocky landscape inhabited by Pit Indians. Wallis warned that these were comparatively hostile and a watch was kept for them at all times.

They had travelled for a week without incident and were congratulating themselves on their good fortune when a new hazard presented itself in the shape of a deep pit dug by the Indians to catch game. Gabby's horse stumbled into it, throwing him and breaking its own neck. Miraculously, Gabby suffered nothing but bruises, but the animal had to

361

be shot and the accident cast a gloom over the rest of the party.

Lily found the new travelling arrangements particularly trying, as she was thrown into closer proximity with Ella and forced to see the way she idolized Moses; however, the baby was thriving and Lily had to admit that Ella was giving the boy all the love and attention that she could have wished for him. She managed an occasional polite word or two, but kept as wide a distance as possible between herself and the happy family group. She was glad that Kate had gone on – the girl's absence made life a little easier. Her horror at Kate's chosen lifestyle had given way to a defeated resignation; if Kate wanted to degrade herself, she was free to do so, but Lily never would understand or condone what she was doing. In a way she felt to blame for bringing Kate with her to California, but told herself it was too late for regrets of that kind.

As the days passed, the difficulties and discomforts of their journey drove out all other considerations and she was forced to live in the present, so that past and future alike lost their significance and gradually she began to regain her perspective on life. Wallis's welcome companionship steadied her and his kindness soothed her injured feelings. She wanted to tell him how much she admired him, but he was not the kind of man to take pleasure in compliments and her few attempts were brushed aside with an embarrassed shake of the head. Each night she rolled herself in a blanket and rubber sheet and slept beside him on the ground, and sometimes in the fading light of the camp-fire she would study his face. Even in sleep he appeared taut and unrelaxed, his brows drawn together in a frown, the lips tight closed, the nostrils slightly flared. He would wake at the snap of a twig but, discovering all was well, would instantly sleep again.

Lily envied him this ability. In spite of her own exhaustion, she often lay awake wide-eyed long after everyone else had fallen asleep. Mostly she thought of Henry, sometimes of Patrick, but occasionally it was her father who occupied her thoughts. She hoped that when she reached Sutters Fort (if she ever did!) she might find a letter waiting from him to

362

satisfy her that he was alive and happy. Her one dread was that he would fall ill and die without her caring arms to sustain him.

Their party still had many miles to go and the extreme mountain cold depressed their spirits and sapped their dwindling energies. Charlie Cooper succumbed to scurvy and with painfully swollen legs and aching joints, was forced – grumbling – to ride in the wagon with Moses and Ella.

November blew in with a light flurry of snow which drastically aggravated their existing problems and created more, but all they could do was to press on though their faces and fingers froze and their limbs grew leaden. Each mile was gained at great cost, but it brought them nearer to their goal and in every heart there burned a fierce flame of resolution which the coldest winds could not extinguish. The more unbearable the conditions of their journey, the more single-minded they became. They had set out in search of gold and they had crossed two thousand miles to find it. Nothing but death would stop them now that the end was almost in sight.

On November the tenth the ragged and exhausted travellers turned a bend in the trail and gazed in disbelief at a straggling collection of cabins and tents. Wallis reined in his horse and waited for the rest of the party to catch up with them so that they could all enjoy the full drama of the moment.

Hester was the first to speak. 'I don't believe it!' she whispered.

Gabby, rendered speechless, gave a long low whistle. A few cabins of split logs, others of rough hand-made bricks and dozens of tents sprawled among willow trees and faced out over a creek. Piles of rubbish lay around and haggard-looking men moved purposefully up and down the muddy 'street'. It was an unlovely sight, but to the small band of onlookers it meant that the journey was over and in their eyes New York itself could not have looked more beautiful.

Long, breathtaking moments passed as they all stared down at the untidy settlement, their hearts so full that mere words could not express their joy and relief.

Lily glanced up at Wallis.

'We've made it!' she whispered.

'We're here,' he said and for once he smiled broadly. 'This must be Lassen's Ranch.'

Impulsively, Lily threw her arms round his neck and kissed him and he buried his face in her hair and whispered, 'Welcome to California, Mrs Golightly!'

Chapter Eighteen

It took the group a few days to assess the situation in which they now found themselves and to which they must all adjust. The winter had closed in and many of the miners had temporarily abandoned their claims and moved into the towns. Some looked for work in Sacramento, the new city that was springing up around John Sutter's fort. Many went further west to San Francisco, adding to the thousands of men who already thronged that busy port; others prepared to wait out the cold weather in the smaller settlements. Everywhere men ate and drank, smoked, gambled or slept, passing the time as best they could, or compared notes in German, Spanish, Chinese or French while they waited for the bad weather to pass so that they could return to their diggings.

In his heart each man *knew* that his own crock of gold waited for him, hidden in a narrow rock crevice, held by the roots of a tree or tumbling along the bed of a creek. Ceaseless erosion had exposed the vast treasure which had laid within the rocks for millions of years and gold was there for those who cared to look for it.

Many of the men had spent a whole summer in the mountains; the later arrivals had only a month's experience about which they could boast, but even these men knew more about the mining process than the Western Hopers. The latter were faced with the agonizing knowledge that unless they were prepared to brave the elements, they must wait until spring for their first attempt to locate gold.

After long and earnest discussions Matt, Gabby and Bart

decided to go ahead, unable to bear the prospect of an uneventful and profitless winter. Charlie was still sick, so it was arranged that he should stay in the comparative comfort of Sacramento with Hester, Ella and the baby. Lily, unwilling to join them, announced that she would accompany the men and nothing they could say deterred her. She told them she would cook and mend and wash their clothes in exchange for a share of the gold when they found it, and at last they were reluctantly forced to agree.

By early December Daniel Miller had somehow rented a large room in Sacramento for himself and Kate. Amos Carp joined forces with the Harpers and they found temporary work in San Francisco, helping to move the stacks of supplies which were daily unloaded on to the waterfront.

January found Lily and her companions installed in a very crude log cabin situated on a stretch of land on one of the northernmost reaches of the Feather River, dubbed Godwin Bar after the man who had first found gold on it. The dozen other hopefuls sharing the bar made no objections to the new party, for it was clear that in adverse conditions safety lay in numbers. The cabin was eighteen feet square and its interior was divided into three by means of cloth walls – a small sleeping area for Lily, a larger one for the three men and another for the shared living room. A rough fireplace had been made of rocks and stones held together with a mixture of mud and mortar, while two barrels and a broad plank of wood served as a table. Tree-stumps made serviceable chairs and Lily's bed was a broad 'shelf' projecting from the wall. She alone had the luxury of a cheap hair mattress purchased in Sacramento; the three men made do with hammocks and declared themselves comfortable enough.

At last the men began to pan for gold and Lily was left very much to her own devices. When the weather permitted, she rode the mule five miles to the nearest 'store' and led it back with their weekly supplies of whatever dried fruit and vegetables she had been able to find. Eggs were almost unobtainable, cheese was in short supply and the prices were outrageously high.

After the initial thrill the men's work became routine and

panning was no more than a back-breaking chore as they crouched beside the water, sifting and swirling the dirt in the pans, unaware of their companions, intent only on the possibility that when the surplus soil had been washed away a small nugget or a few flashes of gold would remain in the pan. It did not happen very often, but the few occasions when it did galvanized them all to renewed effort.

Lily, concerned with her own tasks, paused from time to time to watch as they crouched over their work and marvelled daily at their perseverance. Her own contribution was considerable. The preparation of three hearty meals per day for four hungry people taxed her powers of resilience as well as her ingenuity, but she received plenty of compliments and knew that her efforts were appreciated. They had brought flour, coffee, sugar and beans with them and occasionally one of the men would shoot a duck or trap a few fish in the river. The steep hillsides were thickly clad in forest, so fuel was plentiful and there was good water to drink.

The men treated Lily with respect and she was surprised to find herself reasonably happy in her new surroundings. Her only regret was that she had had no time to look for Henry, and earlier inquiries in Sacramento had produced nothing helpful. Few people seemed to have heard of him and those who had did not know where he was. Lily left a letter for him at Sacramento, where a Post Office of sorts had been established, but so far this had elicited no reply and gradually she resigned herself to spending the winter at Godwin Bar. In the spring, she promised herself, she would take her share of the gold and go in search of Henry. She owed him that.

On the evening of the last Sunday in January, the evening meal was over and Lily and Gabby sat by the fire, the latter composing a letter to Ella. Lily was darning a large tear in her skirt which she had made scrambling through the trees when gathering kindling for the fire. Matt Wallis was rubbing fat into his boots to weatherproof them, while Bart was designing a wooden rocker which would speed up the recovery of gold. Nobody felt the need for conversation – it was enough to be in the warm with full stomachs – but after a while Bart looked up from his sketch, rubbing his eyes tiredly with a calloused forefinger.

'It should work,' he told them, 'and it'll save us near on two hundred dollars. I reckon I could make it in a day. What d'you say? Shall I have a go at it tomorrow if I can find a bit of mesh for the hopper?'

Heaving himself up, he showed the sketch he had made to Matt who considered it carefully and then said, 'You've only got four riffles, but there's room for five if you put em a bit closer together.'

After a moment's thought Bart said, 'You've got it. Five it is. And what about the hopper? Is it wide enough?'

'I guess so.'

Lily laughed. 'I can't understand a word you two are saying,' she said. 'Bring it here, Bart, and explain it to me – and don't grin like that! I'm not entirely without brains and I would like to know what you're doing.'

Bart's grin widened, but he crossed over to her and laid the sketch in her lap.

'It's really just a long wooden box,' he told her. 'Here at the top end there's this square hopper, and the bottom of the hopper is a sheet of mesh if we can get hold of some. The pay dirt goes on this – '

'Aha!' interrupted Lily. 'It's pay dirt today, is it? Yesterday it was just gravel!'

Bart blushed behind his beard at her teasing tone. 'OK, then. The *gravel* goes in here, water is poured on to it and washes it through the mesh to this sloping length of canvas underneath. All the big stones are kept back by the mesh, the finer stuff – '

'The *gold*,' Lily corrected him.

'The finer stuff and the gold if there *is* any,' Bart grinned, 'falls through the mesh and is washed down over these four – or five – wooden riffles . . .'

'You mean these strips of wood,' said Lily.

He nodded. '*But*, when it's running down over the riffles we *rock* the whole thing by means of these rockers underneath and this handle. The water and soil run away at the

368

open end, but the G-O-L-D obligingly tucks itself behind the riffles and we collect it from there.'

Lily nodded. 'So you don't have to stand in that freezing water any more?'

'No – not unless you want to dig up some gravel from the river-bed.'

Matt looked up. 'We won't be able to do that until the level falls in the spring,' he warned. 'While the water's high, we'll have to keep digging along the banks.'

'So how long is this rocker of yours going to be, Bart?' asked Lily.

'About eighteen inches wide and maybe three feet long. It should do the trick.'

'Where will you find your mesh?' Lily asked.

Bart shook his head. 'That's the big question,' he admitted.

'Couldn't you make some?' suggested Lily. 'Take the lid from the biscuit tin, hammer it flat and punch rows of holes in it. It would be just about the right size.'

There was a moment's silence and Gabby looked up from his letter. 'She *has* got brains!' he exclaimed. 'What d'you know!'

Bart grinned. 'Now why didn't I think of that?'

Matt said nothing, but Lily sensed his surprised approval. 'I'll do it,' declared Bart. 'Thanks, Lily. So, what do you all say? Shall I take the day off tomorrow and make it?'

'You've got my vote,' said Gabby. 'I say go ahead and make it. I take it we shall have to work it together?'

Bart nodded. 'One to shovel the pay dirt into the hopper, one to rock it, one to pour on the water.'

'What could I do?' asked Lily.

'You could stagger down to the bank with all the gold in a sack!' said Matt.

Lily caught his eye as they all laughed and she thought how much more relaxed he was now that he was no longer captain of the Western Hopers. When Gabby had called him Matt for the first time, he had obviously been pleased to shrug off the responsibilities which he had borne for so long. Now he could be accepted on an equal footing. Now he was one of them.

Since they had shared the same roof, he had treated Lily with a courtesy which verged on the exaggerated, almost as though he mocked her though in the nicest possible way. She suspected it was a mask for his true feelings, but he never spoke of his regard for her although she saw it in his eyes. If she had not met Henry, she thought, everything might have been very different. Matt Wallis was a man she could respect; possibly she could have loved him. There was no harm in admitting to herself that she found him attractive, but it must go no further than that and Lily was keeping her emotions well under control. She had told Matt she was going to marry Henry, and he was not the kind of man to take advantage of the other man's absence. She supposed that in time more women would travel to California and probably Matt would marry one of them. Would he stay in California? Or would he go home? He never spoke of his future plans, but seemed content to take each day as it came.

A slight sigh escaped her and she turned to look at the two brothers as they pored over the design for the rocker. Their dark, curly heads were close together and Gabby's letter lay unfinished beside him.

Impulsively Lily asked, 'Gabby, are you writing to Ella?'

'Yes.' His tone was guarded.

Lily kept her eyes firmly fixed on her mending. 'Please send her my kind regards,' she requested and was aware that the men exchanged surprised looks.

'I will,' he said. 'She'll be real pleased.'

Lily wanted to add, 'And send my love to Moses,' but try as she would the words would not come. The image of the boy was still painfully strong in her mind and rose unbidden at times to torment her with a longing to hold him in her arms once more. It saddened her that he would never know how much she loved him.

Matt changed the subject. 'That fellow who came by today – Johnny Parks, I think his name was – says there's a chap going round who will bring you mail from the Post Office in Sacramento. Charges two dollars a letter. I guess he'd take one there for the same price.'

'He'll make a fortune,' smiled Lily, 'without panning an ounce of gravel!'

'All the more gold for those who do,' said Bart. 'But good luck to him. Why not?'

'He can certainly take this letter to Ella,' Gabby said. 'Have you written to your father, Lily?'

She nodded. 'Ten days ago. I gave it to Jim Godwin when he pulled out of here last week. I offered him a dollar for his trouble, but he wouldn't take it.'

'He doesn't need it,' laughed Bart. 'Four thousand dollars! That's not bad for six weeks' labour. Struck lucky the very first day, he was telling me. Swung his pick into the ground while he stood back and wondered where to begin. He had this whole bar to himself. Decided to start at the far end, but when he pulled his pick out of the ground there was the gold! Three nuggets nestling together like eggs in a nest. No one's found much since, but it's got to be there.' He shook his head enviously. 'I hope that happens to me.'

Lily smiled. 'If there's any gold, you'll find it in the new rocker,' she told him.

'Not "if", – "*when*", he corrected her.

She bit off her thread and patted the darn. 'Not perfect, but who's going to see it? This poor skirt will soon be more darns than skirt! And my poor boots!' She stretched out her legs to consider them. 'Down at the heel, scratched and stained. I'm beginning to feel like a scarecrow.'

'Ah, but you're a *lady* scarecrow!' laughed Gabby. 'That makes all the difference.'

He was referring to the fact that Lily was the only woman on the bar, and as such aroused a great deal of interest in the rest of their small community. Aware of their lack of feminine company, Lily was at pains not to draw attention to herself, knowing how easy it would be to arouse dangerous jealousies between the men. She looked round now at her own friends with a critical eye. They were all bearded and all decidely lean. Bart's eyes roved restlessly – he was the impatient one, thought Lily. Gabby had his new wife and child to think about and she knew how hard it must be for him to be parted from them. And Matt? He was self-sufficient, quiet and even-tempered. She wondered just how much the journey had affected them all and how they would react to whatever the next six months might bring.

At last, Lily said 'Good night' to the men and went to bed, where she lay under her blankets listening to the low murmur of their voices. She was very fond of all of them and wanted their happiness. If only they could find gold in useful quantities. If only they could 'strike it rich'!

*

By eight o'clock the next morning breakfast was over and it was work as usual. While Bart concentrated on the construction of his rocker, Matt and Gabby worked in the stream. Dozens of pairs of eyes were alert for a glimpse of the precious 'colour' and conversation was virtually non-existent. Engrossed in their labours, they were unaware of the colourful spectacle of which they were each a part; the sun shone from a cloudless sky and sparkled on the shallow water as it rushed over the gravelly stream-bed and bubbled round rocks and boulders. The men's bright shirts stood out against the pale yellow rock of the bar and beyond them steep slopes rose skyward on all sides, dark with trees. A few hundred yards above them, a narrow waterfall burst from a split in the rock and fell into the stream below with a quiet but persistent roar. Closer at hand, smoke curled upwards from various camp-fires and birds wheeled curiously overhead, attracted by the sights and smells of the small encampment. Other sounds completed the scene – the clang of shovel on rock, a snatch of melody or the gleeful shout as gold dust appeared in someone's pan and a pair of tired eyes gleamed briefly with renewed hope. Lily watched them as she pegged three shirts on to a line which Matt had put up for her and suddenly, inexplicably, she wanted to be part of it. She wanted to be out there looking for gold instead of playing her usual role.

'Why not?' she demanded.

There was no one to answer her so she nodded quickly, snatched off her apron and reached for her coat. Taking up a spare pan and shovel, she hurried outside and made her

372

way along the bank of the stream, past Matt (who did not see her) and on to a spot where she would not easily be noticed. For a moment she stared around her. How to begin? Where to dig?

'You can do it,' she told herself. 'I can be as lucky or as unlucky as the men.'

Beneath her feet the ground was a mixture of sand, gravel and soil, but was there also gold hidden within it?

'This will do,' she decided and she laid down her pan and began to dig, throwing the loose mixture into it. When it was a little more than half full, she stopped digging and took up the pan. In spite of the sun the air was cool and Lily shivered, partly with excitement. With a nervous finger she pushed at the heap of dirt.

'Now are you pay dirt or just dirt?' she grinned.

Moving down to the water's edge, she found a flat stone and sat down, trying to keep her feet out of the water. With rapidly beating heart she leaned forward, lowered the pan into the stream and watched as it turned the contents into mud. This she studied hopefully, allowing the light soil to be floated off by the water. Then she swirled the pan, shaking it as she did so, encouraging the gold – if there was any – to sink to the bottom.

She lifted it out and tilted the pan so that most of the water drained away, then carefully she picked out the larger pebbles and began to break up the small lumps of clay in case any fragments of gold were trapped within. After a moment or two she lowered the pan into the water and swirled it again, watching more of the fine light soil drift downstream. She took it out, drained it and looked for golden specks. There were none, but determinedly she bent forward again, repeating the process.

Suddenly she thought of Patrick. 'You should be doing this,' she told his ghost. 'You should be crouched beside this stream with a pan of dirt. Oh, my dear Patrick, how very different everything would be then!'

A great sadness filled her at the thought that he had never achieved his heart's desire and she wanted to comfort him.

'It's no great deal,' she told him. 'Just turning the pan and hoping. It's not as romantic as it sounds and it's very hard work, but if there's any gold in this pan, I promise I'll find it. I know you can't be here, but I'll find it for you.'

She blinked back sudden tears and drew the pan from the water yet again. Much of the fine soil had already gone and she picked out a few more pebbles and stared at the residue. About half of the original panful remained, so perhaps she was getting nearer to finding something. She examined it intently and saw small specks of pale sand, darker finer specks, tiny pebbles, a leaf which she carefully took out and a few shiny flakes which she recognized as mica.

'But no gold,' she said to her husband, 'though I haven't finished yet. The gold will be in the very last teaspoonful!'

Slowly, methodically and with infinite patience, she continued her panning. Her back began to ache and her eyes grew tired from focusing so closely.

'Where are you?' she muttered, swirling the last quarter of the original dirt.

It seemed so very unlikely that in a random shovelful of soil she would find anything of any value, yet she hoped against hope. She had come to California partly for Patrick's sake and partly for her own. She had pursued the path which Patrick had intended to take and now she desperately wanted to find gold.

'Just a speck!' she begged, forgetting her earlier remarks to Kate as to the suitability or otherwise of asking God's help in such an unnecessary venture. Nothing! Determinedly she filled the pan again.

Half an hour passed and as the minutes slipped by, Lily forgot her aching back and cramped legs. She was nearly there. Two tablespoonfuls of dark sand remained in the pan – she dipped the pan into the stream and scooped up a very small amount of water. Gently, hardly daring to breathe, she shook the water up and over the remaining sand, gradually washing it to the lower edge and leaving less and less at the upper rim.

Suddenly she caught her breath and her eyes widened.

'Dear God, it *can't* be!' she whispered. 'It can't be gold.' And yet she knew at once beyond any doubt that it was.

A very small nugget, only half the size of her smallest fingernail, winked up at her with its warm yellow eye. Lily stared at it speechlessly, her heart too full for words. It was there . . . in her pan. Gold!

'Oh Patrick!' she breathed. 'Here's your gold. Isn't it beautiful?'

Unable to take her eyes from it, Lily crouched motionless – thrilled, grateful and hardly able to appreciate her good fortune. She didn't touch it; she had no desire to hold it. Looking at it was enough and more. This piece of gold which had lain hidden for thousands of years had found its way into her pan!

At last she raised her head and looked across at the rest of the miners and understood for the first time what drove them on. It was much more than greed. It was the wild excitement of discovery – the unearthing of a treasure.

'So that's what it's all about,' said Lily and with a sudden lightening of her heart, she winked back at her first nugget. Then she hesitated.

'Oh, blow the washing. It can wait!' she muttered and scrambling to her feet she tenderly wrapped the gold in a corner of her handkerchief and reaching for the shovel, began to dig again.

After a while Gabby raised his head and held something aloft between thumb and forefinger.

'Big as a small pea!' he yelled, 'and smooth as an egg!'

'Wonderful!' cried Lily. 'I found a tiny nugget.'

All heads turned in surprise at the sound of her voice and she found herself the centre of attention.

'What are you doing out here, Lily?' yelled Gabby.

She steeled herself. 'I wanted to try it,' she called back, 'and I found some!'

There was a moment's startled silence while the men digested this remark. It was broken by Matt Wallis. 'Well done, Lily,' he shouted and she waved back in a gesture of gratitude for his understanding.

Influenced by Matt's generosity, the other men also praised her efforts and within minutes the awkwardness had passed and they were all at work once more.

Twenty minutes later Matt found seven nuggets amounting to about an ounce and a half, while Gabby found approximately half an ounce. Then for nearly an hour nobody found anything. At the end of this time a shout from the hill below the bar took them all hurrying down to greet the newcomer, glad of an excuse to stop. Strangers were always welcome, as they frequently brought news of the outside world. The tall, gaunt man with the black beard was no exception.

'Lucky's the name,' he told them by way of introduction. 'Expressman *extraordinaire* – that's French, that is. Take your letter there or bring it back.' He patted the canvas bag which hung on his shoulder. 'There's plenty of mail in San Francisco just waiting to be sorted; thousands of letters. They say fifty thousand came in on the *Oregon* beginning of December, and they're up to their armpits in mail! You never saw such a muddle. Queues a mile long and men getting madder and madder. One or two fellows making a tidy sum queuing.'

'Queuing?' Lily was baffled.

'Sure. They stand in line and when it's nearly their turn they sell their place to a man who's more impatient. Twenty dollars just to give up a place in the queue. Oh, you've never seen anything like it. Mind you, that was before the flood.'

'Flood? What flood?' This time it was Gabby speaking.

The man turned to him. 'Why, the flood in Sacramento. Ain't you folks heard? Water's rising in Sacramento,' he went on. 'Started two days ago and it's – '

Gabby interrupted him. 'You mean the town's flooded?'

'Sure is. That storm on the eighth, that's what did it. More than half the town's under water – hell, not *right* under, but flooded nigh up to the windows and folks paddling themselves round in boats and some on rafts. Oh, it's bad. They even closed the Eagle Theatre and poor Mr Atwater's taken his repertory company down to San Francisco. Tents washed away . . .'

Gabby grabbed him by the arm, his expression tense. 'But is everyone *safe*?' he demanded. 'I mean, there are no casualties – '

The man pulled his arm free. 'Not that I heard of,' he

answered. 'Everyone had plenty of warning, but there's hundreds without a roof over their heads – tents and suchlike washed away. Coming up six inches an hour, it was. The Lord knows what it'll be like when it goes down. Sea of mud I shouldn't wonder. Now, if you had boats to sell, you'd be laughing. Can't get a boat for love nor money. Folks sitting on rooftops and – '

Gabby whirled to face the others. 'I've got to get down there.' he cried. 'I've got to find Ella and the rest of them and bring them back up here. Jesus! What a thing to happen.' He turned back to the man. 'If you've just come up from Sacramento, then presumably I can get down there?'

By now Bart had joined them. They told him about the flood and he listened gravely.

'I must go down,' Gabby insisted, 'and see they're OK. If they're not, I'll bring them back here. Lily could come with me – get a few more stores and save a trip later.'

The stranger shook his head. 'You won't find much for sale,' he told Gabby, 'and all at prices that'd curl your hair. So much stuff washed away and lost. Cattle and hens drowned, flour sodden. If it's stores you want, I'd give it another week if I was you, but as for family – why you'd best go down and see.'

It did seem the only sensible thing to do and it was finally agreed that Bart would go with Gabby in case Ella and the family were in serious trouble and needed help.

Lucky distributed a few letters to the other men on the bar and then they gave him a meal and he went on his way.

By three o'clock the horses were saddled and the two brothers had set off south. Lily watched them go with mixed feelings, because now she was alone with Matt Wallis.

*

Kate sipped noisily from her mug of coffee and her attention wavered from the cards on the table before her.

'Thank heavens we chose this place,' she said. 'Thank heavens we wasn't on the low ground – right mess we'd have been in then.'

Daniel grinned. 'We'd have made out. They'd come in

377

boats or *swim* to visit my two girls. Bees round a honeypot, that's that they are. A few feet of water wouldn't stop them!'

Kate smiled at the third person at the table – an attractive young woman of eighteen with a round face and big brown eyes. Her long, dark hair was wound elaborately around her head and a few curls had been teased out to frame her face.

Belle Staver had been born and raised in San Francisco, but when she was nine her mother died of typhus leaving her father to bring up herself and her brother single-handed. As soon as gold was discovered, father and son departed to the hills to claim their share of it and Belle was left in the care of neighbours. When, five months later, they too went prospecting, she was left to her own devices and was soon in great demand among the menfolk who were arriving in their hundreds. They had endured the miseries of a long sea voyage and were keen to get to work in the gold fields, but first they craved the luxury of a woman. For a week or two they spent their money on Belle and other girls like her, as well as on liquor and gambling. When Daniel Miller appeared in her life, she was immediately charmed by his roguish eye and winning ways. Then she was introduced to Kate and the two women took to each other on sight.

From there on it was easy enough. Belle did not need much persuading that a few free drinks were hardly fair payment for her services, and she was soon ensconced with her two friends in a three-roomed apartment above a liquor store. The cramped accommodation consisted of two small rooms each containing a bed and a chair, plus another larger room where all three lived and Daniel slept. This room contained two easy chairs and a huge sagging sofa which served Daniel as a bed; also a table covered by a fringed cloth, a cupboard for food and an ancient chest for clothes, in addition to three upright chairs and a smaller table. The walls were covered in a dark red paper and light was provided by candles and an oil-lamp.

With accommodation at a premium, they would have been lucky to find even one room and had only secured three by offering an exorbitant rent. It was boom time in Sacramento and everyone was entitled to make their fortune however

378

they chose. If the landlord's wife guessed what went on upstairs, she kept her own counsel and banked the absurdly high rent without a murmur.

Daniel had laid out thirteen cards, all spades, in two rows and he was endeavouring to teach his two companions the rudiments of faro.

'Now I'm the dealer,' he went on, 'the ace is on my left and the seven is on my right. You, Kate, or maybe Belle – you could take it in turns – are my assistant and you sit on my left and "keep case" by moving the buttons on this block.'

The two girls eyed it dubiously. 'How do we know which one to move?' asked Kate.

'You'll learn it,' Daniel assured her. 'Now, they can bet on a single card or more than one – that's called "squares" or "figures". Are you listening, Belle? The first card I deal is called the "soda" and the last is the "hock".'

Belle rolled her eyes. 'I'm tired,' she complained. 'Do we have to do this now?'

'Got to learn it some time,' said Daniel firmly. 'Might as well be now as later. We can make a lot of money out of gambling. They could come in early and lose a few dollars before they – '

'They might *win*,' Kate suggested, drinking the last of the coffee.

Daniel tapped the side of his nose and grinned. 'They won't,' he said, 'take my word for it! Now, I deal two cards and that's called "a turn" – the first card is mine and that's "a loser", the second one is for the players, so that's called a – ?' He waited expectantly.

Belle looked at Kate and they both giggled.

'A card?' asked Kate innocently.

Belle giggled again as Daniel groaned.

'Course it's a *card*,' he agreed, 'but what's it called in faro? Belle?'

Belle said, 'Seven of hearts?' and they both exploded into laughter at the disgusted expression on Daniel's face.

'I thought you two ladies had grey matter here,' he said, tapping his head. 'I thought you had *class*.'

379

'We do,' said Kate. 'We just don't understand faro.'

'It's just like poker,' Daniel insisted. 'It's poker with a few variations.'

'Well, I've never played poker before,' protested Kate.

'I know you haven't,' said Daniel. 'That's why I'm trying to teach you. The first card of a turn is the loser, so the second card must be the – '

'Winner!' shouted Kate and Belle together.

'Right!' He beamed at their success.

'How d'you know they won't win?' asked Kate. 'You're not going to cheat, are you?'

'Cheat? Of course I'm going to cheat. Not much, but enough.'

Kate was intrigued. 'What, stuff an ace up your sleeve?'

'Nothing so vulgar,' Daniel told her. 'I shall round off a corner here and there.'

'They'll have to win sometimes,' Belle pointed out.

'They will,' agreed Daniel. 'They'll win quite a few times, but I'll win more.'

'It's dishonest,' said Belle.

'Certainly is.'

Kate yawned. 'I'm half dead on my feet,' she complained. 'My mind won't work.'

Daniel got up from the table, fetched the coffee and refilled the mugs.

'Drink up,' he said. 'It'll wake you up.'

He persevered with the lesson but he was waging a losing battle. Belle and Kate were losing interest and at last he decided to give in gracefully.

'That's enough for tonight,' he told them. 'We'll have another go tomorrow – you'll get it in time.'

He gathered up the cards to the accompaniment of thankful sighs.

Suddenly Belle giggled. 'That fellow last night – the one with the funny eyes. Soaked through he was. Paid three dollars for the boat to get him here and then fell out half-way across. Like a chick in a thunderstorm, poor lamb. Still . . .' she patted her hair approvingly, 'he said it was worth it.'

Daniel returned the cards to their box. 'That's what I like to hear,' he said, 'a satisfied customer.'

Kate laughed. 'They're such babies,' she said. 'Even the old boys. Did you see that one with the big ears and not much hair? Enoch, his name was. Must have been fifty if he was a day. Wouldn't take his hat off at first. I had to coax him out of it; I told him it was a sign of virility.'

'What, keeping his hat on?' asked Belle.

'No, being bald. That pleased him. Funny how they are about names – must tell you their names. I suppose out here if you're just one of thousands, it matters that someone calls you by your name. Poor old Enoch.'

Belle said, 'Might not be poor Enoch much longer. Might be very rich Enoch! Might come back in a few months' time with his pockets full of gold nuggets.'

'I hope he does,' said Kate. 'He can spend some on me. He was no trouble.'

She put down her mug and yawned. It was just before nine o'clock in the morning and soon she would go to bed for a well-earned rest. But she enjoyed the hour between the departure of their last clients and the luxury of solitary sleep.

Getting up from the table, she crossed to the window and pressed her nose against the glass, still fascinated by the scene below her. The street was no more. In its place a broad muddy river swirled and eddied in and out of the doorways of the mostly abandoned houses. The wind had dropped and the leafless trees reached up out of the flood-water towards the leaden sky. As she watched, a small boat passed by, expertly propelled by a boy who looked no more than twelve years old. His passengers were two elderly men, one clutching a carpet-bag, the other holding a small poodle. Next a home-made raft appeared from the other direction; loaded with boxes and bags, it promptly collided with a half-submerged cart.

'That's the fifth one to hit that blooming cart,' Kate announced. 'They ought to move it, it's dangerous. Nearly had the raft over then. I don't know how that poor chap kept his balance.'

Belle joined Kate at the window and grimaced as a dead

381

mule floated by, the bloated body turning slowly as the water eddied. A barrel followed it, bobbing erratically, and behind that a dog zig-zagged through the muddy water in a purposeful way as though it knew exactly where it was going.

Belle looked across the road. 'That man's gone,' she said. 'The one that was clinging to the roof hollering. Been rescued, I guess.'

'Or drowned,' put in Daniel.

They both turned towards him. 'Don't say that,' said Kate. 'How would you like it?'

'I wouldn't,' he replied imperturbably, 'but then I wouldn't get myself into such a mess. I'd use this . . .' He tapped his forehead. 'Getting yourself stuck on a roof has to be a dumb thing to do.'

Kate gave him an exasperated look and then turned back to the flood.

'Here comes that boat with the fat man in it again,' she reported. 'With two passengers. He must be rolling in it by now – money, I mean. Backwards and forwards. Proper little ferry service. If I've seen him once – ' She stopped. 'He's coming here!' she cried. 'God almighty, it can't be.' Her voice rose. 'It *is!* It's Gabby and Bart! Daniel, he's got Gabby and Bart with him! Crikey, I bet I look a mess.' She turned to Belle who was looking bewildered. 'They're friends of ours. Western Hopers,' she explained. 'We came across with them.' She rushed to the mirror and fiddled desperately with her hair. 'How do I look, Belle?'

'Just fine,' said Belle and then she, too, rushed to share the mirror.

By this time Kate was back at the window, forcing it upwards. She leaned out. 'Gabby! Bart! It's us. Come on up.' She turned to Belle. 'Gabby adopted my little boy – I told you.'

Light dawned and Belle smiled. 'Oh, *that* Gabby,' she said.

But Kate was already at the door and then hurrying down the stairs. Half-way down she reached water level and saw the boat nose in at the doorway. The store was still flooded to a depth of four feet and the landlord had temporarily moved out, taking his liquor with him. Dirty water lapped against the stairs and counter. Sticks, grass, leaves and other debris floated on the surface and the rank smell of mud filled the room. The shelves around the shop were empty, so there was nothing to encourage looters. The absence of a tidemark around the wall showed that the water was still rising and the large round clock on the wall had stopped.

Kate crouched down until she could just see Gabby's anxious face.

'You'll never get the boat in,' she shouted. 'It'll get stuck. You'll have to wade through it.'

Gabby shouted back, 'I'm looking for Ella; I'm not stopping. I've been to the room where they were, but they've gone and no one seems to know where. I thought they might be with you.'

'They're not,' cried Kate. 'How did you know where we were?'

'Just asked around. I'll be off then – got to find them.'

'But Gabby . . .' wailed Kate. 'How is everyone? Can't you come up?'

'We're all fine,' he called. 'So long.'

'Gabby! Wait a minute!'

But to her dismay, the boat began to withdraw and she heard a muttered conversation between the two brothers. Frantically, she ran back upstairs and leaned out of the window.

'Gabby!' she shouted. 'Give him a kiss from his ma!'

Belle gave Kate a sharp look as she withdrew her head and closed the window. 'But you're not his ma,' she reminded her. 'You gave him away and he's got a new ma.'

Kate looked shocked. 'I'm still his ma,' she argued. 'I'm his *real* ma.'

'But if he's adopted – '

Sensing trouble, Daniel intervened hastily. 'Now, now, ladies. That's enough of that. Isn't it time for your beauty sleep?'

But Kate was still glaring at Belle and she ignored him. 'I'm still his ma,' she insisted.

'If you say so!' Belle shrugged.

'I do say so.'

'If I had a baby – ' Belle began.

'God forbid!' said Daniel, horrified. 'You'll tempt Providence talking like that.'

'You'd what?' Kate demanded, her fists clenched.

'I'd want to make sure it wasn't drowned in this flood.'

Kate's mouth fell open. 'Drowned?' She turned to Daniel. 'He's not drowned, is he, Daniel?'

Daniel gave Belle a warning glance. 'Course not,' he said. 'Take no notice of her; he's OK.'

'But where are they, then? Gabby says they're not where he left them.'

He shrugged. 'That's Gabby's problem – he's the boy's father, not me.'

'And Ella's his mother,' said Belle rashly.

Abruptly Kate swung round and brought her hand up. The blow was as hard as she could make it and it knocked Belle off her feet. She fell backwards on to the floor with a scream and a swish of petticoats.

'Cut that out!' cried Daniel.

His voice cut like a whip and Kate burst into tears as he pulled Belle back on to her feet.

'Now you two, make up,' he told them, 'like two good friends. What *are* you thinking of!'

'But she said – ' Kate sobbed.

'She hit me,' wailed Belle. 'She knocked me down. I hate her!'

'No, you don't,' said Daniel. 'Now make it up and you, Kate, stop hollering. All this fuss over a kid you didn't want, wouldn't feed and wouldn't even *look* at!'

Kate fumbled for a handkerchief, failed to find one and sniffed loudly.

Belle handed Kate her own handkerchief. 'I'm sorry, Kate,' she said. 'I didn't mean it. Friends?'

Kate dabbed at her eyes and blew her nose. 'Friends,' she agreed. 'I'm sorry I hit you.'

'It didn't hurt. Caught me by surprise, that's all.'

Belle put an arm round Kate's shoulder. 'I guess we're both tired,' she said. 'Get some sleep and you'll feel a whole lot better.'

Kate whispered, 'But the baby . . .'

'He'll be fine. Like Daniel says, Gabby will find them. Cheer up, Kate. Come into my room and bathe your eyes.'

Kate nodded and allowed herself to be led from the room and Daniel watched them go.

'Women!' he muttered. 'I shall never understand them.' Then he shrugged and smiled. 'But I love 'em just the same!'

*

Twelve days had passed since the rising of the river and still the water level remained high. Warmer weather melted the snows on the mountain tops and this, too, found its way into the flooded valley. Many homeless people had fled to the high ground and these areas were now crowded with makeshift shelters of every description. The Coopers were luckier than many, for they shared a tent which they had purchased at an inflated price. Ella sat on a log of wood outside this tent with the baby at her breast, watching her mother trying to coax a blaze from a few damp sticks. Behind her in the tent, Charlie Cooper lay sleeping.

'Will he get better, Ma?' Ella inquired. 'Pa, I mean. Will his legs get better? Will he ever be like he was?'

Hester twisted her mouth bitterly and said, 'God knows! I'm beginning to wish we'd never come. Things seem to go from bad to worse in this damned country. Nothing's gone right since we left home and that's the truth. First Jess and Will and then your baby. Now Charlie's legs. Where's it all going to end?'

Ella's face crumpled. 'Oh, don't start, Ma. It gets to me. It's not like you, all this moaning. You usually look on the bright side of things.'

'What bright side?' Hester demanded. 'There's no bright side as I can see.' She blew harder into the sticks, where a small red spot glowed half-heartedly; she puffed vigorously for a minute or two and then sat back dizzily, one hand to her head. 'Damned fire, I'm sick of it,' she went on perversely, ignoring Ella's plea for cheerfulness. 'I'm sick of California, if you want to know!'

'Oh, Ma!' wailed Ella, her lips quivering.

'And don't start bawling,' Hester warned, 'or I'll join you.'

Faced with this dire threat, Ella struggled to keep back the impending tears and searched her mind for something cheerful to offer.

'There's Gabby,' she suggested hopefully. 'Gabby's a good thing that happened in California – and little Moses, he's a good thing. Some good things have happened, Ma.'

Hester stood up and watched the few flames that she had produced.

'Ma, I said a few good things have happened,' Ella repeated.

'I heard you,' said Hester wearily. 'If Gabby's so good, how come he's not here when we need him? We'll all die of rheumatism if we have to perch here much longer.'

Ella's mood veered suddenly. 'I never wanted to come to California' she cried. 'It was you and Pa – you would keep on until in the end Jess gave in. It was you as wanted it, you and Pa, so don't go blaming me if you don't like it.'

Her raised voice disturbed Moses and he pulled his face away from the nipple and began to whimper.

'Poor kid,' said Hester. 'What chance has he got in a place like this?'

'He's got *every* chance,' cried Ella, 'because when Gabby finds the gold, we'll be rich. Then he'll eat the best food and wear the best clothes. He'll have a better chance than *I* had – '

'Thanks a lot!'

'Oh, Ma, I didn't mean – '

'Yes, you did. You – ' She broke off suddenly as she realized that their conversation was being overheard by several people in neighbouring shelters. Glaring round defiantly, she demanded, 'Can you all hear or would you like us to speak up?'

An elderly man said, 'We can't help hearing, the way you're carrying on, so don't start on us, you old misery!'

'Ears bigger than elephants, some folks!' muttered Hester, mortified.

She lifted up the tent-flap and asked Charlie if he wanted anything.

'A gallon or two of whisky,' was the surly answer, so she left him to his miseries and returned to the fire.

'Gabby would come if he knew we were in trouble,' said Ella. 'You know he would, Ma. I wish we'd gone with him; I wish – '

'If wishes were horses then beggars would ride,' Hester told her.

Ella put the baby to the other breast.

'This baby's putting on weight,' she said. 'I can feel it. Getting really bonny. Better off with me than all that goat's milk Lily was giving him.' She smiled down into the blue eyes. 'You're going to be handsome, you are. I wonder what his Pa was like? Kate did say he was sort of handsome.'

'She would, wouldn't she?' rejoined Hester. 'Such a waste, the way she's carrying on with Miller and all that.'

'I wonder if they *have* got another girl, like that chap said.' Ella sighed. 'I bet they're high and dry. She always falls on her feet, Kate does. If they're near Sutter's Fort, then they must be on higher ground.'

Just then a young man whom they knew only by sight came up to them. 'Did you two ladies hear the news?' he asked. 'About the war?'

'War?' cried Hester and Ella together.

'It'll cost you,' he told them. 'Bite to eat – that's what it costs.'

'You got it,' said Hester.

He grinned, showing broken teeth, then took off his hat, clutched it to his chest with both hands and began to gabble. 'Well, it ain't a real war but folks is calling it that. Broke out along the Calaveras River a day or two back. Seems there's a Chilean name of Concha and some Americans – they want to push him off his claim. He goes to Stockton and gets himself a writ all legal and proper, then he goes back with some friends and they beat the hell out of the Americans. Killed two of them!'

Ella and Hester waited open-mouthed while he took a gulp of air and resumed his tale.

'They captures the rest and hauls them off to the judge, but on the way they break free and turn on *them* and this

387

Concha – *he* runs off and gets himself killed two days later down in Fandango. The other Chileans goes before a miners' court and two of them get hanged by the neck, some get their ears lopped off and others get lashed half to death. Could you throw in a cup of coffee?'

They stared at him for a moment as he twisted his hat in his hands.

Hester said. 'I'm just going to make some. You're welcome to a cup – sit yourself down.'

'Thank you kindly, ma'am.'

He slapped the hat back on his head and sat down on the wet ground. Ella looked at him curiously, noting the bony hands which clasped frayed braces and the threadbare shirt. His eyes were sunken in their sockets and his cheek-bones protruded.

'Is that what you do, then?' Ella asked him. 'Tell folks bits of news in return for a bite to eat?'

'What if I do? No law says I can't.'

'I just wondered. Broke, are you?'

'Flat broke,' he agreed, 'but I'll be fine once the weather turns. I'll be up there in them hills with my shovel and pan. I've waited all these months, I can wait a bit longer.'

'You trek across?'

'No. Come by boat and sick as a dog the whole way. The *William Ivy*, that was my ship. Slow enough, but faster than most of the others. Put in at San Francisco on the sixth of July and I swear I'll never set foot in a boat again long as I live.'

'So you've been here six months or more?'

He nodded. 'Found a fortune and lost it again gambling, but I'm not grieving. No, sir! Don't do to grieve over money. There's plenty of gold still for any man that'll work and I'll make another fortune 'fore I'm through. Fourteen hundred dollars I made in six weeks!'

'Fourteen hundred!' gasped Ella. 'And you lost it all?'

'Lost or spent it,' he amended. He took off his hat, scratched his head and put it back on again. 'Mind you, I lived like a lord for a long, long time. Oh boy, did I live well! Never lived so well in my life before. All the liquor I could

388

drink and the best of everything. Lobsters fresh out of the bay and champagne – real French champagne – and tongue and turtle soup. Pickled oysters – now they was really something! – if you've never tasted a pickled oyster, you'll have to take my word for it. And candied fruits! Ate and drank myself sick many a night, but what I threw up was quality stuff!' He sighed and shook his head. 'And here I am, telling yarns for a bit of dry bread. But it's no big deal, you see, because I *know* the gold's there. I've seen it. I've had it and spent it and I'll get it again.'

Ella's eyes shone as she turned towards her mother. 'D'you hear all that, Ma?' she demanded. 'About the gold and all them oysters and champagne and suchlike?'

'I heard,' said Hester.

'We'll get our share, Ma. We'll be rich.'

'Hope to God you're right,' Hester said. 'It can't happen soon enough for me.'

She handed the man a slice of bread and he began to eat and drink, blowing on the hot coffee and sucking it noisily into his mouth.

'Where did you find the gold?' Ella asked.

His expression changed abruptly and he glanced at her suspiciously.

'That'd be telling, now,' he said, 'but it was there right enough. Me and my partner did well out of that claim, but then one evening we got to thinking about a few home comforts and we headed for Sacramento. Just for a day or two, we reckoned, but it didn't work out like that. Enjoyed ourselves too much and couldn't bear to leave. He's given up, but I'll go back.'

'Given up?' asked Ella. 'What – gone home, d'you mean?'

'Home? He's got no home, that one. No, he's opened a store in San Francisco, selling fish. He's welcome to it. I'm not minding no store. No sirree!'

He finished his meal in silence, then stood up to go.

Ella asked, 'Haven't come across a man by the name of Smith, have you? Gabby Smith?'

'Nope.'

'Or Bart Smith or Matt Wallis?'

'Nope.'

'Never mind.' Ella shrugged to hide her disappointment. 'He'll come,' she said stubbornly. 'I just know he will.'

Chapter Nineteen

After leaving the Western Hopers, Henry Simms had travelled at a furious pace, spurred on by his anger, urging his unfortunate animals in order to put as much distance as possible between himself and Lily. He was expecting her to regret her decision to stay with Kate and come after him, and he wanted to make her search as difficult as possible. Humiliation still burned within him – she had chosen that worthless, no-good Kate instead of the man she loved. In Henry's book, that was unbelievable. Either she was stupid – and he knew that was not the case – or she did not truly love him.

'She's made her bed and she can damned well lie in it!' he told himself firmly whenever the slightest doubt assailed him as to the rightness of his own decision to leave her. He had offered her marriage. He would have worked all his life for her – *slaved* for her almost – to give her a good home and Patrick would have lived on in their shared memories of him. This romantic notion began to assume immeasurable importance in Henry's mind and his thinking became a little distorted as a result. As he mulled it over, he fancied that Lily had not only rejected *him* but her dead husband also, for Lily had given up the perfect opportunity to keep his memory bright for ever and he began seriously to doubt the quality of her love. If the memory of her dead husband was of so little value, had she ever really loved *him*, he argued. Would she ever truly love Henry Simms, or was hers a shallow love to be discarded so lightly? He managed to ignore the fact that he had expected her to feel deep and lasting love for *him* so shortly after Patrick's death.

However, these illogical and confused lines of thought fuelled his energies and carried him through the worst few days and nights, and by the end of the week he had regained his equilibrium to a large extent, if not altogether. He began to see himself as an interesting figure, a star-crossed lover striking out alone with nothing left but the lure of the gold fields, and this soothed his wounded feelings. Lily's image appeared less and less to trouble his conscience and he began, cautiously, to enjoy life again.

One day he chanced to meet another solitary adventurer and the two men struck up an immediate friendship. The man's name was Charlie Cookson, but he went by the name of Chuck. He had been a fur-trapper, he had had three 'wives' and fathered seven children.

'Me, I love 'em all!' he told Henry earnestly. 'That's the Goddamned truth. I'd keep 'em all in perfumes and furs if I could, but I'm not a rich man. But I will be! Hell! When I get to those gold fields I'm going to work these hands to the bone. Oh, I'll get rich – you'll see if I don't. Trouble is, the first one's left me. Run off with a travelling preacher, more fool her! Took my little princess with her. Oh, that girl was real pretty. Prettiest little girl I ever did see. Took after her ma, she did. Well, I don't need to tell you that!'

He was not quite ugly but certainly unprepossessing, with small almost yellow eyes, a clumsy nose and over-large mouth. Life as a trapper had coarsened and darkened his skin and his mousey hair was noticeably thin on top. Henry, in his less charitable moments, wondered how he managed to attract so many women – all of whom, according to Chuck, were great beauties.

'Even the squaw,' he insisted. 'Oh yes, my third wife was an Injun. I never did go much on Injun women but this one, why, she was something else! Real pretty little thing. Gave five blankets and fifty dollars for her and she was cheap at the price. You see, you can't move in Injun country without some security and an Injun wife's the best security a man can have. They won't attack a man that's got a squaw for a wife. The way I saw it, it couldn't do no harm and she sure was pretty. Long dark hair twisted like into them braids and very loving. And dark eyes and pretty white teeth. I never seen such white teeth in all my life and that's the Goddamned truth! You could do a lot worse out here, believe me.'

The two men made good time and by the third of November they found themselves in California; after a few more days they rode into Guy's Diggings – a rapidly growing community on the north bank of the middle fork of the Feather River.

At first sight it was a haphazard collection of half-finished timber cabins and about a dozen crude tents each consisting of a few poles roughly hewn from newly-cut timber over which an assortment of canvas and cotton cloths had been tied with string. Some formed wigwams, others were box-shaped, even more sloped on one side and strongly resembled a slab of cheese! A few had been strengthened with a half-wall of split logs; one had an additional covering of buffalo skins draped over it to keep out the cold. Most would have been flimsy enough in summer and in late November they provided a very poor shelter, but the miners – totally engrossed in their work – simply donned additional clothing and ignored the rigours of winter. Already the huddle of dwellings had taken on the essentials of a town. A signboard on one tent announced that Doc Pettigrew would stitch wounds and set bones for a dollar. Infectious diseases were more costly. 'Guts' were a dollar and a half! Fires burned outside each home and over them a variety of pots and kettles bubbled and steamed. Furniture was made from tree-stumps, logs, barrels and even large boulders, while in the centre a flag fluttered at the top of a tall pole which was kept in place by three guy-ropes. To augment his findings, one man had set up shop as a letter-writer, another as a blacksmith. There was also a 'brewery' selling ewes' milk and applejack!

Henry and Chuck asked to be allowed to stay for a few nights and this request was granted. Henry would happily have stayed there, but Chuck insisted that the creek was being worked by too many men already and advised that they should move on and find themselves somewhere more remote.

'If we strike lucky we don't want every Tom, Dick and Harry muscling in on it,' he told Henry. 'Me, I'm a believer in small numbers. I'm a loner at heart. No offence, but after a while I get itchy with other folks round me. Kind of fenced in – know what I mean?'

Henry didn't know, being a more gregarious soul, but he pretended that he did and two days later they moved higher up the creek, testing the gravels as they went along and looking for a likely spot to start panning in earnest.

Chuck, of course, knew exactly what they were looking for.

'You've got to find the inside of a bend of a river, where the current flows more slowly!' he informed Henry. 'Outside of a bend it's going too fast – especially in the winter – and it can carry the gold along. Momentum, you could call it. Then there's tree-roots. All tangled, see, so small pieces of gold get lodged between the roots. Course, the finer dust and flakes could be anywhere along the banks where the water's overflowed but the best bits, the worthwhile bits, they lodge in certain spots and that's what we're looking for. We call it rough-gold and if we find them we're most likely near to a seam. You see, the bigger the nuggets, the quicker they fall through the water and settle. And there's rocks, too. Gold gets lodged in the lee of rocks and wedged into crevices in the boulders. My pa looked for gold on and off all his life. Never found so much as a pinch of dust, but I will. Oh yes, I'll find it or die in the attempt.'

He told Henry how to deal with gold dust too.

'You get a pan full of dust, there's no way you can pick it out. So you got to use mercury. One blob in a pan of dust and you've got it. It amalgamates with the mercury. Then all you got to do is get the damned gold out of the mercury – and that's simple enough. Cheapest way I know is to cut open a large potato and scoop out a hole big enough for the blob, then tie it back together again with a bit of fine wire. Bung it in your camp-fire and cook it! The heat evaporates the mercury, see? Leaves a lump of gold dust like a little gold button!'

On the fourth day they reached a spot which Chuck decided had most of the requisite features and there the two men set up their small camp. It was a gravel bar beside a narrower section of the same creek they had left at Guy's Diggings. Less broad, it was enclosed by steeply sloping sides covered in large and small rock fragments. These slopes made it shady for a large part of the day and Henry argued against it, urging that as the weather grew colder they would value whatever warmth remained in the sun. But Chuck would have none of it and Henry's objection was sharply overruled; he saw that Chuck had a steely side to his nature that he had not seen before. The small altercation led to a deterioration in the relationship, but they carried on as planned although Henry did wonder on more than one occasion if he had been wise to team up with this man who admitted to an aversion to his fellow men.

His doubts proved well-founded a few days later when he fell ill with a severe chill and could no longer carry on with his share of the work. He woke on the third morning, shivering violently and too weak to stand, to find himself alone. Chuck had decamped leaving a brief note tied to a bottle of water. The note said: 'Moving on. Will fix you up. Cheers, Chuck.' Henry cursed him with all his rapidly dwindling strength. He was now alone on the mountainside, unable to protect himself and with very little food. He lay there for the rest of the day convinced that his luck had finally run out. First Patrick's death, then Lily's rejection and now Chuck's desertion. As the hours passed he drank the last of the water and then, despairing, sank into a deep and feverish stupor from which he did not expect to recover.

*

'You drink.'

Henry heard the words through a painful, throbbing haze and they meant nothing. He groaned.

'Drink.'

Someone was telling him to drink. He tried to think rationally, but his head ached and his mind was a frightening blank. Where was he? What was the matter with him? Another groan escaped his parched throat and he wanted to drink, but could not marshal his thoughts sufficiently. Was it cholera? Who was the woman? A surge of unwelcome memories made him frown. His jumbled thoughts began hesitantly to arrange themselves in some kind of order while he struggled to open his unwilling eyelids.

'Drink water.'

He tried to speak, to say that he wanted to drink, but his parched lips refused to form the necessary sounds and he shook his head instead. That was a mistake; the slight movement provoked fresh waves of pain and he heard himself say, 'Hell and damnation!' It was his own voice, yet he hardly recognized it. How long, he wondered, had he been ill? He *must* open his eyes! Or – a terrible thought struck him – was he blind? The shock gave him strength and he raised a shaking right hand to his face and rubbed clumsily at his eyes. To his intense relief his lids parted and he then had to shade his eyes from the unfamiliar brightness.

A woman's head was outlined against the opening of the tent and he fancied that she was dark-skinned. But that was impossible, he told himself – a trick of the light. His eyes closed once more. It was coming back to him, slowly, that he was in his own tent somewhere in the mountains. But the woman? Was it Lily? A small firm hand slid beneath his head and lifted it from the rolled blanket which served as a pillow and a tin mug was pressed to his dry lips.

'Lily?' he whispered. 'Is that you?'

'Drink water, white man.'

As the cool liquid trickled into his mouth, he was vaguely aware that Lily would never call him 'white man'. Only an Indian would do that. He opened his eyes again and saw her face more clearly – narrow dark eyes, flat nose, broad shoulders. The eyes looked into his impassively as she coaxed a little more water into his parched mouth. Then she gave a little nod and allowed his head to return to the blanket. As she turned to go he managed one word – 'Wait!' – but she had gone. For a while he tried to make sense of it all, but in his weakened state the effort proved too much and he sank back into a fitful sleep. His dreams were vivid and he struggled to waken, but each time he slipped down into nightmares of noise and fear and colour.

When at last the spectres retreated, he opened his eyes once more and knew he was on the way to recovery from whatever illness had struck him down. One at a time, like the pieces of a jigsaw puzzle, the events of the past weeks returned and with great clarity he recalled his parting from Lily Golightly, but was surprised to find that his bitterness had gone. It all seemed such a long time ago and his sickness had left him strangely indifferent. Had he really felt both murderous and suicidal? Was it possible he had allowed any woman to bring him so low? No woman should be allowed to matter that much, he told himself.

'I don't need you, Lily Golightly!' he whispered and felt cheered by this small proof of his independence.

His back was stiff and he moved slowly and carefully into a new position. How long had he been ill? Days or weeks? Did it matter? He wondered briefly about the Indian girl and decided she would come back to him. He was thirsty and hungry, but when he raised his head to look around him there was neither water nor food. Yes, she would come back.

He lay back again and, holding up his hands, examined them critically. They were pale and bony; he must have lost a lot of weight. He explored his face with his fingers. 'I'm a skeleton!' he said aloud and managed a wry smile at his predicament. Weak as a kitten, miles from anywhere in a strange country, dependent on an Indian for his survival. It was ridiculous, but he felt much too frail to do anything about it. When the girl returned she would probably bring him food. He hoped she would come alone.

Startled, he considered the alternative – that she might bring her menfolk. This was a disquieting thought. But, he argued, if they wanted to kill or rob him they could have done so easily while he was ill. And they had not done so . . . or had they? Anxiously, he eased himself again into a sitting position and surveyed the interior of his tent. Rifle, pan, cooking utensils, boots – they were all there. Suddenly he

397

remembered Chuck's note: 'Will fix you up.' Was the Indian girl Chuck's idea of a nurse? He wanted to hate Chuck for his desertion, but had no energy for such emotions. It was enough that he was still alive. He had enjoyed Chuck's company and learned a lot from him. If a relationship offered no more than that, it was worthwhile. He now felt strangely relaxed and at peace both with himself and the world around him.

'I don't hate you,' he told the absent Lily. 'I simply don't give a damn.'

He felt extraordinarily good about everything and wondered if the euphoria would last. He was convinced that he was regaining control of his own destiny and that was better than being dependent on anyone else for his happiness.

So far he had found no gold, but his new-found confidence encompassed that too and he knew without a shadow of doubt that he would be one of the lucky ones.

'It'll come, all in good time,' he assured himself and an expansive smile lit up his gaunt features.

A sudden picture presented itself unbidden to his mind's eye – a picture of Antoine Robidoux, the Frenchman at the trading post with his Indian wife and family. Henry had envied him his contented lifestyle. An Indian wife? Was that a possibility? No, perhaps that was going too far; he tried to recall the girl's face, but she had been silhouetted against the light and the only likeness he could summon was a hazy one.

'Beauty isn't everything,' he said aloud and grinned broadly. 'Yes, things could be a lot worse. A whole lot worse!'

Still smiling, he settled more snugly into the blankets. She would come back with food, he knew it. Still smiling, he drifted back into a dreamless sleep.

*

Darkness had fallen by the time Lily and Matt settled down to their evening meal, a roasted sage-hen eaten with beans and soda bread. They sat in a comfortable silence, their faces lit by the light of the fire which separated them. Matt wiped his plate with bread to mop up the last of the juices and gave a sigh of contentment that made Lily smile.

'They say the way to a man's heart . . .' she quoted.

'I guess it's true!'

Around them on the bar other groups were also eating. Fires glowed in the darkness and the occasional shower of ascending sparks illuminated the surrounding trees. One group of men was getting drunk on a home-made brew known as 'Tanglelegs'. Further over, eleven miners shared one huge fire and, having finished their meal, were singing their way through all the well-loved songs – 'There's a good pile coming, boys', 'On the banks of the Sacramento' and even 'Hangtown gals' which, being saucier than most, made Lily's cheeks burn. Somewhere nearby a wolf howled and was promptly answered by another. One of the drinkers, registering the familair sound, sent a burning brand from his fire arching through the darkness towards it, shouting, 'Knock it off, you mangy critter!'

Lily took a surreptitious glance at the man who sat opposite her and fought down rising panic. Matt Wallis was rapidly becoming part of the fabric of her life but soon, maybe tomorrow, she would have to leave him. She had promised to go after Henry and she would keep her word, but the prospect of parting from Matt depressed her. If only she had not promised herself to Henry Simms . . . but she had done and she had also done him a great hurt by deciding to stay and nurse Kate. It was ironic that, after making such a difficult choice in Kate's favour, Kate herself had then betrayed her, but if the clock was turned back Lily knew she would make the same choice again. Her father had brought her up to recognize the call of duty and to put the needs of others before her own, and she still held to his teachings. Her aunt had once told her that 'Do as you would be done by' was as good a precept as any by which to live. Now Lily's instinct was to stay with Matt Wallis, but she could not allow herself such a luxury. Somehow she had to tell him that she was going away and it would not be easy; she had been putting off the evil hour because once she had told him, she would be committed and the prospect saddened her. She knew that her feelings for Matt had grown into more than admiration, but she was afraid to analyse her emotions too deeply for fear of what she might discover. She had promised to marry Henry and if he still wanted her, she would stand by her promise and do her best to make him a good wife. Making up her mind suddenly, she looked across at Matt.

'I have to go, Matt', she told him. 'Maybe tomorrow.'

He was sprawling back now, his arms folded underneath his head. For a few seconds he gave no sign that he had heard her, then he sat up.

'I knew you would,' he said. 'Even though you know you should stay!'

Lily looked across the fire into the shrewd grey eyes and thought, 'He will never plead as Henry did. He will never ask me to stay.'

'I shall miss you,' she admitted, 'but I must find him. A promise is a promise.'

'I hope he deserves you.'

The grey eyes seemed to probe her very soul and Lily had the uncomfortable feeling that he could read her mind, yet his expression seemed inscrutable. She found herself making excuses for Henry.

'He loves me,' she said. 'He's a good man at heart and he only went off like that because he was so upset. It was natural in the circumstances, I think.'

Matt gave no sign that he agreed with her reading of the event and she added, 'Lots of men would have done the same. In a way, I think I deserved it. Why should I hold him back? He was so keen to . . .'

She fell silent and lowered her eyes, aware that somehow by her efforts to excuse Henry's behaviour she was making it appear worse. When she looked up again, Matt had resumed his earlier position and was staring up at the stars with apparent unconcern.

'Anyway,' she went on, 'I've made up my mind to go and tomorrow is as good a day as any. There's also another reason – '

She broke off again and he said, 'Gabby will be bringing Ella back and you don't want to see her with the baby.'

Lily sighed deeply. 'I'm sure you think that's very foolish of me, but I can't help it. I don't expect you to understand.' She bit her lip. 'I *know* I'm being illogical and I'm ashamed of myself, but that's the way I feel. That baby meant so much to me that when I lost him, it – ' She stopped.

'It broke your heart,' he finished gently.

'Yes.' The word was no more than an anguished whisper and Lily put her hands over her face.

'You'll have a child of your own one day,' said Matt, his tone matter-of-fact. 'The boy's in good hands and you could hardly have raised him with no husband to support you.'

'But Henry would still have married me,' Lily cried. 'I know he would.'

'You think so?' He considered this, his head on one side. 'Yes, I guess he might have done the honourable thing.' He said it without malice, but with perhaps a touch of sarcasm. Lily couldn't be sure.

'He's nice enough, Lily,' continued Matt, 'but he's not the right man for you.'

The words were almost a reprimand and Lily felt a rush of irritation.

'I think that's for me to decide,' she retorted. 'How can you know that he's not right for me? You know very little about either of us.'

After a pause he said, 'You know you're making a mistake, but you won't admit it.'

Lily was shocked by his perception, but too stubborn to admit that he was right.

'If I had promised to marry *you*, you'd expect me to keep my word!' she protested.

'Sure I would, but that doesn't mean it would be the right thing for you to do.' His voice softened a little. 'People make mistakes, Lily, and sometimes they go along with it rather than admit the mistake. But going along with it is *another* mistake. I like and admire you and I'd hate to see you marry the wrong man.'

Lily could find no answer and the silence lengthened uncomfortably.

'Maybe you should go back to England where you belong,' he suggested quietly. 'Go back to your father, Lily, and marry a respectable God-fearing Englishman.'

Lily was mortified. She had expected Matt to offer himself as an alternative husband, but instead it appeared he had no such intentions towards her. She swallowed and hoped her disappointment was not too obvious. 'Pride comes before a fall,' she told herself wryly.

'And what will you do?' she asked, with an attempt at lightness. 'When you've made your fortune, I mean?'

'Oh, I shan't make my fortune,' he said. 'I won't stay long enough. I've told my father I shall go back. I never did intend to stay in California for long, but thought I'd swirl a few pans since I was here. I have a home to return to in Virginia.'

Lily stammered, 'A home? You mean a *family?* I didn't know –'

He smiled. 'A *home*. No wife,' he said. 'My wife ran out on me a long time ago, but my father is still alive. We farm in Virginia,' he added. 'My father is nearly seventy and he has arthritis pretty bad. He needs me, so I have to go back. My younger brother is at the V.M.A.'

Lily looked puzzled.

'Virginia Military Academy,' he explained. 'He wanted to be a soldier. My sister married a banker, so there's only me.'

Lily was surprised by these revelations, having always imagined Matt Wallis as a lone wolf.

'Is it a big farm?' she asked curiously.

Matt grinned. 'It's sizeable,' he said. 'I guess we have near on five hundred head of dairy cattle, give or take a few.' He shrugged. 'We grow some corn and there are a couple of orchards.'

Lily hesitated. 'Do you have slaves?' she asked.

'No,' he said evenly, 'because we have enough local labour. If we grew cotton it might be different, but so far we've managed well enough without.'

'I thought everyone in Virginia grew cotton.'

'No,' Matt said again. 'Many do, of course, and the

number's growing each year, but someone has to grow food and that's what we do.'

'So if more people grow cotton, they need more slaves?'

'They do, yes.'

Lily fancied that his tone was carefully non-commital, but perversely she went on with her questions.

'Would you have slaves?' It was suddenly important to her that he should answer in the negative.

'No, I don't fancy the idea. I know some slaves are well-cared-for, but others are not. I shouldn't care to *own* another man or woman.' He shrugged. 'It's a matter of conscience. Any more questions?'

Secretly relieved, Lily shook her head.

'I'm sorry about your wife,' she said.

His expression did not change. 'She took off one day with one of the cow-hands,' he stated. 'She was a city girl and she hated the farm. She left me a note, which said that Roberts was going to take her back to the bright lights. I should never have married her – my folks told me it wouldn't work out. It needs a special kind of woman to live that sort of life. It can be very lonely and it's very hard work.' He shrugged. 'There were no children – at least, not to my knowledge.'

'How long were you together?' Lily asked.

'She stayed for eight months. After she left I just wanted to get away, so I took a horse and pushed off. Wandered around, did a bit of trapping, trading and suchlike. No big deal, but I guess for eight years I enjoyed my own company. Then last year I brought a group of settlers over to Oregon. That was some trip! Afterwards I went home and found my father eaten up with this damned arthritis, but too stubborn to give up – didn't trust the foreman and was hauling himself around on two sticks.' He shook his head. 'Stubborn as a mule, that man, but I have to hand it to him. He's got guts.'

'What about your mother?'

'She's been dead for years – died when my sister was born. My father's on his own now. When I got back from Oregon I had a letter waiting for me to say my wife was dead. Run down in the street. That really shook me up. By that time

Marshall had found his gold and I knew there'd be a rush west. I told my father I'd take one more trip and this is it. I aim to be back by late spring. I shall take a ship home.'

'Do you want to go back?' Lily asked curiously.

'In a way I do. It's a good life.'

'And your sister – is she near you?'

He laughed. 'Near us? Lily, *nobody's* near us! It's a big spread. No, Elena is to the north of us, in Pennsylvania, if that means anything to you.'

Lily had to admit it didn't and Matt laughed. 'It's far enough,' he told her. 'We're not close, either, as sister and brother. She's seven years younger than me but doesn't approve of me, especially over the last few years. I guess she finds it hard to explain me to her husband, who's a stuffed shirt at the best of times, at least in my book. Still, what can you expect with a name like Humphrey?'

They both laughed and Lily was relieved that her own situation was no longer the topic of conversation. His comments on the subject of Henry had worried her but, she reminded herself, he obviously had no selfish reason for wanting her to think again. Recalling his kiss, she was annoyed to discover that the memory of it could still move her. Love was a fickle, fragile emotion, she decided, full of pitfalls for the unwary. She was aware of a growing confusion . . . but it was too late now. Matt Wallis would take a ship at San Francisco and in a few months would be back in Virginia and she, along with all the other Western Hopers, would become part of his past. Occasionally recalled, perhaps, but of no further consequence.

'I can at least wish you a safe return then,' she said. 'When do you plan to leave?'

'A week or so, maybe less,' he told her. 'I'll wait for Gabby and Bart to return and see them all safely installed before I go. They are such greenhorns! Then I shall make my way down to Sacramento, on to San Francisco and be on the next boat out.'

'You won't stay and look for gold then?' asked Lily.

'No. If I strike lucky in the next few days I shan't complain, but we're comfortable back home and I'm not greedy.' He sat up and looked at her directly, his face serious. 'And what will you do if you don't find Mr Simms?'

'I *will* find him,' she insisted.

'And if you find him and discover you've made a mistake?'

'I don't know,' she said, 'but I'll think of something. I'm fit and I must learn to take care of myself. I might even find gold,' she laughed. 'If not, I'll find a job. I could always give piano lessons.'

He looked decidedly unhappy with this prospect. 'Go back to England, Lily,' he said. 'You're an English rose and America is not the place for you. You could travel back with me most of the way if you make up your mind in time. At least that way I could satisfy myself you were safe.'

'Do you care, then?' she asked and at once cursed her stupidity.

'Yes, I care, Lily,' he answered quietly. 'I don't want to leave San Francisco knowing that you are wandering around alone looking for the elusive Mr Simms.'

'Don't worry about me,' said Lily. 'I'll be fine. I'll find him because I shan't give up until I do.' She hesitated. 'I'm very sorry ... about the way everything is working out. I can't explain, but I hope it makes some sense to you?'

'It doesn't,' he said bluntly. 'If you've something to say, come on out with it.'

'I can't do that,' she protested, unwilling to put her confused emotions into words; reluctant to face up to the gathering doubts.

'Jesus, Lily!' he exploded. 'You're so damned English! Pussyfooting around!' He shook his head. 'I'll never understand you people.'

Lily's mouth tightened. 'You obviously don't like the English – ' she began.

'Did I ever say that I *did*?'

Offended, Lily withdrew into an icy silence. Tears pricked at her eyelids, but she would have died rather than shed them.

'I'm sorry,' he said. 'But how the hell can I tell you how I feel about you while you're still hankering after Henry

Simms? Your trouble is that you don't know your own mind.'

Suddenly, perversely, Lily wanted to throw herself into his arms, but pride prevented her from making such a rash move and, tightlipped, she answered, 'Since your opinion of the English is so low, I hardly think I could make you a good wife – Mr Wallis.'

She added the last two words out of childishness and instantly regretted them.

'I haven't asked you to be my wife,' he pointed out.

'I don't want to be anyone's wife!' she cried and as she uttered the words, it dawned on her that perhaps at last she had spoken what was in her heart. Patrick had died and she was in no proper state of mind to marry anyone. She was full of uncertainties and running into a second marriage for the wrong reasons was the very worst thing she could do. This knowledge brought a feeling of relief as well as a thrill of fear. Being left alone by circumstances was one matter; choosing to be alone was another, and infinitely more disturbing, yet she felt intuitively that it was right for her. She stood up abruptly.

'I'm sorry, Matt,' she said. 'I don't want to quarrel with you and I think I ought to go to bed before I make matters worse. We're both tired.'

He stood up also, his face unsmiling. 'And will you go after Simms?'

'Yes. I must find him and talk to him, but most of all I have some thinking to do and to do that I must be on my own.' Her voice softened. 'The longer I stay with you, Matt, the harder it will be for me to break away.'

Lily could sense his disappointment but he said, 'Do what you must, Lily. You don't need me or anyone else to tell you what to do.' A brief smile lit up his face. 'I take back what I said about the English.'

'Thank you.' She looked into his eyes for a long time and read there a longing to hold her. If she allowed that, she would be lost. 'Good night, Matt,' she said.

'Good night.'

Chapter Twenty

The following morning Lily woke early and made preparations for her journey. Matt wanted her to take her rifle, but she refused, though she did agree to take a mule instead of a horse on his insistence that it was more sure-footed and more suitable for the rough tracks she would be using.

At last, after a hurried breakfast, she stood beside Matt with a lump in her throat and an overpowering conviction that she would never see him again. He took her hand and kissed it lightly, almost humorously, but his expression was tense as he gave her last-minute instructions.

'Follow the trail down to Sacramento and don't try to go into town unless the water's gone down. No heroics, please, Lily. I don't want to hear that they've fished your body out of the flood-water.'

Lily said, 'I'll take care.'

'And *don't* set off into the hills,' he went on, 'until you have a definite lead on his whereabouts. Never camp out overnight without a good fire and if you see any Indians before they see you, give them a very wide berth.'

'I will,' promised Lily, 'and thank you for all your advice. Please give my kind regards to the others when they return.'

He held out cupped hands for her foot and helped her up into the saddle.

'Goodbye, Matt,' said Lily. 'God bless you.'

'And you,' he said.

'By the way,' added Lily, 'I don't think I ever thanked you

properly for getting us all safely across America. You were wonderful and I am truly grateful.'

His features relaxed into a brief smile. 'My pleasure, ma'am,' he said.

He turned away and Lily tugged at the reins and dug her heels into the mule's sides. Several of the other men called 'Goodbye' and wished her well as she passed them, but most were already hard at work and did not even raise their heads as she rode by.

The rough trail descended erratically between low, dark rocks and Godwin Bar was soon out of sight. To her left she could still hear the splashing of the stream, but after an hour that sound had faded. For the first few hours Lily felt distinctly anxious and found the solitude unnerving, but she prayed hard for courage and as time passed her fears receded a little and she began to relax and enjoy the novelty of her situation.

She had chosen a fine day for the start of her adventure, for there was no wind and she found the winter sun warm and comforting to both body and spirit. The countryside through which she rode was varied and beautiful and the views over the mountains made her catch her breath in awe. From dark rocks she passed under dappled oak trees where squirrels sported themselves, pausing only to chatter at her as she passed below, her face upturned in delight.

For a time she rode along a narrow path that was little more than a ledge in the mountain-side, with a steep wall of red rock on one side and a sheer drop of seventy or eighty feet on the other. Here the little mule proved invaluable, picking its way carefully among the stones while Lily closed her eyes and hung on grimly. The track now rose a little and passed through a grove of wild fig trees before turning sharply and descending further into a small valley densely lined with tall bushes. Here she found another group of miners busy at the water's edge, the inevitable pans in their hands, their eyes intent on the swirling gravel. Two men sat on a tree-stump, one writing and one smoking, while another staggered towards a rocker with a pailful of gravel in each hand.

It was getting dark by this time and Lily ached all over from the efforts of her long bone-jolting ride. To her surprise, a middle-aged woman came out of one of the larger tents and before she could explain the purpose of her visit, insisted that she stay overnight.

'I haven't seen another woman for weeks,' she told Lily. 'We could feed you and you could sleep over if you're not in too much of a hurry.'

Lily accepted gratefully and the woman, whose name was Sarah Burnes, helped her dismount.

Briefly Lily explained her business and Sarah frowned. 'Simms? The name's familiar,' she said, 'but we'll ask the menfolk when they come in to supper. My husband's that tall man at the end – ' She pointed. 'We all came out with Becher and the Brown Bears outfit. You heard of them?'

Lily told her that Henry and Patrick had travelled with that same company.

'Patrick Golightly?' asked Sarah. 'The Englishman? The one who – ' She stopped uncertainly.

'Yes,' said Lily, 'he was my husband. Henry Simms was his partner.'

Light dawned in Sarah's eyes. 'So that's where I heard the name,' she said. 'What a tragedy for you. But there, it was a cruel journey and plenty of good men perished. I recall Mr Simms. Fair, wasn't he? Tall and skinny – nice-looking man. Gone off on his own, has he? Well, there's plenty do that. 'Fraid of sharing it if they strike it rich. Me, I reckon there's safety in numbers – but I'm talking too much. It's such a rare treat to have a woman to talk to, but you'll be wanting to wash your face and hands, no doubt. I'll get my lad to see to your mule.' She put two fingers into her mouth and whistled expertly and within seconds a young boy appeared from the slopes above and scrambled down towards them.

'Jeffery Hallam Burnes, junior,' Sarah muttered proudly. 'Spitting image of his pa, he is. Nearly ten and growing faster than a pile of bills!'

Lily was made very welcome by Sarah and her husband and at intervals throughout the evening other members of the group sidled up to ask for news of any new strikes, or to exaggerate their own findings.

'Don't tell 'em if you've heard of a richer find,' Sarah whispered. 'They'll be up and off! Never can stay in one place for more than a week or two. Talk about itchy feet! Soon as I get used to one place, we go some place else. I shall know these hills like the back of my hand before we're done!'

That night Lily slept soundly and awoke refreshed to the sounds of early morning camp life. They were so familiar that for a moment she thought she was back at Godwin Bar with Matt. Realization brought with it a sense of loss, but with an effort she pushed the thought of him out of her mind and applied herself to the search ahead. She decided that as soon as she reached Sacramento she would go straight to the Post Office, where hopefully she would find a letter from her father and could answer it before setting off to look for Henry.

After a good breakfast of salt ham and fried cakes, she fed and watered the mule and reluctantly remounted. Her muscles complained but she gathered up the reins and, after thanking her kind hosts, turned the mule's head towards the trail and began her second day's journey. Once again she began to enjoy the solitude. The ever-changing scenery never failed to delight her and her thoughts were free to roam at will. The longer she considered her future, the more she worried about her forthcoming meeting with Henry. Would he want her to honour her promise, and if so would she take the easy way out and marry him? Towards noon she passed three Indian women, two with babies slung on their backs, and at once her throat tightened. What was Moses doing now, she wondered? She longed to see him again, but knew she could not trust herself to behave dispassionately towards Ella. The Indian women unslung the babies and held them up for Lily's approval and she gave them a handful of corn meal which was all she could spare. They seemed satisfied with her offering and smiled broadly by way of thanks. Lily rode on somewhat nervously, expecting to encounter the men of the tribe, but to her relief none appeared.

The weather was deteriorating as she crossed an area of scrub where little grew but pale, twig-like bushes without leaves. Without the benefit of sunlight they looked lifeless, almost eerie, and the mule (which was proving surprisingly biddable) found it quite difficult to pick a path through them so that they made slow progress for the best part of an hour. As the run set, Lily could make out the blurred outline of Sacramento and began to hope that she would reach it before darkness fell. Over the sprawling town, smoke from countless fires hung in the still air. Lily breathed a sigh of relief. She would never have admitted it, but the solitude was beginning to depress her and she did not relish a night sleeping alone in the untamed hills.

Ten minutes later she reined in her mount and a wave of apprehension swept over her. Below her, on the winding trail, she could see a small group of riders making their way up towards her. Her first panic-stricken thought was that a party of Indian braves was returning to wherever the Indian women had gone. Flight seemed the most sensible solution, but she knew that if they had seen her they could easily follow the mule's tracks.

While she hesitated, glancing around her for an escape, the voices below became audible and she had a second shock which, in a way, was worse than the first. They were not Indians at all, but Americans – Gabby and Bart with Ella and her parents! Lily was torn between relief and dismay. She did not want to meet them, however, and impulsively she jerked the reins and plunged up and over a low ridge of rocks and down into the pine trees on the other side. From below a horse whinnied and she heard a shout, but no one attempted to follow her. She felt safer in the shadow of the trees and the lichens and mosses dulled the sound of the mule's hooves, so she began to breathe more freely and moved on through the trees which grew on steeply shelving ground, occasionally ducking her head to avoid the lower branches which dripped moisture. A quail ran out from behind a tree, startling the mule and almost unseating Lily, but she watched the small bird with affection until the neat

411

tufted head had once more vanished amongst the undergrowth.

Lily's plan was to take the next trail downward – there would certainly be another, for the wild creatures always made tracks towards the many small pools which dotted the countryside – but when eventually she found one, it led downwards for barely a mile and then began to climb steeply in a northerly direction. Lily hesitated. She did not want to go north, but neither did she want to strike off away from the track in case she got lost. She could retrace her steps, but that would lose a lot of time and she still hoped to reach Sacramento before dark.

'Damnation!' she muttered, sliding from the mule's back to stretch her aching limbs while she pondered the problem. A sudden cracking of a twig startled her but it was only a deer, gazing at her calmly from a distance before retreating once more into the shadows. After a few moments of reflection, Lily decided to follow the trail – almost certainly, she thought, it would take a downward turn sooner or later. With a sigh, she hauled herself back into the saddle and urged the unprotesting mule forward.

To her dismay, the path became narrower and wound tortuously and much later was still climbing. She was on the point of turning back when she heard voices and another turn in the track revealed a muddle of tents and rough dwellings and the familiar sight of men panning for gold.

They greeted her rapturously, introduced themselves with great courtesy and asked eagerly for news. They did not know that Sacramento had been flooded and Lily racked her brain for as many details as she could recall to satisfy their curiosity. They gave her coffee and a slice of bread which one of the miners claimed as his 'speciality'. Lily assured him it was the best she had ever tasted – although whether because of its superior quality or her ravenous appetite, she did not know!

When she told them she was looking for a Mr Simms, they spoke about a lone miner living higher up the creek.

The maker of the bread added, 'They say he's got an Indian wife. Would that be your Mr Simms?'

'No,' said Lily, her hopes dashed once more. 'That can't be him.'

'Tall fellow,' he went on. 'Fair hair.'

One of the men called Beany volunteered, 'Took sick with a fever, so I heard.'

'Mr Simms is tall and fair,' said Lily, 'about as tall as you.'

The man grinned. 'My ma used to call me "bean-pole" and I've been called Beany ever since. My real name's Franklin, but folks don't call me nothing but Beany.'

Lily smiled, but she was thinking rapidly. The blond man could not be Henry, but he might have news of him.

'How much higher up the creek?' she asked.

'A mile or so,' said Beany, 'wouldn't you say?' He appealed to his colleagues and they nodded agreement. 'Go on up and check him out, ma'am. If he's not your man, come on down again. You can spend the night with us. You'll be quite safe; there's not a man here as don't respect a lady. And English at that! We'd be real proud – cook you a real good supper.'

'Thank you,' said Lily, finishing the last mouthful of coffee. 'I might accept your kind offer. And then I suppose I shall have to retrace my steps. I'm sure I'm getting further away from Sacramento and not nearer.'

'You are, ma'am,' said one of the others, a small wiry man with thinning hair. 'But we know a track as'll take you down to Sacramento. It's a bit rough, but shorter than going back through them pines.'

Lily thanked them and set off again, her thoughts on the promised meal and a night's rest. She was finding the journey much more exhausting than she had expected and decided that when she finally reached Sacramento, flood permitting, she would rest for a few days before continuing her search.

After nearly two miles the path brought her back to the creek and she followed it for a few hundred yards to where she could hear the sounds of singing. Her natural caution made her dismount and she tied the mule to a tree and went forward on foot. An Indian girl was kneeling by a blazing fire, stirring something in a pot which hung over the flames. She was singing in a strange chanting voice and she swayed slightly from the waist, nodding in time with the music. She

413

swung round just as Lily caught sight of a man standing in the creek about twenty yards beyond her and for a moment the two women looked at each other. To Lily's inexperienced eye the Indian was very young, perhaps sixteen or seventeen. She was naked except for a skirt of deer-skin and a necklace of teeth of some kind. Her body was long and her sturdy legs were short in proportion to her height. Her black hair hung untidily to her shoulders and her narrow eyes above broad flat cheeks regarded Lily with calm curiosity.

'White woman,' she said and pointed to Lily.

Lily nodded, fascinated. In her turn she pointed to the man whose back was turned towards them.

'White man?' asked Lily and the girl understood and nodded.

'White man,' she said by way of explanation. 'En ree.'

Lily shook her head, not understanding.

'White man. En ree,' the girl insisted.

Lily smiled at her and began to walk away towards the man, who suddenly straightened up and stepped out of the water on to the bank. Lily's heart missed a beat as the girl's voice came back to her. 'En ree!' Was she trying to say *Henry*? Unable to go on, she stood still, one hand to her heart which was now hammering furiously as though to compensate for its earlier omission. There was something so familiar about him, but surely . . . the man turned and Lily gasped. It *was* Henry! His face registered delight and then dismay, but for Lily the meeting brought an overwhelming sensation of relief. Some of the old attraction was still there – the familiar lean body and the large blue eyes still tugged at her heart-strings – but inexplicably he was a different Henry Simms from the man Lily had met at Fort Kearny all those weeks ago.

'Lily! By all that's holy!'

He walked towards her uncertainly and she could see the shock in his eyes even as he smiled. 'He is wondering if he wants me back,' she thought to herself, 'and if so, how he will explain the girl.'

'I never thought you'd come,' he said. 'This is terrific!' He looked around. 'Who else is with you?'

'No one,' answered Lily, allowing herself to be embraced. 'I came alone. I promised I'd search for you.'

His gaze darted past Lily and back and he smiled nervously.

'My nurse,' he said, 'the Indian girl. I've been very ill – but how did you find me?'

Lily explained briefly what had happened to the Western Hope Miners after he left and told him of the new set-up at Godwin Bar.

'Are they finding much?' he asked anxiously and seemed relieved when Lily said, 'Not much yet, but they're hopeful.'

Then they both fell silent for a while and the silence lengthened awkwardly.

'She seems very pleasant,' remarked Lily at last.

At first he pretended not to understand, but then said, 'Oh, the girl. Yes, she's very willing. She nursed me. I meant what I said; I nearly died and I was all alone – then suddenly, there she was. Came out of nowhere and fed me . . . and stayed.'

'That was lucky,' said Lily carefully.

It was at once strange and sad to be talking to him in this way. Two strangers making polite conversation. In a way Lily's heart ached for the Henry she had known and loved and almost married, but this was another man altogether and she fought back a foolish need to weep for what might have been.

Henry looked down at the pan which he still held in his left hand. Automatically, his right forefinger explored the remaining sand and his mouth twisted with disappointment.

'This gold's damned elusive, but I'm finding a little,' he told her.

Lily smiled shakily, but could not speak.

'Lily, that girl . . .' he began. 'I don't know how to explain, it will sound so bizarre. I didn't ask her to come. Truly. She just turned up out of the blue and saved my life.' He explained briefly about his meeting with Chuck and the unfortunate outcome of their brief partnership.

'I should have known,' he told her. 'He did warn me –

said he got ichy with folks around him – but I thought he'd taken a shine to me. Vanity, I guess.'

Lily nodded. 'So the Indian girl found you and then stayed on?'

Henry tried to meet her eyes, but failed and dropped his gaze. 'It wasn't quite that simple,' he said. 'I don't quite know how to tell you this. She came back again several times and brought me food and water. The fourth time she came, she brought her father. I was terrified at first – I thought he'd kill me – but he just stood beside her, impassive, with his arms folded. You know the way they are. She handed me another note from Chuck. It said he'd sent her to look after me and had told her father I might want to buy her . . . as a wife.'

Lily gasped, but he shook his head earnestly. 'It's the truth, Lily. Chuck bought himself a wife that way and it's not uncommon. Remember Robidoux?'

'You mean you *bought* her?' Lily looked at him incredulously.

He nodded. 'What else could I do with her father standing there? I didn't want the whole tribe after my blood for compromising his daughter. I reckoned I *had* to!'

Lily was speechless as he went on, 'Chuck meant it for the best. He probably reckoned I'd be safer with an Indian wife and she *did* save my life. I'd have starved to death without her.'

'Oh, Henry – ' began Lily helplessly.

'Don't say "Oh, Henry" like that,' he begged. 'I'm telling you, I had no choice.'

'I'm not saying anything against her,' said Lily hastily. 'It's just . . . well, a bit of a shock. Do you love her?' she asked curiously.

'Love her? I don't know.' His expression was disconsolate. 'Sometimes I think I do, other times I wonder. I never expected to see *you* again. Hell, Lily – '

'What did you pay for her?' Lily asked, momentarily forgetting her manners.

'My pistol – the Colt – and about ninety dollars. That was all I had left. Don't look at me like that. I tell you it's

416

the way they do things out here and it's not so weird as it sounds. She cooks and sews. She's *company*.'

'But when you've found enough gold and you go back East, then what will happen to her?'

'I'm staying here,' he said quickly. 'In California. I don't want to go back East.'

'But your parents?'

'I'll write them one day.'

'Maybe you'll grow to love her,' said Lily. A deep sigh shook his long frame. 'Lily, I don't know what to say. I *am* fond of her, but if I'd thought for a moment that *you'd* turn up – '

'Like the bad penny!'

'No, *not* like that! Lily, I loved you. I mean, I do love you. At least, God knows I did, but . . .' He scowled. 'That damned Kate! I never could see why you had to – '

'Henry!' Lily stopped him in mid-sentence. 'Let's make this as easy as possible. We both know it's over. I came after you because I promised I would, and because I thought you loved and needed me. Now I realize you don't love me any more or you wouldn't have . . .' She gestured helplessly towards the girl, who was watching them unashamedly. 'And you don't need me either, so I can go my own way with a clear conscience. Maybe we just weren't meant to stay together. We met and we helped each other along, but now it's time to go our separate ways. It's for the best, Henry.'

His eyes narrowed suddenly. 'Are you and Wallis getting together? Is that it? Is that what you came to tell me?'

Lily shook her head. 'He's probably on his way home by now' she replied. 'He's going back to Virginia. If he and I were "getting together" as you put it, do you think he would have let me come all this way alone to find you?'

'I guess not. I'm sorry.'

'I had to come.' she said slowly, 'to find out whether what you and I felt for each other was really love. The lasting kind, I mean. I think we wanted to love each other because of Patrick, but we've found out in time.' She held out her hand. 'Let's part good friends, Henry. I shall always be glad I met you.'

417

Unwillingly, he took her hand. 'Lily,' he whispered, 'I want you to know I'm sorry about walking out on you the way I did. If only I'd waited for you, none of this would have happened. What will you do?'

'I don't quite know,' said Lily. 'I think I shall go down to Sacramento. I'm not helpless and I won't starve. I can give piano lessons – or take in washing! I'll probably get a ship back to England as soon as I've saved up the fare. At least my father will be pleased to see me.'

'Don't say it like that, Lily,' he protested. '*I'm* pleased to see you. It's just that . . . well, nothing ever pans out the way you think it will.'

'What a terrible pun, Henry!' cried Lily. 'Oh, don't let's part on a gloomy note. You'll strike it rich one day, I feel it *here!*' She put a hand on her heart and then impulsively leaned forward and kissed him lightly on the cheek. 'Goodbye, Henry. Be happy,' she said and, gathering up her skirts, hurried back the way she had come without another glance at either Henry or the girl. She unhitched the mule with fingers that trembled and pulled herself up into the saddle.

'Life goes on, Lily Golightly,' she said sternly as she headed back along the path. 'It's not the end of the world, so don't you *dare* cry!'

*

When Lily reached Sacramento, she stared round her with dismay. The flood-water had gone down, but it had left a thick coating of foul-smelling mud over everything and an inch of water still remained to form vast puddles. Fortunate people paddled through it in boots, but the not-so-fortunate made do by wrapping rags or paper over their shoes and lower legs. Here and there a dog splashed through it distastefully, but the cats which had survived the deluge surveyed the unsavoury scene from the safety of roofs or tree-tops. Improvised boardwalks straddled the worst of the mud, crisscrossing the street and forming a network of connections between major buildings. Dead animals and a few snakes lay embedded in the mud amongst a tangle of other debris, and three men struggled to pull a dead horse up into the back of a cart by way of a makeshift wooden ranp. Homeless men searched amongst the wreckage for anything they could find which could be utilized in the building of a new shelter.

Lily inquired for the Post Office and was told it was open for business as usual. She made straight for it, the mule picking its way distastefully through the mud with Lily clinging on more tightly than usual, reluctant to be dislodged if the animal should stumble over some hidden obstacle. Outside the Post Office nearly a hundred men queued patiently, some carrying letters which they wanted to send home, others waiting hopefully for news. Discouraged, Lily decided to find some accommodation first if she could, but this was not at all easy. At last, after a dispiriting hour – during which Lily came to understand at first hand how Mary felt when she rode into Bethlehem – she finally found a sympathetic hotelier. He was tubby and talkative and he took an instant liking to her.

'Find you a room?' he boomed. 'I doubt it, ma'am, but find you somewhere to lay year head, that I certainly will, even if I have to sleep you in my own bedroom. English, are you? I like the English. My niece married an English soldier. Yes, you shall sleep in my own bedroom if I can't find you anything else!'

Lily began to protest that she would not hear of such a sacrifice, but he laughed loudly and gave an enormous wink.

'Don't you worry, ma'am,' he reassured her. 'I won't sleep on the floor. I've a sofa as'll do me fine for a night or two and business is business. I've slept on a lot worse than sofas, I can tell you! Now, where shall we put you?' He stared thoughtfully at the ceiling and drummed podgy fingers on the counter-top. 'Don't suppose you'd want to share, would you? With a *lady*, of course. I've a lady in number six who's waiting for her family to come back. Up in Frenchman's Bar, he is, and been there for months. Poor woman, she'd be glad of someone to talk to. She's not at all happy – shouldn't care to be her husband when he finally gets back. He promised to be here to meet her when she reached Sacramento, but a promise isn't worth much in these difficult times. "You be patient", I told her. "He's doing his best to make you a fortune", but she gave me a look that would've froze the tail off a mule! Wouldn't like to be in his shoes . . . but I mustn't ramble on. She'd probably share the room if you'd share the cost, there's two beds in that room. None of the downstairs rooms are usable yet, as you can see!' He pointed to a brown stain which extended up the walls to a height of six feet. 'Some had it worse,' he told Lily. 'Some were under ten feet of water and that's no joke.'

He paused for breath and Lily said quickly, 'If you don't have an empty room, I'll share with Mrs – ?'

'Keller. Mrs Annie Keller.' He began to write something in his book, then hesitated. 'I'd best ask her before I enter it,' he said, 'but she's sleeping at present. Always sleeping, she is – morning, noon and night. Nothing else to do, she says.'

'If I could unsaddle?' asked Lily. 'Do you have a stable?'

'We did and do, but it's as muddy as everywhere else,' he told her. 'Still, there's several horses in there already and they're surviving. Can't give 'em dry straw because there isn't any!' He laughed again, apparently finding the calamity a great joke. 'Still, they're not complaining. Too many of the poor critters drowned, so what's a few inches of mud to those that are still alive and kicking?' He brought his hand down sharply on a small dome-shaped bell and almost immediately a young Mexican boy appeared in the doorway.

'Help the *señorita* unsaddle her horse.' The boy flashed Lily a wide, white smile. 'His name's Juan.'

'Thank you, Juan,' said Lily and followed the boy outside.

An hour and a half later she had moved her few belongings into number six, had introduced herself to Annie Keller, had washed and eaten and was on her way back to the Post Office. She wore her rubber boots and held her skirts as high as she could as she teetered precariously along the various walkways which eventually delivered her to the end of the queue. To her dismay, it had grown noticeably longer in her absence, but she finally took her place behind an elderly, white-whiskered man. It took over two hours for the queue to shorten appreciably and the long wait was punctuated from time to time by shouts of delight from those men lucky enough to be given mail and explosive curses from some who were not. Many of the disappointed men passed Lily with despairing expressions, their shoulders slumped miserably – lonely men, far from home, to whom a simple letter would spell instant happiness. Lily felt a great compassion for them. What price all the gold in California, she thought, when there was no word from a loved one?

Her own turn came at last and the official's face brightened. A woman was still sufficiently rare to bring about a softening of the tough attitude he normally adopted.

'Golightly,' Lily told him. 'Lily Golightly. The letter will be from England.'

'Golightly,' he repeated. 'Let's see what we can find for you.'

Lily crossed her fingers for luck and then uncrossed them. This was no time for superstition, she told herself. If God intended her to have a letter from her father, it would be there. It was! She took it with stammering thanks, noted that it was again written in the housekeeper's handwriting and hurried back to her hotel with hands which almost trembled with joy. All the difficulties of the last weeks melted away with the prospect of news from home.

She did not go up to her room, but ordered coffee in the tiny hotel dining room which after several washings was relatively free of mud and restored to some semblance of normality. A row of rickety chairs stood along the wall and half the tables were upturned on the others. Lily sat down on one of the chairs and opened the envelope. As she unfolded the letter, a lock of white hair bound at one end with black cotton fell into her lap and she stared at it, frowning uncomprehendingly.

Her father had sent a lock of his hair . . . but why? True, she had left him a lock of hers, but – cold panic seized her and she could not bring herself even to touch it.

'Oh, no!' she whispered and straightened the letter with fingers that trembled.

'Dear Miss Lilian,' she read, 'I write with a sad heart . . .'

'*Please* God, *no!*' Lily cried. She resisted the temptation to crumple the letter; she dreaded reading any further, but with a deep, painful sigh she forced herself to read to the end of the short letter.

... to tell you of the passing of your poor dear father, who was as good a man as ever walked this earth. We buried him yesterday with a full church and so many flowers you would have been proud to see it. He was taken ill soon after you left, which is why I had to write his letter, he would not have you worried. The doctor did what he could, but it was his heart and then pneumonia, but he was in no pain only very weak and spoke constantly of you. Your name was on his lips when he went. He said over and over, "Tell her I've repaired the summer-house and not to grieve, it is God's will and we will be reunited in Heaven. God rest his soul. Mr Downey was with him much of the time. I will wait here, hoping for your speedy return until the new parson comes. Mr Downey says that would be best. Then I will go to Devon to join my sister Ivy. Your belongings will have to be stored, Mr Downey will see to such matters.

I feel for you in your sad loss. You must not blame me, believe me, I did all I could, the doctor will tell you.

I am yours truly,

Agnes Spencer (Mrs)

Lily felt her senses withdrawing and she was grateful. She could no longer hear the voices in the next room and there was a dark mist in front of her eyes. She was aware only of her heartbeat and found no consolation in the fact that she was obviously still alive. Her father, her beloved father, was dead. He had died without her arms around him and without the joy that her presence would have given him. He had died thousands of miles away of a broken heart, because she had been selfish and impulsive and had set off half-way round the world after Patrick Golightly, a husband she hardly knew.

Patiently she waited with bowed head for the grief to well up and overwhelm her; she waited for retribution. It seemed to her shocked mind that she had personally brought about her father's death by her stupidity, and that she must be punished for her callous behaviour. She must suffer for her past mistakes and then maybe she would deserve forgiveness.

With bent head and unseeing eyes, she waited for the press of tears which would preface her break-down, but it did not come. She remained dry-eyed, with a hard knot of misery somewhere inside her chest which made it difficult to breathe properly. With a gulp, she filled her lungs with air.

'Oh, Papa!' she whispered at last. 'My dearest, most precious Papa!'

A great weight of darkness seemed to settle over her, imprisoning her and isolating her from the world around her.

'Papa, I love you,' she said and her voice sounded ridiculously normal.

She thought sadly how much her few letters must have worried him, and wished that she had not caused him so much anxiety. If only she had never met Patrick Golightly – but no, that too was unfair. She *had* met him and fallen in love with him and, against her father's better judgement, she had married him. She had only herself to blame if blame there was. If only Patrick hadn't been planning to go to the United States. If only he could have found a job in England . . .

Slowly she shook her head. Regrets were worse than useless. 'What's done's done!' Someone had said that – probably Shakespeare, she thought vaguely. There was no undoing the past, no matter how much one wished it undone.

'But I'm so sorry, Papa . . . and you repaired the summerhouse!'

She swallowed hard and felt as though her grief was choking her – a physical thing, threatening her life. If only she could die now, they could be together again and she could compensate him for all the anguish she had caused him. But what had Mrs Spencer said? 'Tell her not to grieve.'

Suddenly Lily was aware of a man standing in the doorway. Lifting her head with an effort, she was astonished to see Daniel Miller leaning against the door-jamb, surveying her with his head on one side and his usual quizzical look.

She felt pathetically grateful for the sight of the familiar face, even *his*.

'So Kate was right!' he exclaimed. 'She said she saw you, but I said "Never".' His eyes narrowed slightly as he saw the expression on her face.

'You look a bit peaky,' he said. 'You ill or something?'

Lily forced her frozen lips into movement. 'No,' she said faintly, 'I don't think I am. It's ... this letter.' She held it up. 'It's from Mrs Spencer, my father's housekeeper.'

'Oh yes?' She recognized the concern in the button-brown eyes. 'What news then?'

'It's Papa,' she stammered. 'He's dead. My father is *dead*.'

Her voice shook and the letter fluttered from her trembling fingers to the floor. They both looked at it.

'Dead? Ah, that is bad news,' Daniel sympathized promptly. 'Died in his bed, did he?'

Lily nodded.

'Lucky man, then,' said Daniel firmly. 'Mine died in a fight. I found him stretched out on the bar-room floor with sawdust all over him.' He crossed the room, picked up the letter and folded it carefully. 'That's tough, news like that.'

She nodded again.

He sat down on the chair next to her and dropped the letter into her lap.

'Gave me a shock when mine went,' he told her. 'We'd had words in the morning, too – last time I saw him alive. That hurt, that did, but you can't turn back the clock.'

Lily stared at him. 'How awful for you,' she said.

He shrugged. 'That's life. These things happen.'

'I should have been with him ...' she began.

He raised his eyebrows. 'How could you? Can't be in two places at once – none of us can.'

Lily found his blunt common sense disconcerting yet strangely comforting, and felt herself emerging slowly from the state of acute shock into which the letter had plunged her. Now the tears which had been locked within her surfaced without warning and ran down her cheeks.

Daniel Miller handed her a none-too-clean handkerchief

424

and then patted her knee. 'Cry away,' he said. 'Don't mind me.'

As soon as he gave her permission to cry, the tears dried up again.

'Or don't,' he said humorously. 'Please yourself!'

'He repaired the summer-house,' said Lily. 'It was one of the last things I asked of him and I only said it to cheer him up. "When I bring the grandchildren home," I told him, "they'll want to play in the summer-house." You see, the shingles were all rotten and he said he'd get it repaired for when we visited.' She took another gulp of air. It seemed she could not stop talking and the words tumbled from her lips. 'We used to play croquet together on the lawn. He loved croquet. Sometimes Mr Downey would give him a game, but mostly it was me. The day before I left, he said "Who's going to play croquet with me?" Have you ever played croquet, Mr Miller?'

'Not as I've noticed', he grinned. 'So Kate was right. "That's Lily Golightly," she said. "I swear it is." But by the time I got to the window there was no sight nor sound of you. "You imagined it," I told her, but she was that certain. In the end, just to satisfy her, I said I'd have a look around for you. And here you are! Always looking out of the window is Kate. She doesn't miss much, that one. Likes to watch the world go by, she says. We're lucky; we live upstairs. Nice little place.'

Lily, busy with her memories, paid him no heed.

'We were always so close,' she said, 'because my mother died when I was born. Papa used to spoil me dreadfully. He was not like other fathers. Aunt Florrie used to grumble at him – she came to look after us. "You'll ruin the girl", she used to say, and Papa would smile that lovely smile of his . . .'

Her voice faltered. 'He took me on a picnic once, to the river, and there were some small white flowers growing on the water-weed, I suppose it was. I wanted some and he took off his shoes and socks and rolled up his trousers and waded in. He slipped and fell into the water and I couldn't stop screaming. It only came up to his shins but I thought he'd be drowned – but he climbed out laughing, *with* the flowers.

We had to go home and Aunt Florrie was so cross. She said it was my fault for wanting the flowers – poor Papa! I can't believe he's dead. And buried, too, and I wasn't even there. I wasn't with him.'

Her eyes filled with tears again and she made no attempt to blink them back. They coursed slowly down her cheeks as she continued, 'He was always taking me out. We went to the zoo. Oh, so many times. And we fed the ducks on the village pond and went up to London to see the Thames!'

'The what?'

'The Thames,' she repeated, wiping her eyes. 'It's the river that flows through London. He said everyone should see the River Thames – England's life-blood, he called it. And we went to the fair and to the seaside.'

'Lucky little girl,' commented Daniel. 'It's a wonder you weren't ruined.'

'Is it?' Lily looked up in surprise. 'Maybe I was,' she conceded. 'But no, I don't think so. How can a little girl be ruined by knowing her father loves her?'

Daniel ignored the question, which was too deep for him. 'So what brings you to Sacramento?' he asked. 'Looking for "His Nibs"?'

It required deep concentration on Lily's part before she could remember anything about her present situation, for the news of her father's death had driven everything else from her thoughts.

'Simms,' Daniel prompted. 'Looking for Simms, are you?'

Eventually Lily said dully, 'Henry? No, I'm not looking for him. I've already found him. He's happy enough and I came away.'

He made no effort to hide his surprise. 'Who, then?' he insisted. 'If you've lost someone, Kate'll know where he is. She lives at that window and she's got eyes like a hawk. When she said she'd spotted you, I should have believed her. Then it was "Go after her, Daniel". She's a real slave-driver, that one!'

Lily sighed deeply. She was grateful for Daniel's presence, grateful that his questions were making her think about the present and not the past. The black nameless horror which had engulfed her earlier had retreated just a little, and for the moment she could just about bear the knowledge that her father lay in his coffin below the ground and she would never ever see him again.

'I'm not looking for anyone,' she said slowly. 'I don't really know what I'm doing. I was going to look for work and then go home to England. That's what Matt said I should do.'

'Matt Wallis?'

She nodded and his eyes rolled wickedly. 'Oh, it's *Matt* now, is it?' he teased.

Lily shook her head wearily without rising to the bait. 'He said I should go back to England, that California is no place for a woman on her own.'

'So you need a job to get money for your fare.'

Even in the midst of her grief she recognized the look in his eyes and tried to smile.

'Please don't offer me a job in your "establishment", Mr Miller,' she said. 'I thought I might give piano lessons; I used to do that before I married Patrick.'

Daniel looked at her in amazement. 'Teach piano – who to?'

'Children. There must be some.'

'Mrs Golightly!' he exploded. 'This is Sacramento. It's a raw, rough town of raw, rough *men*. Piano lessons!'

Lily's jaw tightened a little. 'There must be some children somewhere – ' she began, but suddenly Daniel thumped the table and his eyes lit up.

'Maybe you could play the piano in one of the saloons!' he cried. 'You couldn't do worse than some of the fellows I've heard – two left hands, some of them.'

Lily's eyes widened in horror. 'In a saloon!' she exclaimed. 'Are you mad? I couldn't possibly.'

'Why the hell not?' he challenged. 'A piano's a piano wherever it is. You must be able to play or you couldn't teach.'

Lily began to protest, but he was too pleased with the idea to give it up.

'Leave it to me,' he said, 'and I'll ask around. If there's a

427

job going, I'll put in a good word for you. They all know me!' He beamed at her. 'Take your mind off your Papa,' he said. 'And don't take it too hard. We've all got to go some time. My ma always says that if your conscience is clear you've nothing to worry about.'

'Is your conscience clear?' The question slipped out, but he did not take offence.

'Put it this way,' he answered. 'Maybe my halo could do with a polish, but my heart's in the right place!' His smile disappeared briefly. 'Still mad at Kate, are you?'

Lily could not answer.

'OK,' he said quickly. 'She'll understand. It was a rotten trick.'

'I don't want to talk about it,' Lily told him.

'You English,' he said, 'you take everything so personally. Ever heard of water on a duck's back? You've got to learn to let things wash over you. That way you don't get so wet! Look at me now. I've taken some hard knocks in my time, and I could've gone under if I'd *let* myself. But I don't, I look on the bright side. Know what I mean?'

She nodded and put a hand to her eyes. 'I'm sure you're right, Mr Miller.'

He stood up. 'I'll tell Kate I found you. If you change your mind, just ask for Miller's place. They mostly know me. We've got another girl – Belle Staver. Pretty little thing. She and Kate get along fine. You in Sacramento long?'

'I don't know. I have to think, to sort things out.'

'You do that.'

At the door he paused. 'Wallis was here a few days ago asking after you. He's headed for San Francisco and home. Kate spotted him and called out from the window. Said he looked pretty sick.'

Her head snapped up. 'Matt's ill?'

'Sick at heart, I meant. He was on his way to the shipping office. I don't think he's taken to California.'

'He has a lot to go back to,' said Lily.

'Lucky man!' observed Daniel.

Then he had gone and Lily was left alone, staring at the

428

empty doorway. At last she glanced down at the letter in her lap, unfolded it slowly and began to read again.

*

That night Lily cried herself to sleep and she woke the next morning with a severe headache. Annie Keller brought her a cup of coffee, for which she was very grateful.

'I heard you crying,' Annie told her, sitting on the edge of Lily's bed, 'but I thought it best to let you get it out of your system. Better than bottling it up. Bottle up grief and it turns sour inside you and you never get over it.'

She was a dumpy woman in her late forties, with a homely face and long grey hair which hung down her back in a single plait.

Lily could not bear to talk about her father's death, so she asked her new friend about her family and Annie willingly launched into a lengthy account of her own adventures. Her husband and three sons had travelled overland to California, but when they sent word for Annie to join them she had baulked at the idea of travelling through Indian country without them. She decided therefore to travel by sea, and lived to regret her choice, but when at last she reached San Francisco late in December she realized that her troubles were not yet over.

'The whole town was crowded out like always,' she told Lily, 'and I thought myself lucky to find a room on the east side of Kearny, two along from Dennison's. You heard of Dennison's?'

Lily stared at her without comprehension and Annie repeated the question. Lily thought about it. 'No,' she said, 'I haven't.'

'It's a gaming house,' Annie enlightened her. 'Or rather it was – will be again.' For a moment she enjoyed Lily's mystified expression, then she continued. 'Early hours of Christmas Eve, darned if it didn't catch alight. *Set* alight, most folks reckon, but that place went up like a torch. Painted cotton ceiling, that had, and a tarred roof. Stands to reason it would burn. I looked out of my window and there was hollering and shouting and folks dashing up and down

429

the street. Just on daylight it was, and smoke billowing everywhere. Next thing you know, the buildings are ablaze on either side! Never seen anything like it. I got dressed in a hurry, I can tell you. I went outside and the restaurant was burning too – the "United States" they called it. Went up with a great roar. I could see my lodgings would be next and I was right. Ran back in and got my stuff out – folks up and down the stairs, bags and boxes everywhere. You ever seen a real bad fire?'

By this time she had caught Lily's interest.

'No,' said Lily. 'It must be terrible.'

'It's that all right,' Annie agreed. 'It's terrifying. The heat! You can't imagine it, and the crackling and crashing of timber and sparks falling on folks' clothes. Some pushing to get a closer view and others trying to get back from the heat – fellers hollering out orders and no one heeding them!' She shook her head. 'If you've seen a fire like that, you're never going to forget it.'

Lily asked, '*Did* your lodgings burn down?'

Annie snorted. 'Certainly did – saw it with my own eyes. Burned to the ground. I thought, well, that's me homeless again. Welcome to California, Annie Keller!' She sighed. 'You know the Portsmouth Plaza? Oh no, you wouldn't. Well, folks was crowded into it, all goggle-eyed, when a rumour started that there was gunpowder stored in the Parker House just along the street. Never seen so many folks move so fast in all my life. Screaming and shouting like crazy that she was going to blow; well, she didn't, but by midday the whole block had gone from Washington clear through to Montgomery. They reckon it'll cost a million and a half dollars to put it right, but do you know – they started right in rebuilding while the timbers was still smouldering. What d'you think of that for pluck? You've got to hand it to them. Those San Franciscans have got guts.'

'They certainly have,' Lily agreed. 'So then you came on to Sacramento?'

'Had to, didn't I?' said Annie. 'So many folks homeless 'cause of the fire, I reckoned I'd do better to move on. Get a bit nearer to the gold.' She laughed. 'I thought my troubles

430

were over when I got a room here, but there's no sign of my old man and the boys, so I'm kicking my heels in this dump when the water rises and nearly drowns me! Woke up to hear this slopping noise and everything pitch-dark, so I swing my legs over the side and splash! I'm up to my knees in water!' She shook her head at the memory. 'Course I was in one of the downstairs rooms then. I let out one almighty holler, I can tell you. I went to the window and there's all hell let loose – folks blundering about in the water in the dark, with their belongings in bundles. I took one look, collected my bits and pieces and headed for the stairs – and there I stayed for near on two weeks. I only went down a few days ago, several hours before you turned up. Took 'em a whole day to sweep out the worst of the mud.'

'Are the people insured?' asked Lily.

'Insured? Course they're not! Still, you've got to hand it to them. Here in California they just pick up the pieces and start in over again. Like I said, they've got guts. Gold and guts – that's what's going to make California great!'

'Will it be great?' Lily asked.

'I sure as hell hope so!' cried Annie. 'We've nothing to go back to, so it's *got* to be great. There's plenty more folk like us who sold up everything and staked it all on California. My husband reckons there's enough gold to make California the greatest state in America.'

'I hope you're right,' said Lily.

She let Annie chatter on, but gradually her attention wandered and she returned to a consideration of her own problems. During the long hours of the night she had woken several times and taken stock of her immediate options. She did *not* want to remain in Sacramento earning her keep as a piano-player in a saloon. She had very little money but she *had* got the mule, her mining equipment and a few blankets. It might be possible to sell all of them to any one of the prospectors who arrived in the town each day eager to equip themselves for the big adventure. Hopefully, she would get enough money to pay her passage down river to San Francisco, which presumably was a little more civilized than

Sacramento and where she might be able to give piano lessons.

Lily thought wistfully of Matt Wallis and at once his image rose up to torment her. She had finally admitted to herself that she loved and needed him, but admitted also that through her own lack of vision she had allowed him to walk out of her life. She had only herself to blame. The memory of him remained bright and clear and the cool grey eyes haunted her as she recalled the sound of his voice, his smile, the powerful set of his shoulders and the confident way he handled both man and beast. Matt Wallis was not a man to be trifled with, she reflected ruefully as once again she cursed her stupidity. Now that it was too late she realized exactly what she had lost and the knowledge was bitter to her. Life with Matt would have been exciting and full of love – an adventure. Intuitively she knew that she could have made him happy; together they would have raised a family.

When she thought of his first wife her heart ached for him, for she remembered her own recent betrayals and could imagine how deeply he had been hurt by the desertion. Lily longed for the chance to make him happy again, but there was no way now that she could mean anything to him. If only she had never met Henry Simms; if only she had not insisted on following him; if only . . . but such speculation was pointless. Matt offered the chance of happiness, but she had turned him down and he was now on his way back to Virginia. Presumably he would marry again eventually, but the prospect gave her no comfort for the thought of Matt with another woman in his arms was unbearable . . . No, it was over and done. Lily squared her shoulders. She had engineered her own tragedy and now she must face up to a solitary future. With an effort she turned her attention away from what might have been and tried to concentrate on her immediate predicament. She must make plans.

She would stay on in California, but for how long? A month? A year? Yes, maybe a year. Her father was dead and she had no one to return to. England without her father would be an empty and sad place for her. A new parson would move into the house she had called home, and she would have nowhere to live. Why not stay in California and see what the new state had to offer? It was only fair to give it a chance. Yes, she would go to San Francisco and look for work.

She made up her mind so suddenly that Annie was slightly offended when Lily put down the empty cup in the middle of her story and threw off the bedcovers.

'I have to sell my mule,' said Lily and less than an hour later she was discussing the price with an eager buyer.

The young man bought all that she had to sell for a fair price and Lily made her way to the shipping office to inquire about the next steamboat to San Francisco. By two o'clock she was standing on the deck of an ancient paddle-steamer watching Sacramento fade into the distance, her heart still aching but her spirits determinedly high.

The next day she was still making plans when the steamer's paddlewheel stopped turning and to the accompaniment of the inevitable calliope, Lily and the rest of the passengers were hurried ashore by the impatient crew, all of whom were anxious to explore the heady delights of San Francisco.

Lily stood on the landing stage with her bag beside her and stared around at the extraordinary city which sprawled around the bay and encroached on the lower slopes of the surrounding hills. The bay itself was filled with a forest of masts which rose from countless abandoned vessels whose crews and passengers had long since departed up river to look for gold. The city itself boasted a surprising number of fine buildings, but the rainy season had turned the dusty streets into mud and the sidewalks reminded her of Sacramento. The quayside itself was a confusion of crates, boxes and rotting sacks as cargoes, once unloaded, waited in vain for men to collect and distribute them. The balconies of many of the buildings were hung with washing. Some of the finest buildings were either hotels or gambling halls. As Annie Keller had warned her, the process of rebuilding was already under way and the air rang with its clamour.

'San Francisco,' said Lily, awed in spite of herself. She had heard so much about it and yet the reality fell short of her expectations. She sighed, bemused, then shook herself out of her reverie, wearily picked up her bag and straightened her shoulders. She must find somewhere to spend the night. One step at a time, she told herself. Tomorrow she would look for a job. She had taken only a few steps, however, when a familiar voice called her name, freezing her where she stood. She turned slowly, unable to believe it, afraid to find herself mistaken. How could it be Matt Wallis – yet there he was striding towards her, a smile of relief on his face.

'Matt!' A tremendous sensation of joy raced through her as she looked at him and thought, 'All I want is to touch that bright curly hair and kiss that mouth', but with an effort she held out her hand instead. He took it in a grip that was so firm it hurt.

'I don't believe it!' she said. 'I thought you'd be on your way home by now. I saw Daniel Miller in Sacramento and he said he'd seen you on the way back.'

'I should have been,' he told her. 'I booked a passage on yesterday's ship, but at the last minute I changed my mind and cancelled it. I just couldn't go without satisfying myself that you were safe.' He looked around in surprise. 'Are you alone?'

Lily smiled. 'It seems that Henry found someone else who has healed his broken heart.'

His eyebrows rose. 'So *soon*?'

Lily nodded. 'It made me feel rather small,' she confessed, 'but in a way I was relieved. You were right, Matt. He was not the man for me. I knew it before I went, but I had to go. I know it was foolish, but my conscience troubled me.'

'I'm glad you found out.'

She nodded. The calm eyes looking into hers revealed nothing of his thoughts.

'So are you on your way back to England?' he asked.

'No,' answered Lily. 'Not yet.' Some of the animation left her face. 'I've nothing to go back for. My father's dead, Matt; there was a letter waiting for me in Sacramento.' Her voice trembled and she saw the concern in his eyes.

'Poor Lily,' he said quietly. 'That's really tough. I know how much your father meant to you. I'm sorry.'

Lily said, 'I daren't let myself think about it. I'm trying

434

hard to fill my mind with other things. It's much easier if I keep myself busy.'

There was an awkward silence. Lily had so much to say to him, but didn't know where to start.

'So,' he said, 'if you have no one to go back to in England, why don't you come back to Virginia with me?'

Lily wondered if she had heard him correctly.

'Come back to Virginia?' she stammered.

'As my wife,' he added, his mouth twisting into a grin. 'Do you think we'd make out?' As Lily still remained speechless, he took her two hands in his. 'I don't want to rush you. If you prefer to wait a while, you could come as our guest for a few months. I don't want to wait that long, but I will if I have to.'

He pulled her a little closer until their bodies were almost touching and Lily tried to analyse her whirling emotions. She was aware once again of the desire she felt for him and with it came a fierce need to love and care for him. Matt Wallis was the right person – they were right for each other. She *knew* it with an unerring certainty.

'I'd like to marry you, Matt,' she said quietly. 'I do love you and I believe we could make each other happy . . .'

He made no attempt to kiss her but looked at her steadily; Lily felt suddenly weak with longing and acknowledged it as the stirrings of passion.

Matt's mouth widened into a broad smile. 'Seems I've found myself a wife!' he said.

Lily smiled shakily.

'Let's go find a preacher,' he suggested with a grin.

Lily gasped. 'Find a – do you mean now, today?'

'Why not? You've said you love me. No need to wait!'

She stared at him. 'Oh, but – '

'No more "buts", Lily,' he told her. 'No more doubts. Today's the day. I let you go once, but I'm not going to risk it again. Since you know you love me, it's now or never!'

Lily swallowed hard. 'It's now, then,' she agreed breathlessly. 'If we can find someone, that is. It's rather short notice.'

'I'll find someone,' he assured her.

Lily allowed herself to be led by the hand to the nearest church, a simple building of white clapboard. Inside they found an elderly lady cleaning the brass, but she told them that 'the Reverend' was taken ill with a fever and not expected out of his bed for another week or more.

'If then,' she added. 'He's over eighty and frail as a kitten.'

'Who's standing in for him?' Matt asked.

'You may well ask,' she retorted. 'They asked the Reverend Baker, but he's out of town on business, whatever that might mean. Reverend Mayne said "No" but then he would!' She lowered her voice conspiratorially. 'They've never liked each other. Said he was too busy, but *we* know better.'

Matt and Lily looked at each other.

'There must be someone,' Matt insisted. 'You're not telling me that in the whole of San Francisco there isn't a single preacher who can conduct a wedding!'

The old woman scratched her head. 'You could *try* the Reverend Mayne,' she suggested, 'only best not to say you tried here first.' She breathed heavily on to the stem of the candlestick and resumed her polishing. 'He'll want proper notice though,' she warned. 'He's a bit of a stickler that way. Not like our Reverend; he's more obliging. He married one woman on her death-bed. Mayne would never do that.'

'I don't believe it,' said Matt. 'There *has* to be someone.'

The old woman shook her head and after thanking her, Lily and Matt made their way back along the narrow path to the street.

Lily did not know whether she was pleased or sorry, but Matt had not given up hope.

'I've got an idea,' he said and set off down the street at such a pace that Lily had to run to keep up with him.

'Matt, don't be so mysterious,' she begged. 'Where are we going?'

'You'll see.'

He refused to say more but strode on, grinning to himself, and Lily was soon too breathless to ask any further questions. Rounding a corner, they found themselves confronted by a crowd of people who were being harangued by a travelling preacher.

436

He was a tall, gaunt man with a shock of white hair and he stood on an upturned barrel so that he could more easily be seen and heard.

'. . . but the Lord does not glance away,' he assured his listeners in ringing tones. 'He does not turn his head away when we do wrong. No, he does not. I tell you, ladies and gentlemen, sinners all, that he watches us *all the time*.' He threw out his arms as though to embrace eternity. 'And he will go on watching us. He knows not only everything we do, but everything we'd *like* to do! He reads our thoughts. And he notes it down for future reference! No good you and I knocking at the gates of Heaven and hoping he's missed a few of our sins. No, no, no! He sees them all! And that is why I beseech you, one and all – '

'Matt!' cried Lily. 'You don't mean *him?*'

'Him,' Matt echoed. 'He's here most days.'

'But Matt, perhaps we should wait for – '

'I told you, Lily Golightly,' he interrupted, 'no delays and no more ifs and buts. I'm getting to know you and I aim to marry you before you change your mind.'

Before Lily could protest further, he began to push his way through the crowd and for a moment she thought of her marriage to Patrick: the solemn ceremony with her father officiating; the blue lace dress; the throwing of rice outside the church porch and the housekeeper's beaming face as the guests returned to the house for the wedding breakfast. For a moment her heart quailed at the prospect ahead of her, but then she pulled herself together. The man she loved was already lost to view and, throwing propriety to the winds, she pushed through the crowd after him.

By the time she reached Matt's side the sermon had been temporarily suspended and the preacher was leaning down towards Matt and nodding earnestly. A ripple of excitement ran through the crowd as word was passed back that a wedding was about to be performed.

Matt turned fo find Lily behind him.

'He'll marry us now,' he said. 'Right now and right here!'

With a tremendous effort of will, Lily bit back the startled cry that rose in her throat and managed a cheerful nod.

Right now, she thought dazedly, without even time to comb my hair or change my clothes? Right here, in the middle of a muddy street in San Francisco among strangers?

The preacher leaned down towards her. 'You the young woman he's marrying?' he asked. Faded blue eyes looked at her intently from beneath bushy white eyebrows. A moustache and beard completed the picture. Lily never forgot his face.

'Yes, I am,' she answered.

'Name?'

'Er . . . Lily Golightly. I was married before to – '

'You not from these parts?'

'No, I'm from England.'

'Guessed as much!' He looked up. 'She's from England,' he told the crowd and there was a murmur of interest.

Lily stole a look at Matt, who winked at her. Meanwhile the preacher introduced himself as the Very Reverend Albert D. Stringer and he then straightened up and addressed the crowd once more.

'Now this here young couple is wanting to get married,' he announced, 'and there's no time like the present. So if you'll all step back a little and give us a bit more room? Thank you kindly, sinners all.'

As the crowd shuffled obediently backwards and the preacher stepped down, Lily stifled an hysterical desire to laugh.

'You got the ring?' he asked Matt.

Lily's heart sank. Of course they had not bought a ring . . . but Matt was nodding and pulling a ring from the third finger of his right hand.

'It was my mother's,' he told her. 'It might not fit, but it can be altered later.'

She nodded, afraid to speak and nervously aware of a mounting hysteria within her. 'I must stay calm,' she thought desperately. 'This is California and they do things differently.' Life was never again going to be the way it was in England. That had been a different chapter in her life and now, by marrying Matt, she was turning a new page that could never be turned back. The preacher held up a hand for silence and as though at a signal, a slow drizzle began to fall.

Lily thought fleetingly of her father's church with the late afternoon sun slanting through the stained-glass window, and the sight of Patrick's young face turned eagerly towards her as she walked down the aisle towards him. Now he was dead. Tears pricked her eyes for the futility of it all. But then Matt was taking her hand and she turned to look up at him. The grey eyes which she had once thought so cold were now warm with love and understanding.

'It's going to be fine,' he whispered and squeezed her hand reassuringly. Looking down at her own small hand clasped in his, the last of her panic faded away and as she returned his smile, her new-found confidence returned and she faced the preacher with a happy heart.

'It'll be ten dollars,' he announced firmly, 'payable in advance.'

'Ten dollars!' Matt was obviously surprised by this large sum.

'She's English,' said the preacher, as though this fact adequately explained the exorbitant amount.

As Matt reached into his pocket, he winked at Lily and muttered, 'Why quibble? You're worth every penny!' and Lily laughed.

Reverend Stringer produced a small suede drawstring bag and dropped in the money. When the bag was once more secure in his jacket pocket, he returned to the business in hand.

Lily waited for him to produce a prayer book and prepared herself for the familiar and well-loved words: ' . . . to have and to hold from this day forward, for better for worse, for richer for poorer, in sickness and in health, to love and to cherish, till death us do part . . .' She was disappointed.

The Very Reverend Albert D. Stringer waited for silence and then stabbed a bony finger towards Matt.

'You Matt Wallis?' he asked loudly.

'Yes.'

The same finger now pointed to Lily. 'You Lily – what was it?'

439

'Golightly,' she prompted.

'You Lily Golightly?' he roared.

'Yes, I am.'

He turned back to Matt. 'You take her for your ever-loving wife?'

'I do,' said Matt.

Lily stole a quick glance at Matt's face but if he found anything unorthodox in the proceedings, he gave no sign.

It was Lily's turn again. 'You take him for your ever-loving husband?'

'Yes,' said Lily. 'I mean, I do.'

'Now the ring.'

Obediently Matt slipped a large dress ring on to the third finger of Lily's left hand. Broad-shanked in gold and set with seed pearls, it was much too big and she had to close her fingers to prevent it from slipping off again.

Triumphantly the preacher raised his voice for the last time. 'I now pronounce you man and wife,' he declared, 'and may God's blessing be upon you as long as you both shall live.'

Ragged applause broke out amongst the crowd.

'Kiss her, then,' instructed the preacher and as Matt bent his head towards Lily the applause expanded into a cheer of encouragement.

As Matt's arms went round her and his lips closed on hers, the very last of Lily's doubts vanished.

When Matt raised his head again he asked softly, 'Did I ever mention that I loved you?'

'No,' said Lily, 'I don't think you did!'

'Well, I do,' he declared simply.

'I love you,' Lily began, but now the crowd began to drift away and the preacher, unwilling to lose his audience, hastily abandoned Matt and Lily in order to climb back on to his barrel and resume his exhortations.

'Well, Mrs Wallis,' said Matt, 'we'd better see about a bed for the night and then book two passages on the next ship home.'

*

That night Lily lay in Matt's arms with a heart full of gratitude, for they had both found great pleasure in their lovemaking and the spectre which had haunted her for so long had finally been laid to rest. She was a wife in every sense of the word and she wanted to sing for joy.

They lay in a friendly silence for so long that finally Lily asked softly, 'Are you still awake, Matt?'

'Nearly asleep,' he murmured. 'Aren't you?'

'No, I'm too happy,' she confessed, 'and Matt, I want to ask you something.'

'Go ahead.'

'It's about . . .' She stopped and tried again. 'Why didn't you ask me why . . . why I had never – '

'Why I was your first lover?' he asked gently.

'Yes.'

'Because it's none of my damned business! What happened between you and Patrick is part of your past.'

'I didn't refuse him,' said Lily.

'The thought never entered my head.'

'We just couldn't – '

He gave her a hug and said, 'Don't tell me, Lily. I don't need to know. All that matters now is that you and I are happy – and we are. I'm a very lucky man and I'm sorry for Patrick for all he missed, but that's how it goes.'

'I know, but – '

He kissed her to silence her.

'Tomorrow is a new day,' he insisted. 'It's a new road and we have to move on. This is a fresh start and we're going to be fine.' He hugged her again. 'And one day, before too long, you'll give me a son.'

'Or a daughter.'

'Or both!'

They both laughed and were thoughtful again.

'Tell me about home,' Lily said suddenly. 'About Virginia. Do you mind, Matt? I know you're sleepy, but I'm wide awake!'

Matt drew a deep breath, considering how best to describe the country to which he was taking his new bride.

'Imagine a map of the east coast,' he told her. 'Now, find

New York. Washington is south-west of that and further west still is a range of mountains called the Blue Ridge. Parallel to them but even further west is a smaller range called Massanutten. The Shenandoah River runs between them and that area is known as the Shenandoah Valley. Do you follow so far?'

'So far, so good,' Lily assured him.

'Our spread lies between the river and the Blue Ridge mountains, near a small town called Luray – it's all very peaceful and very beautiful. No matter which way you look, you'll see mountains.'

'I shall love it,' Lily assured him earnestly.

'It's your turn now,' said Matt. 'You tell me about your home in England. I'll most likely never get to go there, but at least I'll know.'

Delighted, Lily launched into a description of the parsonage and the small village in Kent where she had grown up.

'I shall write and ask Mrs Spencer to send the best of Papa's paintings,' she told him. 'Then you will see for yourself – Matt? Are you still listening?'

But Matt had fallen asleep.

Lily whispered, 'My darling Matt, I do love you.'

Then she slipped down a little further into the bed so that she rested with her head on his chest and lay in the darkness listening to his heart beating.

She had travelled thousands of miles to find this man with whom she would share her life. Tomorrow they would travel a new road. Lily sighed a deep sigh of happiness and her eyelids fluttered.

'Virginia,' she muttered sleepily. 'The Shenandoah Valley. My new home. Please God, let us be happy there . . .'

Her eyelids closed, but stubbornly she opened them again to repeat Matt's words.

'Tomorrow's road' she whispered and then, with a faint smile on her face and Matt's arms around her, she drifted contentedly into a sweet sleep.